Dawn found the dragon Gonard near the cliff edge, looking down the slope to judge the cleanest drop. To one side, the earth fell away gradually, which would give his claws too many opportunities to catch, to preserve himself. But here, facing back over the river, the cliff was a sheer drop for five hundred meters, the rest of the earth having fallen away long ago. One more stride, and he would follow.

Gonard bent his head, felt an old anger begin to ease. He felt at peace now, ready for what he must do. He lifted his head, limped to the cliff edge. A few grasses tumbled down from a clump of soil, waving in the breeze. Far below, the river shimmered in the weak sun, unwinding like a serpent between the green hills and stark mountains. I forgive you, Father, he thought, his hindquarters bunching beneath him. Perhaps, in time, I could even learn to forgive myself.

He closed his eyes and launched himself out over the cliff.

TSR® Books

F.R.E.E.Lancers
Mel Odom

Yor's Revenge
Roy V. Young

Dragons Can Only Rust
Chrys Cymri

Dragon Reforged
Chrys Cymri

Dragon
Reforged

Chrys Cymri

DRAGON REFORGED
©1995 Chrys Cymri-Tremththanmor
All Rights Reserved.

First Printing: December 1995
Printed in the United States of America.
Library of Congress Catalog Card Number: 94-68161
ISBN: 0-7869-0177-2

9 8 7 6 5 4 3 2 1

TSR, Inc.
201 Sheridan Springs Rd.
Lake Geneva, WI 53147
U. S. A.

TSR Ltd.
120 Church End, Cherry Hinton
Cambridge CB1 3LB
United Kingdom

FOR OMA

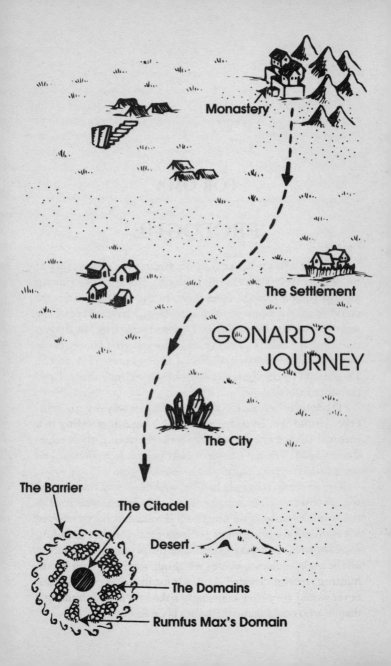

PROLOGUE

He sat alone as darkness came, feeling his joints creak as he deliberately straightened, forcing his spine to line up against the back of the hard chair. In the chilling winds, he could sense the promise of snow. *We will have to spend the winter here,* he reflected. *But I must ensure that the dragon does not become too comfortable with this place, these people. Come spring, Gonard must start back to the Domains.* The medtech allowed himself a slight smile. *I will convince him to do so.*

There had been a time when the dragon was easy to influence. Unbidden, an image appeared: Gonard, standing in a medical laboratory, a leather muzzle encircling the wedge-shaped head. The guards who held his lead were nervous, all too aware that the dragon was accused of murder.

The medical technician had known right away that Gonard was no ordinary Hunt creature. The Lord Citizens who lived in the lush Domains of an otherwise devastated Earth enjoyed occasionally forgoing their technological comforts, trading sonic showers and food processors for the privilege of bouncing on the backs of horses, swords weighing heavily in their hands, hunting creatures created and built for just that purpose. But never would they have knowingly risked their lives hunting a dragon who could flame them into bone and ash.

To ensure that the dragon would be grateful to him—and trust him—the medtech had healed the creature's newer injuries, though he left the crippled forefoot and wing in their twisted state. Then he had convinced the dragon to escape.

What he hadn't counted on was the human woman, Itsa, an Outler who had entered Earth illegally from one of the asteroids. She'd been with the dragon when he was captured and was imprisoned with him. She'd stubbornly insisted on accompanying them on their flight from the Citadel. Though she had occasionally proven useful in the year since they had left the protection of the Domains behind, it was her fault they were presently stuck in this settlement. The medtech started to frown, then thought better of it. She wasn't worth the expenditure of energy the movement would require.

The door to the large hall opened. Gonard stepped in, limping, carrying most of his heavy body on the side opposite his crippled left forefoot. He dipped his long head in a nod to the medtech, then allowed the door to shut behind him as he settled along the tiled floor. His eyes closed.

You have not released consciousness for the night, the medtech thought at him. Not until the Outler has returned will you relax. Why do you welcome that woman? We would be better off without her.

Minutes ticked by, becoming hours. Gonard waited, patient. The medtech waited, more patient still. He had greater practice at patience, had been waiting since the day the Master had abandoned him, half finished.

Finally, the door opened a second time. Itsa pushed her way in, her dusky cheeks flushed with drink and exertion, her reddish black hair curling wildly. "Hiya, dragon, tech," she said loudly, cheerfully. "Ya jig ya don't have to wait up for me, don'tcha? An Itsa looks after herself. She don't need no one."

The dragon raised his head from his forefeet. His snout touched her chest gently, careful not to push her over with a head that was nearly as large as her body. "I know," he said softly.

For a moment, the swagger disappeared from her stance. Itsa's face gentled as she touched one nostril, her black fingers spreading across the red-lined rim. "Yeah." Then she grinned. "See ya in the mornin'. Us humans need our shut-eye."

She brushed past the dragon, grimaced at the medtech, and shut the door to her room behind her. The medtech saw Gonard slowly lower his head back down, finally allowing himself to settle into his equivalent of sleep.

You are concerned as to what happens to her, the medtech thought. I have come to comprehend that, even if I cannot understand why. Perhaps that concern can be used.

The night spun on, quiet as the last voice stilled. The medtech called up his plans, factored the Outler into each step, adjusting words and actions until the outcome was assured. The only part he could not influence was time. And he had so little of it left, he who was designed to be operative for only a short number of decades. He could not allow himself to cease functioning, not yet.

In the end, the dragon would understand. When it was far too late, he would appreciate what had been done for him. He might not forgive, but by then the medtech would be far beyond such immaterial concerns.

CHAPTER 1

Itsa slammed the door behind her, then leaned against the smooth-polished wood, so dark with age that it nearly matched her skin. She'd thought last winter was bad, stuck in a tiny cabin in the wilderness with the dragon and the medtech, but this place was really getting to her. Even Mummer's asteroid seemed like a piece of heaven now that she was stuck in a backward town where a toilet was a hole in the ground and people found happiness by drinking stuff that burned the back of her throat. So much for all her plans about sneaking onto the planet and getting Citizenship and the easy life in the lush gardens of the Domains.

Her first day Earthside, she'd found the dragon and somehow had gotten stuck with him—escaped with him from the Domains, almost died beside him in the desert, saved him from the sentient crystal City. Even when she'd tried to leave him, she'd only succeeded in binding them closer together. Her ankle still hurt a bit, after all these months, as if in reminder.

And now that she'd almost got to like him, the dragon was planning to throw himself into the Changewinds again. Yeah, right, so he came back the first time. But the other Windwalkers kept telling her how that didn't mean anything, how someone could walk the Winds a hundred times and still go benders the hundred and first.

What will I do if he doesn't come back? I'll be stuck in this hole with the medtech. Stupid, stupid, shattin' stupid, she thought, roughly wiping away her tears before anyone could notice them. And who's more dim, me or the dragon?

It took a moment before she realized that two people were staring at her. One person, she corrected herself quickly—a member of the settlement—and the medtech. Couldn't really call *him* a person. "Yeah, and whatcha lookin' at?" she asked.

"Pardon, lady," the man said nervously. "I came t'seek th' advice of th' Walker's Second."

Itsa transferred her scowl to the medtech. "Lots of them doin' that nowadays, ain't there?"

"My expertise in legal issues and moral matters is valued," the medtech said impassively.

"Ya can come back later," she told the man. "Me and the mighty whatnot have things to talk about."

To her annoyance, the man bowed. "Aye, m'lady."

"And I ain't nobody's lady!" she shouted as he slipped through the door.

"That," said the medtech, "is obvious."

"Cut it, tech," Itsa snapped. "I got no stomach for it."

"And why should that be?"

Itsa dropped into a chair, hard-backed and practical like everything in the settlement. "I jig ya got no feelin's, tech, butcha gotta jig I'm ragin'."

The medtech lifted his shoulders in his version of a shrug. Itsa bit her lip, looked away. As time went by, the robot was becoming less and less successful in his mimicry of human mannerisms. His black hair hung lank and lifeless; even the beige technofiber jumpsuit he'd worn since their escape from the Domains was finally beginning to show wear.

"Anger is a very common expression of your personality.

Am I to understand that it is for some reason greater today?"

Itsa snorted. "Don't knock it, ragin's what got me this far. Got me off Mummer's asteroid and 'way from the mines. Got us outta that City, too, 'member? Ya weren't much help when it was tryin' to take over Gonard's mind."

"My advice has been of value," the medtech said calmly.

"Yeah, when?" Itsa leaned back in the chair, scruffing the heels of her boots on the wooden floor. "Gettin' out of the Citadel and leavin' the Domains was a great idea, right?"

"You are well aware that I gain little from arguing with a human of your low intelligence." Itsa gritted her teeth as the medtech's dull silver-gray eyes studied her. "Your latest attempts to persuade Gonard not to reenter the Changewinds have been unsuccessful."

"Least I'm tryin'!" Itsa jumped out of the chair. "Ya're just goin' to let him go back in, ain'tcha?"

"He returned from his first venture into the Changewinds."

"Only just. 'Member that strange story he told, all 'bout some lion chasin' him? What if he gets lost out there this time? What if it makes him benders, like those others, since he won't even sing to keep his head right?" She strode up to the impassive robot, her hands bunching into fists. "Ya're always so keen to keep him alive. Why don'tcha try talkin' to him?"

The medtech held his ground. "You presume I would wish to convince him to remain in the settlement. I may, however, consider a second journey into the Changewinds necessary for the achievement of his goal."

"Oh, yeah, I forgot," Itsa said sarcastically. "Ya wanna see if he's got a soul. And goin' into the Winds is gonna help do that?"

"I have a theory."

"Yeah, don'tcha always? What's it this time?"

To her surprise, the medtech instantly answered. "You will recall that he claims to have heard the Master's voice when the City attempted to conquer his mind. There is ample evidence that Lord Citizen Rumfus Max was killed by Gonard; a dead man should be unable to communicate, even with his creation."

"The dragon calls Lord Max 'Father,' not 'Master,' " Itsa pointed out.

"One of his mental aberrations."

"Like stickin' with me?"

As she'd expected, the medtech didn't contradict her statement. "There are unresolved issues between Gonard and our Master. It is my theory that the chemicals borne by the Winds reach into the subconscious, and will perhaps assist Gonard in freeing himself of the guilt of killing Lord Max."

"Yeah, and that's a real good reason for him to go out again, right?" She strode angrily out of the hall. If the medtech was for Gonard going out, then she was against it. She was against anything the tech wanted. That much she knew, though she still didn't quite know why she distrusted him so strongly.

The setting sun was washing the stone buildings with a sheen of orange, but Itsa only absently noted the golden hues. A breeze brought the smells of evening fires, where dinners were being cooked for the Singers in their confine. And at the gate stood Gonard, facing the direction of sunset. The direction of the Changewinds.

Itsa found herself slowing, then stopped. Gonard's shadow stretched away from him, long and dark. In contrast, the remaining light picked out points of fire on his blue scales, tangled bright in the fringe lining his pricked ears. The golden edges of the whole wing were outlined with red, the crippled one hidden in darkness. His nostrils flared, exposing small hairs; then his head turned, acknowledging her presence.

For a moment, Itsa stayed where she was and studied him. It was hard to believe that the man who had built the dragon had also built the medtech, a robot without emotions, slowly falling apart under the strain of their journey. What had Rumfus Max done to make the dragon so different?

Straightening her shoulders, Itsa marched up to him. Her head was just high enough to cast a shadow onto the top of his foreleg.

"Ranalf's tribe got back today."

"The tribe is no longer Ranalf's," Gonard said heavily. "It was removed from his control after my trial."

"All right, Naylor's tribe," Itsa said irritably. "Look, it ain't yar fault Ranalf lost bein' Headman. He decided to come back here before the huntin' season was finished, just to get back atcha."

"He had good reason."

"The trial settled all that," Itsa snapped. "It's not yar fault Ranalf's son and those other tribe members died in the Changewinds. They shouldn't of expected ya to sing, 'member? Yar not a Singer, so ya couldn't protect them. It's not yar fault they went benders and had to be killed."

"Perhaps not," he said. His ears flicked, the crystal earring he had received in the City jouncing in the folds of the left. "But I will never sing again. That much I promised, when the City would not have me."

The sudden sound of the medtech's voice startled Itsa. "We will have the winter to discuss that statement." The pale eyes twisted to Gonard. "It will not be possible for us to begin our journey back to the Domains until spring. What are your intentions for the duration of the season?"

"Yeah, like what'm I s'posed to do all winter?" Itsa complained. "Why don'tcha two get bored?"

"The capacity for boredom is not within our programming," said the medtech. "It is a counterproductive emotion, and therefore the Master wisely decided to retain it."

Gonard blinked. He looked down at the medtech. The golden wings rustled. "*Retain?*"

Itsa glanced between them, lips thinning. "What's up?"

"It was a strange word to use," Gonard explained.

She shuddered as he left one eye on the medtech's inscrutable face, rolling the other back to look at her; seeing him do that always gave her the chitters.

"Retain. What do you mean by that?"

"An imprecise word," the medtech said. "It may be preferable to substitute it with 'withhold.' "

"It is not preferable." Gonard lowered his head, bringing his blue eyes level with the medtech's. There had been a time when the dragon had always deferred to the medtech. Not now, after all this time outside the Domains. Itsa was suddenly reminded how much he'd been changed by his experiences. "You do not use imprecise words. Why 'retain'?"

The medtech calmly stood his ground. "It is not for me to explain, but for you to discover. The discovery may take place shortly."

"When the Changewinds next blow," Gonard rumbled. Itsa, feeling the sudden tension between the two robots, stepped back. "You always know. You're always ahead of me."

"No," said the medtech wearily, "I am behind you, always behind you, even as I was designed to be. I was first so that you might be best. I was failure so that you might be success. I was hope, but you are reality. It was only rational to abandon hope for reality."

Gonard lifted his head. "What is it you want of me?"

"Prove my Master was right. Prove to the Lord Citizens that he created a being with a soul."

"And how's he gonna do that?" Itsa asked sharply,

knowing all too well what would probably happen if they returned to the Domains. The dragon would be turned into scrap by the Lord Cits, and she'd be sent back to the mines. The medtech, the way he was going, wouldn't even last that long.

"It is my duty to determine that action." The medtech straightened; his shoulders were developing a tendency to slump. "It is your duty now to face the Changewinds and, in the spring, to return with me to the Domains."

Itsa kicked at a cobblestone. "Still don't see why ya gotta do this Winds thing again."

"The Winds revealed something to me last time," Gonard said slowly. "They might do so again."

"Yeah, just make sure ya come back. I can't take the tech on my own."

The medtech almost smiled. "It is interesting to note the common direction of our opinions, Outler." He turned and stalked away, his uneven footsteps making Gonard's nose wrinkle into a frown.

"He'll be okay," Itsa said sharply, annoyed that the dragon still worried about the tech. How many times had she warned him not to trust his brother-creation? She thrust her hands farther into the pockets of the tattered green vest she'd worn since leaving the mining asteroid, scowled as her fingers dropped through the bottom of one. "When're the next Winds?"

Gonard lifted his head, took a deep breath. She watched his nostrils flutter as he sorted through the scents on the evening air. "It will rain tonight. The Winds will come a day later."

"Oh." She studied him, wondering if she should try to talk him out of it one last time. A last touch of sunlight caught the bone whistle around his neck, the one she had carved for him from a buck he had accidentally killed in his first stire hunt. "Ya're gonna keep wearin' that whistle?"

"Not if you don't want me to."

"It's yar whistle. Ya can do whatever ya want with it."

Gonard cocked his head. "I *will* come back."

Itsa started to turn away. Then her hands clenched. "I never knew my Dad, ya jig," she said quietly. "Ran out 'fore I was born. And Rammelly—he died on me, 'member? The City pulled that from my mind and showed it to ya."

"I remember."

"I'm gettin' real tired of losin' people." She waited a moment for her heart to settle, her breathing to ease. "Don't go, dragon. All right?" She looked up at him. He seemed so solid, indestructible. But she knew how fragile he could be, how close she'd come to losing him several times already. "Don't go."

For a moment, she held his gaze. She could almost hope that he might do as she asked, not risk life and sanity in the mind-altering Changewinds.

Then he glanced away. "I have to go. You must see that."

"Go, then!" she flared. "Just don't expect me to come after ya, right?" Angry and humiliated, she hurried away into the night.

* * * * *

Coffee, Itsa found herself thinking as she munched the warm cake. I miss coffee. And syntho-ale. Never mind tooth gel. Bet my teeth got loads of holes. That's the prob growin' up with mod tech. Ya get used to it.

She yawned. Dawn was only beginning to gleam on the buildings of the settlement. Itsa found a seat on an as-yet-unoccupied market stall and watched with mild interest as the traders prepared for another day. She was rarely out of bed this early, but she'd not slept well last night.

Yeah, and I wonder why. She tossed away the rest of the bread, no longer hungry. Gonard never needs to eat. Shattin' dragon.

Itsa stood, stretched. Someone else other than traders was awake this morning. She watched the man scratch the several days' worth of stubble on his chin as he stared at a stall, his lips moving silently. He seemed familiar; she racked her brains for his name. Rygor, that was it. He was Rygor, one of Naylor's tribe. After all those months with the tribe, she ought to know the members. She wandered in his direction, bored enough to talk to anybody.

Rygor glanced at her as she stopped beside him. "M'lady," he said curtly.

"Get back yesterday?" she asked nonchalantly.

"Th' tribe could nae wait much longer." His broad shoulders lifted in a shrug. "Th' hunt season be o'er."

"And how'dcha do?"

By the expression on his face, Itsa knew that she shouldn't have asked. "Th' clan will live."

"Right." She knew what that meant. Each tribe depended on a good hunting season to buy the comforts of the settlement to see them through the winter. The time Ranalf had lost by bringing his people back early to have Gonard stand judgment had cost the clan dearly. They'd be housed in the bare wooden buildings at the edge of the settlement, and would probably have difficulty affording the new spears and whatnot they'd need for the next season.

With a shrug, Itsa put it behind her. Wasn't her problem, after all. "Whatcha doin' now?"

"A new knife be needed . . ." He suddenly hesitated. "M'lady, could ye read th' signs fer me?"

Itsa glanced at the list of blades and prices, propped against the stall. The spelling was different than what she was used to, but she could guess what 'broz' and 'stel' were. "Sure. Why, can'tcha read it for yarself?"

"Th' reading be settlement work, women's work."

"Like huntin's for men," Itsa said, recalling the separation of duties by the sexes. In the settlement, the women were in charge; out on the hunt, the men gave the orders. "So, where's yar woman for woman's work?"

He met her gaze squarely. "Dead o' th' Winds."

Itsa felt her face warm. Of course. Now she remembered. His wife had been one of those who'd gone benders and been killed when the dragon had refused to sing against the Changewinds. "All right, I'll read it for ya. Whatcha lookin' for?"

Rygor waited as she haggled over the price of a steel dagger, silently handing over the required payment when Itsa had concluded discussions with the trader. She presented him with the knife, rather proud of her negotiating skills.

He slipped the leather sheath onto his belt. Fiddling with his belt buckle, he said quietly, "Ye be a fine woman, m'lady."

"Sure," she said, thinking of a dragon willing to leave her behind.

"I be grateful fer yer help."

He started to turn away. "Wait," Itsa called, an idea suddenly coming to her. "I've got a trade for ya."

"A trade, m'lady?"

"Yeah, a trade." She hooked her arm through his, leading him away from the market. "It's like this. Ya need to be able to read. I need to be able to hunt. I'll teach ya one, if ya'll teach me the other."

"Yer th' woman o' a Walker," Rygor said. "Why do ye need t' hunt?"

"He's goin' out into the Winds again." Itsa was surprised how bitter her voice sounded. "If he don't come back, I wanna be able to look after myself. Trade?"

"If ye will come t' th' clan's place on th' morrow, I will

do as ye ask. But if ye were mine, m'lady . . ."

Itsa waited a long moment, then prodded impatiently, "Yeah, what then?"

"If ye were mine, I would never leave ye." Then he pulled away, leaving Itsa staring after him, surprised by the strength in his voice. She started back to the Singers' confine, lost in thought.

CHAPTER 2

The rain came and went, dampening the air, leaving puddles on the stony ground. The weak sunlight had only begun to dry the buildings when the old Windwalker who had led Gonard out on his first journey into the Changewinds came for him again.

Gonard pulled himself to his feet, flexing the crippled foot before placing any weight on it. He nodded to the medtech as he limped past, paused beside Itsa. "I came back last time," he reminded her.

"It was different last time," she said tightly. "Ya jig it. I jig it. Even the tech gets it."

"Especially the medtech," Gonard agreed. He studied Itsa for a long moment, trying to memorize the sight of her slim, tall figure, her fear-tainted scent. But his attention was drawn by her eyes, wide with concern, but flaring with inner determination. She's so strong—why does she need me? he wondered. But this was not the time to ask. "I *will* return."

Itsa merely stepped aside. Head held high, Gonard limped out into the early evening.

The Walker's eyes darted to him. "Be ye prepared?"

Gonard fell into step beside him. "I don't know what I'm preparing for."

The man clucked his tongue. "All Walkers should be prepared afore th' Winds. Ye hae walked once. Why do ye walk th' Winds now?"

Gonard glanced thoughtfully at his left forefoot, navigating the twisted toes over an uneven section of cobblestones. "There is something I must know, and I hope the Winds will show it to me."

The old Walker barked a laugh, startling Gonard. "Aye. That they will. How otherwise would a Walker learn t' see into th' souls o' others? Th' Winds first call us t' see inside our own."

The settlement began to stir into action as the bell started to toll in the confine. The streets became deserted, even beasts being herded into strong shelters. The gates were hurriedly opened at Gonard's approach. "Here I leave ye," said the Walker, leaning heavily upon the wall. "Th' gates will be opened after th' passing o' th' Winds, an' I will be here."

With your knife, Gonard added silently, in case I don't come back sane. He recalled sharp blades slicing into the throats of the men and women of the tribe, the ones he had failed to protect. That could be his own fate. Even now it was not too late; he could turn back. He shook his head. No. Over the last two months, he had become increasingly aware of some pressure building up inside him, darkening his dreams and tempering his days. He had chosen to go into the Changewinds, and he would do so.

Gonard trembled, once, the gates towering above him marking the threshold between the firm world of stone behind and the shifting world of mist awaiting him. He called to mind the look in Itsa's eyes, shining with determination and strength. Then he forced himself to step out into the fog.

The gates rattled into place behind him. Gonard wandered away, deciding that he didn't want to be too close to the settlement when—when whatever happened. The warning bell was muffled by stone and distance. Gonard imagined people rushing into homes, bolting doors, clinging to each other as they awaited the approach of the Winds. He pictured Itsa and the medtech, waiting in their hall, and drew comfort from their safety. They were his friends. It was good to have friends. And he would return to them.

The slight breeze began to pick up. Gonard lifted his head, facing the Winds. Tendrils circled around him, playing with the fringe of his ears, ducking into the hollows of his nostrils. Unlike the first time, he saw no bouncing spheres, no swirling colors. Gonard sharpened his vision, almost certain that he could see the molecules of chemicals borne on the Winds. He did not flinch as they settled on him, forced himself to hold still as they trickled past his nostril hairs. He had come to be exposed to them, not to escape their influence.

Sun began to shine weakly through the fog. The plains around the settlement had disappeared, were replaced by the same woods as on his last journey into the Changewinds, the trees as tall and thin as before. This time, Gonard recognized them. He was standing in the clearing outside his Master's cave, under the trees he had for years seen only as a green mass below the ledge outside the laboratory in which he had been created. The knowledge of his surroundings made him suddenly tense, wary.

The lion strode out from the trees. He seemed larger than he had the last time he had appeared to Gonard. The sun seemed to come with him, glinting off the tawny body and burnishing the heavy golden mane. Gonard took an involuntary step backward, the memory of claws aching across his right leg, knocking his crippled wing. Whether or not the creature was a hallucination caused by the Winds, he wasn't going to risk a second encounter.

"Your battle is not with me," growled the lion. "Your

true struggle lies with another, and it is he I have called forth from you."

The beast stepped aside, and then sat, the long tail curling around the powerful forefeet. Gonard eyed him warily for a moment, wondering how long the lion would remain at ease.

Then all thoughts of the beast fled as a man stepped into the clearing. "Gonard."

Gonard's legs seemed suddenly weak, unable to bear his weight. His creator, the man who had built him so many years ago, stood once again before him. The man he had killed, to prevent himself from being dismantled. "Master," he acknowledged.

Rumfus Max tilted back his head. "I am grateful that you can still recognize me, considering how you last left me."

Gonard dropped his muzzle to the damp earth. "I am sorry, Master."

"You should be more than remorseful." The Master came forward; Gonard's skin shuddered as a hand was placed on his left leg. "I reclaim you as my own."

Reclaim? Gonard wondered, bewildered. Have I ever stopped being his? "May I have permission to ask a question, Master?"

The Master was walking around him, brushing fingers down wrenched scales, analyzing healing wounds. "You have not been taking care of the body that I entrusted to you. Ask your question."

"You are dead in body." Gonard flinched as the man tugged at the earring piercing his left ear, a reminder of the City. "Are you truly alive in spirit?"

"So, neither have you been caring for the mind." The Master rapped his knuckles on Gonard's head. "Cast back through your memories. I have been a part of you since long before you became a dragon, when you were nothing more than a glittering construction of brain components on my laboratory table."

The Master was speaking of a time before Gonard's Awakening, when he had been nothing more than a machine, unable to think for himself. All memories before Awakening were hazy, fragmented. But Gonard raised his head, met the dark eyes. A time before he was placed into a body, when only his brain existed. Nothing sensed but that which was placed within him, the feeding of bulk information from other computers, the insertion of connectors to various mechanical parts, the touch of a mind on his . . . He said slowly, "You decided to connect your brain to mine."

"I fed my memories into you," the Master agreed. "You were to be the repository of my knowledge, since the Citadel would not allow me to deposit my 'heretical' theories into the main library. The religious Schools were aghast at my creation of a robot in the image of a man. The thought that I was trying to create a being who might develop a soul . . . That was too much for them."

Gonard found himself breathing heavily. A dim awareness flickered through his mind, not substantial enough to be called memory: an awareness of another mind, of pain, of sudden knowledge. "Your mind, into mine."

The Master smiled. "You do remember. The experience was not a pleasant one for me, and I had thought it unsuccessful."

"You spoke to me," Gonard whispered. "When the City tried to assimilate my mind, you freed me."

The Master shrugged. "Self-preservation. I had no wish to be bound forever to a sentient crystal—though it was her influence that enabled me to gather myself together in your mind." He shrugged again. "But I am ready now; I will take over."

"Take over?" Gonard echoed.

"A perfectly reasonable solution." The Master glanced at the lion sitting calmly nearby. "Would you not agree?"

The beast regarded them both with his golden eyes. "All

Gonard's choices are his own."

"What will happen to *me?*" Gonard asked, trembling.

"Does it matter?" The man strode forward aggressively. "You are merely a creation from my own hands, given movement and the minimum of emotions. You know for yourself that you are nothing more than a structure of metal and rubber. It took the destruction of another dragon for you to realize that you were not a thing of flesh and blood. Do you not remember? Dragons can only rust. I gave you that body, and now I will claim it back at little sacrifice."

Gonard dared to look him in the eyes. "At the sacrifice of my *self*."

"As I said, little sacrifice."

Is that how little you think of me? Gonard felt his chest tightening. "You never believed that I'd be successful, did you? You never thought I could develop a soul."

"Death changes priorities," the Master said harshly.

This isn't real; this isn't happening, Gonard thought frantically. It's only the Changewinds, making me believe that the Master is talking to me. But the words of the medtech, spoken after his first venture into the Winds, came back to him. Even if he were only imagining everything, did that make it any the less real? If he gave in now, would he be one of those destroyed by the Changewinds? "I can't let you."

"Have you forgotten how we came to this pass?" asked the Master grimly. "You killed me. You destroyed your own Master. You cannot find forgiveness for your action—you cannot even forgive yourself. I offer you a means by which to atone for your crime."

"But what about *me?*" Gonard cried out, the tension snapping his voice. "What about your plans for me? Aren't they important?"

"Important?" The man sneered. "Why do you believe that they were ever important?"

"You created other dragons for the Lord Citizens to hunt,

but you didn't let me be hunted—"

"No Hunt would have a crippled beast."

"You named me, the only one of your creations you ever named—"

"A name? An anagram of 'dragon.' I could not waste more time than that."

Gonard took a deep breath. The crisp scent of pine restored a measure of strength to his body. "You never believed in me, did you? You never believed that I could really develop a soul."

"You don't even believe in yourself," the Master rasped. "No one believes in you."

"No, you're wrong," Gonard said slowly. "Itsa believes in me." He felt the world shift back into order. "Itsa believes in me."

"Not important," the Master snarled. "You are not important!"

Gonard drew himself up to his full height. "But I am."

The Master smiled, folded his arms across his chest. "Then you must kill me again . . . *Son.*"

Gonard winced at the heavy sarcasm on the last word. Then anger flared through him, opened the fire chamber in his chest. "You are no father to me!" A gush of flames followed the words, surrounded the mocking figure. The body was covered with dancing fire, but still the mouth grinned, the dark eyes laughed with scorn. Gonard expelled more and more flame, until the trees behind the man were ablaze, the acrid scent of burning green wood filling the clearing. For a second time, the figure of his Master disappeared into ashes.

Finally the man was gone, borne away by the smoke. Gonard hung his head, weary both in body and in mind. He heard the lion stand, stretch, then pad over to him, power hanging like a spice in the rich mane. "The Master—my father," Gonard mumbled. "He never—he never—"

He lifted his head, seeking an answer in the golden eyes.

But the lion merely asked softly, "He never what?"

The answer trembled on the edge of Gonard's awareness. "No." He backed away, refusing to acknowledge it. "He must have, or how could he have created me, protected me. He was my father, how could he not—"

He bit off the last words, banished the thought. But his father's scorn still burned through his mind, the memory biting deep. "No," he whispered again. He would not, *could* not accept it. Then he turned, and the bunched muscles of his haunches threw him into a gallop as he sought escape from the realization being thrust upon him.

* * * * *

His legs had finally given out, refusing to keep running. Gonard lay where he had fallen, earth turfed up by his collapse, a few grains of dirt dripping steadily into his half-open mouth. Consciousness came and went, so that one moment he felt the warm sun upon his scales, and the next a cold frost bound his ears to his skull.

I am—running from—something. He pieced the thought together slowly, painfully, over the course of a number of days. But why—hasn't it—caught me?

It can't find me. If I stay quiet, it can't find me. He moved strained, stiff muscles, pulling himself unsteadily to his feet. Then he coughed, clumps of earth flying from his mouth. I must keep quiet, keep moving.

But he had no sooner taken a step than the memories rushed up to him. A dark-haired man, flames, angry faces, a dark-skinned woman—and he threw himself into a gallop again, trying to drive them all from his mind by the sheer effort of running. I will not think. The words pounded through his feet, striking the ground in grim determination. I will not think. I will not remember.

The plains disappeared behind him. The sun took longer

each day to drive the chill from the earth. Gonard's pace slowed, until he spent days walking, noting with simple delight the red-brown tinges of the falling leaves. He was calm, but only uneasily, his mind threatening time and again to shift back to his past. I will not remember, he promised himself. It is better not to remember. I will not remember.

He awoke one morning to find snow falling. Large white flakes spun slowly to the ground, covering hollows and leveling out humps, throwing the world into a featureless land of white. So be my mind, Gonard thought fiercely. Even as the snow blankets the earth, let my mind be covered. As each flake shields a leaf, let a memory be shielded. So I won't remember anymore.

The snow trickled to a halt by midday, but Gonard's nose wrinkled as he smiled. It was all behind him. He was free, his past slipping from his shoulders like snow disturbed by his movement. He was nameless, untroubled. With a heavy burden lifted from his mind, he resumed his journey, breaking through the fresh snow.

A few days later, he came upon a herd of large animals. Their dark bodies moving slowly across the snow filled him with a sudden sense of loneliness. He gingerly picked his way down the hill slope, stopping a good distance away from them on the valley floor. A few tails flicked at his presence, and the does gradually grazed away from him. But he was tolerated, for which he was grateful.

The snows came again, burying the ground even more. Gonard noted the futile digging by the animals, their worried whistles. He limped into their midst, ignoring their quick departure, wide hooves skimming them over snow that his heavier weight broke through. He laid down a sheet of flame, melting the snow away to reveal the brown grasses underneath. Then he withdrew, allowing the herd to return and graze in peace.

Despite his efforts, several of the animals weakened and

died, their bodies avoided by the still-strong herd members.
Gonard stood by one fallen buck, feeling memory struggle
to break free from its moorings. Another large herd,
whistling, blood streaking down his snout . . . He had killed
one of their kind. Part of its horn hung around his neck.
Gonard lowered his head, knowing that their simple peace
would never be his. So he turned and left the valley, his rest-
lessness driving him on.

More snow fell. Trees groaned under the weight. Gonard
kept to the higher, windswept grounds, where the drifts
were thinner and he could still struggle through. He heard
predators howl their hunger in the distance, spotted the
dead bodies of those starved by the winter littering the
snow. He wondered sometimes, dimly, why he felt no
hunger, but that threatened to bring memory back, and so
he turned his thoughts away.

But the cold was beginning to affect him. He could feel
knee joints stiffening, circulation slowing. One day, casting
an eye up at the gray, snow-threatening sky, he turned
toward a canyon appearing between two hills. Caves, he
sensed, could be found in such places, and caves were fit
shelter for a dragon. He could wait out the rest of the winter
there and continue his journey when the snows had thawed.

The canyon began promisingly, dipping down sharply
from the hills. Gonard limped along the uneven floor,
relieved to be free of snow for the first time in weeks. He
took deep breaths, noting the various musky scents of the
small animals hidden in crevices lining the cliffs. I will be
your neighbor, he thought to them. And we will awake to
the spring together.

But the floor began to climb again, and the walls to narrow. Gonard was forced to admit that there might not be a
cave or, if there were, the walls would become too narrow to
permit him access to it. He halted for a moment, breathing
hard, trying to decide if he should turn around.

A growl echoed from above. Gonard's ears flicked, but he feared nothing from predators. Forward, he decided, for a little longer. I can always shelter in the bottom of the canyon.

A growl came again, and then a heavy weight dropped to his back, sinking sharp fangs into his neck. Gonard whipped his head around, found himself looking into bright, hunger-maddened eyes. The rangy smell of canine seared his nostrils.

Another wolf dropped to the ground before him, slashing at his legs with yellowed teeth. Gonard attempted to rear, but the canyon walls penned him in. The beasts had followed him, he realized dimly, waiting to attack until he was hampered by the narrow walls. Loud growls told him that more canines waited to join the assault from above.

With a desperate wrench, Gonard threw himself backward. The back claws scrabbled furiously on the slick ground, his wings scraped against the cold rock walls. The wolf on his back was pitched forward, dropping heavily to the ground. It came quickly to its feet, head held low, tongue rolling between bright teeth.

The other canines leapt into the canyon, several dropping into place behind him. Gonard felt their hot breath against his legs, their teeth slashing futilely against his stiff scales. But for every nine slashes that slipped harmlessly away, the tenth brought a tooth underneath a scale, and it was ripped loose to expose vulnerable skin underneath.

Teeth. The world was filled with teeth, snapping at his ears, tearing into his skin. The walls were narrow, too narrow for him to turn. He struggled to back away, to return to a wider section where he could turn and run. But the wolves hampered his every step.

He paused finally, head hanging, legs splayed. His breathing was hoarse, drowning out even the sound of canine growls. There had once been a voice, he dimly realized. A voice that would have shouted at him to continue fighting, to never give up. But that voice was gone now. And he was tired, so tired. . . .

I won't even make a meal for you, he wanted to tell the wolves. They were becoming more proficient, learning to first tear scales away before slashing at the exposed skin. I won't fill your stomachs, because I'm not—I'm not—I'm not alive.

But I *am* alive! He heaved himself onto his hind legs, forefeet straining up the canyon walls. The wolves snapped at his exposed belly, ripping at the long scales. Gonard dug claws deep into the rock, pulled himself close, exhaled all breath from his lungs. Bit by bit, he twisted himself around, the harsh rock scraping his cheek and down his belly.

The wolves danced before him, still fresh, still eager. They would not leave him, Gonard realized. Even if he reached the mouth of the canyon, they would follow him. And on the open snow, the advantage would be theirs, their wide paws carrying them over the snow while his heavier weight broke through the crust.

He suddenly hated these laughing creatures, these beasts that held his life in their teeth. All eight stood ahead of him now, awaiting his next move, breath misting on the cold air.

A blind fury possessed Gonard. They would not have him! He growled his loathing at the beasts. His chest grew, swelled, reflecting the heat of his anger. Then, with a roar, he released the contents of his fire chamber, spraying the waiting canines with flame.

The wolves howled, blackened, died. The smell of frayed hair and charred flesh filled the air, and ashes sprayed across the canyon. Gonard closed his eyes, unable to watch as constricting muscles twisted the bodies in a mad dance. When his fire chamber was empty, he forced his eyes open.

Eight humps stretched across the ground. Here and there a strip of red muscle was bright against blackened bone. An empty skull grinned in Gonard's direction, the muzzle melted back to the empty eyes.

Stiffly, Gonard moved forward. You would have killed me, he wanted to plead in his defense. You would have killed me, and still be left starving. Was it wrong for me to defend my own life?

A whimper drew his attention. He limped unwillingly toward one of the mounds of flesh. The wolf raised its head at his approach, eyes wide with pain. Flame had crisped its forelegs, burnt the skin away from its left side. There was no way it could survive for much longer—but it was alive now, and suffering.

The green eyes sought Gonard's. A question burned deep within them, a request that Gonard could not comprehend. Then he understood. The wolf wished him to release it from its pain. Just one more blast of flame . . .

The words someone had once spoken hung heavily around him. *That's your purpose, to kill.* What else could his flame chamber be for?

"No." The sound of his own voice startled Gonard. "No. I will never kill again. I promised. I will never kill again!"

He gathered his weary legs under him to spring away, once again running from the scene of failure, away from memories that threatened to break loose and confront him.

CHAPTER 3

"Three days." Itsa scowled at the misty world outside the settlement. "Where the shat is he?"

The medtech gazed through the gates. "His tracks indicated that his intention was to leave the area as quickly as possible."

"So, what're we s'posed to do, go after him?"

The medtech grasped her arm, although she had not moved. "It is not prudent for us to begin now. The first snows will come upon us in the next fortnight. If Gonard does not return here within that time, it will behoove us to remain in the proffered hospitality of the Singers until the spring. We may begin our search at that time."

Itsa pried the fingers from her arm, grimacing at their cold, rubbery texture. The medtech seemed to be getting less lifelike with each passing day. "Yeah. Maybe. What do ya jig's happened to him this time?"

"I have no method by which I could discover the effect of the Changewinds upon Gonard."

"No, but ya've *hypothesized* somethin', haven'tcha?"

"I have formed some initial theories." The medtech's eyes slid to her. "I have, however, nothing of any consequence to share with you."

"Sure ya ain't," Itsa snapped. "Ya just don't wanna."

"I have nothing of any consequence," the medtech repeated. "It is not feasible for you to have been totally unaware of Gonard's development."

Itsa shrugged, forced herself to sound casual. "He's gotten more interestin'."

"Even as humans develop a personality throughout childhood, whether for good or ill"—the medtech flashed her a sharp glance, leaving Itsa in no doubt as to what category he placed her in—"so has Gonard struggled to differentiate himself. I hypothesize that he is slowly evolving more complex emotions and a correspondingly more intricate understanding of himself. It was to force a conflict within himself into the open that he once again walked into the Changewinds."

Itsa felt her throat dry. She swallowed, then said, "So, him not comin' back ain't a good sign."

"He may require healing." The medtech's hands twitched—in helplessness, Itsa suddenly realized. "A healing that I cannot give to him. He has moved beyond me."

Yeah, Itsa child, and what 'boutcha? she wondered bitterly. Maybe he's moved beyond ya as well. "That's what happens when dragons grow up."

"We will wait out the winter," the medtech said firmly. "Then we will follow his trail."

"Maybe," Itsa said again. She felt the medtech's sharp glance, but ignored it. Rygor would be waiting for her, ready for another exchange of lessons. Leaving the medtech to stand at the gates alone, she headed back into the settlement.

* * * * *

Rygor flipped his wrist. The knife flew from his hand, turning neatly in the air, sunlight flickering along the bright blade. The dagger thudded into the target with a satisfying *thwack*. He nodded, stepped back. "Now, throw yers."

Itsa licked her lips. She hefted her own knife, the smooth metal between thumb and forefinger, heavier hilt a good fifteen centimeters away. Make the blade an extension of yar will, she recalled from Rygor's instructions. The target is already hit, all ya have to do is let go of the knife. She let go of her breath and flung the dagger. The tip buried itself alongside that of Rygor's own knife. "Yeah!" Itsa shouted, thrusting a fist into the sky. "Suck that one!"

Rygor smiled. "Yer words be strange, but th' meaning be clear. Ye hae an affinity wi' th' knife."

"More'n ya with readin'," she agreed, rubbing chilled fingers together.

"I hae problems wi' reading close t' signs," he agreed. "But nae when far away."

"If ya were in the Domains, ya could have an operation for that. Quick cut with a laser, and ya'd be perfect." She shrugged at his lack of comprehension. "Maybe ya don't wanna be perfect."

"I be meself," he said equably. "That be enough."

Itsa grinned. "That's what I like 'boutcha, Rygor. Ya got no swagger on ya."

Rygor walked over to the target, removed their knives. He offered Itsa's back to her, hilt-first across his arm. She accepted it and, with a glance at the darkening sky, slid it away. "Th' clan be meeting this eve fer speech an' song. Ye be welcome."

"Ya jig?" She pulled her cloak tighter around her shoulders. "Me bein' the Walker's woman and all that?"

"I would hae forgiven ye," he said seriously.

Itsa snorted. "Yeah, like what've I gotta be forgiven for? It wasn't me who didn't do no singin'."

"Ye were part o' his house," Rygor explained. "Ye are then part o' his crime. But he were said t' be free o' any crime, by th' Triune. So ye hae nought t' fear." Then, more seriously, he asked, "Be ye his woman?"

Again that note she had occasionally caught in his voice. "No," she said quietly. "I'm not."

His face eased. "Then ye'll come?"

Yeah, why not? Get her away from the medtech, at any rate. "Yeah, I'll come."

* * * * *

At her first step into the communal building, Itsa knew she should have turned down Rygor's invitation. Conversations stilled, mugs of drink were lowered as heads twisted in her direction. Silence rippled through the room. For once she regretted her dark skin, such a contrast to their winter-whitened faces. Standing her out in any crowd.

Boot heels clicked against the wooden floor. Rygor made his way forward, calmly moving past gaping watchers. He stopped before Itsa, studied her for a moment. Then, with a pleased nod, he held out his hand.

"Nae." Another arm knocked his aside. Itsa took an involuntary step back. It took her a moment to recognize the man standing between her and Rygor. Ranalf, the former Headman of the tribe. The death of his only son and the loss of his former position had taken their toll; she almost felt a twinge of sympathy for the man. Then she remembered how he'd brought Gonard to trial, hoping the dragon would be sentenced to death, and she scowled back at him.

"I hae invited her t' be here," Rygor said evenly. "That be me right."

"She be nae welcome here," Ranalf replied grimly. "Hae ye forgotten what her lord did t' th' tribe?"

"That be again a wrong." Rygor glanced at Itsa. "What said t' me this eve? Be ye his woman?"

Itsa found the clan hanging on her response. She straightened, held her head high. Other people had tried to judge her, and she'd showed them wrong. Never try to put an Itsa, she thought. "No, I'm not his woman. I'm my own, right?"

"It be nae th' tribe who speaks in th' settlement," another familiar voice said crisply. Ranalf was pushed aside by his wife, her dark eyes angry. "It be th' clan's place. What says th' Headwoman?"

"Th' judgment be gi'en," said a woman farther away, Naylor's wife, Millan, and now Headwoman. "Th' Walker hae proven hisself. An' th' woman wi' him was ne'er on trial. She be not unwelcome here."

"Yeah, thanks," Itsa muttered. She'd heard better at lynchings.

Conversations began to rebuild, helped along by new servings of ale and the thick stout called Devil's Black. Even the dragon got drunk on that, she suddenly remembered, then wished she hadn't. She didn't want to think about Gonard, not now.

Rygor walked to the rack of ale barrels. Itsa followed, pleased that he hadn't tried to lead her by the arm or anything. At his glance, she nodded, and he filled a mug with creamy ale.

"Do ya get together like this a lot?" she asked, keeping a wary eye on the room. Not everyone seemed to have forgotten she was there.

"We be a clan," Rygor answered.

"Like that explains everythin'," Itsa said.

"Th' brothers o' me sire be here," he continued. "An' th' mother o' me first mate. Me daughter—"

"Daughter?" Itsa interrupted sharply, rapidly revising his age upward. She followed his gaze to a young girl, standing shyly with a group of children her own age. "Ya got any other kids?"

"She be me only one." The note of sadness in his voice reminded Itsa why, and she quickly took a gulp of the dusty-flavored ale.

Time passed slowly. Itsa occupied herself with sipping her drink and matching children to parents. *Wonder what they do with the kids durin' the hunt season?* she thought idly. *Shat, I must really be bored, to be thinkin' 'bout somethin' like that.*

Rygor had left her to talk to a relative, the thick nose and thin lips of both proving their common lineage. Itsa refilled her mug. *Now, the miners,* she thought, *we knew how to party. Rammelly . . .* She took a deep breath and almost choked on a gulp of ale. *Rammelly always had the best jokes.* So long ago, he'd died, and she still missed him.

She came out of her musings to find Rygor's daughter looking up at her. The brown eyes were serious, lips turned down as she studied the taller woman. "Ye be th' one wi' th' Walker?"

"The dragon was with me," Itsa countered. The girl's frown deepened. Itsa grimaced. "Right, we were together, okay?"

"Then ye can tell me." She straightened. "Tell me, how did me mother die?"

Itsa saw again the blade, bright in Rygor's hand, sliding across the throat of his delirious wife. "What did yar dad say to ya 'bout it?"

"He says nae a thing." The girl turned her head, but not before Itsa saw the angry tear. "Nae one says."

Where's Dad, Mom? Itsa stared down at her drink, the words as fresh as if she'd said them only yesterday. *Why don't I have a dad? All the other kids've got one.*

"She died brave," Itsa lied quietly, trying not to remember the delirious ravings as those caught by the Changewinds screamed that they were being altered, changed. "Ya would of been proud of her."

The girl turned back. "I do nae listen t' what th' others say," she declared. "Ye be nae a stranger t' me."

Itsa stared as the girl hurried away. Then she started as Rygor was suddenly back at her side. "I thank ye fer nae telling her."

"Ya'll have to tell her, one day," Itsa said fiercely. "Kids got a right to jig things."

"When she be o' age," Rygor answered amicably.

A hush suddenly settled over the gathering. Itsa watched as Millan stepped into a clear space in the center of the room. "A man hae but two tasks," she announced. "T' hunt well, an' t' sire young. Who can speak fer her man?"

A woman joined her. "I speak fer me mate. Two stire did Chaffen bring down in th' hunt, an' I carry his third child."

The room burst into cheers. "All hail Chaffen!" the Headwoman urged them needlessly. "Hunter an' father both! Who else speaks fer her man?"

One by one, the women of the clan joined their Head-woman. At last, only a few were still standing apart, their thin bodies showing that they were not among the pregnant ones.

"Th' clan be increased by th' hunt," Millan said, "an' by th' children t' come. Ye who be nae wi' child, come t' us an' pledge ye will help th' mothers wi' their young."

"Wait." Ranalf's voice broke strongly through the cele-brations. "We forget them who are nae wi' us, lost in th' past season."

For a moment, Itsa stared at him, puzzled. Then, as his eyes came to hers, she understood what he meant. Her fists clenched at her sides, longing to wipe that smirk from his face.

"This be nae th' place," Millan said angrily. "Ye speak out o' turn, hunter."

But Ranalf refused to move. "Let their names be spoken. Let us hear th' names of them who will ne'er bear a child again."

She'd had enough of this. Itsa strode forward, hardly noticing that people hurriedly moved aside for her. She stopped beside the Headwoman, then turned, staring at Ranalf. "Lanorlan o' Lanal. Notgar o' Lisbeth. Debor o' Susa. Melitta o' Susa." She flicked a glance at Rygor. "And Meredith o' Haladan." Then she glared at Ranalf. "Is that whatcha wanted?"

"It be enough," Allida said firmly. She laid her hand on Ranalf's arm, pulling him away. But the look in Ranalf's eyes told Itsa that it wasn't over yet. He had other plans. Yeah, Itsa thought at him, ya and what army?

"Let all hear," Millan said firmly. "Th' Windwalker be tried, an' proved hisself in th' Winds. He an' his be part o' th' tribe, an' part o' th' clan. I will hear nae more said 'gainst them."

I don't need nobody's help, Itsa wanted to say. But she merely shoved her fists into her pockets as the Headwoman gave her a nod. As the women not pregnant came forward to stand with those who were, Itsa made her way back to the ale barrels.

"That be brave o' ye," Rygor said quietly beside her.

"That?" Itsa took a deep swig of Devil's Black, then wiped foam from her lips with the back of her hand. "I've seen down worse than Ranalf."

"Aye," he agreed. "But nae, methinks, in a place nae o' yer own choosing."

Itsa found herself smiling. "Ya got that right."

"An' as th' Headwoman said," he continued, serious again, "ye be welcome here. Ye be tribe an' clan t' us."

"Right." Itsa grinned around her mug, the room starting to haze around her. Maybe passing winter in the settlement wouldn't be so bad after all.

* * * * *

A groaning noise woke her the next morning. Itsa blinked into her pillow, only slowly becoming aware that the groans were her own. Must of been that third mug of Black, she thought muzzily. And no recovertabs either.

"And a pleasant time was had by all."

Itsa grimaced at the medtech's voice. "Come back later, tech. Like ten years from now. Right?"

"We have standards to maintain," he continued. "You will rise from your bed and prepare yourself for the day."

Itsa muttered several suggestions for alternative uses for parts of his anatomy. Then, turning over on her mattress, she stared up at his pale skin. "Ya sound like my mom. Standards? Whatcha mean?"

"We are seen to be part of Gonard's household." Itsa gritted her teeth as he talked; movement had set her head throbbing. "That is why we have been permitted to remain within the Singers' confine. We must, however, continue to present ourselves as a Windwalker's Second and his mate, or risk expulsion to a less desirable portion of the settlement."

"Yeah, yeah, yeah." Itsa closed her eyes. "Leave it to ya, tech. Ya'll sort it out."

"Thank you for your confidence in my abilities."

Despite herself, Itsa laughed. "Ya jig I'm just too gone to bother, so don't pretend it's somethin' else."

"And you must desist in your attendance on that hunter from the clan."

Reluctantly, Itsa dragged herself awake. "Ya got a problem with me seein' Rygor?"

"You are thought to be the mate of a Windwalker," the medtech persisted. "It is therefore unacceptable to be seen accompanying another man."

"Look, tech." Itsa sat up, then paused for a minute to let her head settle down again. "First off, the dragon's a dragon, not a man. So let's get that straight. I ain't his mate. Second, if I wanna go 'round with someone, I won't be askin' ya first. Ya got no claim on me."

"I may not." The dull eyes held hers. "Does Gonard also have none?"

"If he did, it ran both ways," she snapped. "Sorry if ya missed it, but he left me, not the other way 'round."

"He had no choice—"

" 'Course he did." Itsa slid back down, throwing the covers over her head. "Now, go 'way. I got some sleepin' to do."

He waited a long moment; Itsa scowled under the heavy blankets, willing him away. Finally his boots clicked against the tiles. She sighed, turned over. What was that Old Earth word for what she had? Something about hanging. She thought muzzily about ropes and knots, trees and branches, arrows and spears. . . .

"Shat." She forced herself upright, shivering as the warm blankets fell away and exposed bare skin to the cold air. Spears. Rygor was supposed to give her a lesson in spear throwing today. "Shat, shat, and super shat." With what felt like a monumental effort, she heaved herself from bed and groped for the clothes she'd dropped to the floor last night.

* * * * *

The day outside did nothing to improve her head. Itsa drew her cloak tighter around her shoulders, the thick material slowly darkening in the damp. Fog softened the outlines of the buildings. She carefully counted turns in the twisting paths from the confine, more concerned with not getting lost than actually finding Rygor.

"I said t' ye, nae t' hae that last drop o' Black."

Itsa managed not to start at his sudden voice. "Right, so how'd ya jig I was here?"

"Every person hae his own walk." Rygor appeared out of the fog, lips bent in his slight smile. "Yers more than most."

"Thanks," Itsa said dryly.

"Ye walk like a hunter."

Itsa accepted the proffered spear, experimentally hefting the long shaft. She found herself remembering her first sight of the tribe, the hunters surrounding her and the medtech, with spears like these aimed at their hearts. Well, *my* heart, she amended. The tech ain't got a heart, in more ways than one. "And a woman shouldn't walk like a hunter, right?"

Rygor shrugged. "Ye be nae an ordinary woman. Ye be wi' a Windwalker, an' a wanderer from a distant land."

"So it's okay to teach me how to hunt."

"I teach ye fer th' reading." Then he smiled again. "An' I like t' teach ye."

Itsa drew back, wondering again at that note in his voice. Before she could question him, another figure emerged from the mist. The girl slipped a hand around Rygor's arm, looked up shyly at Itsa. "Hi."

"Yeah, hi to ya, too." Itsa glanced a question at Rygor.

"She be getting old fer long hours wi' me mother," he explained. "An' me mother be getting old fer teaching a young one. Will ye teach her th' reading wi' me?"

Ya don't jig how much I hate kids, Itsa thought at him. But two pairs of dark eyes were watching her hopefully. Deciding that she was definitely getting soft in the head, she said, "All right, both of ya."

A wide smile broke across the face of Rygor's daughter. "My name be Rydeth," she said. "Rydeth o' Meredith."

"Itsa." She paused, then added reluctantly, "Itsa of Sharit."

Rygor nodded, looking more pleased than she would have liked. "Right," she prodded. "So, how're ya gonna teach me anythin' 'bout throwin' a spear in this weather? Ya can't see far 'nuff for a target."

He sighed. "Hae ye learned nought? Th' spear, or knife, or arrow be but a part o' ye. It hae already touched th' target, afore ye sent it on th' way."

"Easy for ya to say," Itsa grumbled. "Prove it."

Rygor took back the spear. "Go t' th' target. Stand one arm length 'way, to th' right, then call t' me."

Itsa studied him. Then, with a shrug, she strode away. Her cheeks were getting cold, and she rubbed them with only slightly warmer hands. She'd call him over to the target, then suggest they call practice off for the rest of the day. Maybe the rest of winter, if this was what it was going to be like.

The square piece of wood loomed out of the fog. Itsa touched the wet side with a finger, stepped to the left and turned. "Yo," she called. "Come on, then."

Something slipped through the air. Itsa blinked; the spear was suddenly humming beside her, tip buried deep into wood at the center of the target. "Shat," she swore without thinking. "Ya might of hit me!"

"Nae wi' me aim." Mist rolled back from Rygor's shoulders as he came to pull the spear free. "Did ye wish t' take a turn?"

"No, I've had 'nuff," Itsa said firmly. "It's bleedin' cold."

It took a moment for her to realize that the soft sound she heard was his version of laughter. "I cannae say I disagree."

"Must ye quit, Father?" Rydeth stopped beside him. "So soon?"

Rygor touched her cheek gently with the back of one hand. Itsa turned away, swallowing against a sudden surge of envy. "On th' morrow, Daughter. Then will Itsa teach us th' reading."

"Aye." Rydeth gave Itsa a smile, then hurried away.

"She could of stayed with us," Itsa said, almost meaning it.

"Nay." Rygor hefted the spear, began to lead the way through the fog. "Methinks a hot drink were th' best fer us, an' she cannae come to me house."

"Why not?"

"She is nae o' age," he explained patiently. "It be nae proper fer her t' be wi' me in th' small house wi'out a wife fer watching us both."

"So when do ya get to see her?"

"In me mother's house." His voice remained steady. "We also meet oft in th' evenings. That be allowed."

So, Itsa found herself thinking, he'd not only lost his wife, he also lost his daughter. She shrugged the thought away; it wasn't her problem if these people had strange customs.

The path became muddier underfoot as they traveled from the wealthier regions of the settlement to the poorer, trading stones for bare earth. Itsa was once again glad that the Singers' confine employed servants. She'd hate to be the one to clean her boots after this trip.

Itsa's nose was almost numb by the time they reached the clan's set of buildings. Rygor pushed open the door of a small cabin, leaning the spear carefully against the wall before striding to the fireplace. As he built up the fire, Itsa studied the one-room house. A table rested against one wall, several bowls indicating that its surface was used for preparing meals not taken with the rest of the clan. At the other end, a bed sagged on wooden legs. A couple of camp-stools similar to those used by the tribe when out on the hunt were set up by the fire.

"Th' last season o' Ranalf's sire," Rygor said quietly, "we wintered in th' grandest houses o' th' settlement. Rooms aplenty, tiles on th' floor, stone fer th' walls."

The fire was growing, flames burrowing into the dark lumps Rygor had placed onto the embers. Itsa took a sniff, decided not to ask what they were. Warm, anyway, she

decided as she took a seat in front of the fireplace. Her nose
began to thaw, and, annoyingly, to run.

Rygor brought two mugs over, placing them on the
hearth. Lifting a poker from the fire, he lowered it into one
drink, then the other. The liquid hissed, releasing a thick
scent. Itsa accepted one, took a tentative sip. It was some
kind of concentrated alcoholic drink, and very warming.
She wrapped her chilled hands around the warm mug and
felt herself begin to relax.

"Where do ye come from?"

Itsa grinned. "Hardly anyone asks me that."

He glanced away. "Be it wrong fer ye t' tell me?"

"It ain't a secret." She leaned back, stretching her legs
out in front of the fire. "I come from one of the asteroid
colonies. We do all the grot, and the Lord Cits get the
rewards, livin' on Earth in the Domains with their gardens
and things."

"Yer words are very strange t' me," Rygor admitted. "Ye
come from a settlement set apart from th' Singers?"

"Yeah, whatever." How could she explain tech like trans-
mats and force-field barriers to someone who thought that
using an arrow was a great step up the intelligence chain?
She wasn't even going to try. "I guess it's like that. We kept
the Cits goin', ya see. Workin' our lives out on some bit of
rock in space so's they could try to get back bits of Earth by
movin' out the Barrier. 'Cause they jive everythin's dead
outside their bit, the Domains. Ya're s'posed to pass a test
to get there, but I cheated. Found my way into a transmat.
If ya don't get put back together wrong at the other end,
the Cits say the Ultimate's on yar side and ya get to try for
Citizenship. That's what I was gonna do."

"Then why be ye here?"

"Blame the dragon." Itsa shrugged. "And the medtech, I
guess. Bumped into one and then the other just after I got
to Earth." And after Gonard had killed his Master, but she

decided Rygor didn't need to know that bit. "Things got a bit hot at the Citadel, so we got out sharpish."

"And came t' th' tribe's lands."

Itsa laughed. "Shat as like. No, we first got caught up with that City thing."

"I hae heard say o' th' City." Rygor leaned forward, fire-light sparking in his eyes. "Be it true, th' tales th' Singers tell?"

"I don't jive what they say." Itsa took a long sip of alcohol, finally feeling warm again. "But I ain't gonna go back there 'gain."

"Th' Singers tell o' its beauty."

Itsa snorted. "Oh, yeah, she's pret all right. She's got that goin' for her. But she also wants a lot. The tech and me, we only found out when the dragon was s'posed to be made a Singer. She takes her Singers' minds away, and fills them instead with herself."

"She be alive?"

"Alive, the bitch." Itsa began to smile. "I had to ride Gonard out of there, to get him 'way from her. Don't jive she was too happy 'bout that." The smile turned into a frown. "Got him through the winter and all. He didn't want anythin' for a long while, like the tech and I didn't matter. We got attacked by yar tribe after that."

"We did nae attack ye," Rygor contradicted mildly. "Ye were on th' lands o' th' tribe. We asked ye fer yer reasons."

"And ya always do yar askin'," Itsa retorted, "with spears pointed at somebody's heart?"

Rygor said, seriously, "I would nae do it t' ye now."

" 'Course not," Itsa replied, deliberately brushing away the implications of his statement. "I jive how to handle a knife now."

He leaned back, nodded. "An' it were me who taught ye."

"So ya jive how sharp I am."

"Aye. I know how sharp ye be."

He got up to refill their mugs. Itsa studied him, wondering at the strange undertones in his voice.

* * * * *

The medtech was standing in the center of the hall when Itsa returned. She scowled as she shut the door behind her. Like one of the investigators in the mines, she thought, waitin' to pin somethin' on ya. "Sorry," she said sarcastically. "Did I forget to get a night pass?"

"You have once again spent a day in the company of that hunter."

"Don'tcha get twisted, tech. We ain't tumbled." Itsa smiled. "Is that what's up ya? Whatcha care, jealous 'cause ya ain't got the right bits?"

He strode up to her. The flickering light of the oil lamps wasn't dim enough to hide the sags in his skin, which was breaking away from the metal structure underneath. She wondered what the people of the settlement thought of his slow deterioration. "We have been summoned by the conclave of the confine. They have announced their intention to discuss the nonreturn of Gonard."

"Ya'll have a great time doin' that." Itsa yawned. "Tell ya what, ya can even give me the whole story 'bout it afterward. I might even listen to ya."

The medtech tried to straighten his shoulders. Itsa glanced away, hating the way even that small motion seemed to be slipping from his control. "It is imperative that we present a united front if we are to contain any unfortunate rumors."

"Yeah? What kind?"

"There are those who maintain that Gonard will never return."

"Well, maybe they're right. And ya jive what else, tech?" Itsa took a deep breath. "Maybe I just don't care.

Right? Maybe I just don't care what he does." Then she brushed past him, heading for her room and the dinner she knew would be awaiting her there.

CHAPTER 4

The bells had finished ringing, marking the end of compline and another day. Brocard's shoulders ached after the afternoon he had spent instructing the novices—by example—how to clean the stables of the coursairs. He could see the questions in their eyes, unspoken in deference to their vow of silence. The internal struggle against curiosity had made many of them awkward, scattering straw across the floor rather than into the beasts' stalls. Brocard had patiently shown them again and again how to gather the grasses on a fork and pitch it into the loose box. Later, the men would learn that the straw provided comfortable bedding for the coursairs, a layer between their hides and the cold stones. But a novice first had to learn to obey with his questions unanswered. For now, obedience was of greater importance than knowledge.

Brocard stretched, and his back cracked. He bent his head respectfully to the crucifix on the wall as he entered his cell. The room and its furnishings were plain: a wooden bed, a stool, a table that acted as his desk. Three books were spread out across the table, the only sign of his rank. All brothers, novice or professed, were expected to read during the appointed times, but few were permitted more than one of the books from the precious collection stored in the chapterhouse library.

Brocard washed his hands carefully in the small basin of water beside his bed. Only when the last stains of the stables were gone did he dry his hands and lift one of the books. He perched himself on his stool and applied himself to the text, which he was slowly translating from Latin to Anglish.

A knock on his door broke his concentration. Brocard carefully laid his pen aside, closed the book. Then he took the few steps to the door. A brother in the brown robe of a novice stood outside, his mouth working frantically. But he remembered himself enough to place a palm over his mouth, the gesture requesting permission to speak.

Brocard stepped aside, allowing the young man into his room. "Permission granted. Speak."

The brother bobbed nervously. "Dom Brocard, there is a dragon in the cathedral."

Brocard rubbed his beard thoughtfully, hiding a frown. "What is a 'dragon'?"

"A large, serpentine beast, Dom. It is lying in the choir."

"And how come you to know its species?"

The novice shuffled his feet nervously and stammered, "I—I asked it, Dom, and it—it replied as such."

Brocard rubbed his beard again. The weeks of silence in the winter were not unknown to affect the minds of first year novices, but he had expected better of Thresalym. That there was some beast in the cathedral, he did not doubt; this would not be the first winter that some creature pressed open the doors and sought shelter inside. So had the chapter gained one of its coursairs. "We will examine this beast," he assured the novice. "Your silence is reinstated."

The cathedral was only a short distance from the brothers' dormitories, but it was far enough to allow the winter winds to swirl up long robes, chilling the skin through several layers of woolen cloth. Brocard once again was grateful for the Abbot's decree last winter, that the brothers' traditional footwear of sandals could be exchanged for sturdy boots while the ground was snowbound. There should be other changes, he thought once again, as he watched Thresalym shiver in his thin robe. But even a brother on the Abbot's council could go only slowly.

They paused for breath in the warmer air of the cathedral's entrance. The novice pointed at the wide doors, indicating that, while he had closed the exterior doors, he had left the interior doors as he had found them. Brocard nodded. He studied the extent to which the doors had been knocked ajar. A large coursair, he decided. The harsh winter had claimed two of the chapter's six beasts, so a new one would be welcomed. He motioned Thresalym to wait, then stepped softly into the cathedral proper.

The thick stone walls muffled the sounds of the winds outside. The tall windows of stained glass were dull in the darkness of night. The only illumination came from the recently replenished candles along the side chapels and in the choir—Thresalym's task, Brocard decided. He was amused to note that the novice had completed his duty despite his discovery.

There was indeed a creature stretched out along the tiled floor of the choir, its hulk squeezed between the wooden sides of the stalls. Brocard walked up the nave, waiting for his eyes to adjust to the dim, yellowish light. The beast was larger than any coursair he had even seen, and—his heart sank at the realization—it was either deformed or injured, with what appeared to be large sacks of skin pressed against its sides.

The beast stirred as Brocard's steps broke the silence. It lifted a large head as he stopped beside one foot. Candlelight revealed a long, thin muzzle, with the protruding teeth of a carnivore. Blue eyes glittered as it looked down at him. Nostrils flared as the beast drank in his scent.

Brocard found himself stroking his beard and forced his hand to drop back down to his side. Facing an injured and possibly hungry carnivore was not the best time to spend long in analyzing its physical attributes. He found himself reflecting that he had had a good twenty out of forty years of life, should he now be called to meet his maker. "Thou art in the House of the Lord," he said to the beast. His voice echoed more strongly through the cathedral than he felt. "You will not harm any being herein."

The beast dipped its head, as if in a nod. It stood, with difficulty. Now Brocard saw the many slashed wounds gaping across strangely bloodless skin, and his tone was tempered with pity. "Nor can you remain here, for this is a chapter for the healing of humans."

"I am sorry," rumbled the beast in a deep voice. "This place reminded me of another sanctuary I once knew."

Brocard was not a suspicious man, but he had to restrain an impulse to cross himself. "You can speak. What are you, for you are not human."

The beast sighed. "What is human?"

Indeed, what is human? Brocard looked up into the blue eyes. "The division betwixt human and beast," he said softly, "is the divine gift of a soul. Have you a soul?"

The beast glanced away. "I don't know. I-I can't remember anything. I don't know who I am anymore."

And yet he can speak, question, reason. Brocard was suddenly reminded of a small youth who had taken shelter in this same cathedral, many years ago. What would have happened to him if the then Dom Pernay had not taken him in? He hardened his heart. "I cannot help you. The chapter is here to care for humans, not beasts."

The blue eyes came back to him. " 'Yet the dogs eat of the crumbs that fall from their master's table.' "

Brocard found himself staring dumbly at the beast. No, not a beast, to be able to speak and to quote from the Holy

Book. Coming to a sudden decision, Brocard stepped forward. "A cathedral is not the place for a winter shelter. Come with me, and I will lead you to somewhere more suitable."

The novice stared, wide-eyed, as Brocard paused beside him, the beast following docilely. "To your bed," he told Thresalym. "And do not ask permission to break silence on this."

The young man nodded and hurried out into the wind. Brocard followed more slowly, conscious of the beast's halting steps. Snow swirled around their ankles, and more snow was promised by the dark clouds hanging low above their heads, but for now the community buildings were comforting hulks in the dim light. Brocard led the beast to the disused stable block, prying open the tall doors. "I will obtain bedding and bandaging for you," he promised as the creature sank exhaustedly to the hard floor. "What are your dietary requirements?"

"I don't eat."

Almost enough to restore belief in changelings, Brocard thought, despite Dom Avery's persuasions to the contrary. But he prided himself, above all, on being a practical man. He collected bundles of straw from the nearby stables, spreading it across the walkway between the empty stalls, the beast moving obligingly out of his way. Then he lit more candles to bandage up the torn skin, wondering again at the lack of blood and the glistening muscles underneath.

The beast lowered itself onto the straw, tail curled around its body. "Do you require anything further for your comfort?" Brocard asked formally.

The beast brought its head on a level with his own, the large eyes blinking. "You've done more for me than many would. Thank you."

Brocard looked deep into the blue eyes. Something stirred in the depths, a lost soul struggling to break free. "I shall heal thee," Brocard promised, the ritual words welling in response to the need he saw in those deep eyes. "I will see thee whole."

*　*　*　*　*

Between collation and compline was the time set aside for brothers to approach the Abbot in his chambers, bringing news of new patients admitted to the chapter's care. Brocard found himself climbing the creaking stairs alone as he finished his cheese; few men came to the chapter in winter. The snows usually claimed those who made the attempt, and their bodies would be found in the spring thaw. Brocard had often argued for patrols to be made around the chapter borders, to find and lead these poor souls to safety. As yet, he had been unsuccessful in changing tradition. The wounded must seek out their healing.

As the beast had last night. Brocard wiped his mouth and frowned. No, he is not a beast. What did the novice call him? A dragon. He is a dragon. He rubbed his hands on his gray robe, then knocked on the Abbot's door.

"Blessed be the Lord," a voice acknowledged inside.

"And those who serve Him in the healing of others," Brocard responded. He entered the chamber, finding the Abbot to be slowly finishing his daily ration of wine. The old man smiled as he saw Brocard and unhurriedly selected a second slender glass, pouring a measure of red wine from a bottle at his elbow.

"I have had my seasonal portion," Brocard said, though he eyed the glass wistfully.

"I grant you dispensation." The Abbot smiled again as Brocard accepted the glass. "This is the first evening in a month that a brother visits me with the name of a new soul come to us for healing. Tell me of him."

Brocard twirled the glass stem between his thumb and

forefinger, contemplating the swirl of the red liquid as he searched for an answer. "May I first remind you of my own history, most Reverend Father?"

"I know of it, my son."

"I was found in the choir as a cold, unwanted youth." Brocard cast back his mind to the painful memory of the child he had been. "Here I found warmth, healing, love. And here I remained, pledging my life to the Lord's service, so that others might be touched by the same love that had transformed my own life."

The Abbot sighed. "What sort of man has come to us, my son?"

"Not a man at all, or, if so, one that has been severely deformed." Brocard met the Abbot's pale gray eyes. "To all appearances, he is a beast, going about on fours."

"This is a place for the healing of the bodies and minds of men," said the Abbot sternly. "Our sister house attends to the healing of women. But neither is the place for a beast."

"He may be a changeling," Brocard said, reluctant himself to accept the idea.

The Abbot waved that aside. "Brother Avery has disproved that falsehood. The Winds have not that power. You must offer me better reason than that to accept a beast for healing, when the harsh winter makes great demand on our stores."

"He has the appearance of a beast." Brocard took a sip of wine, mentally rehearsing his arguments. "But he speaks; he has reason. When I said to him that the chapter was for humans, not beasts, he quoted from the Holy Book. I believe he has a soul. What else does he require to be worthy of our care?"

The Abbot leaned back in his chair. "Indeed, we do not ask the value of any man before offering him what healing we can. You are correct, my son, in that all humans are equal before the Lord." He flicked a glance at the crucifix, as plain as Brocard's own, on his wall. "Tell me more of your beast."

Brocard related the discovery in the cathedral, leaving out nothing, not even his fear. The Abbot stirred again as he finished. The old man stared moodily into the remains of his wine. "You come to me under a false pretense," he growled. "You have already sworn yourself to his healing."

Brocard bent his head. "I ask forgiveness of my Abbot."

"Bah!" The Abbot put his glass down heavily. "You always skirt the edges of our traditions, Brocard, reinterpreting as you feel may be barely permissible. Since the day I found you huddled in that choir, I knew you would be a challenge to this chapter."

"I have never attempted to presume on our bond," Brocard said stiffly. "You are my Abbot first and foremost, only secondly the father of my soul."

"No, I know you would never presume." The Abbot got up from his chair, his white robe swirling around his thin frame. "But it was the gentling of a young man that gave me the insight to be Abbot." He paced to a small window set beside his bed and placed his palms against the wall on either side. "I am growing old, Brocard."

Brocard put down his wine glass, shaken suddenly by the white hairs he had not noticed before, the deep lines etching the smooth-shaven cheeks. "You will be Abbot yet for many more seasons."

"The Lord's voice becomes clearer as the years pass." The Abbot stared out through the window. "And it becomes more difficult not to answer. One day, my body will join those of our previous brothers in the crypt below the cathedral. And you, Brocard, are my choice as successor."

Brocard tried to speak, but no words would come.

"But, you must take care, my son. A beast with a soul—few will believe you, even as few believed me when I took an abused and frightened youth into the chapter. This may be the challenge to bring you to the wisdom you will require to be Abbot. But if you are mistaken, if you fail, all eyes will see you fail and know you to have been mistaken. You could lose the respect that is also required to be Abbot."

"I would never sacrifice another soul for my own gain," Brocard said quietly.

The Abbot glanced at him. "Ah, but to gain this position would finally free you to forward the new ideas you hold for the order. You would no longer need to force them past old men, eh?"

" 'If you would wish to rule men, you must first rule yourself,' " Brocard quoted. " 'Your care in small things will reveal your ability to care for the great.' "

The Abbot nodded. He came back to his chair, resumed his seat. "Blessed be the Lord."

"And those who serve Him," Brocard responded. "Most Reverend Father, I have admitted a penitent to the care and protection of the Order of St. Thomas. I ask for your blessing upon my administrations for the healing of his soul."

"You have my blessing, my son." The Abbot sketched a cross in the air. "I will add my prayers for his recovery to yours."

Brocard bowed, then left the room. How long, he wondered, before news of the dragon rippled through the chapter, despite the vows of silence? When would the council demand an explanation?

The council. Brocard shrugged the thought away as he prepared for compline. He was a fully qualified soul-healer whose very background was controversial. Those who thought ill of him would always do so, and those who supported him before would stand beside him now. Even as the Abbot had done.

* * * * *

The first task Brocard set for himself was the healing of the dragon's wounds. The crippled foot and wing, he decided, were ancient scars, long healed if never fully mended, but the marks of a recent battle covered the dragon's legs and belly. Brocard talked in a low, constant voice as he changed bandages and bedding, talking about everything and nothing, knowing from experience that merely the sound of a friendly voice could begin the process of healing.

Strength slowly came back into the large body. But the dragon's head still hung low, and he spoke not a word. His ears followed Brocard, however, so the man knew the dragon was listening to him.

After a fortnight, Brocard began to notice an eagerness in the dragon when he approached the stables. The beast snuffled with interest at the healed skin, touched with his bright red tongue the spots where new scales grew.

After tierce one morning, the raw taste of communion wine still fresh in his throat, Brocard entered the stables to find the dragon standing, his eyes bright and alert. He halted, held his breath as the dragon studied him. How do I look to you? he wondered. The chapter did not possess any mirrors. Do dragons grow gray hairs as they age, or gain rounded bellies from winter rations of ale?

"Why?" asked the dragon finally. "Why are you caring for me?"

Suspicion trembled in the deep blue eyes, agitated the long tail. "The purpose of our order is to bring healing to this suffering world," Brocard said quietly. He wanted to go up to the dragon, to lay calming hands on his muzzle. . . . But he knew that he was not so trusted. Not yet. "We seek to do so by healing the bodies and the souls of those who come to us."

"No." The dragon's tail slammed against a stall door. "Why you, for me?"

Brocard rubbed his beard. "A soul-healer can enter only the shadows he himself has confronted. He can be a guide only for lands he has once traversed within himself. Even as you are now nameless, your history locked away from you, so I was when I was discovered, also in the cathedral choir."

The dragon took a step toward him. "What happened to you?" Then he ducked his head and looked away. "Sorry."

Brocard dared to take a step closer. "Sorry for the asking? If we are to help one another, we must be honest to each other. We must be free to ask, and to answer."

The dragon swung his head back, lowering it so their eyes were on a level. "Do you now remember what happened to you?"

"As much as I can bear to remember." Brocard forced his voice to remain steady. "When I was five years of age, our tribe was attacked by some of the barbarians that inhabit these regions. Most of the men were killed, but I was considered pretty by the barbarians, and was their plaything when they were tired of captured women. I was with them for many years, a witness to their attacks and atrocities."

The dragon moved restlessly. "Do you hate them?"

"For many years, I did," Brocard admitted, his voice still steady. "But hatred is an emotion that saps at the heart and serves no purpose but to wound one anew. I escaped from their camp one night when they had drunk themselves into a stupor. I was found in the choir several months later, the memory of my time with the barbarians deeply buried, hidden from even myself."

"Wasn't it better that way?"

Brocard noted the hope in the dragon's voice. "Such things may be hidden from the waking mind, but the memories still fester beneath. Until they are exhumed and faced, any peace is a false peace, built upon rotting foundations."

"I don't want to remember."

"Then what is it that you do want?"

The dragon sighed. "I don't know."

Brocard allowed a moment of silence to grow between them, not removing his gaze from the dragon. The dragon shifted again, ears twitching. "I don't know," he said again, finally. "Will I never know, unless I get my memories back?"

That is for you to answer, Brocard thought. Aloud, he said, "Brother Angles, our chapter physician, is to visit you tomorrow morning. I have asked him to confirm that your recent physical wounds are now healed."

"Will it hurt?"

"I can never promise that you will not feel pain," Brocard said softly. "Pain is often part of healing. Even as a leg wrongly set must be rebroken so it can heal properly, so must the past be confronted so a future can be built." He finally closed the gap between himself and the dragon. "You do not travel this path alone. I will be with you."

The dragon lifted his head and turned it away. "And if I don't want to?"

Brocard stepped to one side, pointed at the stable block's doors. "The doors are only closed, not bolted. You are free to depart at any time. We only offer healing; we do not force it." He glanced back at the dragon. "But I ask you, how long can you continue to flee from your past?"

The dragon studied him for a moment, then lowered his head. "I will stay."

* * * * *

Brother Angles gave his report to the chapter meeting after prime. The other brothers with patients under their care had already summarized their current conditions, answering such questions as were presented. Past mornings, Brocard's report had been as succinct as theirs. But, as

Angles concluded that the dragon appeared to be in full health, his old injuries notwithstanding, Brocard sensed that his latest update would be questioned.

Indeed it soon was. No sooner had he returned to his seat than Dom Cherril stood. "He agreed to stay," the man rasped. "How kind of him. You tolerated such reluctance?"

"Dom Cherril," another council member, Dom Acton, chided. "You can hardly expect a man to thank you while his arm is being reset."

"We give our gifts too easily," Cherril continued loudly. "Have you spoken to him of the Lord?"

The eyes of those brothers not on the council were wide at this public argument. Brocard gave them all a reassuring smile, but his eyes met the Abbot's. The Abbot would rather that such debates took place in council, doors barred to the other brothers. But are we not all of one order, brothers in one Lord? Brocard thought. Should not all the brothers, lay and novice as well, know of the discussions that will affect the chapter? "Brothers, this is an argument that has long set my will against that of Dom Cherril. He sees the purpose of a Holy Order to be that of preaching and conversion—"

" 'Go ye into all the world,' " quoted Cherril, " 'and preach the gospel to every creature.' "

"Whereas I believe that we are to serve those who come to us, in the name of the Lord who shed His blood so that all may know healing. 'With His stripes we are healed.' It is not our place to demand anything in return."

Cherril stood to speak again, but the Abbot came to his feet, silencing them all. He swept the gathering with his gray eyes. The candles lighting the room stood behind him, their yellowed light turning his wisp of hair into a halo. "My sons," he said, "you have heard today the two views that exist on my council. No doubt, some of you have faced similar doubts in the privacy of your own souls." He paused for a moment.

Brocard dared to glance around the room, finding the same look of reverence and awe on each of the fifty-odd faces lifted to the Abbot. The thought of himself possibly being the recipient of such regard made Brocard shift uneasily.

"You would now have me offer you the answer, even as we give an answer to our novices when the questions become beyond their bearing. But I do not believe there to be an answer. Nor do I seek it. Both insights are required in our wounded world, and both are to be valued. 'But the manifestation of the Spirit is given to every man to profit withal.' "

The Abbot returned to his seat, nodded to the chapter secretary. Dom Elias struck a small bell, announcing the end of the meeting.

Dom Cherril waited in the corridor outside for Brocard. "My only concern, Brother," he said, walking beside Brocard as they headed for the novices' dormitories, "is that you do not exclude the Lord from your work. The only true healing comes from the Lord."

"My work is in His name," Brocard responded. He slipped his hands into his robe sleeves as they stepped outside, the sky pale with dawn. "I am but a channel for His healing."

Cherril ducked his head in a half-nod. "I only pray, my brother, that you will know when to stand aside and allow the Lord to heal directly."

* * * * *

The dragon awoke slowly. The bells rang in the cathedral. Tierce, he decided, glancing at the amount of light creeping under the door of the long stables. Brocard would come soon.

He slowly got to his feet. Muscles he had once thought would never recover were once again supple, ready. The slashes inflicted by the wolves—his mind shied away from the ending to that battle—were now closed, and new scales were quickly growing to replace those that were lost.

I could go now, he thought. I could leave, but . . . Where? Where would I go? Who would welcome me? He sighed, his breath scattering straw across the stone floor. Brocard wants me to stay. Brocard wants to help me remember.

His tail twitched. The past was a shadow. Why not leave it so? Why not enjoy the present? But I can't, he thought. He took a deep breath of the musty air, the fresher, dry scent of straw mingling with the older rank smell of coursair. There is someone I promised . . . something. I must remember, so I can keep my promise. I keep my promises.

He lifted his head at the sound of footsteps—Brocard's footsteps. He stepped forward, standing at the edge of the straw bedding. Brocard gave him a smile as he opened the doors, and the dragon felt an answering welcome leap in his chest as he wrinkled his nose in return.

"You feel well today?" Brocard asked.

"Yes." The dragon's eyes were drawn to the doors, still open. For the first time in weeks, he saw the world outside stone walls, smelled the freshness of snow. His ears flicked to the sounds of coursairs grunting.

"Would you like to go outside?"

In answer, the dragon limped forward, pausing for a moment in the doorway. A courtyard stretched before him, mostly cleared of snow, open to the west. On the other side of his stable, a long, rectangular building stretched, two rows of small windows announcing the presence of rooms. Another building, squarer, stood at a right angle to the dormitory. To his left was another stable block; his nose confirmed that it held coursairs. And ahead of him . . .

He stepped outside to gain a better look. The cathedral, he decided. Unlike the dark stone of the other buildings, only light gray brick formed the foundations, rising high into the air to support the tall windows.

The windows. He followed the patterns, telescoping his sight to better study the many pieces of colored glass. They were set together to make pictures that he felt were familiar, like stories he had once heard told. He pulled back his gaze, noting the arches of stone that leapt from pillars to the roof, supporting the weight of the building.

"The cathedral appears to fascinate you."

The dragon had almost forgotten that Brocard stood beside him. "Yes. She is beautiful." He felt a twinge of disloyalty. Once, there had been another holy place, even more beautiful than this. . . . But the memory slipped away.

"Come. I will show you inside."

He limped obediently after the man. The skies were more gray than blue, sunlight muted, but he still rejoiced in the feel of light on his scales, fresh air in his lungs. He almost resented entering the cathedral, stone once again cutting him off from the world. But he watched with interest as Brocard opened the second set of doors and led him up the nave.

Even in the dull light, the windows glittered. Gonard remembered the dark night he had hidden in here, nursing his wounds, wanting little more than to be left in peace. But Brocard had found him, was going to help him. He took a deep breath, nostrils twitching at the bittersweet smell of incense.

"You do not know your name," Brocard said quietly, his voice slipping easily into the stillness. "But it is not proper for any child of the Lord to go nameless through the world. I have brought you here to choose a name for yourself, to use until you remember your own."

The dragon shuddered involuntarily. "I should carry

only the name my father gave to me."

"We are all named at birth." Brocard waved past the stone supporting pillars to the many small chapels that were set back from the cathedral proper. "Many men, upon entering the order, choose new names for themselves, often taking the name of one of the saints that waits upon the Lord. Thus a second birth is celebrated. View the chapels. See the saints. Choose a name."

"My father named me," the dragon said stubbornly, not understanding his reluctance.

"You are always free to reassume that name," Brocard said soothingly. "Will you not take another name for the present?"

"I will look," the dragon conceded. He limped around a pillar into the south aisle. The chapels were set back into the thick walls. Each held an image: some a painting, others a sculpture. One statue showed a man carrying a child on his shoulders; Saint Christopher, the inscription chiseled onto the marble read. Another chapel held a painting of a man kneeling, large lions crouched around his body; the dragon felt a shiver of memory trickle down his spine, then disappear.

He dutifully circuited the cathedral, entering the south transept, bowing to the high altar with Brocard as they passed outside the sanctuary. He could not feel any connection between himself and these pious, holy men. What did they know of his history, his pain? How could he name himself after one of them?

Then, in the north transept, he halted. A statue stood in a small chapel, a single, weak candle throwing a deformed shadow on the wall behind it. He limped forward, holding his breath lest he be mistaken. The statue seemed to meet his eyes mournfully, hands clenched together over the hilt of a sword, tip buried in the earth. "What is his name?" he asked Brocard.

"He has one name, but with two pronunciations. By some brothers he is known as Saint Michael. Others call him Saint Michel."

"I like Michel. It's a softer sound." He swallowed. "He has wings like mine."

Brocard came to his side. "The left wing of the statue was shattered long ago. The true angel has two whole wings."

"He is more like me than any of the others." The dragon glanced at the man. "May I be called Michel?"

Brocard studied him for a moment. The dragon moved back slightly. He had the sudden, uncomfortable feeling that the man was listening to something other than his spoken words. "The naming is for you to perform. Name yourself."

The dragon shook his head. "I can't."

"Why not?"

"It is not permitted." He felt the walls around him change, meld into those of darker stone, a smooth white floor beneath his claws. "No. Only the Master can name."

"The Master?"

"My father. Only he can name." The dragon turned his head. The cathedral spun past his vision; the windows became tall, glittering cabinets, the wind outside the hum of machinery. "I can do nothing without him. Only rust. Dragons can only rust."

"And what name did he give you?"

"A stupid name! A joke!" The dragon took a deep breath, incense tickling his throat, ashes burning his nostrils. "Something he could laugh at, nothing else. And I thought it was a gift!"

The world seemed to spin around him. He dug his claws deep into the stones, willing himself back to the cathedral, to Brocard's comforting presence. The cold walls of gray slid away, the reek of burnt flesh cleared from his nostrils.

"But I can't remember it," he said at last.

Brocard nodded thoughtfully. "Could your father not give you another name?"

"No." He shuddered. The ashes were back, coating his mouth, swirling in the air. "He can't."

"Why not?"

Flame, erupting from his jaws. A small man, twisting in the fire. Soot staining a white floor. "Because he's dead. I killed him."

CHAPTER 5

The medtech moved stiffly from the corner of the hall in which he usually stood to pass the nights. Not for the first time he regretted the loss of his laboratory, left behind in the Citadel. He had been programmed to bring value to the lives of humans, either by serving as a medical technician or by the research he carried out when his medical skills were not required. But there was little for him to do at night while humans slept.

Gonard sleeps, he reflected. His hands ran down his beige coveralls, noting the stains and wear. A weaver was due to call this morning with a new set, just in time to present himself before the conclave and argue on behalf of the dragon.

Yes, Gonard sleeps and thereby renews his energy levels for the next day. The medtech dispassionately studied one gray hand, more stained and ragged than the clothes he wore. I was built with only a limited amount of energy stores. Once they have been depleted, I will cease to exist. Gonard could possibly continue existence limitlessly. In that alone, I am more human than he.

A diffident knock on the door echoed through the hall. The medtech moved unhurriedly to answer it. As he had expected, the weaver waited outside, a folded garment resting on his arms. "M'lord," he said humbly, "I hae brought yer suit."

"You may leave it with me."

"Yer pardon, m'lord," the man continued, "but it be fer me t' check th' fitting."

The medtech stepped back, allowing him to come inside. The weaver glanced at the high walls of the hall, then down at the polished tiles underfoot. Dragon claws had left marks on many of them. Then, remembering why he was there, the man offered the coveralls to the medtech.

Yes, they would do. The medtech shook them out, the fabric slightly darker than that of those he currently wore. The material was a wool and cotton mixture, warmer yet less hard-wearing than the synthetic coveralls he had brought with him from the Citadel. It would suffice.

The weaver's efficiency made the medtech willing to be sympathetic. "It would be my suggestion that you turn your head while I exchange garments."

The man smiled. "M'lord, I hae seen many a man in th' flesh, from the great o' th' Singers t' th' lowest o' th' street sweepers. I would see th' fit."

The medtech lifted his shoulders in a shrug. He pressed down the side of the coveralls he wore, releasing the molecular bindings. As the material fell away, he saw the weaver swallow, back away uneasily. Without a word, the medtech stepped into the new outfit. The buttons took a few minutes to fix into place, giving the man time to recover his composure.

"M'lord," the weaver said apologetically, coming forward to check the fit, "I did nae know that th' Winds had so changed ye. T' nae be a man . . ."

"I was never anatomically complete," the medtech answered. "My Master left me when I was only partially finished. The assistant who finally assembled my components decided that the materials could be better used elsewhere."

The man nodded, pretending to understand. The medtech lifted his arms, allowing the length of the sleeves to be measured. "Yer arms be th' same length. I oft see one o' them shorter than th' other."

"There are portions of my construction that are superior to the human body," the medtech said. "My skeletal structure is composed of a synthetic form of titanium. Unlike Gonard, the one your people call the Windwalker, I am not susceptible to corrosion should my interior be exposed to moisture."

"Yer words be strange t' me, m'lord," the weaver said, voice muffled by the measuring tape held between his teeth. "I do nae understand them."

"I never expected you to do so." The medtech watched the man rise to his feet. "The garment is satisfactory. You will receive payment for your services."

"Nay, m'lord. It be a pleasure t' serve ye." The weaver managed to sound sincere, though the pounding of his heart, obvious to the medtech's sensitive hearing, told otherwise. "Do ye require aught else?"

"You may depart hall and confine," the medtech confirmed. Even the Outler offered more stimulating conversation, limited as her intelligence might be.

* * * * *

Clothes were easily changed. The medtech found himself shuffling as he left the hall, and he forced the aging servos in his legs to lift his feet higher. If he had access to his laboratory—even an hour would do—he could tighten up the skin, inject lubricants into the joints. The steady disintegration would continue, but it would be less obvious.

Winter sun was struggling weakly through the cloudy sky. The medtech felt a few rays touch his face, sparking a chemical reaction that further relaxed the lining from metallic bones. I may have to consider taking to the wearing of a hat, the medtech reflected, although it would be regrettable to give the Outler such ample justification for amusement.

The conclave's chamber was located in the exact center of the confine. He was due to meet the Singers there "near t' th' mid o' th' day." To one with an inbuilt clock, this meant noon. However, bearing in mind the usual relaxed attitude the people of the settlement held about time, he could expect a number of fellow attendees to be early, and the rest to file in later.

Only once before had he had occasion to visit the most important structure in the settlement. Then, as now, he was intrigued by the lack of distinguishing marks. Other than its size, there was nothing to indicate the stature of the building. The golden stone was plain, the entrance the standard double doors. It must be recalled, the medtech mused, that only Singers would see this chamber, so far into the confine. There is no need to impress the clans.

Two guards stood before the doors. They nodded respectfully to the medtech and stepped aside. He noted their deference. The Outler had showed little interest in his growing importance within the settlement; unlike himself, she had not examined the uses to which it could be put.

The door swung open into the chamber proper. The medtech let it swing shut behind him, the Singers sitting nearest him glancing up curiously. The rest, arranged on benches along one long wall, were listening to the debate between a man and a woman, which was taking place on the open floor.

The medtech's timing mechanism told him it was noon. He shuffled past the benches and onto the clear area. "The medtech of Rumfus Max," he announced, cutting through the woman's speech. "I was summoned."

The woman nodded to the man, who took a seat. The Singer turned to the medtech. "I be Callin o' Macall. Ye were called t' us fer ye hae come t' be a voice in th' settlement."

"There are those who have come to value my advice," the medtech admitted.

One of the seated Singers leaned forward. "And by what authority hae ye set yerself so forward?"

As his body deteriorated, so did his programming. The medtech felt the present shunt to one side, to be replaced by one of his stored experiences. Another questioning by self-important, self-elected humans, seated on tiered rows in a round chamber. The air there was artificial, heavy from constant reuse, and the bright colors of the Lord Citizens' robes made the white walls seem even brighter.

"Although I have been constructed in the human form, declared as holy and sacred by a number of your Schools," the medtech declared, "I do not consider that I am an abomination against the Ultimate. My form was chosen to reflect my function, which is that of a medical technician to Citizens and Lord Citizens of the Domains. My ability to serve you would be impeded by a form that seemed unnatural in its design, as humans demonstratively prefer to be served by humans."

Then the past swirled away, stored once again in the appropriate memory capsule. The medtech found the Singers muttering and staring, confused by his response. "I am able to speak in terms that none of you can comprehend," he said smoothly. "I am, however, also able to provide advice and interpretations of which those who have lived always in the settlement could never conceive."

"But by what authority?" the Singer repeated.

The medtech straightened. "By my position as Second to the Windwalker, Gonard of Rumfus Max."

"Ye do nae understand," a woman said. "There be some question about th' Windwalker. There be question whether he be a Walker. He hae nae returned from th' Winds."

"I have been given to understand," the medtech said

stiffly, "that not all Windwalkers do return."

The humpbacked Windwalker who had escorted Gonard out into his first Winds rose. "A true Walker would always return. E'en wi'out his mind, he returns."

"Gonard may still return." The medtech flopped his shoulders in a shrug. His optical units analyzed the varied expressions of the several dozen Singers watching him, and he concluded that *he* was being tested in this interchange, not Gonard. "Winter has only just begun."

A general relaxation in the room confirmed his suspicions. The Windwalker resumed his seat, and Callin nodded. "So say we. Th' Walker will return, fer he be Walker. So did we declare after th' trial and his first Walk. We cannae hae th' clan say otherwise."

The medtech gave them one of his rare smiles as he recalled the outcome of the trial. "For if he were to be declared never to have been a Windwalker, the clan could press claims against the Singers for the loss of the tribe's hunting time. The confine would have to pay compensation."

"Aye," Callin agreed grimly. "Fer th' entire tribe."

"Which could be very costly."

"An o' danger fer ye an' his woman. Ye would be held as guilty as he, an' suffer at th' hands o' th' clan. They would take t' revenge." She raised her chin. "Also, yer place here be from th' Windwalker. If he be found t' be other, yer place be forfeit."

The medtech executed a stiff bow. He preferred humans who were direct. "Then it would appear that I have good justification to support belief in Gonard's eventual return. I also, therefore, gain additional reason for the request I bring with me to this conclave."

"Name it, Second."

The medtech paused, acknowledging the reminder of his rank. "Indeed, I am only the Second to a Windwalker."

Second to Gonard in more ways than these humans would ever know. "I have, however, noted that my services have not been unappreciated by those to whom I have supplied them. I now seek formal confirmation of my abilities, in order that I may be of further service to this community."

"I do nae trust him," one of the Singers growled, his voice carrying through the chamber. "He be too full o' his own words fer trusting."

"Its form is blasphemous," the Lord Citizen countered, robes swirling against the white balcony as he stood. "The machine must be destroyed!"

The medtech waited as past merged once again into present. "Then whose words would I use, if not my own?"

A few chuckles rose from the listening Singers. But his challenger remained persistent. "Th' words o' yer master."

"We can see that its own designer left it incomplete," the voice of the Lord Citizen echoed around the chamber. "Perhaps it would have been better if his assistant had also recognized the error of his ways."

"What I offer is complete within itself," the medtech said evenly, forcing his attention to remain on the present. "If this conclave had felt otherwise, the guards would have been instructed to prevent clan members from entering the confine to seek my advice."

"In th' absence o' his master," said another Singer thoughtfully, "we may wish t' hae him wi' us, fer our guidance."

"And how can we prevent it from destroying the faith of our younger Citizens?"

"If what I do destroys that which already exists," the medtech answered to both of his accusers, past and present, "then what exists was too weak to survive long at any rate." He tipped back his head. "What is it that you fear?"

"Oh, let it continue, then," another Citizen snapped, waving a dismissive hand. "This argument bores me. All the robot wants to

do is be useful. So let it be."

"Aye, indeed," said his present interrogator. "Th' man hae as much reason as we fer supporting th' confine. I say, bring him into th' conclave. Then will he be wi' us. He hae th' necessary learning, an' no need t' sing."

"Besides," added another Lady Citizen dryly, "how long can a robot operate for? A few years should see us rid of it."

Callin raised her voice. "An' all who be fer th' Second joining th' conclave, stand now in yer place."

The two events might be separated by years, but the looks on the human faces were the same. Grudging acceptance, permitting a robot's existence merely because it was less awkward than the alternative. The medtech heard once again a Lord Citizen's voice announcing that he could leave, the cultured tones blending with the rougher vowels of the Singer as she pronounced the date for the medtech's entrance into the conclave. The medtech gave them a respectful bow, then left the building.

The sunlight had disappeared, to be replaced by clouds carried across the sky by strong upper winds. The medtech bent his head as rain began to fall, soft, large drops that soaked his hair and clothes in the few minutes it took for him to walk back to the hall granted to him as Gonard's Second.

A knife thwacked into the wood beside him as he opened one of the double doors and stepped inside. The medtech studied the long blade, then lifted his eyes to Itsa. She shrugged. "Got to keep workin' on my aim," she said, striding forward to reclaim the dagger.

The medtech measured the centimeters between the metal and himself. "If I was meant as the target, you have much more work to do."

Itsa barked a laugh. "Nay, hardly. 'Sides, wouldn't of mattered if I hit ya, anyways, would it? Ya've got no feelin's."

"I possess no pain receptors," the medtech acknowledged.

"Ya jig that's not what I meant." Itsa walked back to her original position. "Come on, tech, outta the firin' line."

"Would I not be less likely to encounter damage should I remain here?"

"Stop joshin'." Before he could move, Itsa flung the knife again. The tip buried itself alongside the previous mark. "Hey, like yer new getup. All ya need now is a new haircut."

"My hair," the medtech said, shuffling away from the doors, "is incapable of growth."

"Yeah, that's the prob." Itsa ran her fingers through her own dark, shoulder-length hair. "It's startin' to look real tatty."

"My master found it easier to emulate skin than hair."

"That's not much better." She pointed the knife at his arms. "Good thing ya've got long sleeves to hide that."

"There is no need," he said stiffly, "for me to hide anything."

"Sure, tech. Look, we all hide somethin'." She slipped the knife away, brushing back her dark cloak to reveal the leather sheath. "Ya might be a 'bot, butcha ain't told me everythin'. I'm still watchin' ya."

He looked down at her, a sudden loss of control sending his fingers twitching. "You are wise to do so."

"Yeah, yeah, I jig." The cloak was drawn closed, hiding the bright trousers and long shirt. "See ya later."

"Do you recall Gonard's first appearance before the Council?"

As he had planned, his soft tone stopped her before she had reached the doors. Itsa turned, scowling. " 'Course I do. I was there, 'member? Ya saw the whole thing yarself."

"The trial was only postponed, not concluded," the medtech continued. "When we return to the Citadel, Gonard will need to appear before the Council for a second time. He will find it necessary to prove that he possesses a soul, or the Council will order his destruction in retaliation for his murder of the Master."

Itsa shrugged. "That's yar prob, not mine. I just came 'long for the ride."

"You came because Gonard requested you to come."

"And 'cause the Lord Cits were breathin' hard behind us!" Itsa snapped. "I wasn't gonna stay behind and be blamed for him gettin' 'way, was I?"

"You came because Gonard requested your presence," the medtech persisted. "You remained with him through a year of trial and hardship."

She shoved hands into trouser pockets. "Does this have a point, tech? 'Cause I'm gettin' jaded, standin' here."

"I merely question your loyalty." He turned his head. "We must prepare to search for Gonard once the winter has passed, should he not return before that time. Yet you seek the companionship of a clan member in Gonard's absence."

"Maybe ya missed it, tech." Itsa's rough voice brought his gaze back. Her cheeks were red, eyes bright. "I begged him not to go. Ya hear me? I *begged* him. I don't beg nobody for nothin'. And he still went out there. So that's it, right? If I don't mean that much to him, then he sure don't mean that much to me."

"He had no choice but to face the Changewinds again."

" 'Sides, what's the point, me and a dragon?" She snorted. "Ya've tried to break us up lots before this. Well, maybe ya ain't gotta try no longer. The dragon's done it for ya."

She slipped out the door. A chill wind blasted briefly into the room, scattering the damp locks curling on the medtech's head. Then she was gone, leaving him staring thoughtfully at the scarred wood.

The door opened again. The medtech studied the face of the woman who entered, her hesitancy giving him time to confirm that she was not in his database. He gave her a grave nod. "Welcome to Gonard of Rumfus Max's hall. It is my duty to hold it until such time as he returns."

"I be Lissa o' Sanna." The woman introduced herself quietly. "It be said, ye hold th' hall 'lone."

"Itsa of Sharit also occupies a room in this hall."

"But she be nae yer woman."

The medtech all but smiled. "If she is anyone's woman, it is of the Windwalker."

"I thought it said that she be wi' Rygor o' th' Clan o' Millan."

"It will not be possible for her to remain with him."

"It be an unlikely pairing," Lissa admitted. "But if they love one another . . ." She shrugged.

"I have neither the time nor the programming," the medtech said sharply, "to indulge in useless gossiping. What is your purpose here?"

"Ye hae nae woman." Lissa smiled. "Ye need one t' do yer cooking an' th' cleaning, t' barter fer clothing an' t' set th' fire. I be that woman."

The medtech shrugged. Considering how long he and the Outler had already lived here, it seemed strange that only now was a woman being assigned to take on such duties. "It is acceptable. You may begin by cleaning out the ashes from the fireplace." Itsa steadfastly ignored such tasks, and he was finding it more and more difficult to wash the black soot from his skin.

"Aye, m'lord." Lissa started her tasks with a possessive smile that the medtech found unsettling. He moved to his room, leaving her to the work.

*　*　*　*　*

The ceremony was short and direct. The medtech was surrounded by the Singers and Windwalkers, who laid a dark green cloak over his slumped shoulders. An earring of green metal slid coldly through his left ear. Callin nodded, and the medtech knelt stiffly, joints creaking in protest. He lifted folded hands to the assembly.

"Do ye swear, on th' lives o' those ye cherish," she asked, slowly, seriously, "t' protect an' t' serve th' settlement, t' protect all an' t' counsel them who come t' ye?"

"I will protect every member of tribe and clan of this settlement," the medtech intoned. "I will offer reasoned counsel to any who seek me out. In everything, I shall remember that I represent the confine and the Singers and Windwalkers within. So do I swear, on the lives of those I cherish."

"Now ye are one o' us." Callin waved him to rise. "An we welcome ye t' th' confine."

The medtech stood. Reluctant welcome, he thought, little better than no welcome at all. "It is my pleasure," he said calmly. Speaking untruths was daily becoming easier. "Have I the freedom of the settlement?"

"All that be ours," Callin assured him, "also now be yours."

"It will be mine to cherish." He bowed, then shuffled away through the misty afternoon.

Snow was falling in the distance. The sensitive olfactors along his nasal cavity picked up the crisp, frozen smell. He predicted that the fall would continue over the settlement, coating the buildings in white within two days' time. Gonard would not be able to return through the drifts, even if he were in a state to do so. Once again, the medtech felt his fingers twitch, angry and helpless.

"I would speak wi' ye."

The medtech halted at the creaky voice of the Windwalker. Glancing back, he met the eyes of the old man, still bright under the hump bending his spine. "I know of nothing we would wish to discuss."

"I sent Gonard o' Rumfus Max back into th' Winds fer th' sake o' a darkness he bore. Only then could he name it, an' by th' naming be free o' it." The Windwalker spoke thoughtfully, and the medtech felt his close scrutiny. "Ye hae a greater darkness yet, an' ye also know th' reason fer it. Why do ye nae let it go?"

The medtech gave him a slight, mocking smile. "Save your breath for those who can use it."

"Ye carry a great darkness," the man persisted. "Speak its name, an' be free o' it."

The medtech turned back, resumed his steady pace. "Then take great care!" the Windwalker called after him. "Take great care, else th' darkness may harm them closest t' ye!"

That is what I am planning for, the medtech thought grimly. Still wearing the gaudy cloak, he passed through the gates of the confine and into the settlement proper. It was necessary to ensure that many humans saw him in the stature of his new role.

Despite the chilly day, few clan members had stayed in their homes. Children played in the streets, throwing counters onto the stones or engaging in mock battles. Women haggled with market traders, their husbands standing meekly nearby. There was laughter as two men shared a joke, tears from a boy who had fallen onto the hard ground. The medtech strode on. His programming had not included emotions, and what little he had developed still gave him no insight into why humans had to carry such a wide variety of reactions to the world. As ever, he felt no affinity with the creatures with which he shared a form, but little else.

His steps slowed as he picked up Itsa's distinctive, dusty scent. She was sitting on an empty market bench, her legs swinging as she whistled an absent tune to herself. A small knife flicked between her dark fingers, slicing away at a piece of stire horn. From the male Gonard had killed, the medtech decided as he came closer. He knew that the Outler had carved a whistle for the dragon from the first horn. It appeared that she was now working on a second one.

"Just the person to ruin my day," she said as he stopped

before her. "Go 'way."

"Where is your paramour?"

Itsa looked up at him. "My whatamore?"

The medtech wondered why she persisted in her pretense. They both knew she was far more intelligent than she chose to appear. "The clan member to whom you have attached yourself."

"We've finished lessons for today." She leaned closer, then grinned. "Hey, ya got an earring! Very flashin'. Still don't look much like yar brother."

"The City's earrings were created from crystal, not metal."

"Off it, tech, don't act so dim," Itsa retorted. "Why aren'tcha a dragon, like Gonard?"

"Form follows function."

"Whatcha mean?"

"You know precisely to what I refer," the medtech said calmly. "I was built in human form to better serve humans. Gonard was most likely built as a dragon to fulfill whatever purpose our Master had for him."

"To be able to kill." Itsa shrugged at the medtech's glare. "That's what I told the dragon, once. Why else make him a walkin' flamethrower? That's his purpose, to kill."

"Then why does he possess wings?"

" 'Cause they look pret?" Itsa grinned. "Well, they would, if one weren't all twisted."

"Then why did Lord Citizen Rumfus Max not make him aware of the function of wings?"

"Maybe he wasn't that nastic. Why tell the dragon when he couldn't use one of them anyways?" Itsa slid to the ground. "Ya jig somethin', don'tcha? Ya jig, and ya won't tell me." Her nostrils flared. "Spill it, ya shattin' robot."

The medtech said nothing, merely smiled. She swore and marched away, boots scuffing against cobbles. Of all the humans who might have been necessary to my plans, he thought, why did it have to be an infuriating Outler?

A man cleared his throat. The medtech turned, finding a member of the clan of Millan at his elbow. "M'lord," he said quietly, "I seek a word wi' ye."

The medtech bent his head. "I am at your service, Shan of Shannus."

Shan smiled. "I be honored that ye 'member me name, m'lord."

"It is the place of a Second to know all the names of those entrusted to his lord's care," the medtech demurred. "It is his place to provide for them, even if his lord cannot fulfill his duty."

The man blinked. "Th' Windwalker were cleared by th' triune, me thought."

"Of course he was," the medtech said smoothly. "And the triune judgment never errs."

"Nay, it ne'er be wrong," Shan said, though without confidence. "Th' Walker will return, will he nae?"

"Of course he will," the medtech affirmed. "He must, or he was never a Windwalker."

"Aye." The man chewed his lip, troubled. "If ye would come wi' me, m'lord, I would hae me words under me roof."

The medtech followed the man, pleased with his sudden hesitancy. And so it begins, he thought. So it begins.

* * * * *

The medtech returned to the hall several hours later, pleased with the day's work. He had spoken to several clan men, leaving them with new thoughts, new concerns. Now he needed a few minutes to file away the information he had gathered.

Itsa was near the entrance, her body stiff with anger. The medtech followed the direction of her glare. Lissa stood near the fire, a mop in her hand. "What," Itsa asked icily, "is this?"

"I be Lissa o' Sanna—"

"I wasn't askin' ya." Itsa transferred her glare to the medtech. "What's she doin' here?"

"It is evident," the medtech informed her, "that you were never taught the principles of polite behavior."

"Manners don't save yar throat in th' mines." Itsa took a step forward. "Who is she?"

"Lissa o' Sanna, who has offered her services."

Itsa's eyes returned to the older woman. "To do what?"

"Th' Second be wi'out a woman," Lissa pointed out. "I hae offered t' be woman fer him."

For a moment, Itsa simply stared at her. Then she began to laugh, quietly, glancing between the woman and the medtech. "Ya don't jig, do ya?" she finally asked him. "Ya just don't jig. Ya're so dim, sometimes."

The medtech began stiffly, "It would be of assistance if you would explain—"

"Go 'head," Itsa told Lissa. "Prove yarself to him. Just don't make too many plans." Still chuckling, she went to her room.

The medtech stared after her. Levity from the Outler always alarmed him.

"Methinks she be jealous," Lissa offered. She propped the mop by the fireplace and crossed over the hall to his side. Her fingers touched his cloak. "Be ye now a member o' th' conclave, m'lord?"

"The ceremony took place today," he confirmed.

"Then come wi' ye," she said, smiling up at him as she wove her arm through his. "Ye must hae some better clothes t' wear wi' that cloak. Ye be o' th' conclave now. Ye must be proud t' wear th' colors."

Proud? the medtech mused as she led him back out into the afternoon. A search of his memory stores revealed that pride was another emotion he had never experienced.

Lissa appeared happy enough to exhibit it for both of

them. She kept her hand on his arm, her shoulders straight and her chin high as she marched along the tailors' stalls. "Green," she told the women by the bolts of fabric. "He be now o' th' conclave. What hae ye t' offer in green?"

Heads turned as they passed. Even the medtech's hearing wasn't sharp enough to catch the comments muttered by others nearby. He felt current awareness slip again, the past weaving common threads with the present.

The stale, many-times breathed air of the Citadel. A man shorter than the medtech holding a hand on his elbow, offering encouragement as the robot took his first hesitant steps. Activation was an event only hours old, and the bombardment of sensations was almost overwhelming new circuits.

"You'll get used to everything," the man beside him said. "Human babies take years before they even walk."

The medtech looked at him and found that he was once again using wrongful interpretation. The man's round, red face sounded like a flute, the gray shirt adding a violin accompaniment. "Am I not human?"

"You're a robot." The man's sigh was tinged blue-green. "I've put you together from Lord Max's plans—I'll explain that later."

Faces. The medtech was slowly sorting out his senses. Now he saw faces, rather than heard them. Men and women were slowing as they came down the corridor, the skin around their eyes and mouths wrinkling as they looked at him. The medtech glanced down at his co-creator. "Do humans look at robots differently than they look at other humans?"

"Yes." The medtech's circuitry interpreted the man's tone as one of sadness. "Yes, unfortunately, they do. It's something you'll have to learn to live with, I'm afraid. But I'll help you as much as I can."

A slight push against his chest brought him back to a chill day in a society hundreds of years removed from the technology necessary to build a robot. Lissa was pressing a shirt against his chest, smiling at the near fit. She nodded at him, noting that his thoughts had returned to her. Surprised at her easy acceptance of his mental lapse, the medtech watched her haggle for his new clothes. When she smiled at him, he found his mouth twitching in return.

CHAPTER 6

Brocard unwillingly left the dinner table. He had forced himself to eat his ration of meat and cheese, but left his bread untouched. As he left, he tapped the shoulder of Brother Kern and pushed his plate in front of the other man.

He made his way down the corridor joining the refectory to the chapterhouse, reflecting that it was only in obedience to one of the order's rules that he was now reporting to the Abbot. Poverty, chastity, obedience, he thought. The foundations of the order. We may possess a modicum of furniture, we may be forgiven a past history of unwilling debauchery, but obedience must always be followed.

And what would you sleep on, the floor? he argued back to himself. Would that better prepare you to counsel patients? Nor did all willingly overlook your past when you presented yourself for profession. Obedience only rankles when you wish to act against what the order rules is best for its members. So, be a good brother and report to the Abbot.

He strode through the empty chapterhouse, a few candles lighting his way. Then, up the stairs to the Abbot's chambers. He found himself wondering, as he knocked on the door, how much longer it would be before the old man left his seat, to retire to live with the lay brothers. I will miss him, he thought with a pang.

"Blessed be the Lord."

"And those who serve Him." Brocard entered the room, glanced with concern at the half-finished supper resting on the polished table. He smoothed his face as the Abbot turned away from the window. "The soul in my care has today revealed a great sin to me, most Reverend Father. As the rules of our order oblige me, I come to report it to you."

The Abbot grunted, eased himself into his chair. "And you would not have done so otherwise. It can only be one of three things, then. Which?"

"Murder, most Reverend Father."

"How many?"

Brocard found himself staring at the Abbot, startled by his easy acceptance. "Only one. His father."

"Ah." The Abbot waved him to a seat. "My neck is too old to strain with looking up at you. So, that is his great sin?"

Brocard obediently took the stool. "I think not. As you yourself taught me, it is not the deed that injures, but that which lies behind the deed. I could not ascertain anything further after his confession."

The Abbot nodded thoughtfully. "Do you believe him to be a danger to our community?"

"No, I do not." Brocard had thought long and hard about the dragon after sext, when he should have been examining his own conscience. "The murder of one's father is not an indiscriminate killing. I do not believe he would harm another creature."

"I accept your conclusions." The Abbot glanced at his dinner, then shoved the plate farther away, resting his arms on the table. "And I will add my prayers to yours for his healing. Has he taken a name?"

"Michel, most Reverend Father."

A smile eased the Abbot's face. "The wingéd saint. An

apt choice."

"The statue in the cathedral has a broken wing," Brocard explained. "The dragon felt a kinship." He hesitated, then added, "It appears that Michel does not realize his loss."

"Surely he must be aware that his crippled wing prevents him from flying?"

Brocard shook his head. "I believe that he does not know. If he is human by birth and has never seen a bird . . . The most Reverend Father is well aware that few alive have seen a bird. That species was affected harshly by the world's wounding."

"Those who have are brothers of this chapter." The Abbot clasped his hands together, stared at them thoughtfully. "I would not presume to direct the paths of your healing, my son, but I would suggest that you do not permit Michel to wander into the hills. Do not allow him to witness what he has lost. Unless—do you believe that the wing could be reconstructed?"

Brocard closed his eyes for a moment. He visualized the pair of wings, one straight and proud, the other bent back upon itself, skin hanging in tatters. "Brother Angles bears some hope. It is my intention to heal the soul first."

"Yes." The Abbot lifted his eyes, meeting Brocard's own. "But you may find that one does not proceed without the other."

Brocard gazed into the gray eyes. "I value your sight into souls, most Reverend Father. What do you see?"

The Abbot shook his head. "I recall to mind only that as is the soul, so is the body. The body often bears testament to the soul's ills." He stood, signifying that the meeting was at an end. "I would ask, my son, for you to consider whether it is now time to draw Michel into the life of our community."

"I will consider it, most Reverend Father," Brocard replied and turned to leave the room.

"My son." The Abbot's tone of warning made him halt. "The emotional bond of father to son could indeed cause one to rise up against the other. Take care in your healing, lest you cause the same anger, and to the same result."

* * * * *

"You have been with us for a month," Brocard stated.

Gonard stood slowly. Was he already unwelcome? "It's because I killed my father," he said numbly.

"No, no." Brocard lifted a hand in reassurance. "This is a place of healing, not condemnation. The most Reverend Father of our chapter, Dom Abbot Pernay, has taken me to task for not inviting you to participate in our services."

There was a sudden tension around the man that made Gonard uneasy. "I'm sorry. I didn't meant to cause you any trouble."

Brocard rubbed his beard, then gave Gonard one of his small smiles. "No, it is I who must seek forgiveness. When I am with you, you are my only concern. All else is unimportant."

"No," Gonard felt compelled to say, "I'm the one who's unimportant."

Brocard's eyes narrowed. "And why do you say that?"

"That's what my father said. I am nothing without him. All I can do is rust. Dragons can only rust."

"A spade rusts and is then thrown away," Brocard said softly. "But you are a living creature, Michel, a child of the living Lord. Your life is precious—*you* are precious. Did your father tell you otherwise?"

"Yes." Gonard ducked his head, another part of the puzzle sliding into place. He said, learning even as he spoke, "That's why I had to kill him. He was going to destroy me."

"Why was he going to destroy you?"

"I don't know." The crack into the hidden recesses of his mind had closed again. "I can't remember."

The man stirred, bringing Gonard's eyes back to him. "In time, you will remember."

"Yes." Gonard blinked. "These services—are they in the cathedral?"

"Yes." Brocard accepted the change in topic. "You are welcome to sit before the choir, though, as you are not a professed brother, you cannot partake of Communion." The term meant nothing to Gonard, and he allowed it to slide by for the moment. "However, the singing of our choir is worth any preponderance in the sermon."

"Singing?" Gonard lifted his head. The concept spoke to some deep part of him, filling him with sudden eagerness. "Is there—singing—at all services?"

Brocard shook his head. "Plain chant for the morning psalms and vespers. At tierce, when conventual Mass is celebrated, the choir sings in full polyphony."

Gonard's ears twitched at the unfamiliar words. "Polyphony?"

"Come and listen. You know the bells for tierce?"

"After the sun rises, when the bells toll three times," Gonard said. "It's after that that you visit me for the second time in the day." He paused, finding his throat suddenly aching with longing. "They—the others—won't be afraid of me?"

"All men fear the unusual, the unexpected." Brocard leaned back against one of the closed stall doors. "I will not lie and say that it is otherwise. But we are all strangers until we come to know one another. Let the brothers see you, greet you, and in time they will accept you. Some readily, others at greater length." He cocked his head. "It is time you ventured beyond these stone walls, Michel."

"I will come," Gonard promised, torn between fear and longing. If others should see his crime, back away in horror . . .

But the singing. He had to hear the singing. "I will come soon."

Singing. Gonard stood near the shut doors after Brocard left. He was suddenly aware of faint notes he had heard before, muffled by cathedral and stable walls. Now he pricked his ears forward, straining and waiting impatiently for vespers.

The day dragged by slowly. All was quiet after Brocard left, until a single bell rang. Footsteps shuffled across the still-frozen courtyard, pouring from dormitories to the main hall. Gonard caught the faint clink of pottery and metal, the sharp scent of cheese and the drier scent of bread wafting through the air.

The bell sounded again. Gonard moved away from the door. Brocard appeared a short while later, a book under his arm. He resumed reading aloud to Gonard, from a volume entitled *The Silence of the Heart*. On other days, Gonard had interrupted the reading with questions, and they had discussed the author's thoughts. Today, he wandered restlessly, paying little attention.

Brocard left two hours later. Gonard waited until the doors were shut, then resumed his place just within their confine. Another hour of silence passed, broken only by the occasional brother walking from chapterhouse to dormitory.

Then the bell tolled, its deep tone echoing twice across the courtyard, washing up against the buildings. Footsteps came from the dormitories again, this time crossing to the cathedral.

Gonard held his breath, pressed his ears closer to the doors. There—a faint tremble on the air. Voices, raised in song. Much plainer than he was used to, chanting words in unison. But singing, nonetheless. Singing.

I could do better, Gonard thought scornfully. Then he backed away from the doors, ears pressed flat against his skull. But I cannot. Singing is forbidden to me. I cannot sing. It would be wrong—I don't know why, but it would be wrong.

Why? Why is it wrong? Why would it hurt so much to sing again?

He slept restlessly. His dreams haunted him with faces of men and women singing, each of them wearing an earring like the one weighing down his own ear. A man shouted, urged him to sing, while a wind whipped the hair over the man's eyes and disturbed the fringe in Gonard's ears. And, finally, he dreamt that he was singing, standing alone on a cold winter night, his heart breaking as he pleaded with another who would not, could not, accept him.

He awoke when Brocard came in for his first visit of the day, a candle in his hand casting soft shadows through the stable. Gonard knew the routine well enough to stand, blinking groggily, as Brocard examined the regrowing of his scales. The man had learned not to ask whether he could also examine the crippled foot or wing. After the initial appraisal, Gonard had not allowed any further inspection. The old injuries felt too much a part of some deep, dark secret he was as yet unable to share.

There would be no more singing, not until tierce. Gonard moved restlessly, alone in the dark stable. The longing to go to the cathedral, to witness the singing at close hand, fought with the fear of how the others would react. Would they turn away, disgusted by his crime? He seemed to remember a white chamber, many faces glaring at him in silent condemnation. Another had stood beside him then, giving him the strength to bear their loathing. . . . But she was not here now. He was alone.

The bell tolled. Once. Twice. Thrice. Gonard lifted his head and, with a gulp of breath very like a sob, he pushed the stable doors open. He limped out into the courtyard.

Brothers were striding across the stones, hands sheltered

inside the wide sleeves of their robes. Gray-robed men led
the way, those in brown following. Gonard came last, placing himself at the end of the procession.

He had to hang back at the cathedral entrance, however,
for another group of men came up from the other side of
the cathedral. He saw now that there was another set of
buildings down the hill. These men were dressed in robes
of black, and they waited deferentially until the other
brothers had entered the cathedral before they took their
places.

They all know where they belong, Gonard thought dis-
consolately as he stopped before the cathedral's inner doors.
Every brother had silently, confidently gone to his place in
the choir, with those in the black robes taking seats on several pews set up in the nave. Where do I belong? Do I
belong?

He started to turn, to walk away. But then the choir
began to sing. Six voices began low, then climbed with
intensity, echoing gracefully through the cathedral's
depths. Then the rest of the choir joined in, their higher
voices soaring above the chant, blending for a moment,
then lifting away.

As once before, Gonard found himself being called forward by the sound of singing. He stepped slowly into the
nave, limping along the stone slabs, until he was halfway to
the choir. Then he sat down, allowing the music to travel
through him.

The longing built up in him again. He felt his throat
strain with the effort of keeping silent. I can't sing, he
thought. It's not allowed. I can't allow myself. I can't—I
can't face the pain, not again. He dropped his gaze, wondering if he had any place here.

Colored light glittered at his feet, like so many jewels
cast across the stones. Wonderingly, Gonard lifted his eyes,
searching for the source of the pattern. A shaft of sunlight

was shining through the large window at the front of the cathedral, spilling the colors at his feet.

He looked up at the window, at the design formed by the many colored pieces of glass. It was a man, he now saw. A man, arms spread wide and legs pinned to a dark structure. A crucifix, like the one that hung around Brocard's neck on a leather thong.

The hands. Gonard felt a sudden sense of kinship. Both the hands and the feet were red, bloody, damaged by a strip of metal pinning them to the dark cross. No, not like me, Gonard realized. I have only two wounded limbs, and he has four. Why has he four to my two?

The arms were flung back, the bare chest strained with pain. Gonard could imagine the agony of the unnatural position, being fastened to a dark structure of wood, held up from earth to the bare heavens. But the face was clear of sorrow; in fact, it appeared to smile at Gonard, to welcome him.   •

To welcome—what? Gonard shuddered. The arms no longer seemed to be held back by force, but opened deliberately, as if the man welcomed into his embrace any creature who suffered, even as he suffered. *A man of sorrows.* The words came to Gonard, though he knew not from where. The arms were stretched forth to gather him in, to gather in his own pain, so that he could give it into the scarred palms and be made whole.

Gonard lifted his head, closed his eyes, and sang. He sang into the great cathedral, his voice joining that of the choir, then arching above it, higher than any man could reach. He sang, but not as the City had taught him, from the mind; he sang from the heart. He mourned the loss of the City, sang of the heartbreak of rejection and separation, and the man seemed to take it into himself. Gonard, without pausing, opened his eyes and saw that the man still smiled, still welcomed. And Gonard, struck by the wonder of it all, finally understood why he could not have served the City. He could not relinquish his soul.

His voice lowered, deepened, as he now sang to the man. He sang in the wordless language of the City, but felt understood. A longing to heal the man grew within him, along with a longing to heal himself. *I want to be whole. I want to know who I am. I want to be myself.*

He brought his singing to an end, sending one last, high note soaring up through the vaulted roof. Then, as he fell silent, he realized that the choir was also still, the men's faces turned to him, eyes wide with awe. Gonard dipped his head apologetically, then limped from the cathedral, his steps lighter than when he had entered.

Footsteps hurried after him. Gonard halted in the courtyard, turned his head back to the cathedral. The singing had begun again, but more subdued, as if afraid that he might return. Brocard walked up to him, his face grave. "You would have been welcome to remain for the rest of the service."

"I came for the singing."

Brocard's mouth quirked. "Theirs or yours?"

"I don't know." Gonard's ears twitched as the singing ended and a monotone voice began to speak. "Maybe I should not have sung."

"The choirmaster approved of your performance."

Gonard blinked, realizing that he hadn't even considered what anyone else might have thought of his singing. "I once promised never to sing again."

"To whom did you make that promise?"

"Myself." The peace that had settled upon him in the cathedral still remained, enabling him to speak with a calmness he would not have expected. "If I break one promise, what is to stop me from breaking others?"

"What other promises have you made?"

Gonard took a deep breath. The air was tinged with

incense, drifting through the cathedral doors. "Not to kill again, after I killed my father. But I've already broken that one," he added, almost as an afterthought. "I killed again."

Silence. Brocard merely waited, a slight breeze waving the hem of his robe. Gonard shifted, his last words seeming to hang in the air like a question unanswered. "A stire," he finally said. "I killed a buck. That's where the whistle around my neck comes from." His skin twitched where the piece of horn rubbed; he had forgotten about it. Who had put it there? "And a pack of wolves."

"Why did you kill the stire?"

The calm was leaving him. "By accident." The words came slowly as the recesses of his mind revealed the answers. "I tried not to, but my foot hit its head."

"And the wolves?"

"They were hunting me."

"So, you have killed once accidentally." Brocard rubbed his beard. "And twice to defend yourself."

"But it was wrong!" Gonard protested, stung by the calm summary.

"Why was it wrong?"

"It's wrong to kill!" His tail slid across the cold stones. "One shouldn't kill!"

"The lay brothers slaughter herd beasts so that we might have meat on our table. Is that wrong?"

"That's different," Gonard said. "You have to eat to live."

"And to sometimes kill to survive?"

Gonard backed away. "It was wrong for me to kill my father," he said stubbornly. "The stire was an accident, the wolves I had to fight, but it was wrong to kill my father."

"What is the difference?"

"Because the reasons were different." Gonard paused, surprised by his own answer. He repeated it again, slowly, "The reasons were different." Brocard nodded, urging him to continue. "It's not—killing—as such, that's wrong, on its own. It's also the reason for the killing. And promises— it's not wrong to break one that's no longer necessary. Or one that shouldn't have been made in the first place." He shook his head; his thoughts seemed to be tangling. "But shouldn't things be either right or wrong?"

"Should they?"

Gonard closed his eyes, lifted his snout to the sunlight, taking a moment to calm himself. "You answer my questions with questions."

The scratch of bristle against skin told him that Brocard was rubbing his beard. "You assume that I have the answers. Even if I had, would the answers mean as much if I simply gave them to you?"

"Maybe." He dug claws into the ground, opened his eyes. "I think—things aren't just right or wrong in themselves. It's *why* something's done, the reasons behind it." Again, the silence, but now he was comfortable in it, used it to support his struggle to put growing understanding into words. "I killed the stire by accident, so there was no reason for blame. The wolves—I killed them to save myself. Except one. One lived."

"You permitted one to live?"

Gonard swallowed. "It was injured and in pain. I couldn't kill it; I thought it was wrong. But maybe it was more wrong to leave it in pain, when it was going to die anyway. I should have been—merciful."

The cathedral began to empty. Brothers strode past, giving them both wide berths. Gonard glanced thoughtfully at the large building. "It was wrong to kill my father."

"Was the act wrong? Or the reason?"

Gonard felt an answer almost within reach. But his mind shied away, refusing to accept it. "I don't know."

Brocard shook his head. "You do know. You are merely not yet ready to admit it to yourself. It was not the killing alone that has wounded you, is it? There was something far greater."

Gonard simply met his eyes, unable to answer. But he felt the truth in the man's words.

* * * * *

The bells had rung once for sext. Gonard cocked his head, analyzing the distance of the other buildings from the cathedral by the time it took for the echoes to return.

A patter of footsteps made his ears flicker. Few men crossed the courtyard away from the cathedral at this time of day; nor were these the steady strides of Brocard. He came to his feet as someone fumbled at the latch to the stable doors.

"Yes, yes, I'm certain you didn't expect a visitor." The voice became clearer as the doors swung away, revealing a gray-robed man. "Most brothers spend this time examining their consciences. I have as little trouble with my conscience as my stomach, so I have come to see you." Gonard drew his head back as the man closed the doors, then rubbed his hands together, chuckling to himself. "Indeed, after your performance yesterday, I knew that I must come to you."

"Who are you?" Gonard asked bluntly.

The man laughed. "Of course. You were too busy challenging the expertise of my choir to take note of me. I am Dom Lybrand, the choirmaster."

Gonard swallowed, suddenly recalling the quiet, awed choir. "I'm sorry I interrupted yesterday."

"What? An apology?" Lybrand laughed again. "You did my choir much good. Getting too complacent—I have said so many a time. But would they listen? No. Takes a—what are you?"

"A dragon," Gonard supplied helpfully.

"Takes a dragon to bring them up. They'll work harder

now." The man nodded sharply to himself, his black, uneven hair waving wildly. "But I have not come here for chatter. I wish to take your measure!"

"Measure?" Gonard echoed, glancing down the length of his body.

"No, no, your vocal range!" Lybrand peered at him. "Treble, was it not? Give me your range."

Gonard obliged, somehow knowing that he had once practiced scales endlessly, under another teacher. . . . A place of green crystal came to mind. He steeled himself for the sorrow that usually accompanied the memory, but was startled to find instead a faint glow of joy.

"Yes, yes, very impressive," the man finally interrupted. "Too many men fall into the middle range. Trebles only with boys. Too many tenors, not enough baritones."

"Baritones?" Gonard shifted voice and did the note scale in baritone, enjoying the throb of the low tones through his chest.

"Enough," Lybrand said after several minutes. Gonard watched, puzzled, as the man shook his head. "With a few like you, I could do away with all my choir. You could assume all the parts."

If that's what he wants, Gonard thought. He was starting to like this brisk, cheerful man who so clearly admired his singing. Closing his eyes for better concentration, he opened his jaws and sang an exact copy of the choir's song he had interrupted. First six voices, laying the foundations. Then the four higher voices, lifting above in high counterpoint, alternatively melding and countering the six baritones. But, as he had not heard the song end, he reluctantly had to trail off, allowing the voices to die away.

"Wondrous!" Lybrand clapped his hands together. "Marvelous! Such a talent. 'Tis a crime for Brocard to lock you away from singing!"

"He didn't know I could sing," Gonard said, feeling a

need to defend his mentor.

"No, no, of course not, singing is too near to levity. Not
solemn enough of an enterprise for him." Lybrand grinned,
taking the sting from his words. But Gonard shifted
uneasily as he suddenly found himself comparing Brocard
to this lively man. "Can you read music?"

"I could learn."

"You cannot sing in services," Lybrand explained. "Only
professed brothers are trusted with that task, or promising
novices! But you could assist me with new compositions—
so difficult to experiment with harmonies with these brothers. Would you be willing to assist me?"

"I would be honored," Gonard said.

* * * * *

The bells had rung for dinner. Brocard was crossing the
courtyard to the refectory when he heard the dragon's voice
rumble within the stable block. He changed direction mid-
stride, noting that the doors were partially open.

Gonard's head swung toward him as he stepped inside.
Dom Lybrand straightened, folded his arms over his ample
belly. Brocard gave him a nod. "You have finished your
examinations early, Dom Lybrand."

The other man grinned. "Dom Brocard, my conscience
troubles me as much as ever—less than my stomach will,
should I forgo dinner." He bowed to the dragon. "I will
return this time tomorrow, if I am welcome."

Gonard nodded. Brocard stood aside to allow Lybrand to
leave, then turned back to the dragon. "What have you
agreed to do?"

"To sing his new compositions." Gonard cocked his long
head, studying Brocard with glittering eyes. "Do you
mind?"

Brocard realized suddenly that he was frowning. He

released the tension in his face, forcing himself to relax. It was not his place to approve or disapprove. "You would be of great assistance to Dom Lybrand, so long as he does not tax your patience."

"I like him."

"Oh, yes, he is well liked." Brocard regretted the bitterness of his words as soon as he had spoken them. "Your forgiveness, Michel. I should not have spoken so about Dom Lybrand. He is a hardworking member of this chapter, and you will enjoy singing his works."

The dragon's head was still cocked, and he looked thoughtful. "You don't like him because he laughs."

I am here to heal *you*, Brocard almost said. But he sighed instead, knowing that he was merely trying to escape Gonard's question. "*They* laughed," he said finally. "The barbarians. They laughed at every cruelty, laughed the louder when their victims begged for mercy. So I have little tolerance for laughter. I find it is always at the expense of another, in response to their pain."

"Can't it ever be just from happiness?"

"I have yet to witness such laughter." Brocard straightened. "I shall return after none."

"Can't let your stomach trouble you," Gonard agreed, his eyes shining. Brocard left with the definite feeling that he was being mocked.

* * * * *

"Michel. Have you heard a word of what I have read?"

Gonard pulled his thoughts back to the stable. " 'And so should be the heart, silent before the Lord, in awe of His ever—loving forbearance. So should be the mind, stilled before the Lord, awaiting His words.' "

Brocard closed the book. "You have heard, but have you listened?"

Gonard shuffled his feet, disturbing the straw. "The draft under the doors smells different. I think—has winter broken?"

"The ground has begun to thaw." Brocard stood up, carefully placing the book on his stool. "If you wish to go outside, you do not need my permission."

Gonard ducked his head. "I thought I should ask, first."

In answer, Brocard pushed the doors open and stood beside them. Gonard limped forward, and together they stepped outside.

The sun felt warmer than before. The ground was losing its chill beneath his feet, the stones glittering in the sunlight. Gonard took a deep breath, cocked his head curiously. The scent of fresh-turned earth came to him. He decided to follow it, across the courtyard, past the cathedral, down the hill to the buildings beyond. Brocard followed him without complaint, his pale skin shining in the sun.

"These are the dwellings of the lay brothers," Brocard explained as they passed the squat dormitories and long barns. "Lay brothers are those who do not feel called to the strict life of the order, but still wish to serve the chapter. A few are healers, but most work to support the chapter in other ways. They till the fields, and raise and guard the communal flocks. Two of them are our cooks, and one brother is our librarian. In return, they are fed, housed, and clothed by the chapter, and join in what services they wish. But they have no voice in chapter proceedings."

Past the buildings were the fields of which Brocard spoke. Four were being plowed and were the source of the damp earth scent. Three plows were drawn by pairs of coursairs, the beasts' black skins glistening. Large nostrils were opened wide, bristling the horns rising behind the ridges.

Gonard stopped, watched with interest. "Why are two men pulling the fourth plow?"

"Two coursairs died at the onset of the winter."

Gonard watched the men rest a moment, then throw their weight once again into the leather harness. They were only sixty meters away; he could hear the leather creak, the men's labored breathing as they fought to pull metal through hard earth. "Can't they wait until they get replacements?"

"The traders will not start their trains until later in the season." Brocard pointed to the southeast, where a range of mountains rose into the blue sky. "The River Strand lies between them and us, and the waters will be swollen with the thaw. It will be a month before we can expect any traders, and that is too long to wait before turning the earth to air, I am told."

Gonard nodded, winced as one of the men pulled too hard and lost his balance, stumbling against one of the plow arms. The man guiding the plow from behind called to his companions. They halted, breathing heavily, their faces red with exertion. Their black clothes were darkened with sweat.

Gonard frowned. He glanced at the coursairs in the fields beyond, measuring their width and height. Then he stepped forward, limping across the uneven field.

Brocard lifted a hand, then let it fall. He forced himself to stand still, to watch the dragon leave.

The lay brothers backed away as he approached, gathering together beyond the plow. Gonard paused. Three pairs of eyes met his, wary but unafraid. He nodded, as if to himself. Then he backed into the plow's shafts, his body nearly filling the space meant for two coursairs.

Brocard held his breath. The lay brothers bent their heads together in consultation. Then one of them went up to the dragon. For a long moment they simply looked at each other. Then the man lifted the harness, throwing it across Gonard's back. The straps meant to go across two beasts were combined into a makeshift harness for one. When all was in place, the man stepped into place behind the plow.

Gonard lowered his head. Brocard watched as muscles rippled under the tight-fitting scales, marveled as the dragon flicked his tail to one side and pulled the bright metal blade of the plow, turning the dark earth to the sun.

CHAPTER 7

"What d'ya mean, he's not here?" Itsa scowled down at Rydeth. "Why not?"

The girl backed a step, startled by the anger in Itsa's voice. "Me sire had t' attend t' duties, so he said. Do ye wish me also t' leave?"

Yeah, Itsa thought. Make the brat leave. She took a deep breath, wondering why her palms were wet with sweat. "All right, ya can stay. Ya got yer board?"

"Aye, m'lady." Rydeth settled on a seat, pulling a sheet of slate and a piece of chalk from a carry pouch. "I be ready t' start."

Still scowling, Itsa sat near her. "Okay, where did we stop yesterday?"

"Ye were tellin' us o' th' difference 'twixt vowels an' consonants." Rydeth pronounced the words carefully.

"Then write out all the vowels." Itsa watched her bend her dark head over the slate, tongue caught between lips as she obeyed. A strand of hair slipped free from one shoulder, catching against the hand clenched around the chalk. Was I ever that young? Itsa found herself wondering. She's twelve years old. By the time I was that old, I had the Supervisor chasin' after me. I bet she's always had it easy, a great dad, a mom who looks after her—

A grandmom, Itsa corrected herself. Her mom was killed after the Changewinds got to her.

"Finished," Rydeth announced. She held up the crude scrawls for Itsa's attention.

"Almost right." Itsa pointed at the third letter. "It's an *O*, not a *C*. *C*'s a consonant." Even here, among people who'd been separated from technology and Earth history for hundreds of years.

Rydeth nodded, erased the incorrect letter. She carefully drew the vowel, complete with the little mark those of the settlement made across the top of the circle. "Like that?"

"Yeah, like that. Ya've got it right." Itsa watched the round face beam at the faint praise. "Now, try those words I was teachin' ya. 'Member? Write out yar name an' clan."

Pulling a rag from her pouch, Rydeth rubbed out the marks. Then she applied herself to obeying the instructions.

Yeah, I was like her, Itsa decided. I was breakin' my back over 'puter books and lessons, tryin' to get ready to pass the Theological Examination. The T. E. was s'posed to be my ticket to Earth, my ride to the easy life. I got here anyways, and what happened? I threw it all 'way, decidin' to come with a dragon 'stead of stayin' in the Citadel and provin' my claim. I could of been a Cit by now, 'stead of slummin' it in some pretech civilization where the women get a say only when they're in the settlement. All the interestin' stuff happens on the hunt, and the men make the rules there. What a bummer of a life.

"Be this right?" Rydeth held up the slate. She'd not only listed her name and that of the clan, but she'd also added the name of the tribe. Itsa nodded. "An' I can write something more."

"Yeah, then do it." Itsa glanced away, watching members of the settlement walk past, making their way to the nearby market. Winter was gradually easing, the air warming, and many of the women waddling by were obviously near the end of their pregnancies. Bet they got no nerve blockers here, she thought. Like the miners, they're goin' to feel every bit of the kid comin' free.

"Finished." Rydeth sounded shy again. Itsa accepted the slate, tipped it back to read the scrawl. *I be Rydeth o' Meredith,* spread across two lines. And below, the chalk continued, *Itsa o' Sharit be me frind.*

Itsa felt her mouth dry. Rydeth was smiling up at her, though there was a hesitancy around her mouth as if she were unsure of the older woman's reaction. And, shat, I am older, Itsa found herself thinking. Old enough to have kids of my own—my mom was younger than I am now when she had me. "Yer all right," she told the girl. "Yeah, I guess we are friends."

Rydeth ducked her head, looking pleased. Then her head came up again at the sound of a familiar tread. "Father!"

Itsa deftly caught the slate as the girl jumped up to greet Rygor. He lifted her with his strong arms, swinging her around once before lowering her back onto her feet. "Ye be learning wi' th' Lady Itsa?"

"Aye, Father."

Itsa quickly rubbed the slate clean, then came to her own feet.

"Be ye finished wi' yer work?" Meredith asked.

"All but." Rygor picked up her pouch, handed it to Rydeth. "Now needs I t' speak wi' th' Lady Itsa. See yerself t' yer granddam's."

Rydeth's face creased in protest, but she nodded obediently. Sliding slate and chalk away, she trotted down the road, calling cheerfully to several boys leaning against a stall.

"Me daughter hae taken a liking t' ye," Rygor stated quietly.

Itsa shrugged. "I guess so."

"An ye t' her?"

"She's okay." Itsa rubbed her hands against her trousers. "I've met worse kids."

Rygor sat down heavily. As he remained silent, Itsa took a seat near him, wondering what was on the hunter's mind. "She be near t' coming a woman," he said finally, staring at his hands. "Soon, she shall be grown."

"How do ya decide that?" Itsa snorted, then answered herself, "Ya mean, she's soon goin' to start her monthlies."

"Yer words be strange as alway, but I understand th' meaning." Rygor took a deep breath. "Th' others who come to womanhood wi' her hae t' be presented t' th' clan. That be a woman's place, th' presenting. It be th' place o' a mother, but she hae not a mother."

"She can't be the first kid to have lost her mom," Itsa said, wary of what Rygor might be suggesting.

"Nay. One who be wi'out a mother is t' choose another in her place." Finally Rygor met her eyes. "She hae asked if ye would so be."

Itsa started to her feet. "Look, I ain't nobody's mom, and I never wanna be. Got it? She can get somebody else."

Rygor continued to look at her, his gaze steady. "M'lady, what do ye fear?"

Itsa forced a laugh. "Me? Nothin' gives me the chitters. Right? Nothin'."

"Ye lie."

The calm brashness of his statement cut through her anger. Itsa dropped back down beside him, ran a hand through her dark, curly hair. "All right, I hated my mom, right? Ya jig, the good old 'She was a terrible mom and I've been screwed by it' shat."

"What were her crime?"

"She took up with the Supervisor." Itsa shrugged. "He thought I'd be a replacement for her once she got too old for him. But I showed him. I made sure I failed the T.E., so's he couldn't take me to Earth with him."

Rygor studied her for a long moment. Then he said, "It be th' place o' a mother t' protect her young."

Itsa laughed bitterly. "Only when she's not tryin' to get somethin' outta it for herself."

"Yer mother did nae protect ye," he continued. "That do nae mean ye would nae protect yer own."

Itsa's hand balled, flew toward his face. Rygor caught it in his own fist, met her gaze. "How'dcha jig?"

"I hae seen ye wi' me own daughter." He lowered their entangled hands. "I hae seen ye fight 'gainst yerself. Now I ask ye 'gain, will ye stand in th' place o' her mother, an' present her t' th' clan?"

Itsa shivered. Suddenly, she felt old. "Yeah, all right," she said reluctantly. "I'll do it."

* * * * *

Why in shat did I agree to do this? she thought only a day later, scowling inside the dark building. Other girls and mothers sat around her and Rydeth, intent on the lecturer at the front of the room. Millan stood before them, explaining that a woman became pregnant when her mate's spirit mixed with hers. Yeah, Itsa thought, that's why the men wear bits of guts from stires when they get into women's tents while on the hunt. They wanna stop the spirits from gettin' free.

Beside her, Rydeth was listening intently. Itsa suppressed a yawn, remembering the 3-D presentations that had been her sex education. They'd been a lot more interesting than this. Made her and a boy in her class try it all out afterward. She found herself smiling at the memory.

"An' now," the Headwoman concluded, "th' assignments."

Assignments? Itsa straightened, back aching from sitting so long on the hard floor. Pregnant women filed into the room. Millan began to list the girls present, giving each the name of one of the women. As the other pairs had done before them, Rydeth and Itsa moved to the woman Millan named.

"Ye are now t' be their hands an' feet," the Headwoman said once all the girls had been assigned. "Ye will be there at th' birth, an' carry th' babe after."

Oh, yippie, Itsa thought. Does this get any better?

It did. Women, mothers, and girls were ushered into a larger chamber, lined with beds. There, Itsa was given to understand, each trio would stay until the woman gave birth. As Rydeth fussed self-importantly around their charge, Itsa flopped angrily on a nearby cot. This, she decided, ain't goin' to be one of the more excitin' times of my life.

Her mood lightened as mugs of Devil's Black were brought in. Then it dropped again as the drinks were handed only to the pregnant women. "Fer th' blood," said Rydeth's charge.

Our charge, Itsa reminded herself sourly. What's her name again? Lindea, right. "I hope ya enjoy it."

Lindea laughed. "It will one day be yer turn, m'lady."

Itsa snorted. "Shattin' likely."

Quickly glancing to one side to ensure that Rydeth was out of earshot, Lindea asked quietly, "Yer wi' her sire, are ye nae?"

To her annoyance, Itsa found herself blushing. "No, I'm not," she snapped. Coming to her feet, she left the room for the one trip allotted to her, ducking briefly into the hall at the confine to retrieve a few personal articles.

The other women settled into a comfortable pattern of gossip and storytelling. Itsa scowled from the periphery, occupying herself with carving the stire horn. The first birth came the third day, and then the women began to come due with increasing frequency.

"I hate to break this up," Itsa said dryly to Lindea and Rydeth as another trio hurried to the separate birthing room, "but I guess ya usually have mothers and their kids help out 'cause the mom should know 'bout givin' birth. I know nothin' 'bout it."

"I know," Rydeth said quietly.

"Why?" Itsa grinned, prepared to be relieved. "Ya've helped out 'fore?"

"At me mother's second birthing." The voice had sunk even lower, and Itsa found herself leaning forward to pick out the words. "Two year ago. Th' birth o' her son."

"I didn't jig ya had a brother." Even as she spoke, Itsa saw Lindea shift back, wincing. "Ya don't, do ya?"

"Th' boy died soon after th' first touch o' th' sun." Rydeth stared down at her hands, folded in her lap. "In me arms, as I carried him t' th' hall o' men."

"It were nae yer fault," Lindea said quickly. "Th' Singers say so. Th' boy were weak. Th' heart were nae right."

"That's right," Itsa added, wondering if this was why the girl always seemed so quiet. "It wasn't yar fault, not if he was goin' to die anyway. It just happened while ya were carryin' him."

Rydeth shook her head. "He were in me arms. Mine be th' blame."

"No, it's not." Itsa took a deep breath, swallowed her anger. "Look, kid, I once knew someone who blamed herself for killin' someone. She was standin' in a cave by the edge of a long drop. The guy she loved was standin' beside her, and she moved suddenly, knockin' into him. He fell, and died at the bottom. She said it was all her fault, just like you do."

Rydeth slowly lifted her face, eyes bright with unshed tears. "Nae if she but pushed him unawares."

"Right. That's what other people told her. Took her a long time to jig it for herself." Itsa shrugged. "Sounds to me like the kid was goin' to die anyways. Least he did it held by his sis. Rammelly—the guy—he died down a deep mine shaft. Alone."

Rydeth considered. "It be wrong t' die alone."

" 'Xactly. Yar brother didn't get that. Ya were with him."

A voice called out that lunch was ready. Rydeth moved away to gather three portions. Itsa leaned back, finding her jaw tight with the strain of that conversation. She stretched her mouth, releasing the tension.

"Rammelly be th' name o' yer first love?" Lindea asked.

Itsa shrugged. "Yeah, I guess he was the first."

"T'were brave t' tell Rydeth o' him."

"Nah, not for real." Itsa shrugged again. "Just didn't wanna watch the kid tear herself 'part over somethin' that wasn't her fault."

Lindea reached out, touched Itsa's arm. "I hae seen how Rydeth looks at ye. Ye be more than friend t' her."

"Yeah?" Itsa snarled, pulling herself free. "And who asked ya?"

"A truth," Lindea answered steadily, "does nae wait fer th' asking."

Itsa marched away, annoyed. She'd let the girl get close, and that was something you learned not to do in the mines; you never let anyone get close. Worse yet, someone else'd noticed. Itsa leaned against one wall of the long room and glared at the world.

* * * * *

"Ye must push 'gain," Rydeth said calmly, leaning close to Lindea. Itsa wiped sweat from her forehead, wondering how long they'd already been here. She never knew giving birth could take so long.

"Aye," Lindea answered grimly, hands clenching the sides of the birthing chair.

Itsa gulped a quick breath of air and resumed her position near the floor. A streak of color distracted her; with a start, she realized that the sun had risen and dawn was shining across the floorboards.

Lindea grunted. Itsa glanced back at her charge, then grinned in sudden excitement. "Hey, I see somethin' comin' through. We've got baby comin' out!"

"It be all but there," Lindea confirmed, panting with exertion. "Be ye ready?"

"Yeah, I'm ready, but for——" Itsa lunged forward as the head broke free, quickly followed by a chest and arms. Instinctively she caught the small body before it could hit the floor, a mixture of blood and fluid all but slipping the baby from her hands. "Got it," she confirmed, loosening her tight grip as the child began to wriggle.

Rydeth handed her a bright knife. "Ye must cut th' cord, an' bring th' babe t' life."

Itsa stared at the thin tissue still binding child to mother. *This was me, once,* she found herself thinking as she obeyed Rydeth. *I was once this close to my own mother.*

Lindea accepted the boy, pressing him close to her breast. Looking at the tender smile on the older woman's face, Itsa decided, *No, I was never that close to her. She never smiled at me like that, like . . . like I was important to her.*

"Be ye able t' go fer presentation?" Rydeth softly asked Lindea.

"I be able." Itsa accepted the boy back and wrapped him in several soft blankets. Lindea dressed herself, accepting Rydeth's fussing with a tolerant smile. Then, Itsa leading the way, carrying the baby, they filed out into the morning.

The air was still cold. Itsa felt the sweat on her forehead
chill, and she cursed whoever had invented this stupid cus-
tom. Lindea followed behind her, and then Rydeth. Those
few on the streets at this time of day moved to one side
and bent their heads in respect, honoring the birth party.

At least we weren't the only ones 'wake all night, Itsa
thought malevolently as they halted before the clan's meeting hall. The man outside straightened, spear tip glistening
in the sun as he lowered it to her. "Who comes t' th' clan?"

"Itsa of Sharit, Lindea of Minnera, and Rydeth of
Meredith," Itsa answered. "Come to present a new hunter
to the clan."

The spear dropped away, and the man pulled open the
door. Itsa marched inside, past the yawning men. At the
front of the room waited Naylor and Synon, Lindea's mate.
As she'd been instructed, Itsa walked up to the waiting
pair. "Headman," she said, nodding to Naylor, "I present a
son to the clan of Millan, the tribe of Naylor."

Naylor accepted the bundle, smiled down at the boy.
Then he raised him high for all the men to see. "A new
hunter for th' tribe o' Naylor!"

"A new hunter for th' tribe o' Naylor!" the men roared
in response. "An' what be his name?"

Lindea lifted her chin proudly. "Synlin o' Synon." She
took the boy back from Naylor, handed him instead to her
mate. "An ye, Synon o' Synlor, do ye swear t' be a father t'
him, t' teach him th' ways o' th' tribe, e'en as I will teach
him th' ways o' th' clan?"

"Aye," Synon breathed, touching the face of his son. "So
I do swear." He raised his head. "Me thanks t' th' birth
mothers."

Birth mothers? Itsa drew back, not liking the sound of
that. Before she could say anything, Naylor was again
speaking. "An now, t' Devil's Black, t' see in th' new
hunter!"

In the sudden bustle and cheering, Itsa was able to separate herself from the other two women. She made her way to the back of the room and poured a mugful of ale. It was heavy on an empty stomach, but the alcohol started to relax her.

"Methought ye did nae like that o'ermuch."

Rygor's calm voice made her tense again. "This's all yar fault. Birth mothers, for shat's sake."

"It be a title o' respect. Did ye nae bring th' child into th' world?"

"Someone had to," Itsa snapped, not quite understanding herself what she was trying to say. Slamming the mug onto a wooden table, she shoved her way to the door and to the fresher air outside.

"What be bothering ye?" Rygor asked, catching up to her.

"I don't wanna be a mom," Itsa said furiously, her strides long and stiff. "Not in title, not for real. Got it?"

"I ne'er sought t' be a father." He shrugged. "Ne'er thought o' it. Nae till I held Rydeth in me arms. Then I be changed fore'er. Felt ye nought, when ye held Synlin in yer arms?"

Itsa glanced away. Yes, there had been . . . something. She found that she was gritting her teeth. "It's not for me."

"Ye would nae be alone, were ye t' be a mother," Rygor said quietly. "Ye would hae birth mothers from th' clan—"

"Yeah, I've seen that."

"An ye would hae th' father." He waited until she met his eyes. "Ye would hae me."

Itsa halted, felt her mouth dry. Several things came to her at once. They were still in the clan's portion of the settlement, her responsibilities to Lindea were over for now, and she had never before noticed how broad and strong Rygor's shoulders were. The breeze brought her his sweaty scent, the smell of an honest man, miners' smell. Not like

Citizens, wearing perfume to mask their humanity. Her usual confidence was suddenly gone. She asked softly, "Why haven'tcha said anythin' 'fore this?"

"We be in th' settlement, th' place o' th' clan." He gave her his slight smile. "It be th' place o' th' woman t' hunt here."

Itsa found herself laughing. It was the first real laugh she'd had for years, and she savored the lightness in her chest. Rygor stood, waiting patiently. In answer, Itsa threaded her arm through his and led him toward his house.

The fire had nearly died down, leaving the interior dark and cold. As Rygor busied himself with poking the embers back into life, Itsa gathered blankets from the small bed and spread them across the floor. Rygor rocked back on his heels and looked up at her, a question on his face. Itsa laughed again. Right, the woman did the hunting. She dropped her overcoat, kicked it to one side. Shirt and trousers followed.

Rygor studied her, nodded. Itsa lifted her chin proudly. Life in the settlement had put the weight back on that she'd lost last winter, when the medtech had struggled to scrounge up enough food to keep her alive. Summer with the tribe and the lessons with Rygor had tightened her muscles, and she was the fittest she'd ever been. She flicked her fingers at him.

Smiling in return, he also removed his winter layers. Itsa raised an eyebrow at the scars across his chest, wondering what could have caused them. Such questions were unimportant now. She closed the distance between them, pleased to discover that they were nearly the same height. Laying a hand on his cheek, she kissed him.

Rygor responded, eagerly, hungrily, but holding back, waiting for her lead. Itsa suppressed a chuckle, wondering how strong his self-control was. She pushed him down onto the blankets, then lifted her head away. Slowly, deliberately, she trailed her hair down his chest, listened to his deep-breathed protest. "M'lady, ye try me."

"My lady?" she repeated, looking down into his dark eyes. "Still?"

He answered firmly, "Ye will always be th' lady o' me heart."

Itsa gave him a mock growl. Rammelly had finally caught her with a similar line. She never could resist a man who made soppy statements. Burying Rygor's mouth under hers, she finally stopped teasing him.

* * * * *

The clouds had lifted when Itsa emerged from the house. The afternoon sunshine reflected her mood perfectly. She found herself whistling as she strode back to the confine. It's been a long time, she thought. You'd of liked Rygor, Rammelly.

The medtech stood waiting in the center of the hall. Itsa suddenly felt as she had when she'd come back to her mom's apartment, disapproval dragging down her mother's finely trimmed eyebrows. The medtech, lacking emotions, still managed to convey the same sense of outrage without moving a muscle.

"Go on," Itsa said, marching up to him. "Whatcha goin' to say?"

"It was merely my intention," the medtech said in his usual, infuriatingly calm voice, "to inquire after the child born to the clan today. It was my understanding that you assisted in the birth."

"Yeah, it went all right." Itsa studied him. "So, that's all?"

"Should I inquire after anything else?" The voice became steely. "Such as where you have been since the birth?"

"Celebratin'," she answered sharply.

"Alone?"

Itsa grinned, straightened. Let him have it on the nose. "No. I went back to Rygor's place with him. And, yeah, it was great."

The medtech stated flatly, "You engaged in sexual relations with the man."

"Sure did." Itsa shrugged. "Whatsa matter, tech, jealous 'cause ya ain't got the right bits yarself? Have ya told Lissa yet?"

"Do not become emotionally involved with a man of the clan." The warning in the medtech's voice was unmistakable, and Itsa felt her teeth set on edge. "Do not become emotionally involved with any man in the settlement."

"And why not?"

The dull eyes slipped away from her face. "It will only give you cause for regret."

As she had said before, long ago, Itsa snapped, "I'll do whatever I want, tech. Ya got no hold over me." He said nothing further, merely turned away. She stomped to her room, furious that she'd lost her temper.

* * * * *

It started so slowly that Itsa hardly noticed at first. She did realize that members of the clan had started pointing her out to each other, but that seemed hardly surprising. With her skin color and accent, she never could blend in. And she was spending more and more time at Rygor's house, finding his company far preferable to the medtech's.

Then the strange accidents began. Itsa would be jostled on the street, but a swift apology always followed. And when one clan member turned too sharply, and she ended up in the mud at the side of the path, he offered to buy her a new set of clothes. Itsa, grimly smearing mud from her eyes, declined. It was only when the load of hay fell on her, despite her determined acrobatics to miss it, that she finally decided the happenings couldn't be occurring at random.

"I will bespeak Martin," Rygor said that evening as she picked stalks from her clothes. "He be nae that clumsy."

"No," Itsa said angrily, "he wasn't clumsy. He aimed too well for that."

She felt the disbelief in Rygor's silence. Looking up from her seat before the fire, she saw the stubborn denial thinning his lips. "Do ya jig I can't get outta the way of a turnin' wagon?" she demanded. "And it's not the first thing that's happened."

"All from th' clan?"

"Yeah, from yar clan." Itsa dropped the shirt, deciding it was ruined anyway. "I ain't funnyin' ya."

Rygor glanced away, but she saw the troubled look in his eyes. "Th' Tribunal said th' Windwalker t' be clear from guilt. Th' clan were told." Then he shook his head. "It be all yer imagining."

"Sure it is." Itsa rose, grabbing her cloak from the ground. "Like I jived ya might believe me."

She strode from the house, slamming the door behind her. Men, she thought, glancing up at the dark sky. Always jive they've got it right, and ya've got it wrong. Even Rammelly tried to decide what was best for us, never mind askin' me.

A storm was coming up. Itsa pulled the hood of the cloak over her head and hurried away, hoping she'd be able to reach the confine before the rain did. She'd had enough aggravations today without a soaking on top of it.

In her haste, she didn't hear the footsteps behind her. When a hand suddenly clamped around her mouth, her first reaction was startled paralysis. But then, as an arm tried to drag her off the path, the reflexes learned in the harsh life of an asteroid mine took over. A kick, a duck, and a punch, and she was dancing back, looking for the face of her attacker.

Shat, I've been out of it too long, was her thought as another pair of arms reached for her. Should of seen that comin'. But her body was quicker than her mind. She used the man's momentum against him, flipping him over her body and sending him sprawling onto the ground. "Anybody else?" she shouted, whirling around.

Several bodies shifted in the darkness. At that moment, the rain broke. The heavy drops splattered across the road, and Itsa braced herself against the slippery mud. But the men turned away, disappearing back into the darkness.

Itsa took a deep breath, then bent down to her first two attackers. One was groaning where he lay, a hand rising to his head. The other was sitting up, gasping for breath. "Ya're lucky," Itsa told them grimly. "I've done worse to men tryin' to catch me."

A pair of hurrying footsteps made her crouch again. "Itsa?" Rygor's voice called.

Itsa relaxed slightly. "Over here." She shook her head, the rain beginning to weigh down her hair. As Rygor came close, she stepped back, pointing at the two men. "Ask them what they were goin' to do to me, will ya? I might be imaginin' them."

Rygor gave her a quick look, then crouched by the seated man. "Larson," he identified quietly. "Why be ye here?"

"Nay," Larson retorted, "why be ye wi' her? She and hers killed yer mate."

"Th' Triune—"

"Th' Triune said him t' be Walker," Larson sneered. "But a Walker returns from th' Winds. He hae nae returned! He be nae Walker!"

Itsa pulled her cloak tighter around her, chilled by the

pronouncement. Could the dragon really have lost his mind in the Changewinds? He could be dead already, buried under the snows.

"Get on wi' ye," Rygor said sternly. "Get back t' yer mates 'fore I tell them how ye hae attacked a woman."

Itsa's fists clenched, but she stepped back and allowed the men to hobble away. "Now," she asked between clenched teeth, "do ya believe me?"

Rygor looked away. "I cannae protect ye."

Itsa grinned. "Did it look like I needed protectin'?" Then she sobered, realizing that he had more to say.

"Ye be nae o' th' clan. Were ye o' th' clan, none would raise hand 'gainst ye."

Itsa studied him for a moment. "Whatcha tryin' to tell me?"

"Ye be nae o' th' clan." He straightened his shoulders. "Think on it."

She watched him set off through the rain. Now, what was that supposed to be about? Adjusting her cloak, she bent her head to the wind and headed for the confine. She'd think on it over a warm drink and an open fire, even if it meant getting glared at by the medtech again.

Wind gusted through the door as she stepped inside, the fire spitting in response. Itsa firmly shut the storm outside, then turned to drape her dripping cloak over a nearby chair. Only when she turned back did she realize that the medtech was not alone. Rydeth waited beside his taller figure.

"Be ye bound t' any man?" she asked without preamble.

Itsa blinked at the formal tone. "No, I'm not."

"Would ye be a good mate?"

"If ya jig—" Itsa cut herself off. Think 'fore ya talk, she told herself sternly. There's somethin' goin' on here. "Yeah, I'd make a good mate."

"Would ye serve a man on th' hunt, an' look after him

in th' settlement? Would ye raise his children an' take yer due?"

Itsa said evenly, "I could do all that."

Rydeth nodded curtly. "I hae nae yet been presented t' th' clan. When I be declared a woman, I will return an' ask ye t' be th' mate o' me sire."

Itsa stepped aside as the girl let herself out. As the door shut, she lifted her gaze to the medtech. "Right. The women rule in the settlement. Didn't jig it even went to arrangin' marriages."

The medtech's face was set. "It is of course impossible for you to accept her proposal."

His matter-of-fact tone raised Itsa's temper. "And why's that, tech?"

"It is our intention to leave the settlement and search for Gonard once winter has ended."

"Maybe that's whatcha plan to do." Itsa lifted her chin. "I ain't goin' to."

"It is imperative that you and I, together, find Gonard."

Itsa waved his statement away. "Ya go, tech. He's probably dead and buried by now. I've got more to do with my life than go runnin' after a dragon. Right? Lots more."

"And," his suddenly quieter voice halted her, "you will undoubtedly be expected to bear children to a hunter. Are you willing to be a mother, daughter of Sharit? After the way in which your own mother treated you, are you willing to risk that you will be equally as callous toward your own offspring?"

Itsa closed her eyes briefly, waiting for her mother's face to swim up from her memories. Instead, she saw the baby she'd helped deliver, remembered again how the small body had nestled against her own. "Maybe," she said softly, "I'm not so scared of tryin' anymore."

Lissa appeared in the entrance to the hall, her face creased with confusion. Itsa glared at her, wondering once again if she should warn the medtech. Nah, let him find out the hard way, she decided angrily. She brushed past a silent medtech to her room.

CHAPTER 8

Brocard turned restlessly on his hard bed. The sheets had become twisted from his sleeplessness; he sat up and fumbled them into some order. It was still too cold at night not to have the woolen covering.

Michel doesn't appear to feel the cold, he reflected. Then he frowned. Michel. That was the reason for his inability to sleep. The dragon was coming to be accepted by the community. He attended services, sitting quietly in the nave, eyes glowing. At other times he wandered through the courtyard, always willing to be a beast of burden when the water tanks required refilling.

Michel appeared happy, at peace with himself. Brocard rubbed his eyes. But this was not a real peace. Too many questions still hung unanswered. His cautious probings in his visits to Michel had so far brought them no further.

What could he try next? Brocard turned, felt along the rough wall beside him. His hand touched the cross that hung there; he lifted it from its hook, held it between his hands. The wood was smooth between his fingers, and he rubbed it, calming his thoughts. What next, Lord? he thought. You see into his soul.

Brocard blanked his mind, waited for an answer. He found himself thinking back to his first sight of the dragon, lying between the choir stalls. He tried to move away from the image, but it refused to leave him. The dragon, in the cathedral. What had Michel said? He had been reminded of another sanctuary. He had known from the first where to go for his healing.

But he visits the cathedral daily, Brocard argued. He goes to all the services.

And the voices of the brothers echo around him, while he must remain silent. Brocard shook his head. Of course, he is silent. Only those in vows were permitted to sing in the services.

The answer came to him, so audacious that it took his breath away. Then let him profess. Let him become a brother.

He spent the rest of the night arguing with the decision. So the morning went by in a daze, until he found himself in the chapter meeting, resting his head against the high chair back, awaiting his return to report.

"You have been quiet today," the Abbot commented, turning to Brocard. "Tell us of Michel. He appears well."

Brocard leaned forward, clasping his hands together on the table before him. "My brothers, most Reverend Father. I have spent the past night in prayer, searching for guidance."

The Abbot's forehead creased with concern. "Tell us of your difficulty, my son."

Brocard stared down at his hands. "At the first, Michel's mind revealed much to him, enabling his inner healing to progress rapidly. As the other soul-healers among my brothers could attest, such early progress is not unusual. Nor would they be surprised to learn that this growth has now slowed. The later steps are often greater, more difficult, and require greater time and preparation."

Dom Acton stirred in his chair. "Or is Michel perhaps already healed?"

"No." Brocard shook his head. "He has not regained his

full memory."

Acton nodded. "Have you come to a conclusion as to the next step?"

Brocard's mouth quirked. "Yes. To permit Michel to profess."

The reactions, as he had expected, were quick and varied. Dom Cherril stood first. "How much knowledge does Michel possess of our order? More importantly, what does he know of the Lord?"

"He knows very little," Brocard admitted. "However, most novices know little except that our order offers a life of contemplation, learning, and service. Michel's ignorance is no greater than theirs, and he would attend the same teaching sessions as all novices."

Brother Elias came to his feet. "Will the simple profession lead to permanent vows?"

"Is that a consideration?"

Elias spluttered. "Of course. Provisional vows are intended to lead to permanent vows!"

"Then why does our order insist that all novices first bind themselves with only the simple vows? Why not force them all to take only the permanent?" Brocard's eyes traveled around the faces at the table. "Provisional vows are designed to allow novices to explore their calling, to decide if they wish to spend their lives in the order. Equally, the order must decide whether to accept the novice as a brother. Whether Michel eventually professes as a brother is not my concern. I am a healer, and I desire to see him whole. I believe he requires a structure in which he can feel secure, so that he can once again struggle with the chaos in his soul. The order of our days will give him that structure, and the chapter will provide him a community in which he can take part. And, he will be permitted to sing with the choir."

Dom Lybrand, who was known to doze through chapter

meetings, straightened at Brocard's last remark. He came to his feet. "I support Dom Brocard's submission. Let Michel profess."

Another stood as Lybrand returned to his seat. His black robe marked him out as a lay brother, one of the two who were permitted a seat in chapter meetings. "Reverend brothers, most Reverend Father," he said, bowing to the Abbot. "I realize that, as lay brethren, neither I nor my brother may have a vote in this meeting." Brocard noted with interest the tension in the man's voice. "But we do have the right to speak, and I beg your reverends' pardon as I use this right to also speak in Michel's favor."

He paused, one hand nervously twisting the knots of the white cord around his waist. But no one spoke to stop him, so he bowed to the Abbot again and continued. "A few of my religious brothers are aware of the difficulties we have faced this spring. Though the coursairs come under your care, two died early in the winter, leaving us a team short for the spring plowing. We were forced therefore to use our own bodies to pull the plow—a laborious process, as I can myself testify."

Brocard leaned back in his chair, certain he knew what was coming. "We had heard of, but not seen, the Michel of whom you speak," the lay brother said. "So that, when he strode to us over the fields, we were suspect of him. But he offered himself, my reverend brothers, offered his own self to draw the plow! Accepted the lowly role of a beast of burden and asked for naught in return." The man took a deep breath, visibly calming himself. "I would not claim to have your greater spiritual understanding, reverend brothers. But to those who labor for the well-being of this chapter, Michel appears to possess the humility the Lord calls from us all. Even as He did not come to be served, but to serve." He paused again. "We lay brothers would offer our own support to acceptance of Michel as a novice."

He sat down again. Brocard wondered how many of the others could sense the unspoken words: *If our support meant anything to this order.* He rubbed his beard thoughtfully. *Did many more of the lay brothers long for a greater voice in chapter matters?*

"Any further comments?" Silence followed the Abbot's question. "Then, in three days' time, the vote shall take place in the usual fashion. Should any of you feel strongly against this proposed novice, you are free to share your concerns with me."

*   *   *   *   *

The box was placed in the refectory three days later. The beans were handed out at the chapter meeting, one black and one white to each brother, the Abbot included. As soon as the meeting concluded, Brocard strode to the refectory, and dropped his black bean through the box slit.

But he had a few reservations, though he mentioned these to no one. Michel had almost too readily accepted the suggestion of entering the novitiate, especially eager once he discovered that he would be able to sing with the choir. *They will be only temporary vows,* Brocard reminded himself, leaving the building as the bell tolled for tierce. *You yourself took the simple profession so that you could remain with the chapter. The Abbot wisely extended your probation until a deeper commitment came into being.*

The box was emptied by Brocard and the Abbot in the Abbot's chamber that evening. Brocard was relieved to see only two white beans shining in the midst of black. Michel had been accepted.

The Abbot sighed, startling Brocard. "How many professed brothers have we, my son?"

"Fifty-three religious, most Reverend Father."

The Abbot ran his fingers through the pile of beans.

"Strange. By the number of votes cast, our size would seem to be double that count."

Brocard studied the pile. "Each brother was given only one black."

"I have no doubt of the number given to the religious brothers." The Abbot glanced up at him. "I am merely considering the source of the beans, whether dried for voting or present at our supper table. I am also recalling an unusual number of lay brothers in the courtyard during the day."

Brocard nodded. "They appear to desire a voice in chapter proceedings."

"A desire that has been long growing." The Abbot swept the beans back into the box. "A desire that, I fear, my successor will find it necessary to face. However, the votes against are too low for the extraneous votes to affect the outcome. We will welcome Michel into the order in a day's time. Prepare your candidate, my son."

"Yes, most Reverend Father." Brocard accepted the box and left the room. He walked down to the kitchen, emptying the beans into a pot of vegetables simmering over a low fire.

* * * * *

Gonard glanced at the shadows stretched across the courtyard by the setting sun. "I should now tell you to examine your conscience," Brocard had told him earlier, "and ask the Lord for His guidance on the step you now propose to take. However, though that is what the rules of our order stipulate, I will not pretend to you that they always apply perfectly to the time in which we now live. The rules were written in an earlier age, before the world was struck with the Great Death. Few who come here know of our Lord; the novitiate is now a place to learn and to discover a calling, rather than a threshold into final dedication. So,

take this time to calm yourself, and do not fear what is asked
of you."

Then he had left the stable block. Gonard had followed
him out, stopping outside the doors as the man walked on
to the dormitory. His thoughts were random, flitting
through his last day in the fields, the songs he had practiced
with Lybrand, the patterns made by the sun on the rough
walls of the chapter's buildings. But, as vespers drew nearer,
he began to reflect upon the coming ceremony.

The profession of those entering the novitiate, Brocard
had told him, was usually made in the chapterhouse, in the
presence of the Abbot and his council. However, Gonard
would not have fit through the door. Therefore, the ceremony would be held in the cathedral, preceding vespers.
And all of the chapter would be present.

The bell rang. Gonard lifted his head as the dormitory
doors opened. Brothers began to file into the courtyard,
crossing the paved stones to the cathedral. Several turned
their heads and smiled encouragement to Gonard as they
passed him. The novices followed. Gonard placed himself
behind the last one, as he had been instructed.

The lay brothers stood outside the cathedral, ready to
enter behind the novices. As Gonard approached, they all
raised hands in benison. He paused, taken aback by this
show of support. A few he knew from his mornings in the
fields, but only by sight; sensing their uneasiness, he had
always kept a distance between himself and his fellow work-
ers. But he felt none of that tension today. He dipped his
head, gratefully accepting their well-wishes, and stepped
into the cool interior of the cathedral.

The brothers stood in their places in the choir. Gonard
limped down the nave, his eyes on the Abbot standing in
the sanctuary, his white robe gleaming in the light stream-
ing in through the clear western windows. The brothers
straightened as Gonard passed them. He stopped in the

middle of the choir, careful not to catch a claw in the grates lining the beginning of the stalls. The transepts stretched out on either side of him. He felt, as he lowered himself to his second knees, as if he were in the center of the world.

" 'This is the thing which the Lord hath commanded,' " the Abbot read out into the quiet cathedral. " 'If a man vow a vow unto the Lord, or swear an oath to bind his soul with a bond; he shall not break his word, he shall do according to all that proceedeth out of his mouth.' Michel, is it your sincere and solemn joy to enter into the service of the Lord, binding yourself to Him for an initial period of four seasons?"

"Yes, most Reverend Father, by the help of the Lord and the assistance of your prayers," Gonard dutifully answered.

"During this time, will you seek to consecrate your whole being to Him?"

"Yes, most Reverend Father."

"During this time, will you renounce the striving after material gain, seeking instead the goods of the spirit?"

All he possessed was the whistle around his neck and the crystal weighing down his ear. "Yes, most Reverend Father."

"During this time, will you seek to be always available to serve with your brothers and, in order to give yourself completely to the Lord, remain celibate?"

Gonard thought of his large body, his awareness that he was the only one of his kind in existence. "Yes, most Reverend Father."

"During this time, so that the order of our community be maintained and we move in common purpose to the glory of the Lord, will you abide by the decisions made in the chapter and as expressed by the Abbot?"

Obedience has always been my strength, Gonard thought, surprised by the bitterness he suddenly felt. But he replied evenly, "Yes, most Reverend Father, by the help of the Lord and with the assistance of your prayers."

There was a pause. Then the Abbot announced, "Let

those who have sponsored this candidate take their places in his support."

Gonard lifted his head as they came to stand before him, Brocard on the left, Lybrand on the right. Brocard stretched out a large, opened book to Gonard. "Let the candidate give his petition," said the Abbot.

Gonard took a deep breath. He shifted his weight, lifted his left foreleg. Slowly, reluctantly, he lowered the left foot, placing it onto the book. The twisted toes draped across the pages, a dark blemish against their white clarity. "I, Michel, swear that I will strive to live in charity and love for the time of my vows, and that I will obey the words of my brothers and my Abbot."

Then he was allowed to return his foot to his side, hide it under his bent leg. The Abbot came forward. Lybrand placed into his hands a braided cord in the dark brown color worn by a novice. Gonard lowered his head, and the Abbot stretched to place the cord around his neck, lifting a neck spine to lay rough wool beside the thong that held the whistle in place. Lybrand moved forward, kneeling to fasten the ends together.

"Michel," the Abbot said, "I welcome thee to the service of the Lord and accept thy pledge in His name. May thou always serve Him in love and faithfulness."

"Amen," intoned the congregation.

Gonard bent his head again, the cord heavy around his neck. The brothers in the choir stalls began to chant a psalm, sides alternating with the verses. Gonard closed his eyes, letting the words carry him.

I will lift up mine eyes unto the hills,
from whence cometh my help.

My help cometh from the Lord,
which made heaven and earth.

He will not suffer thy foot to be moved:
he that keepeth thee will not slumber.

Behold, he that keepeth Israel
shall neither slumber nor sleep.

The Lord is thy keeper:
the Lord is thy shade upon thy right hand.

The sun shall not smite thee by day,
nor the moon by night.

The Lord shall preserve thee from all evil:
He shall preserve thy soul.

The Lord shall preserve thy going out and thy coming in
from this time forth, and even for evermore.

The Lord will watch over me. Gonard raised his head as the psalm ended. There was a strange, nagging doubt in his mind, which he forced away for the moment.

Brocard and Lybrand had stepped aside for the chanting of the psalm. Now they returned, Brocard holding a new candle, as yet unlit. A thurible swung from Lybrand's hands, the metal gleaming dully. The Abbot came forward, carrying a lighted taper. He touched it to Brocard's candle, and it spluttered into life, casting yellowed light into Brocard's face. "Receive this light," said the Abbot as Brocard moved to stand on Gonard's left, the candle in his hands. "So hast thou passed from Darkness to Light, to shine with the glory of our Lord."

Lybrand lifted the top of the thurible, the metallic clang echoing loudly through the hushed cathedral. The Abbot touched the taper to the incense inside, then nodded to Lybrand. The choirmaster replaced the lid. "Receive this scent," said the Abbot as Lybrand came to Gonard's right. "So hast thou made a sweet sacrifice of thyself to the Lord, and thou art pleasing in His sight."

Gonard bowed his head. The beeswax candle was a sweet, fresh smell to his left; the incense was a darker, smokier one on his right. Tendrils of gray scent curled past him, like spirits on the air. They twisted past his nostrils, teared his right eye. Then they disappeared, unwinding into nothingness.

The Abbot lifted his arms. "We are called to be the community of the Lord, to shed His love upon His troubled world, even as He once shed His own blood for our healing. Will you support Michel in his novitiate, and uphold him in his ministry?"

"We will," responded the congregation.

At the Abbot's signal, Gonard rose shakily to his feet. The old man came forward, laying hands on either side of Gonard's muzzle. "I welcome you as a son, Michel, and the chapter welcomes you as a brother. Turn and accept the welcome of your family."

Family, Gonard thought. I have never had a family before. He turned slowly, limped down the choir. The brothers stretched forward, their hands touching him in greeting. He paused so that each one could whisper a welcome or a benediction. Then he took up his usual position in the nave, the lay brothers in their pews on either side of him. The Abbot returned to his seat in the sanctuary, but Brocard and Lybrand came down to stand beside Gonard, remaining with him for vespers. Gonard lifted his head high. The service seemed lovelier than ever before, now that he knew himself to be part of the community for which it was held. My family, he thought again. I have a family now. I have many brothers.

A face suddenly came to his mind. A grim face, with sagging skin and dull gray eyes. My brother? Then the image was gone, sunk back down into his subconscious. I have a brother—somewhere. I wonder where he is now?

* * * * *

His domicile was still the stable, and his daily visits with Brocard continued. But otherwise, Gonard's life changed with his acceptance into the order. He quickly learned the schedule of both workdays and Sundays, an internal clock more accurate than the chapter's own, ensuring that he was never late for a service. He discovered that there were seven services a day, four of which only novices and professed religious attended. His favorite was vigils, held at 2:30 A.M. by his clock. When the waking bell rang, he would open the stable doors and watch the brothers stumble out into the dark night, one at their head leading the way with a candle. In silent pairs they would enter the cathedral, featureless in their long robes, cowls raised over their heads against the cold. The candle that led them there was the only light in the cathedral, handed to the Abbot to hold as he stood in the choir to lead the service. The psalms and antiphons were chanted softly between the two sides of the choir, crescendo and diminuendo, and Gonard forced himself to keep silent when a sleepy brother missed a note or forgot a word.

Lauds would follow, then a simple Mass, the brothers receiving the bread and wine in their places in the choir. Brocard had explained to him that only those in permanent vows could partake of Communion. Gonard had accepted this without murmur; neither the small portions of bread nor the dark wine, which soured the breaths of the receiving brothers, appealed to him.

Other portions of his new life were more confusing. Every workday morning after prime, all novices gathered together for instruction under the novice master, a Dom Petri. Conscious that these meetings were held in the courtyard for his sake, Gonard tried to listen dutifully. But Dom Petri's teachings often gave rise to questions that Gonard found difficult to hold back.

"I understand that you have been querying the novice master," Brocard said one afternoon, leaning back against the stable wall.

"I try not to," Gonard said apologetically.

"No, no, you should ask questions. The novice master is there to teach you, and asking questions is part of learning."

"But he isn't very good at answering them." Brocard raised an eyebrow, and Gonard drew his head back, surprised at his belligerence. "I mean, when I ask, he answers, but not enough."

Brocard rubbed his beard. "Give me an example of one of your questions, and his answer."

Gonard thought back. "Five days ago, Dom Petri read to us from the Holy Book. 'If we confess our sins, He is faithful and just to forgive us our sins, and to cleanse us from all unrighteousness.' "

"The promise of the Lord to His creations."

Gonard frowned. "That's what Dom Petri said. But I asked, 'Why didn't God forgive me when I asked Him to?' "

Brocard lowered himself to his stool. "I imagine his first response was to remonstrate you for blasphemy."

"Yes, that's what he said, that I shouldn't use the name of the Lord."

"We do not use His name to show our respect for Him."

Gonard's frown deepened, creases spreading up his snout. Old teachings came to him. "But the Ultimate is known by many names, each as inadequate as the other."

"We call the Lord," Brocard said quietly, "by the name He gives Himself in His Holy Book."

Gonard noted the arms crossed over the chest, the sternness underlying the man's words. Even Brocard can't be fully questioned, he realized, deflated. He moved on. "After

Dom Petri told me I'd blasphemed, he then said of course the Lord would forgive me, if I was sincerely repentant. I said I had been, but—the Lord—hadn't forgiven me. He asked how I was sure, and I said, 'Because He told me I wasn't forgiven.' He said, 'You mean, you simply did not feel forgiven.' And I said, 'No, He spoke to me. He said, "No. Not yet." ' " Gonard took a deep breath. "Then Dom Petri said I was to consider that I hadn't been truly repentant and that's why I thought the Lord was speaking to me. And he finished the lesson there."

Brocard sighed. "Dom Petri is committed to the welfare of his novices. But few, in my experience, have questioned him so closely."

"Why not?"

"Most novices are younger than you are, with less experience of the world."

Gonard protested, "But I'm only twelve years old!"

"Your species must mature more quickly than ours." Gonard stared at him. Species? His species? He had come from a human, thought like a human—was he not human? But Brocard was continuing, "Tell me what you said to the Lord, before He said that He wouldn't forgive you."

Gonard closed his eyes, wondering if he'd be able to remember. But the words came easily to him. "I said, 'I didn't plan to kill him. I know I did wrong.' And then I said, 'I only ask to be forgiven.' "

"And the exact response?"

" 'No. Not yet.' "

"What do you think the Lord meant by that?"

"If I knew," Gonard said bitterly, "do you think I would have asked the novice master about it?"

Brocard straightened. "Strong words, Michel."

"I know." But Gonard found himself unwilling to apologize. He gazed at a stone wall, feeling suddenly restless. "I'm not an animal, Brocard. I'm not a different species. I'm as human as you are, only I'm in a different kind of body. My father was human, and I killed him, and with him dead there can't be any forgiveness between us. So I went to his Creator and didn't receive forgiveness from Him either. So, what am I supposed to do? Say nothing when someone tells me something I know isn't true, that God forgives everything?"

"You don't know it to be untrue," Brocard pointed out placidly. Gonard risked a glance; the man was still calm, despite Gonard's outburst. "The answer was, 'Not yet,' not strictly 'No.'"

Gonard realized that he'd been holding his breath, expecting a stronger reaction to his words. "But why 'Not yet'?"

"If I knew, do you think I would have asked you?"

"Yes," Gonard retorted, "because you'd want me to realize it for myself."

Brocard's mouth quirked; then he smiled. "You are learning." Then the smile faded. "I do not know how to answer, Michel. But, perhaps I can suggest something from the book you are currently reading."

Gonard's right eye flicked to a small book lying on another stool. Reassured that the precious volume was still intact, he refocused both eyes on Brocard. "What?"

"Do you not recall a statement made by the writer? That sometimes our own screaming need for the Lord deafens us to His voice."

" 'Perhaps your own reiterated cries deafen you to the voice you hoped to hear,' " Gonard said, quoting automatically.

"The Lord longs always to grant forgiveness, for through forgiveness comes a soul's healing," Brocard continued. "But it may be that He so answered you because it is not His forgiveness that you truly require. Perhaps another's forgiveness is struggling within you."

"What would that be?" Gonard asked, confused. "I can't ask my father's forgiveness—he's dead. I told you that."

"No." Brocard leaned forward. "What you actually said was, 'with him dead there can't be any forgiveness between us.' Is it simply a case of him forgiving you? Why did you kill him, Michel?"

Gonard felt the man's question open up his mind, push him back to an earlier time. He shook his head, felt his legs tremble. But the laboratory was around him, the memory so strong that he seemed to be living it again. "He was going to kill me." The rod lifted in his father's hand, pointed at his head. "Can't you see? He was going to kill me."

"Why was he going to kill you?"

Farther back now. A red head swung toward him, wedged like his, scales glittering in the setting sun. "He killed Vomer." The words were dragged out of some deep, dark place. "He killed her, took her apart as if she were nothing. And then he was going to kill me, because her death wasn't enough. He was going to kill me, and I was all that was left of her."

Brocard stood, moved closer to him.

Gonard backed away, the image of the gray-robed man blending with the smaller shape of the Master. "Your life is mine," said the man slowly. "It is mine to take, and yours only to give."

"No." Gonard backed away farther, down the length of the stable. Rows of computer panels slid past his gaze, flickering into stable doors when he attempted to look at them. The far wall stopped him. He shuddered as the man came nearer. "No. My life—my life—"

The man halted. "What? Is what? Why should it be of any concern to me?"

"Because you're my father!" Gonard bellowed. "Because you created me! Aren't I important to you? At all?"

The man regarded him for a long moment. Gonard felt

the seconds pass, heard his own breathing echo harshly from the walls. Then the man said finally, softly, "No."

And anger swirled in Gonard's chest, fury at this man who could so callously throw his life away. *She is not important. You are not important.* His chest swelled, chemicals pumping through his body, making him feel lighter, more powerful. He drew his head back, opened his jaws.

And saw, in the split second before the gases from his chamber burst into the air, that he was in a stable, and it was Brocard who stood before him. He whipped his head to the side, flames spreading across the straw, the wooden stalls, into the stone wall. The straw caught on fire, red flames dancing quickly through the dried grasses. The dry wood of the stall blackened, then it too began to burn. Gonard expelled the rest of the gases in a blast that cracked stones in the wall. Brocard stepped back, smoke curling around him. Gonard strode forward, snapping his head down to close his teeth on Brocard's robe without breaking his stride. Lifting the man high into the air, Gonard leapt over the flames and threw his shoulder against the stable doors. They burst outside, the fire in the stables roaring into power behind them.

Brothers had begun to gather in the courtyard. "Water!" Lybrand was yelling above the confusion. "Water! The fire must not be allowed to spread! Move!"

Gonard stopped by the cathedral. He carefully lowered Brocard to his feet, noting the rips his teeth had left in the gray cloth. But Brocard appeared unaware that the breeze was ruffling against bare skin. He stared at the blaze engulfing the stables, the chain of brothers passing bucketfuls of water to throw upon the building. Then he slowly turned to Gonard, his eyes shadowed. "Michel, is that how your father was killed?"

Gonard nodded, not trusting himself to speak. They stood together in silence for a long time, neither moving as the fire was extinguished, the stable block reduced to a pile of blackened stones and a few bits of charred timber.

Maybe, Gonard thought heavily, not knowing where the thought came from, my purpose is to kill.

CHAPTER 9

"An' then," the man said, his voice ragged with pain, "I did draw th' blade 'cross her throat, 'fore she could change 'gain."

The medtech leaned forward, nodding in the approximation of human encouragement. His mind took a second to locate the man's name, which reminded him once again of the slow deterioration of his faculties. Ramos, that was it. It had taken many sessions with this hunter, Ramos, to bring him to this point, to speak of the death of his mate, brought on by the Changewinds.

"She might have recovered," the medtech said softly.

Ramos shook his head, eyes closed against tears. "Nay. None taken by th' Winds recover. They be changed e'ermore."

"Nor can anything prevent the madness."

"Naught." Ramos looked up at him, sadness suddenly transformed into bitterness. "Naught but singing, an' we had but a Walker fer th' tribe."

"It is true that the Headman engaged the services of one since declared to be a Windwalker, and therefore not expected to protect others against the Changewinds." The medtech permitted a small smile to crease his stiff lips. "A Windwalker could not be expected to sing."

"Aye," Ramos agreed glumly. "Nae a Walker."

"It would be an easement to you," the medtech mused, "if Gonard were here to discuss the matter further with you."

Ramos lifted his shoulders in a heavy shrug. "But he be nae here."

"You know why not?"

"Aye. He stepped into th' Winds an' hae nae been seen since." A thought slowly darkened the man's round face. "If he be a Walker, why hae he nae returned?"

"It is impossible to respond to that question." The medtech felt his back supports creak as he straightened in his chair. His olfactory receptors registered the change in the man's sweat, from fear to anger. "It might be possible to present the same query to the conclave. It was they who decided that Gonard was indeed a Windwalker."

"The conclave." Ramos spat onto the tiled floor. The medtech grimaced. He would never come to accept the uncivilized manners of these hunters. "They ruled t' protect their own coffers. Ye know what I think, m'lord?"

"I do not," the medtech lied.

"I think that th' Lord Gonard ne'er be Singer nae Walker." The man drew back, as if afraid of the medtech's reaction. "What say ye?"

"I choose not to respond to that statement."

"But ye be his Second," Ramos persisted. "Ye be bound t' defend him."

"I was once his Second." The medtech allowed another smile. "I am now a member of the conclave."

Ramos paused a moment to digest the implications of that statement. "Then ye be nae longer beholden t' him. Ye can tell th' truth o' this matter."

The medtech spread his hands. "It is not my place to tell you anything."

"Nay, m'lord," Ramos said with a grim smile. "It be th' place o' th' tribe. We be th' ones t' seek fer justice."

The tribe, the medtech reflected. So, the men would act alone in this. "Justice was given by the Triune."

"Triunes hae been wrong 'fore." Ramos rose, bowed to the medtech. "Me thanks, m'lord. Me way be clear now."

The medtech remained seated as the man let himself out of the hall. Another name to cross off his mental list. But he felt no sense of accomplishment. Itsa still spent most of her time with the hunter Rygor, and no longer showed any interest in leaving the settlement in the spring. This despite half the clan being turned against her.

A knock on the door made him raise himself to his feet. "Come in."

One of his fellow counselors waved a hand at him as she came through the door. "Ye should sit, m'lord. I do know how th' winter tells 'gainst ye."

Then that is how they explain my weakening, the medtech mused. He lowered himself back into his chair, tipping his head back as he waited for the Singer to speak. Maroll, he reminded himself. She is called Maroll.

"The Clan o' Millan hae nae Singer," Maroll said, taking the other seat. "An th' Windwalker be nae here t' do any speaking fer th' clan."

"It is well known that I have little knowledge of your customs," the medtech replied evenly. "I can, however, deduce that you would request my services in the absence of a Singer, since I served as Second to a Windwalker involved with the clan."

Maroll nodded. "Aye. It be time fer th' girls o' age t' 'come women. A Singer must be wi' th' clan fer th' presentation of th' girls, t' gie them their truth an' t' say that they be now adult."

"It will be my pleasure to perform this duty." The medtech shifted back in his seat. "It would be of assistance if you would outline the course of events at such a presentation."

"It be nae difficult." Maroll had visibly relaxed at his acceptance of the task, and the medtech wondered if he were once again saving the Confine from embarrassment. "Th' mothers will declare their daughters 'fore the clan, giving their lineage an' promising that they be now a woman. Ye hae th' right t' challenge any girl or mother if ye feel aught amiss. After all hae been named t' ye, ye will take each one 'lone t' a room an' gie her a truth she must take wi' her. When she hae nodded t' it, then ye both return t' th' hall an' ye take th' next girl."

The medtech considered the chunk of information. "Then this 'truth' must contain some pain for the recipient. How am I to discover what must be said to each girl?"

"Their mothers will gie it t' ye. They will come here, one by one." Maroll stood, rubbing her hands together briskly. "I will gie th' Headwoman th' word."

A final question from the medtech stopped her by the doors. "What is the procedure for those girls who have lost their mothers?"

Maroll shrugged. "Another be asked t' take th' place. That be th' way."

"Of course," the medtech murmured to himself, once again alone. "That is the way."

* * * * *

Itsa stood by the fire, staring into the flames. There was something different about her; the medtech paused in the entranceway to the main hall, analyzing what it could be. The ragged vest she had worn since smuggling herself from the asteroid colony was finally gone, leaving her in the fine clothes made available to those living in the Confine. Her face was clear of her customary anger, replaced by the wrinkles of a near smile. And she stood straight, almost at ease with herself. The medtech felt cheek attachments twitch in an attempt at a scowl. This was not as he wanted.

"Yeah, look, it's the medtech." Itsa grinned up at him. "Ya look like ya've swallowed somethin' twisty. But I forget, ya never eat, do ya?"

The medtech remained where he stood. "The presentation of the new women of the clan is due to take place tomorrow. The mothers of the other girls have each come to give into my keeping the truths I am to speak to them. All except for the mother of Rydeth, who is unable to perform that duty. Is it to be my understanding that you have accepted this task on her behalf?"

Itsa laughed. The ease of her levity made the medtech frown. "Ya jive I am."

"It is then obvious that we must embark upon a similar discussion."

Her smile disappeared. "I saw some of the women ya sent outta here. They were cryin'."

"Truth often cuts both ways."

"That's what they say 'bout swords." Itsa leaned back against the wall, crossing her arms. "I jig ya did it on purpose."

The medtech gave her silence in return. Then he asked, "Do you know the truth that I am to give to the girl?"

" 'Course I do." Itsa took a deep breath. "A couple of years ago, her mom gave birth to a boy. It was weaky anyways, but it died while Rydeth was carryin' him to the clan. She blamed herself. I jive she still does. The truth is, it wasn't her fault. The kid would of died anyways. That's the truth she needs to jig."

"It was her wish that you knew this information?"

"Yeah, it was." Itsa had turned her head to look into the fire again. "We talked to each other 'bout our moms, once, and she told me."

Again, that difference about her. For once, the medtech saw behind the brave stance of the Outler, to the softer core.

He suddenly found himself willing to spare her at least one sorrow. "Leave the hunter now, Itsa. It is imperative that we form our plans for the search for Gonard."

Itsa shook her head, smiling to herself. "Don'tcha jive, tech? Once Rydeth's a woman, she'll be in charge of the family. Then she can offer her dad to someone, and that's goin' to be me. So she's said." She glanced up at him again. "That's what I want, tech. Someone to look after, someone to look after me. I'm goin' to accept Rygor and stay here with him."

The medtech felt his resolve strengthen again. The Outler had brought this onto her own head. He would let her suffer the consequences of her choice.

The door was pushed open, allowing a gust of cold air and Lissa to enter. The medtech saw Itsa straighten, smile to herself. "Welcome, Lissa o' Sanna."

Lissa gave no sign of noting the irony in the Outler's voice. "M'lady, Itsa o' Sharit." She was dressed in new clothing, the medtech noted, and a belt of dark green tightened her tunic against her waist. "I hae come t' petition ye."

"Yeah, I jigged ya might." Itsa was enjoying herself far too much for the medtech's comfort. "Go 'head."

"It be me understanding that ye be th' nearest th' Second hae t' a kinswoman."

Itsa shrugged. "Guess so."

"Then me asking comes t' ye." Lissa stood tall, with the quiet pride the medtech had often noted. "Th' Second hae nae woman. I hae nae man. Fer th' past moon I hae tended t' th' needs o' this hall, an' I hae proved meself well able."

"Ya have," Itsa affirmed.

"Then I ask ye fer th' man. If he be willing"—Lissa's eyes flicked to the medtech—"I will join meself t' him, an' serve him alway."

Itsa sighed. "Ya don't jig 'bout us, do ya?"

"I know that ye will soon be leaving th' Second," Lissa

said softly. "Yer place is t' be wi' th' clan o' Millan, th' tribe o' Naylor. Would ye leave th' man wi'out a woman fer his needs?"

Itsa glanced at him. "Come on, tech, tell her, will ya?"

The medtech studied her for a moment. Little did she seem to realize that her union with Rygor was as unlikely as his own pairing with this woman. But perhaps this was an opportunity to allow the Outler to discover the intrinsic incompatibility for herself. "My lady," he grated, lowering himself to his knees, "I ask your leave to accept the offer of Lissa of Sanna."

"Whatcha up to?" Itsa demanded. The medtech said nothing. "Do ya jig what ya've gotta do at the ceremony? No, 'course not. Ya don't bother tryin' to learn how primitive humans act, do ya?"

"We wait yer answer, m'lady," Lissa prompted softly.

"Then ya'll find out, won'tcha?" Itsa snapped. She turned to Lissa. "Yeah, go 'head. Don't say I didn't warn ya."

Silence hung in the room for a moment. Then Lissa came forward, touching the medtech on the shoulder. "She hae gi'en th' word," she said quietly.

"They work fast here, tech," Itsa added grimly. "She'll have everythin' set up 'ready. Where's the party?" she asked Lissa.

"At th' hall o' me clan." Lissa smiled down at the medtech. "Be ye ready?"

The medtech creaked back to his feet. "It would be preferable to complete this task without delay. Lead us to your hall."

Lissa's tribe had obviously enjoyed a good hunting season. They occupied one of the more desirable areas of the settlement, cobbled streets circling around large stone buildings. Itsa halted outside the hall. "I'll let ya go in 'lone," she told the medtech. "Have fun."

The medtech had an unsettling recall of memory: his co-creator, stopping outside the Council chamber and letting him go in alone to face the ruling of the Lord Citizens, debating whether to allow a robot's continued existence. "Is it not preferable that you attend with me?"

"Not preferable for me."

Lissa opened the door, led the medtech in. Oil lamps were set into the windows, adding to the daylight struggling inside. The medtech saw a half-dozen men and women waiting behind a table, their expressions a mingle of welcome and concern.

"Be this th' man ye would wish t' take as mate?" the woman sitting in the center asked.

Lissa drew herself up proudly. "It be. He be th' medtech o' Rumfus Max, Second t' th' Windwalker Gonard o' Rumfus Max, and also on the conclave o' th' Confine."

One of the men nodded, turned his head to the medtech. "Hae Lissa o' Sanna proved herself t' ye?"

"She has proved herself to me," the medtech replied steadily.

The woman asked Lissa, "Hae ye th' word o' his kinswoman?"

"Itsa o' Sharit hae given her word."

"Then we be ready t' declare ye bound." The woman rose to her feet. "Let ye show one another that ye be well an' untouched by th' Winds."

Lissa unfastened her belt, pulled her tunic over her head. The medtech watched as she stripped, leaving her clothes in a pile at her feet. She smiled at him, and the medtech realized that he was meant to do the same.

Past merged seamlessly with present. Once again he was ordered to remove his coveralls, to stand naked under the scrutiny of others. Lord Citizens pointed, aghast, while the Lady Cits turned their heads. The men behind the table muttered in shock. Yes, I am incomplete, the medtech thought at them, knowing that they saw only smooth skin

where manhood should be. Why build a robot with geni-
talia? He is never expected to feel either lust or love. Only
the dragon was built complete.

"He be Wind-touched," the woman said grimly. Lissa
looked away. "Wind-touched cannae be taken fer mate."

The medtech nodded. He pulled on his clothes again,
now understanding why the Outler had laughed. As before,
he stood alone to be shamed. And his betrayer waited outside. Betrayers always waited outside. He looked at Lissa for
the last time. Then he marched from the room, his hands
clenching and opening, again and again.

He had not been created with emotions. But he was
learning from humans, storing the knowledge he gained.
And one thing he now knew well: betrayal. That lesson had
been provided by several teachers.

*　*　*　*　*

The medtech took the seat ceremonially offered him in
the clan's hall. He flicked one eye at the sagging ceiling, the
other at the wooden floor. The lack of success by the tribe
was all too evident. It was therefore unsurprising that the
men were turning their failure into anger, finding it easier
to blame Gonard for their shortcomings than themselves.
Human nature was so predictable.

One fact he had gleaned about those who spent their
winters in the settlement, however, was that they were eter-
nal optimists. The hunt might have not gone well last summer, but a new spring would come, and they would do
better this time. It was with this hope that the mothers
marched into the hall, their daughters one step behind
them. Smiles stretched every face. A boy became a man by
killing his first hunt animal, when the blood of his prey
would be smeared across his cheeks in celebration. A girl
became a woman upon the declaration of her mother, ready

then to take her place in a society where each sex ruled for one half of the year.

"Th' Clan o' Millan, th' Tribe o' Naylor, be all here together," the Headwoman declared. She stepped back from the line of women and girls, ranged across one side of the hall. "We hae come t' welcome th' ones who would be women. They offer themselves here fer approval. Do we say that these be ours?"

"They be ours," the men and women grouped beyond them chanted.

"Be we ready t' judge, an' t' question any who 'pears unready?"

"We be ready," came the reply.

Millan came to the medtech's side. "Th' duty be yers, m'lord."

The medtech rose. "Let each woman state her name and line, and do so also for the child she claims as her own."

The mother closest to him spoke first, giving her lineage back for five generations, then declaring the father of her daughter and the year of her birth. The medtech nodded, and the same information was provided by the next woman. So they passed down the line, until Itsa's turn came. The medtech waited as she came up with the names of her distant relations, unsurprised that she knew them; she would have had to give the same information at her Theological Examinations.

Once she had finished, the medtech deliberately sat back down into his chair. "Nowhere in that lineage," he said calmly, "do I hear the name of a member of this clan."

Itsa glared at him. "Ya jive I ain't a member. I'm representin' Rydeth for her mom."

"Have you therefore been given her express authority to be her representative for this occasion?"

Several people stirred, but, although the questioning was unusual, it was within the rights and duties of a Singer, or

his Second. " 'Course not," Itsa snapped. "She's dead. Her
husband asked me, and I agreed."

"It is therefore imperative that you prove, to the satisfaction of this proceeding, that you have the necessary knowledge to act in this manner for a girl unrelated to yourself."
The medtech stood again. "Tell me this. What is the most
painful memory held by Rydeth of Meredith?"

He heard knuckles grind as Itsa clenched her fists. But
her voice was steady as she answered, "Two years ago, her
mom gave birth to a boy. It died while Rydeth was bringin'
the boy to the clan. She blames herself. That's her worst
memory, 'cause it died in her arms."

The turn of Rydeth's head confirmed Itsa's statement.

"That be all," Millan declared. Then she glanced apologetically at the medtech. "If ye do accord, m'lord."

"It is sufficient," the medtech agreed blandly, and then
continued down the line.

Once all the girls had been presented, the medtech withdrew to a small side room. There, in the only chair, he
waited as each girl came in alone. He made no attempt to
dispel their nervousness, merely stating the statements
derived from the meetings with their mothers. The truths
varied. One girl only smiled, relieved and amused to discover that her mother had been hoping that she would be a
boy, a son instead of the constant daughters she produced.
Another girl blinked back tears as the medtech informed her
that the man she had thought to be her father was actually
her mother's second husband.

As the medtech had arranged with Millan, Rydeth came
in last. She stood before him, ready and unafraid. The
medtech asked, "Are you unaware as to the circumstances of
your mother's death?"

Rydeth studied him for a moment, then replied, "Me sire
hae told me. She be killed by th' Changewinds."

"The Changewinds affected her mind," the medtech

agreed. "However, it was your father who drew a knife across her throat. He was the one who killed her."

He saw the knowledge sink in, pushing its slow way past the barriers she tried to raise against it. Then, bending her head, Rydeth pushed past him and through the door leading outside.

The medtech rose. As he marched into the room, he saw the concerned faces, the question in their eyes. "Rydeth of Meredith has not returned to you," he stated. "She is unwilling to accept the truth imparted to her. It is regrettable; however we must now continue with the investiture of the remaining girls, who are ready to be declared women."

Rygor thrust himself through the group. "Where be Rydeth?"

The medtech met the angry eyes. "She left by the second door."

"What truth did ye gie her?"

"That," the medtech said, "is for her to impart to you."

Rygor hurried out. Millan stopped Itsa from following, taking her instead to one side before giving the medtech a nod to continue the proceedings. The medtech calmly led the girls through the recitation of their names, the pronouncement of their new status, and the presentation to the clan. All the while, Itsa's eyes never left his face, a dark scowl warning him that she would be demanding explanations later.

*   *   *   *   *

In silence they trudged back to their hall in the confine, rain and wind forestalling any attempts at questions by Itsa. As the medtech opened the door to enter, a dark figure turned away from the fire. Even before the hood of his cloak was thrown back, the medtech had identified Rygor's scent.

"Why?" he demanded of Itsa. "Why did ye gie him that truth fer her?"

Itsa had frozen at the vehemence in his voice. The medtech calmly continued into the room, the man barely giving him a glance. "I didn't jig there'd be anythin' wrong 'bout it. She needed to understand—"

"Aye, she needed t' know," Rygor all but shouted. "But in me own time, at me choosing, nae yers. I be her father, an' it be t' me this falls, fer as ye know full well she hae nae mother."

The medtech quietly added more logs to the fire, building up the warmth. His internal heating systems were wearing down, and the cold occasionally thickened lubricants and jammed his joints. Strangely enough, he suddenly found himself missing Lissa, whose task it had been to keep the fire going.

Itsa said stiffly, "I jive that. But she told me 'bout it herself. What's wrong 'bout tellin' her it wasn't anybody's fault?"

"But it were." Rygor came to her, stiff with anger. "It were th' fault o' th' one who be nae e'en a Walker, t' pretend that he could sing an' save us. An' ye lie further when ye say that she told ye herself. She ne'er knew. She be nae there when I drew th' knife 'cross Meredith's throat."

The medtech watched Itsa's eyes widen at the last statement. "But I never—"

The hunter strode past as she spoke. "Ye be nae longer welcome t' me house," he interrupted. "I must now see t' me daughter." And he stepped back into the storm outside, not waiting to hear her denial.

Itsa turned the look of disbelief to the medtech. "What did ya tell Rydeth?"

"That it was the blade of her father that dispatched her mother after she had been affected by the Changewinds."

"Ya snout-nosed robot—"

"It is regrettable that you left me with no other choice," he continued as her fists lifted.

"I gave ya what to say to her," Itsa growled.

"It was then used by yourself during the challenge that I was required to issue to any woman who stands beside a girl not her own daughter." The medtech expected Itsa not to realize the untruth of that statement. "I was then obviously unable to utilize the same memory for the next portion of the proceedings."

"Ya could of picked somethin' else."

"I could only choose what I myself knew regarding the girl in question," the medtech pointed out. "That knowledge is very limited. It was regrettable that her father had not seen fit to discuss the truth of her mother's death before this time."

"Yeah, isn't it just." Itsa turned and punched the wall. The medtech noted that she had obviously accepted his explanations. "Isn't it just." She leaned her forehead against stone, closing her eyes.

The medtech left her then, to grieve alone for what she had lost.

* * * * *

"That, an' that." Beeran, one of the scholars among the Singers, pointed out the landmarks on the map spread out across the tiled floor. "They be th' mountains o' th' east. Methinks th' Walker could nae hae gone that far."

The medtech studied the circular rings representing mountains, noting the river flowing around their feet. "It is difficult to predict how far Gonard may have ventured. It is my belief that he would seek out human habitations. He has shown several times that he prefers the company of others above solitude. Are you aware of any settlements in this area?" The sweep of his hand indicated the lands eastward; the medtech had already decided that it would be unlikely that the dragon would return to the City. To the south the map indicated a wide ocean. Gonard might have taken the other option and gone north, but the tracks left behind had been heading east.

"Traders travel th' routes." The Singer pulled at his mustache. "There be note o' a settlement here." He pointed at a square near the mountains.

"Does that designate another group of tribe-clans?" the medtech asked.

"Nay." Beeran shook his head in emphasis. "They be— otherwise. It be hard t' explain," he continued apologetically. "They be men, but they be like a clan. They hae Singers, but they ne'er leave th' settlement. It be said they bring healing t' them who come t' th' settlement. Th' Walker could hae been taken there."

Healing. The medtech stared thoughtfully at the square. Could that be possible? They will not have the necessary technology to repair the damage to his foot and wing, the medtech reassured himself. "To arrive at that place will require traveling through much of the intervening territory between this settlement and the mountains. It is therefore a promising destination, as it will entail the exploration of other possible locations."

"Take care, m'lord," the Singer counseled. "There be also barbarians in th' hills. A tribe be too strong fer them t' challenge, but a man 'lone may be taken."

The medtech allowed a slight smile. "I will not be alone." Then he rolled up the map, handed it back to Beeran.

The man stood, then shifted uneasily. "Ye will be taking yer leave soon?"

"Yes, I will take my leave shortly." The medtech waited until the Singer had left before laboriously raising himself onto his own feet. He knew why Beeran's last question had sounded hopeful. Gonard's associates were a growing embarrassment to the confine as spring approached and the dragon had still not returned from his second journey into the Changewinds.

It is imperative that I survive the journey, the medtech reminded himself. As he had done daily for the last two weeks, he walked across the Confine. Although the wall around the settlement was as high here as anywhere else, a protection against the Changewinds, a few precious panes of glass were set into the stone. Age had made the liquid run, but the ground outside was still visible. The snow had melted further.

The medtech heard Itsa's distinctive steps come up behind him. "It will soon be possible to leave the settlement," he told her without turning.

"Yeah, so?"

"It is necessary to have your decision on this matter." He looked back at her. "Will you accompany me, or is it still your desire to remain within the settlement?"

"I've looked for Rygor, ya jig." She seemed to speaking more to herself than to him. "He's gone, him and Rydeth. And nobody'll tell me where. Nobody'll even talk to me."

The medtech held still, awaiting her answer. There were other pressures he could bring to bear, if he must.

"I'll come with ya," Itsa finally said. "There's nothin' left for me here now." And she stumbled away, her shoulders hunched.

The medtech allowed himself a satisfied nod. Then he, too, started back to their hall. There were still several details of their journey that he had to prepare.

CHAPTER 10

"Blessed be the Lord."

"And those who serve Him," Brocard responded automatically. He stepped into the Abbot's chamber, wincing as a sandal strap rubbed against a burn on his foot. But he refused to limp; he made his way carefully to the Abbot, reminding himself that all the burns were only superficial, even if they did sting.

"Sit down, my son." The Abbot leaned back in his own chair as Brocard obeyed. "I am informed that the fire did not spread beyond the one stable block. Neither you nor Michel is injured?"

Brocard shut his eyes briefly, remembering the sheet of flame that had been turned from him at the last moment. "I have only minor burns, most Reverend Father. Michel is unharmed."

"How did the blaze begin? Do you know its source?"

"Yes." Brocard felt his lips quirk. "It was Michel."

"I am not seeking to apportion blame, my son."

"Michel has—capabilities—that I am still in the process of discovering," Brocard said. "One of which is the ability to exhale flames. Such was the means by which he killed his father. I was attempting to force him to acknowledge his anger at his father, by placing him in his mind-set at the time of the killing."

The Abbot nodded. "I have seen such transference used to great success."

"Perhaps too successfully, in this case." Brocard forced himself to relax. "Fortunately, Michel realized in time that I was not his father in truth, but merely representing him."

"In time to save your life," the Abbot acknowledged. "Not in time to prevent the loss of the stables. It will require rebuilding before we obtain more coursairs. And there is the problem of lodging for Michel."

"There are empty barns by the lay brothers, now that the sheep are out to pasture," Brocard said, watching the Abbot closely for his reaction. "The coursairs could be placed under their care. Michel could then occupy the other stable block."

The Abbot leaned forward. "Care of the coursairs is the physical work selected by the chapter for novices."

"They could use the time instead to study healing techniques."

"It is also the tradition of the order that its most valuable assets are under the care of the religious brothers."

" 'Do you renounce the seeking of material gain, seeking instead the goods of the spirit?' " Brocard quoted softly.

The Abbot was silent for a moment. Then he nodded. "I will take your solution forward at the next chapter meeting. However, you may find other suggestions more difficult to put through the council."

Brocard stiffened. "So soon, most Reverend Father?"

The Abbot smiled. "It is not my intention to die in this room, as did the Abbot before me. I will put your name before the chapter tomorrow, with the intention that you should be consecrated Abbot on Easter morning."

"And if the vote is not unanimous?"

"I think you will discover that you are supported by more than you know." The Abbot leaned back in his chair.

"However, an Abbot cannot give the time required of a healer. Will you be free for your new duties by Easter?"

Brocard looked down at his hands, found them clenched. He opened them, studying the contrast between pale skin and gray robe. "The time scale you propose leaves me a little over six weeks to complete my duties to Michel."

"Will that be long enough?"

"It is difficult to judge, most Reverend Father. I believe that I know the cause of his suppression of memory, and I feel that we are near to the next major step in his healing, but"—he looked up—"I cannot speak for certain."

"Will the chapter first need to sacrifice another stable block?"

Brocard ignored the gibe. "The Abbot may be asked to postpone the consecration of his successor. I will not endanger Michel's recovery."

"Very well," the Abbot conceded. "I shall announce my intended retirement and put your name to the vote as my successor. If it so transpires that you cannot take the seat at Easter, I shall continue in office until such time as you have discharged your duties to Michel."

"I thank you, most Reverend Father."

"My son." The Abbot leaned forward, eyes serious, searching. "Do not let your dedication become an obsession. No, hear me, Brocard," he continued when Brocard attempted to speak. "I have ofttimes considered as to whether another brother should have had the healing of Michel. It is true that, having traveled a similar path once yourself, you are skilled as a guide for another soul. But take care that you do not become lost yourself. You and I both know that your own wounds run deep. Michel should be no more important to you than any other who has been under your care. Ensure that this is so, my son."

"Yes, most Reverend Father," Brocard answered. But he dropped his gaze, knowing that Michel was different, that never had he yearned so strongly for any soul's healing. Despite the dangers.

* * * * *

Gonard lifted his head. It was difficult to concentrate on the book he was reading with the smell of coursair dung still fresh in the stables. He missed the other stable block, which had stood a month empty of coursairs before his occupancy.

Footsteps made his ears prick forward. He carefully closed the book with extended claw, and stood waiting, tense, wondering if Brocard would open the doors this time, instead of hurrying past.

The footsteps halted. Gonard heard the man breathing heavily. "I wouldn't have killed you," he said, limping up to the door.

The door swung open. Brocard looked up at him. "I did not realize your anger could be so dangerous."

Gonard backed away, hoping that the man would enter the stable block. "I wouldn't have killed you. I didn't kill you. You're not like my father."

Brocard stepped into the building, closed the door behind him. "No, I am not like your father. Who was Vomer?"

How could he explain? "She was—like a sister. We were together for many years." Flashes of memory: watching the sunset, side by side; her arrival at the laboratory; walking into his cave to join him; lying in a dull red heap, discarded. But so much was still out of reach, in a fog—a fog he was reluctant to penetrate.

"And your father killed her."

"It was his right. We were his."

Brocard nodded, began to turn away.

"Wait." Gonard stepped forward. "Why are you going?

Why aren't you asking me any questions?"

Brocard straightened, his gray eyes meeting Gonard's. "Do I dare to ask, Michel? What if I anger you again, if I attempt to push you to face what you hide from yourself? Will you turn your flame aside this time? And if you do, what about our next meeting, and the next after that?"

Gonard shuffled his feet. "I won't hurt you."

"Can you truly promise that?"

"I'll try not to get angry."

"No, that is not the solution," Brocard said sharply. "You must understand the reason for your anger before you can conquer it. But you do not want to know, do you?"

Gonard glanced away. "I like it here. I like living here. Do I have to remember?"

"The past cannot be hidden away without consequence. It will eat at you, disrupting any peace you attempt to build for yourself." There was a pause. Then Brocard added, "You also told me that you promised someone that you would return to her."

A dark face, teeth startlingly white against brown skin as she grinned . . . Who was she? "Wasn't it right," Gonard began slowly, haltingly, "for my father to decide what to do to us? We were alive only because of him."

"Do you think he had such a right?"

"No." Gonard turned troubled eyes to Brocard. "Not now. I used to think he did."

"You could not have done so then either," Brocard pointed out, "or you would not have killed him. Letting him destroy the one whom you loved was enough."

Gonard pulled his head back in alarm. "I didn't love her. Only someone with a soul can love."

Brocard frowned. "Do you consider yourself to be without a soul? You have told me that you are not an animal. You are human, regardless of outward appearances."

"A soul." Gonard flicked his tail restlessly. "I've been

trying to find out if I have a soul." There was some reason why he shouldn't have one, something about his father, and small hands moving over a long table.

"To have a soul," Brocard said thoughtfully, "is to be able to worship the Lord, to love one's brothers, and to strive to perfect oneself. To have a soul is to be able to feel the touch of heaven in daily life, and to heed the warnings of hell."

"When I sing . . ." Gonard stopped, reflected. "When I sing, I feel as if I'm part of something greater than myself. Like the first time I sang in the cathedral, to the man in the window . . ." He shifted his weight, easing the pressure on his left forefoot. He said, very quietly, "Do you think I have a soul?"

He heard Brocard rub his beard, knew exactly when the man would ask: "What do you believe?"

"I think—I might have a soul." Gonard dared to look at him again. "So I couldn't let him kill me, could I? I acted only to defend myself."

"Then you have no reason to feel guilt over his death," Brocard said. "Nor any reason for your anger."

"It's not that easy," Gonard protested.

"If it is not, there must be another reason behind the deed."

Gonard sighed. "But what? I don't know."

Brocard shook his head. "You do know. One day you will finally tell yourself."

* * * * *

Gonard followed the other novices into the cathedral, once again regretting that he had to walk up the nave singly, and not as part of a pair. You should be thinking about the service, he immediately chided himself. Dom Petri's talked himself hoarse explaining how important Ash Wednesday is.

The brothers went solemnly to their places, the cathedral more hushed than ever before. Gonard stood in his place in the nave. He watched Dom Abelard light the candles with a long taper. Six were lit, one by one, three at each side of the choir.

The Abbot came into the choir from a side chapel. His feet were unshod; Gonard suddenly realized that the feet of all the brothers were bare, their robes old and shabby. All wore the brown of a novice's robe, except for the lay brothers, who still wore their own. Even the Abbot was in brown, the heavy cross of silver he usually wore replaced with a plain one of wood.

Dom Abelard came forward, the Holy Book across his arms. The Abbot read from it, his voice loud and clear. " 'Therefore also now, saith the Lord, turn ye even to Me with all your heart, and with fasting, and with weeping, and with mourning: And rend your heart, and not your garments, and turn unto the Lord your God: for He is gracious and merciful, slow to anger, and of great kindness, and repenteth him of the evil.' "

The Abbot bent, kissed the Book, and Abelard retreated with it to a seat in the choir. I would turn to the Ultimate with all my heart, Gonard thought, watching the Abbot go to his seat in the sanctuary. But it wouldn't have me.

The psalm was starting. Gonard took a deep breath as the choir chanted, their voices starting low, rising, dropping. When they rose again on the third verse, he began the first, his voice coming in high above theirs. The chants for Mass were always sung in Latin; Gonard relaxed, enjoying the feel of the ancient language rolling smoothly from his throat.

All too soon the choir finished. Gonard brought his own verses to their end. The Abbot stood, came forward again. Abelard held another book open to him. " 'My brothers,' " the Abbot read, " 'it is the wisdom of the Mother Church, of which the order of St. Thomas is a part, to observe with a season of penitence and fasting the days preceding our Lord's passion and resurrection. The season of Lent was given to us by the Lord for us to prepare ourselves for His last days, joining Him even as He said, "Stay here and keep watch with Me," to those who were His companions. By self-examination and repentance, sorrowing for the evils of the world and the destruction humanity has caused to the Earth, we seek to acknowledge the sins of our selves, and of our forebears. Nothing must be left hidden to the Lord, so He may bear all upon His cross and wash the effects of sin from us by His blood.

" 'In recognition to all which we owe to the Lord, we will now kneel, showing outwardly the repentance which we feel in our hearts.' "

Gonard curled his legs under him, sinking to his second knees. There was a soft rustle of cloth as the brothers knelt, propping clasped hands onto the choir stalls. "We confess to Thee, our Lord," said the Abbot, "for the love we have failed to show to our brothers, for the forgiveness we have withheld."

"Have mercy upon us, Lord," intoned the brothers.

"For the indulgence of our appetites in denying the needs of others," continued the Abbot.

"Have mercy upon us, Lord."

"For our negligence in prayer and worship, neglecting to give You all honor that is due to You."

"Have mercy upon us, Lord."

"For the waste that our kind has brought to Your world, and the faltering in our determination to bring the world to Your light."

"Have mercy upon us, Lord."

"Accept our confession and our repentance, Lord, and grant us renewed strength to be Your healing hand in a suffering world."

"Accept our repentance, Lord."

"Restore us to Your love, Lord, and purge us from all sin and darkness, that we may carry Your love to all ends of the Earth."

"Show us mercy, Lord, for Your love is great."

The Abbot stood. Abelard carried away the book and returned with a small silver dish. Gonard watched with interest as the Abbot took the dish, holding it in his left hand, and covering it with his right. "Lord of all," he intoned, "from the dust of the Earth were we created. Let these ashes be to us a sign of our mortality and penitence, that we may remember that it is only by Your great sacrifice that we have gained healing and the hope of life beyond this shattered world."

The Abbot handed the dish back to Abelard and knelt. Abelard dipped a thumb into the dish; it came back out gray with ash, which he applied to the Abbot's forehead in the form of a cross. The Abbot stood, and Abelard knelt before him, accepting the same mark on his head.

One by one, the rest of the brothers went forward, returning with the gray smudge of ash on their foreheads. Gonard limped up the nave, dipped his head to the Abbot. The man smeared the cross on a space between his nostrils and the first head spine. "Dust thou art," the Abbot intoned, "and to dust thou shalt return."

Dragons can only rust. That's all you can do without me. The older phrase echoing through his head, Gonard returned to his place.

The choir entered softly into another psalm, their voices sliding easily through the low tones. "*Misere mei, Deus.*" Gonard entered quietly, his voice a murmured counter-chant, his mind translating effortlessly from Anglish into Latin: "Have mercy upon me, O God, according to Thy lovingkindness: according unto the multitude of Thy tender mercies blot out my transgressions."

After the end of the service, the brothers drifted from

the cathedral, each his separate way. The novice master had explained that Ash Wednesday was a day of reflection and self-examination. After Mass, the afternoon was to be spent in prayer and fasting. There would be no further services until compline.

Most of the brothers went to the dormitory, retreating to their cells. Gonard paused outside the stables, nose wrinkling at the thought of spending a day with the sour reek of coursair. He lifted his head, glanced back at the fields of the lay brothers. Hills were hazy beyond, the sides green with trees promising a cool place for contemplation. Gonard turned and limped away from the courtyard.

Even the lay brothers were not at work today; he passed through empty fields. The hills began just beyond, a clear trail marking a path between the budding trees. Others must come here. Gonard found himself hoping that he wouldn't meet anyone today.

Dragons can only rust. The image of glittering brains, metallic muscle. He had been created by human hands. The realization had come to him in the cathedral as the Abbot placed ash upon his head. Did he have a soul? Was he more than a thing constructed from metal and rubber?

He started up the trail. Is the human body any different? Gonard stopped short at the thought. They are formed from nothing, and decompose back to nothing when they die. *Dust thou art, and to dust thou shalt return.* They are born, grow into adults, their souls maturing along with them. Am I that different?

A flash of movement caught his eyes, disrupting his thoughts. Curious, Gonard limped forward into the sun. A cluster of large flowers draped across the path, long, elegant petals of pink-streaked white waving slightly in the breeze. Gonard took a deep breath of their sweet fragrance. He could not identify them. So much has been changed by the Destruction, he thought sadly.

Something moved again. Gonard's ears flicked to the sound of a low hum, barely audible. He searched the flowers with his eyes until he found the source of the noise. A small, thin-bodied creature hovered in the air by one of the petals, a long beak dipping into the flower's center. Gonard watched, fascinated, as it moved from one flower to another. He estimated that the creature was no larger than one of his claws.

But how did it manage to hover above the flowers? There was a blur of activity around its shoulders, a movement too fast for normal sight to follow. Normal sight. Gonard frowned, concentrated. He slowed down the speed of the image interpreted by his mind, reducing the blur until he could see what propelled the creature. Two small structures of feathers flicked back and forth, providing lift to the body, holding it in the air. Wings. It had wings.

Wings? Gonard drew back his head, his vision reverting to normal. Other words came to him now. Flight. Bird. Hummingbird. The hummingbird flitted to another flower, the red feathers at its throat gleaming in the sun.

It flies. Gonard stretched open his own wings, studied them. The one on the right was proud and whole, bones straight, edges taut. On the left wing, the bones were loose, the leathery skin hanging in tatters. Wings are meant for flight. That is their purpose. He looked down into the valley, imagining it spread out below him, his body carried over the fields by the wind under his wings.

Numbly, he glanced back at the ragged wing. I cannot fly. He looked up at the blue sky, a few clouds crawling lazily in the distance. The skies are denied to me. I was destined to fly—and I cannot. I cannot.

The hummingbird finished the last flower, zoomed down the trail. Without thinking, Gonard lunged after it. "Come back!" He stumbled over a tree root, scattered rocks from the path. "Come back!"

He galloped down from the hill, back across the fields. Wings unfurled from his back. His right cupped the air, lifting him from his feet. But his left provided no counterbalance, the skin flapping helplessly. He fell heavily, plowing into the earth. Earth, he thought, feeling the dark ground around him, the fresh smell of young, growing things. I am a creature of the sky, bound to the earth.

"No!" He flailed to his feet, chest heaving with grief. "No!" He broke into another gallop, unable to stand still. He must escape the earth that chained him.

He thundered into the courtyard, his feet drumming an awkward beat against the stones. Then he halted, whirled. The stables were at his side, the cathedral on his left, but he wanted neither. Where could he find peace? Where could he escape the grief sagging both wings to the ground?

Brocard appeared at the cathedral entrance, blinking in the bright sunlight. "What is meant by this disturbance of Lent?"

Gonard backed away, wing-leathers dragging across the stones. "Fly. I was meant to fly. And—" He turned his head to his left wing, which twisted awkwardly from his shoulder.

Brocard walked up to him. "I had wondered if you might one day realize."

Gonard snapped his head back around. "You knew?"

Brothers were starting to appear at the dormitory doors. Brocard said firmly, "Michel, we should continue this discussion in your domicile."

"You didn't tell me," Gonard said, standing his ground. "Why didn't you tell me?"

"What purpose would it have served? There were enough wounds to heal, without delving into those long mended."

"Ones you can't heal," Gonard said bitterly.

Brocard rubbed his beard. "Why do you believe that the

wing cannot be healed?"

Gonard felt his breath catch in his throat. "Can it? Can I be healed?"

Brocard looked up at him. "We can attempt it. The process may be painful, and there can be no promise of success."

Gonard glanced away, back across the fields. The hills were now clear of haze; he could pick out the spot in the trail where the hummingbird had appeared to him. "I need—I want to try."

"And if we are unsuccessful?"

"Then I shall never fly," Gonard answered simply.

* * * * *

The next morning, Brocard came to the stables with Angles. At the physician's insistence, they went into the courtyard, where Gonard obligingly spread out both wings.

"Fascinating," Angles muttered, ducking under the edge of the right wing. "The golden skin is quite striking against the blue phalanges."

"The physician, when he is not diagnosing," Brocard explained dryly to Gonard, "is a master painter."

"Of religious scenes only." Angles reappeared. "Brocard, for example, was the perfect model for Saint Paul—studious and serious. I haven't been able to include you in a painting yet, Michel."

"I look better from my right side," Gonard said.

The physician frowned. "I fear that there is little I can do for your foot. An injury not properly healed is often made worse by constant use. The toes appear to have adapted to their shape. But you have not attempted to use this wing, have you?"

"I've never flown."

"Then the wing should be as it first healed." Angles

crossed behind Gonard, who felt the man's hands probe gently at one lump of skin, curled up under a phalange. "Much of the actual skin appears still to be present, merely twisted and coiled. It must be encouraged to straighten and, where necessary, to grow together again. The right wing will serve as our guide."

"And how are we to accomplish this?" Brocard joined the physician. "For example, this—this—"

"Foresail." Gonard swiveled an eye to watch Lybrand stride up to them. The choirmaster smiled and shrugged. "My father was a fisherman. Michel's wings bring sails to mind."

Brocard nodded, turned away. Gonard wondered once again why he avoided the friendly choirmaster. "Brocard and Angles are trying to decide how to straighten the wing fragments," Gonard explained to Lybrand.

Lybrand looked thoughtful. "The right wing is whole?"

"Yes."

"My father once wished to duplicate an unusual sail design," Lybrand said, speaking to Gonard, but his eyes flicking to Brocard. "He took down the sail and laid it across a bolt of cloth. The outline of the sail was traced onto the cloth, and he used this as his guide."

Angles straightened. He glanced at Brocard. "A piece of cloth, across which we could trace the outline of the right wing. We could then piece together the left, stitching the skin into place."

Gonard winced. As if guessing his thought, Angles asked him, "How much feeling do you have in the sails?"

"Enough." He turned his head around. "If it can help me to fly, it'll be worth any pain."

"The sails may be the portion easiest mended." Angles ran light fingers down the loose bones. "And I believe that these will firm together once the skin is whole. We will discover how well a dragon's body heals."

The operation was carried out that afternoon. Gonard sank to his belly inside the stable block, wings spread out along the section between the stalls. "You won't be able to move while the wing sets," Brocard explained as he and Angles unrolled a bolt of white cloth over stones swept clear of straw. "I thought it better that you be in here than outside."

Gonard nodded. He watched the men use large pieces of a dark, greasy material to outline his right wing. I never knew my wings were so long, he thought, as Angles straightened the cloth under the far tip. Even if they are bulky on my back.

Lybrand came in as the men finished. He held out his hand; without a word, Brocard surrendered his lump of grease. The choirmaster knelt on the stone floor and began to sketch the phalanges on the cloth, Gonard lifting and lowering the wing as and when required. Even the finer bones were drawn in, and markings made where the skin thickened. Gonard marveled at the complexity of his wings. He could see that they were based on the structure of human arms, rising from a point just behind his shoulders. The main bone thinned to a thick elbow, which in turn thinned to a design like an elongated hand. What would have been fingers were long, thin bones, jointed twice, the leathery skin of his wings spreading between them. How would it feel to have the wind sliding past those fingers, the greater pressure underneath lifting him into the sky?

Lybrand stood. Gonard lifted his wing again, glanced at the choirmaster. The man nodded, a pleased smile on his face. He perched the drawing material on a stable door and bent to help the other two gather the cloth together and move it to the other wing, inverting it before spreading the design underneath.

Gonard closed his eyes briefly. The light shining

through the open doors had clearly highlighted the difference between the wings. But he forced himself to watch, to note with interest that the dark substance had penetrated through the cloth so that the design could be read on the other side.

Angles tapped a part of the cloth. "The elbow," he said to Brocard.

"The elbow?" Gonard repeated.

"It has been knocked awry." Brocard pointed at the cloth; the elbow of the right wing, when fully extended, made a smooth, straight line. The left was bent back upon itself, which had torn the small, upper portion of skin leading from the joint to his shoulder.

"Difficult to determine if it has been broken and healed incorrectly, or if it is merely dislocated." Angles probed the joint as he spoke; his fingers were gentle, but the pain made Gonard dig his claws into the stone floor.

"Should we attempt to correct it first?" Brocard asked.

Angles shook his head. "Either a rebreaking or a relocation will take a large measure of force, carefully applied. I suggest that we first attempt to realign the skin and smaller bones. What we learn from this may give us an insight to the correction of the elbow."

The physician went to the stable doors, retrieved a dark bundle. Gonard watched with morbid fascination as Angles unrolled the leather. A series of long needles were revealed, bright against the dark material. "Forged by a lay brother a month ago," he told Gonard. "They are usually used to treat coursairs—the stallion has a habit of rubbing too vigorously against gate posts. He always finds the one nail not fully driven in." Angles began to thread the needle. "I would advise you not to watch."

"I'd rather watch," Gonard said quietly, his throat suddenly dry. I've faced worse pain, he told himself sharply. But he knew that the wing skin was the most sensitive on his body, probably designed so in order to be aware of every shift in air currents. That's what all this is for, he reminded himself, digging claws deeper into the floor. "How're you going to get the skin to grow back together?"

"The same as we did for your leg wounds," Brocard said grimly. "By abrading the edges." He began to unroll the first fold of skin.

Lybrand came to his feet, left the healers. Gonard followed him with one eye as the choirmaster stopped before him. "Both eyes forward, Michel," he ordered firmly. Startled, Gonard obeyed. "Now, we have much work to do before us if you are to sing at the Easter service. Psalm 110 and 111, Michel, from the beginning. *Now.*"

Now? Gonard blinked. Then he raised his head farther from the floor, giving room to his lungs as he drew in a deep breath. The ancient language unfolded in his mind, verses swelling his throat. "*Confitebor Domino in toto corde meo, in consilio iustorum et congregatione. Magna opera Domini, exquirenda omnibus qui cupiunt ea.*"

He kept his voice steady as Brocard roughened the skin edges with a file. But the first jab as a needle went through his skin made his notes waver. Gonard closed his eyes, focusing on the music, forcing the tone to remain steady. Another stab, and another. He concentrated on the meaning of the words he sang, pouring his being into them. "Praise ye the Lord, I will praise the Lord with my whole heart, in the assembly of the upright, and in the congregation."

From that psalm Lybrand ordered him to sing another, and another. There was nothing but the singing and the pain; he felt the song fight with the pain, fight for supremacy over his mind. He put yet more strength into his voice, until there was song, only song, lifting him far above his body, hovering above the stones. He opened his eyes, found himself looking down at a large blue body, three small men dotted around the hulk. The tail was trembling, the claws dug to their roots in rock, but the body remained still, and the golden wings did not move. Piece by piece, the tattered skin of the crippled wing was being unraveled, the edges abraded, then sewn together and into place on the cloth. The small bones were eased back into realignment as the wing was reshaped. With a new form of vision, Gonard could see the bones already beginning to firm, the pieces of skin touching each other stretching to close the gap.

The men were finally done, the patchwork wing stretched along the floor. The elbow was still bent back awkwardly, but the wing was now closer to the right appearance. Gonard blinked—

—and he was suddenly back inside his body, his throat aching, strained with hours of singing. He finished the verse, letting the last note trail away. Then he lowered his head to the floor, exhausted.

"Let him sleep," said a voice, seemingly at a great distance. "It will be a kindness."

"It will be a kindness to me, as well," said another voice. "My shoulders ache, and my ears are deafened."

"Still an excellent idea, to take Michel's mind from the pain," said a third voice. "Lybrand—I thank you."

"No thanks necessary, Brocard. Always a pleasure to drill a young novice in the psalms."

There was a chuckle; then the men left, shutting the stable doors quietly behind them. Gonard sighed. He stretched his head out farther and fell into a deep, dreamless sleep.

* * * * *

The pain eased to a steady throb over the next few days. Brocard and Angles arranged a sling, the ropes thrown over the stable rafters, to lift the wing from the ground and allow Gonard to stand. Both men visited daily to check on his progress.

"Incredible!" Angles exclaimed on the fifth day. "I have never seen skin knit together so rapidly."

"No portions were missing." Brocard sounded puzzled.

"Is that wrong?" Gonard asked.

"No, not wrong." Brocard rubbed his beard. "Merely unexpected. How long ago did you injure this wing?"

"At birth—twelve years ago."

Brocard nodded. "We would have expected some atrophy during that time. But all of the skin was present, merely rolled up or torn."

Gonard said nothing. With a strange wrench, he realized that the true circumstance of his existence was something he could not share with Brocard. The man would not understand; the high technology taken for granted in the Domains would be incomprehensible to someone from the chapter. I cannot share everything with you, he thought, looking down at Brocard. But then, should I?

He had other visitors when the order's schedule allowed. Lay brothers timidly entered the stable, bringing handfuls of young wheat, to show Gonard what his labors had helped bring to pass. Lybrand brought the choir to practice several times, so Gonard could rehearse the Easter psalms with them. Even the Abbot came once, in Brocard's company, showing great interest in comparing whole wing to healing one.

And one afternoon Lybrand, with all the brothers, lay and religious, sang as the Changewinds blew across the chapter's compound. Gonard shivered as he sang, a green City flickering in and out of memory. Why, he wondered, could he remember only in portions, never in entireties?

"Perhaps you are not yet ready to face whole truths," Brocard said thoughtfully, when Gonard finally asked him. "Perhaps you still do not want to remember."

Gonard stared out the open door. Light and shadow alternated on the courtyard as the sun ducked in and out of clouds. "I want to remember."

"You once asked if it were necessary."

"That's when I wanted to stay here always." He brought his gaze back to Brocard, feeling suddenly awkward. "I'm not sure I belong here."

Brocard took the admission calmly. "The life of the order is not for every soul."

"I just can't believe the same as you do." Gonard fought an urge to shuffle his feet; any movement could jounce the wing painfully. "I've tried, but the Lord you speak about, the man on the tree, is not the Ultimate I've spoken to."

"Belief is not a strict formula, Michel."

"I also feel that there's someone I've promised something to. I need to find her again."

"Entrance to the order does not mean the refuting of all past ties."

Gonard blinked. "Are you trying to encourage me to stay?"

"No." Brocard's mouth quirked into his version of a smile. "Though you will be sorely missed. I meant only for you to ascertain your true reasons for leaving. It should not be to escape truth. You should ask leave of your vows only if you cannot find your own truth within the order."

"I don't want to hide anymore," Gonard said wearily. "I'm tired of not knowing who I am. Why can't I remember now, when I want to?"

"Michel, let one wound heal at a time." Brocard let his gaze wander pointedly to the left wing. "You will remember as you are ready to remember."

* * * * *

The stitches were removed ten days afterward. Gonard winced as each piece of thread was pulled through, leaving tiny, clear beads of liquid above each hole. Healing fluid, he thought. The same viscous material had bound skin to skin, once the abraded sections had been placed against one another. He wondered how much more he didn't know about the capabilities of the body his father had designed for him.

"We'll leave the sling in place," Brocard said, dropping the last thread into a bucket.

"Provide support for the wing," Angles agreed. He walked up the length of the wing, checking closely to ensure that no stitches had been left. He said, sounding awed, "I believe that there will be no scarring."

Gonard said quietly, "I wasn't bothered about that."

"Perhaps not, but I was." The physician returned to the right wing, which Gonard helpfully stretched out for inspection. Angles ran a finger down a length of skin. "This is smooth. Scarring would cause thicker tissue, perhaps disturbing your balance as you flew. Brocard took great care when he abraded the skin edges." He smiled at Gonard. "I am certain that it did not feel so to you. However, we cannot take all the credit for your remarkable recovery."

"*Will* I fly?"

Silence. Angles chewed his upper lip. Brocard rubbed his beard. "The elbow joint," the physician said finally, "is still bent incorrectly. Whether broken or disjointed, use will have encouraged your body to compensate."

"Use?" Gonard asked.

"You use it to fold the wing."

Gonard closed his right wing, noting thoughtfully how the wing folded into itself, held close to his back by the elbow joint. "The left wing hasn't folded right—for a while." A memory of a dark night and golden eyes came and went.

"We have looked at the joint carefully," Brocard said. "There is no sign of a healed break, so we have come to the conclusion that the joint has been dislocated."

Gonard gazed out the stable door, imagining the blue skies beyond. "Will I fly?"

"We are trying to devise a method to realign the elbow," Brocard assured him. "But we would first wish to ensure that the sails have fully healed. They will give support to the elbow, once it is repositioned."

Gonard nodded. "You have done a lot for me. I thank you." Angles murmured a few words, then departed. Gonard turned his gaze to Brocard, who was leaning quietly against a stable door. "What aren't you telling me?"

Brocard rubbed his beard. "You have never flown."

"No."

"And you are certain that you are of human parentage, although you now bear this dragon shape, changed by some force that you will not disclose to me?"

"Yes," Gonard said, adding uncomfortably, "you wouldn't understand."

Brocard shrugged. "What instinct, then, might you possess for flight?"

Gonard blinked. "I have wings."

"The chapter's library has an illustrated tome on birds. At least a dozen species possessed wings that were useless for flight."

Gonard pulled his head back, hissing slightly as the movement rubbed tender wing skin against the sling. "I was meant to fly."

"How can you be certain of that?"

"Because my father—" Gonard broke off, thinking rapidly how he could explain. "Because my father wouldn't have helped me develop wings if I wasn't meant to use them."

"Then why did he not heal you?"

Gonard simply stared at the man, staggered by a question he suddenly realized had been gnawing at him for days, but which he had not been willing to admit to himself. "I don't know," he whispered.

Brocard's eyes glittered. "If it was in his power to heal you, not doing so would be a strange way for a father to act."

"He had the right." Gonard wondered why he felt so compelled to defend his father.

"Did he?" A long silence passed, Gonard staring at the stone floor, unable to answer. He raised his head as Brocard moved. "One healing at a time," the man said apologetically. "Lybrand will no doubt attempt to have you rehearse in the hour before vespers. I know he will not be sent away, but try to keep your voice down. The novices are falling behind in their Lenten reading. It appears that they would rather listen to you sing than apply themselves to their studies."

Gonard made a noncommittal sound as Brocard left. *Did my father have the right? Why didn't he heal me? Didn't he want to heal me?* Gonard sighed. *It doesn't matter. I owe everything to him, my creator, my father.*

A flash of anger, of denial, went through him, unintelligible, confusing. Like his memories—fragmentary, glimpses of a crystalline City, dark brown tents, yellow stone buildings. Nothing held together; nothing made sense. There was something—no, *someone*—missing, without whom it was all meaningless. Sometimes, at the end of dreaming, it seemed as if he could almost remember, recall a dark face, a flash of teeth. But the image never revealed anything further.

A . . . woman, Gonard thought, trying to hold on to what he knew for certain. *A human woman. Is that why I ran into the wilderness, because she is in a human body, and I am not?* He seemed to remember some physical longing, which he knew could not be fulfilled. *Why was I made a dragon? Why not human, like . . . like . . .*

Again, it was gone. *Like my brother, whoever he is.* Gonard took a deep breath. His wing ached. "You will remember as you are ready to remember," Brocard had said. He would have to believe that. Gonard closed his eyes, willing himself to believe.

CHAPTER 11

Itsa tried not to think of other times, other departures, as she swung the pack over her shoulder. Something clanked inside the thick leather, but she merely grimaced, not in the mood to once again search through the provisions the Singers had granted them.

Well, granted me. He don't need any. She glanced at the medtech, nodding gravely as one Singer gave him final well-wishes. Say it like ya really mean it, she thought angrily. Soon as the snows had cleared, the questions about when they were planning to leave had become more and more pointed.

Finally the medtech had finished. He lifted a bag to his own back. Itsa looked away, almost hearing the creak of the robot's metal spine. Not for the first time, she wondered if she'd be better off without him. His steps were very slow now, as if he had to consider each one separately. Itsa shrugged. No, she needed him. He carried the maps in his head and had the necessary sense of direction to follow them. Only the medtech could get them to the dragon.

If that's what she really wanted.

Itsa slid her arm through the other loop of leather, then tightened the cords so that the heavy pack rested against her back. The medtech came to her side. Without a word, they left the confine. Several guards fell into step behind them, reminding Itsa how unsafe the settlement was now for one associated with Gonard. She hadn't dared to leave the Confine for weeks, not since one attack had left a nasty wound beneath her ear.

Clan members, tradeswomen, children, even dogs stopped what they were doing to watch them pass. Itsa gritted her teeth and held her chin high. Okay, they might not want her here anymore, but she'd still made her own decision to leave.

At the gates their guards halted, drew back. Itsa strode through the gates quickly, afraid suddenly that Rygor might appear, pushing his way through the crowd, and say—what? She felt the muddy ground squelch under her boots as she waited for the medtech to catch up.

The gates clanged shut behind them. Itsa took a deep breath of the wet morning, felt the cold air sear down her throat. "Right, tech," she said grimly. "Ya jive the way. Go 'head."

The medtech led them without deviation across the soggy plains. Itsa trudged behind him, impressed despite herself at his ability to calculate their heading. He had explained about magnetic poles and compass directions, as usual going on long enough to bore her.

Night still drew in early. When Itsa found an outcropping of rock around twilight, she informed the medtech that they would camp there for the night. He made no protest, merely standing in place while she spread her sleeping furs across one elongated stone.

The days began to blend into one long, dreary trek. Itsa, at first glad that the medtech said nothing, began to feel the silence grind on her temper. Finally, the tenth day of their journey, she spoke over the crackling flames of their weak campfire. "I jig it's yar fault, ya jive."

The medtech turned his head slowly, his dull eyes borrowing

life from the red fire. "It is difficult to respond to such a vague accusation."

"Ya did it on purpose." Itsa threw a handful of leaves into the flames, watched them crumble into dust. "Ya told Rydeth that truth on purpose."

"It was my choice," the medtech admitted calmly. "It was the only one that I had left to give."

"But ya did it on purpose," Itsa persisted, wondering if he were as dim as he pretended. "Ya jigged it would get Rygor 'way from me."

"Why should I possess such a motive?"

"To get me comin' after the dragon with ya."

"Have I ever indicated that I wished for you to remain with Gonard?" Itsa glanced at him. There was a trace of irony in his tone. "It has never been my stated intention to ensure that you remained together."

Itsa bit off a piece of travel meat, chewing the tough muscle thoughtfully. Yeah, the medtech's always tried to get us 'part. "But ya've changed that now."

"It is obvious that I can no longer continue without assistance." The medtech spoke matter-of-factly, without a trace of self-pity. "There was no one else who would be willing to accompany me on this search for Gonard."

"Thanks for the support," Itsa muttered as she used her knife to slice the meat.

"Is it my understanding that you will shortly come to the last of the rations?"

Itsa shrugged. "Yeah, in another week or so."

"It is therefore imperative that we discuss the means of your continued sustenance."

"Nah, it's not." Itsa gave him a grin. "I don't need ya to look after me. I'll do it myself." She patted the spear at her side. "I got this and my bow. I'll get somethin'."

"You are confident of your ability to hunt for your provisions?"

"I had a lot of training." Then she looked away, reminded of what she had lost in the settlement. "Ya'll see."

* * * * *

The ground began to firm as the climate warmed. Itsa could now make out the tall mountains in the distance. "Ya really 'spect the dragon's in this other settlement?" she asked the medtech.

"Gonard has shown his preference for companionship," the medtech answered. He seemed to be regaining some of his strength with the lengthening of the days. "He does not willingly seek solitude. It is my hypothesis that he will have at least visited the settlement, even if he did not remain. In particular, the Singers described this settlement as a place of healing. It could be possible that any tribe discovering him might refer him to a place where his supposed changeling nature could be treated."

They had entered a forest, tall trees blocking the sun with their young leaves. "And if he ain't there?" Itsa asked. "We saw those other campfires, 'member. We ain't the only people around here."

"The ashes were several days cold," the medtech reminded her. "If Gonard is not to be found in one location, we will search another. It is imperative that he be found before the next winter."

"Why?" Itsa demanded, circling around a clump of tree roots. A gathering of mushrooms caught her attention; identifying them as edible, she quickly ripped them up before hurrying after the medtech. "What's the great rush?"

"It is beyond your comprehension."

"Only 'cause ya're not botherin' to explain."

The medtech halted so suddenly that she almost bumped into him. His head swiveled, turning much farther than a human's could have. Itsa swallowed, the sight making her feel slightly ill. "Have you noted the change in the forest?"

Itsa glanced around. "What change?"

"Listen." The medtech tipped his face upward. "There is a wind in the trees. It is warm."

Itsa took a deep breath, felt her guts chill. "Change-winds?"

The medtech's eyes came to her. "It is my belief that they are approaching, yes."

Turning her mind forcibly from the effect she'd seen the Changewinds have on humans, Itsa turned in place, searching for some protection. The medtech had hypothesized that the Winds carried chemical emissions that attacked the brain, causing hallucinations and madness. She knew of only three defenses against the Winds: singing, shelter, and height. Well, from what she'd heard of the medtech's singing she didn't expect any help from that direction. The ground was solid, not offering a cave or even a hole.

"It will be necessary for you to climb into one of the trees," the medtech said, coming to the same conclusion as she had.

Itsa fought down fear as the Winds picked up, blowing through her hair. "How? The branches are up higher than I can reach."

The medtech braced his legs, then offered her his joined hands. "I will lift you. That should enable you to grasp the lowest branches of the tree opposite me."

Itsa was in no mood to argue. She lifted one booted foot into the cracking palms, then grabbed at the tree trunk. The medtech heaved. Itsa flung out her arms, grappling at the nearest branch. Rough bark scraped against her cheek as she leaned too far. Then her fingers curled around the branch, and she pulled herself up onto the bending platform.

"It is imperative that you climb farther!" the medtech called from below. "You will require more height to avoid contamination!"

Itsa carefully braced herself against the trunk. The branch creaked warningly under her feet. The next one up was thicker, she was grateful to notice. She hauled herself across it, then searched for her next grip. An overeager move almost unbalanced her, and she threw her arms around the trunk, heart pounding at the distance already between herself and the ground.

Ya got higher in the mines, she told herself roughly. Ya just didn't notice, 'cause they were dark. So, don't be dim and look down.

Higher and higher she climbed, the smaller branches snagging her clothes, forcing her to leave pieces behind as souvenirs. She only hoped she could get high enough. Gonard had described to her how the walls of the settlement had held back most of the particles of the first Changewinds he'd stood in, and she must be higher than those by now. Still she kept going.

The branches became too thick for her to squeeze through. Itsa lowered herself over one, her back pressing against the trunk, legs hanging down either side. A quick glance down made her feel dizzy, and she closed her eyes.

The Winds had steadily grown in strength. Itsa felt the tree shudder beneath her. The whistle of air through leaves was echoed by the trees around her. Itsa wondered if she'd climbed so far only to be tossed off again. Then she felt her lips thin with determination. She'd not come so far, from asteroid to Earth, through City and settlement, to die now, dropped like a discarded acorn. She tightened legs and hands on the bucking branch, clenching her teeth against the effect the upheaval was having on her stomach.

Her muscles were aching with strain by the time the Winds finally eased. Itsa relaxed cramped fingers, wiped a sweating face. Then she started the difficult process of climbing down from the tree.

A strange, strangled sound almost made her lose her

grip. Itsa paused, several branches from the ground. The noise came again. The medtech, she realized. It was the medtech, and he was laughing. She felt her spine stiffen at the unpleasant grate. "Tech?" she called hopefully. "Hey, tech, help me down, will ya?"

Laughter was the only response. Itsa made her way to the bottom branch, then lowered herself down with her arms, dropping easily to the ground. She winced at the pain shooting through her weary legs, then forced herself to follow the direction of the sound.

The medtech was seated on the ground, resting back against a tree. "At least Odysseus was tied to his mast before sailing past the harpies," he said solemnly. Then he laughed again.

"Shut it!" Itsa shouted, unnerved. "Ya didn't climb, did ya?"

"Climbing is for monkeys. I am not descended from apes." He chuckled. "It is obvious that I do not even look like one."

Itsa felt her fists bunch as he roared at his own comment. "Ya weren't made to laugh, tech!"

"I was not given the capacity for humor," he agreed, sobering suddenly. "It is bitterness for me, and anger, and despair. Laughter and joy are for dragons."

The Winds've got to him. Itsa took a deep breath, trying to clear her own mind. He might recover. Can a 'bot go twisted? she wondered. The tech seems to be tryin' to find out. So, do I stick with him, or leave him here?

"Th' Winds be hard on them who do nae get out o' their way," a low voice commented behind her. "Take yer hand from yer blade."

Itsa slowly, reluctantly obeyed. Six figures emerged from behind the trees, a motley collection of men and women. Itsa turned to face the woman who had spoken, unsurprised to find a spear leveled at her heart. "Who're ya and what do ya want?"

"Drop yer knife." Itsa obeyed, keeping her eyes on the tall woman. "I be th' leader o' this group . . . an' ye?"

"Just a wanderer." Itsa jerked her head back at the still-chuckling medtech. "I'm with him."

"He be Windstruck," a man said. "Do we gie him th' blade?"

The leader's gaze came back to Itsa. "Ye answer him. Do we?"

For a moment Itsa toyed with the idea, wondering how they would react when no blood came from the medtech's throat and he continued to laugh. Then she forcibly rejected it. There was no telling what sort of damage that might cause the tech, and she still needed him. "Nah, I'll take care of him. Thanks. Ya can go now."

"We shall go," the leader confirmed, smiling. "An ye'll come wi' us."

Inwardly, Itsa cursed. But she forced herself to return the older woman's smile. Two of the men picked up the leather packs, and another woman pulled the medtech to his feet. They marched farther into the forest.

* * * * *

Itsa grimaced, unimpressed. Whatever else these people were, organized wasn't one of them. When Ranalf had marched them into his tribe's camp, all the tents had been proudly erect, organized into a circle, bright paint marking the status of the occupants. These shelters sagged loosely on their wooden supports. Rips in the heavy hides flapped in the breeze. Dirty rags and the remains of cooking fires darkened the ground, and Itsa started breathing through her mouth as the stench of rotting meat blew across her face.

Several of the men hurried away as they approached the half-dozen shelters. Their leader led Itsa and the medtech to the largest tent and took a seat on the stool the men had placed in front of it. She was ceremoniously handed a spear, which she rested across her legs. "Now," she said, glaring at Itsa, "who be ye an' what settlement be ye from?"

Itsa glared back, wondering how far this woman would push her. "I am Itsa; that's the medtech. We're not from any settlement."

"Gie me his name," the leader demanded, pointing at the medtech. "Only them o' rank hae nae name."

"What's in a name?" the medtech asked quietly. "A rose by any other name would smell as sweet."

"He ain't got a name," Itsa said stubbornly.

"An' ye must come from a settlement." The woman nodded to two of her followers. Itsa clenched her teeth as the contents of her pack were dumped into the mud, the medtech's alongside. Hands dug through the mingle of clothes and food, snatching away the mushrooms, the shiny cooking pot, her bow. The leader nodded at a bright shirt. "These be th' clothes o' a Singer."

"We used to live in a settlement." Itsa gave her a smile. "We got kicked out."

As she had thought, the leader raised her chin proudly. "We also be outside th' settlements. We hunt where we wish, an' there be no Singers t' take from us what be ours."

"Congrats." Itsa let her eyes roam over the motley group. Their smiles might show a distinct lack of teeth, but the hands holding knives and spears looked competent enough. Forget makin' a break for it, she decided. "So, whatcha want with us?"

"There be little ye can gie t' us," the leader responded haughtily. "Yer man be mad from th' Winds, an' ye be a woman. A woman cannae hunt."

Itsa smiled again. "Let me have back my knife, and I'll show ya what a woman can do." The men and women muttered, unsure. "There's just one of me, and twelve of ya. Are ya scared of one woman 'gainst all of ya?"

"It be ye who hae reason t' fear." The leader nodded to one of her assistants.

Itsa held out her hand, and her knife was given back to her, hilt-first. "That tree," she said, pointing at a trunk a hundred meters away. "See that mark where a branch used to be?"

The blade flew from her hand. Itsa stood straight with a confidence she didn't quite feel. When the steel thwacked into the target, she covered her relief with a grin. "See. Told-cha."

"We do see." The woman's smile was disturbing. Itsa swallowed, not liking the sudden tension in the group. "We be in need o' new hunters. Ye be welcome here."

"Yeah, well, thanks." Itsa shrugged nonchalantly. "Got people to meet and places to see. So if ya'd give us back our packs, we'll go, all right?"

"We be in need o' new hunters," the leader repeated, firmer now. "Whether ye will it or nae."

Itsa started toward her. A half-dozen spears were immediately lowered to her chest. She lifted her hands in innocence. "Hey, maybe we'll stay a bit. Okay, tech?"

The medtech told her solemnly, "One man's meat is another man's poison." Then he calmly led the way to the tent indicated by their captors, Itsa fuming at his heels.

* * * * *

They marched steadily for several days after that. Itsa wondered if the leader had decided not to believe her and was purposely putting distance between her group and any tribe Itsa and the medtech might have come from.

Their packs had been returned, much lighter. Itsa said nothing as she realized that only her ragged green vest and a bent cooking pot had been left inside the hide. It was harder to keep quiet as the leader paraded through the makeshift camp wearing the new clothes. Ya gotta be patient, Itsa my girl, she told herself firmly on the third morning, forcing down her portion of the heavy stew that formed every meal. That much ya've learned, bein' out here.

As usual, she traded her empty bowl for the medtech's untouched meal. As she leaned across him, he said quietly, "It is imperative that we leave this encampment."

"So," she said just as softly, "ya can still speak."

"I have begun to overcome the effect of the Changewinds upon my circuitry."

"And now's a good time to scatter? Funny timin', tech."

"It is only today that we have begun to deviate from the course I had set for us." The medtech looked up; Itsa followed his gaze, finding him studying the leader. "It is also my hypothesis that you will find your position becoming more permanent, and untenable."

Itsa saw the woman glance at them and frown. Swallowing the questions she wanted to ask the medtech, she straightened and started on the second serving of stew. Might as well keep her strength up.

"Ye." The leader pointed her knife at Itsa. "Rise."

Pausing a moment to emphasize her distaste at the sudden order, Itsa placed the bowl on the ground and came to her feet. "Yeah?"

"Ye say ye can hunt." The woman nodded. "Ye can hit a mark. Can ye bring down a beast?"

She hadn't, not yet. But Itsa gave the woman a confident smile. "Sure. No probs. Just give me the spear—"

"Nay, I know better." The leader motioned at another woman. Itsa was handed an old bow, several crude arrows. "Can ye bring down a beast wi' that?"

"No." Itsa straightened. "This isn't my bow. Mine's made for my length, and I'll need it if ya want me to bring anythin' back for ya."

"She speaks true," a young man said from his place beside

the woman.

The leader frowned. "Th' bow now be mine."

"Permit her t' use it," he continued. "Take it back 'pon her return wi' th' beast."

Reluctantly, the woman let the bow be handed over to Itsa, along with three of her arrows. Itsa ran a thumb down the smooth wood, strung the bow. Notching one of the arrows on the gut string, she suddenly aimed the steel tip at the leader. Spears were immediately raised. Itsa grinned, lowered the bow again. "And whatcha jig's goin' to make me come back?"

"We will hae yer man."

Itsa glanced at the medtech. "He ain't my man. For one thing, Winds got him. He ain't a man anyways."

"He be nae yer man." There was a new, calculating look in the woman's eyes that put Itsa on her guard. "But he still be yer friend. If ye do nae come back, me people will hunt ye. An' we will put out his eyes."

Itsa grimaced, not caring to discover whether the medtech had other means of obtaining visual information. "Right. Well, give me a couple of hours, okay?"

Without waiting for a response, she strode into the forest. She'd hoped that the worst result of her first failed hunt would be an empty stomach. *Don't need this pressure,* she thought resentfully. *Okay, so we'll see how good Rygor's teachin' was.*

The sun had risen, a few shafts of light straying past the trees to touch the soft ground. Itsa paused, checking the direction of the wind. She wanted to head upwind from the camp—the smell of the place would have driven any respectable herbivore far away. *And stay downwind of the game,* she repeated Rygor's words to herself. *Don't let the animal catch yar scent.*

She moved quietly through the woods, picking her way past roots and dead leaves matted by winter. Stalking was not new to her; she had followed targets through the tight corridors of an asteroid colony, gathering information for the resistance movement among the miners. The surroundings might be different, but the principle was the same: seek out the target and obtain what you require, without bringing any attention to yourself.

Something dark and moist littered the ground ahead. Itsa paused, studied the small pellets closely. Something had been by here recently. She touched the hoofprint nearby. A small deer, by the looks of it. Small would do. She was here to prove herself to the group, not to feed them.

A soft noise stopped her. Itsa crouched, blinked as she searched past a nearby fern. A doe grazed in a small clearing ahead, the dappled coat gleaming in the sun. Holding her breath, Itsa raised her bow, bracing one leg behind her to keep her balance and her aim true. She drew back the arrow, sighted down the straight shaft.

The arrow is a part of ya, she told herself. Ya've 'ready hit the target, 'fore ya've let it go. Exhaling slowly, she released the string.

The arrow flew silently across the clearing. The steel tip shuddered into the doe's shoulder. She leapt, the force knocking her off balance. Before she could take another step, Itsa had fitted another arrow and let it fly at her flank. With a soft cry, the deer wrenched sideways, flopping to the ground.

Itsa ran forward, bow clenched tightly in her fist. The doe was still struggling, one arrow half-wrenched from her side. Blood pumped from the wounds, and the brown eyes were distended in fear and pain. Itsa paused, her breakfast rising in her throat. No one had warned her about this bit, that the animal might still be living when she got to it. Grimly, she looked for something to finish the job, cursing the lack of a knife.

A nearby rock had to do. Itsa aimed for the head. Even

that took several attempts, and she was surprised that her stomach held up to the job. *Yeah, Itsa, the mighty hunter,* she thought when the animal was finally still. *Better get used to it, my girl.*

She knew she should bleed and gut the animal, but that would have to wait for now, since she had no knife. Just as well the doe was small; she was able to heft it across her shoulders, the body still warm.

Voices stilled as she walked back into the camp. Itsa dumped the doe at the leader's feet. "There. Told ya so."

"Were I t' gie ye spear an' knife," the woman asked slowly, "would ye hunt fer th' people?"

And my pack and a hundred meters head start. "I'd hunt for ya," Itsa affirmed.

The leader chortled. "Ye lie. Gie ye knife an' spear, an' ye'll be o'er th' hill afore a spear could catch ye. So I hae decided. Ye will be taken fer wife by me son."

"Thanks," Itsa said. "But no thanks."

"Ye hae nae say in this matter." She nodded at several of her men. "Put them in th' tent, son o' mine."

As Itsa, scowling, followed the medtech into their shelter, she heard the woman speak to the young man who must be the son in question. "Go ye after, an' make sure o' her. Ye know what t' do if th' man disturbs ye."

" 'Make sure of her?' " Itsa repeated to the medtech when the hide flap had fallen shut behind them. "What's that s'posed to mean?"

"It appears the design of the leader is to draw upon one of the strongest instincts among animals," the medtech responded. "The reluctance of a mother to leave her young."

"But I ain't got no—" Itsa halted as she realized what he meant.

The tent flap rose, then slapped back into place. Itsa glanced up at the man, recalling that the medtech had expected one of Ranalf's tribe to seduce her for the same reason. That was back when the tribe had wanted Gonard to stay with them. All these bods tryin' to get me preggy, and the only one I might of wanted to have a brat with made sure I wouldn't end up that way.

Thinking of Rygor made her lips thin. Itsa marched up to the man. "Look, ya're not my type, got it? So just turn 'round and leave."

"I hae nae wish fer ye," he answered grimly.

Itsa bunched her hands into fists, more angry than relieved. "Why not? There ain't nothin' wrong with me. I even got all my teeth."

"There be another." He shrugged. "O' a tribe nae far from here. She hae said she will come wi' me." Even in the dim light inside the tent, Itsa could see his face darken. "She will nae come if I hae a mate."

"Then help us get out of here," Itsa suggested. "If me and the tech leave ya, then ya'll be free to settle down with that other woman. Whatcha think?"

He pulled nervously at his lower lip. "Th' leader will wi'hold me food if I let ye go."

"We'll make it look like ya had no choice. Won't we, tech?" Itsa grinned. "Hand him yar knife, and we'll play like he got if off ya. Once we're away from here, we'll let ya go again. Ya'll have yar excuse, and we'll be away 'fore yar mom can catch us."

The man looked undecided. With a quick move that Itsa had thought beyond the medtech, the robot was suddenly at his side, the man's belt knife at his throat. "It would appear that you no longer have any other choice."

The dark eyes flicked fearfully at Itsa. "Ye will set me free beyond th' camp?"

" 'Course we will," Itsa assured him. "Now let's go out and say hi to yar mom."

The medtech shouldered the tent open, pushed the man outside. Itsa followed, swaggering one step behind. "Sorry, he ain't my type," she told the leader in the sudden silence that had fallen over the camp. "But I got no reason to see him dead. So, if ya'll put down yer spears, we'll just leave quietly. We'll let him go later on—so long's none of ya come after us. Got it?"

The woman waved at her group, her face grim with anger. "If ye harm him—"

"Got no reason to, have I?" Itsa grinned. "Now, if ya'll hand me my pack, not forgettin' my knife, bow, and bedroll, we'll be on our way. Keep the clothes," she added, deciding that they were probably lice-ridden by now at any rate.

Pack slung across her shoulder and her bow back in her hand, Itsa let the medtech lead the way. "Are they followin' us?" she asked the medtech at one point.

He still had the knife resting against the man's back. "They are not. It is evident that they believed you."

"Yeah, and why not?" She slipped the other arm through the pack's straps. "I got no reason to lie."

The sun set. Itsa cursed as her feet were caught by tree roots. At one point, she glanced up and found the man's face shining pale in the moonlight. That was when she saw the thin line of red across his neck. Obviously, the medtech had been a little careless. She frowned, but said nothing.

They broke suddenly free from the trees. Itsa paused at the start of the plain, noting that the mountains were now a definite bulk on the horizon. "Right, tech," she said. "Ya can let him go now."

"He will return to them," the medtech said quietly, "and report our last known position."

"That's why all the twistin' and turnin'," Itsa snapped. "So's they couldn't follow our trail. Come on, let him go."

"It is obvious that we have only one option." The medtech slipped the knife into his pocket. Then he gripped the man's neck with two wrinkled hands, gave a jerk.

Itsa started at the soft moan, the crack. The man fell to

the ground, his head rolling in an unnatural position. She turned her head, and was promptly and noisily sick. Wiping her mouth clean, she glared up at the medtech, standing calmly, waiting for her. "Ya didn't need to do that."

His eyes were silver in the moonlight. "It was as necessary as your murder of that deer."

"It's not the same thing," Itsa snapped, more afraid than she wanted to admit. "That was an animal. He was human."

"I have never noted a great distinction between the two categories. Now it is imperative that we continue our journey." He set out across the plain, his feet shuffling through the wet grasses.

Taking a deep breath, Itsa followed. If I got in his way, she thought uneasily, would he just get rid of me like that too? She swallowed against the sour taste of fear in her mouth and grimly forced herself after the robot.

CHAPTER 12

Brocard carefully sliced through the ropes of the sling and, with the assistance of Angles, slowly lowered Gonard's wing to the floor. Except for the dislocated elbow and fine tracings marking the joins of pieces of skin, the wings were now a matching pair. Gonard gazed upon the change with as much awe as his healers.

"I do not understand it," said Brocard.

Gonard reluctantly moved an eye from admiring the healing wing. "What don't you understand?"

"You." Brocard quirked his smile. "Your physiology, more precisely. Clear liquid rather than red blood, and the silvery fibers of your wing skin. But who is to argue with the Winds?"

"The Changewinds attack the mind," Gonard said promptly, then wondered where he remembered that from.

"There are not many beyond the chapter who would believe that."

"There are some." Gonard had the sudden image of a grinning, humpbacked man.

The wing could be folded again, though only awkwardly. Gonard was still excused from regular duties, so he spent long hours in the courtyard, opening his wings to even the slightest breeze. As he had realized when the men were reconstructing the wing, the skin contained many minute communication connections—his mechanical version of human nerves. When the back charge of power had gone through his wing at birth, the connections had reacted so violently that the skin itself had been torn apart. Now that the skin was rejoined, the connections had reformed.

Why so many? He closed his eyes as the wind blew against the sails. His body scales registered the pressure of the wind, transferring bulk awareness to his brain. But the wing-leathers . . . To the wings, the wind was not a blunt force, but a series of wind currents, varying in intensity as they eddied around obstructions, or gathered under tight-stretched skin.

And I am meant to use this sensitivity to fly. He turned, exploring the responses of his leathers. Brocard was right. Flying, for me, is not instinctive. But my father packed my wings with connections to allow me to judge every shift in the wind.

And after giving me all this, he didn't see fit to heal me so I could use it.

Gonard shook his head. It's no use thinking like that, he told himself. He's dead, and he can't answer for himself. It was his right to decide what to do and what not to do. He had other creatures to build.

But still something nagged at the borders of his consciousness, something he had run from once before. I have other things to think about, Gonard decided firmly. I've got to practice reading the wind—so one day, I might be able to fly.

* * * * *

Brocard stepped away from the small window of his cell. The image of Michel still burned in his eyes, the dragon's blue scales flashing in the morning sun as he turned himself to the wind. The sag of the left wing wore at Brocard, worried him. To have accomplished so much, and perhaps not to be ultimately successful . . .

But it was his soul that you vowed to heal. Brocard sighed, knowing that it was not so simple. The healing of the wing was a key to the healing of the soul—of that he was certain.

And there was something else. Some understanding just beyond his reach, perhaps the key to Michel's loss of memory. Brocard had confided his difficulty to the Abbot yesterday, after their nightly meeting in preparation for Brocard's consecration.

"To be a father, to have a son," the Abbot had mused, fingers resting on the last volume of the history of their order. "Perhaps it is here that your own childhood fails you, my son."

Brocard shrugged. "I had a father."

"From whom you were violently torn at a very early age." The fingers drummed against the leather binding. "It is not a fault, merely an awareness that you lack. We of the order call one another brothers, our Abbots father, but the love that we vow to show one another is that of an ideal, chosen freely by those who bind themselves to the order. The relationships in a true blood family can be much more complex—and cruel."

Brocard had forced himself to relax, to accept that he was not being criticized. "You came to adulthood in a blood family, most Reverend Father. How would you counsel me to now proceed?"

The Abbot was silent for a long moment. Then he pushed the volume across the table to Brocard. "Your next portion of Lenten reading." Brocard had dutifully come to his feet, enjoying the rich aroma of the cured leather as he picked up the thick book. "You have shared much of Michel's healing with me—I will think on him."

He may not have an answer, Brocard thought now. He turned away from the window. The bell would toll shortly for tierce, and he had completed none of the reading assigned to him.

The last clouds had disappeared from the sky when Brocard stepped out into the courtyard. He glanced at the blue heavens, felt the sun ease some of the tension his thoughts had put into his shoulders. A bright spring day. He had the sudden impulse to walk past the cathedral, through the lay brothers' fields, and up into the hills beyond. He found himself smiling as he imagined the reaction from the brothers, the ever-serious Brocard acting so—frivolous.

He found his place in the line of gray-robed men shuffling into the cathedral. Out of the corner of his eye he saw Michel take his place among the novices, towering over them all. Perhaps it is just as well that he feels no calling to permanent vows, Brocard found himself thinking. Michel could never attend chapter meetings, nor visit the Abbot, nor join the other brothers in the common meals.

Then he was entering the cool interior of the cathedral, and two decades of habit wiped all other thoughts from his mind as he bowed to the altar and took his place in the choir. Michel, as usual, sat down in the nave. Brocard suddenly realized that this was the first time Michel was attending a service since his healing. Then, startled by this temporary lapse, he firmly banished all thoughts of the dragon from his mind and concentrated on worshiping the Lord.

The service began ordinarily enough, with the additional Lenten verses that all present sang, before the choir went on to sing alone. Michel's powerful voice responded and then rose above the men's. Brocard closed his eyes, sensing that in this alone did Michel feel whole, at one with himself.

The reading announced by Abelard surprised Brocard. It was usually an advent reading, declaring the coming of the

Lord. He shrugged inwardly; the Abbot had the right to depart from the set readings, if he felt that another would serve the lesson to better effect. Brocard leaned against the hard, wooden back of the choir bench, puzzled further by the Abbot's tone. Unlike the usual, studious reading, the Abbot's tone was elated, as if celebrating the joy in the verses.

> *The people that walked in darkness*
> > *have seen a great light:*
> *they that dwell in the land of the shadow of death,*
> > *upon them hath the light shined.*
> *Thou hast multiplied the nation,*
> > *and not increased the joy:*
> *they joy before Thee according to the joy in the harvest,*
> > *and as men rejoice when they divide the spoil.*
> *For Thou hast broken the yoke of his burden,*
> > *and the staff of his shoulder,*
> *the rod of his oppressor,*
> > *as in the day of Mid-i-an.*
> *For every battle of the warrior*
> > *is with confused noise, and garments rolled in blood*
> *But this shall be with burning*
> > *and fuel of fire.*
> *For unto us a child is born,*
> > *unto us a son is given:*
> *And the government shall be upon his shoulder:*
> > *and his name shall be called Wonderful—*

A commotion made Brocard straighten, turn with a frown to admonish the novice who would dare to interrupt the reading. Then the frown deepened as he saw that it was Michel, backing away from the choir, his claws scraping against the stones in the nave. The dragon's nostrils were flared, eyes distended. He turned and fled from the cathedral, his tail thumping against the doors.

Brocard glanced at the Abbot. The man was still reading, unperturbed, but he flicked his hand at Brocard, urging him to follow Michel. Brocard stepped out of the choir and hurried after the dragon, ignoring the novices who gaped at the unusual goings-on before Mass.

He found Michel standing straddle-legged in the courtyard, his chest heaving, the bright sunshine glinting from his eyes. He swung his head toward Brocard, who halted, remembering a plume of flame, a burning stable block. Then, remonstrating himself for his lack of courage, he strode forward to stand before the dragon. "It is usual," he said, forcing himself to speak calmly, "to remain seated through the reading."

" 'For unto us a child is born,' " Gonard quoted, " 'unto us a son is given.' Don't you see? He was my father, *but I was his son.*"

"You were his son," Brocard acknowledged, wondering to what conclusion Michel was struggling.

"I thought he couldn't do anything wrong." Gonard shook his head violently, ears flapping, earring flashing in the sun. "I thought he had the right to do anything he wanted to me. But he didn't, did he? He didn't."

"And why didn't he?" Brocard asked softly. "Tell me."

Gonard straightened, so that Brocard had to crane his neck to meet the blue eyes. "Because I was his son. Because I didn't ask to be created. He created me. He had a responsibility to me. He—" The voice broke, body sagging. "I wasn't important to him. He never loved me! Why didn't he? Why didn't he love me? And I killed him, so he can never learn to love me, I can never prove I'm good enough, that I am important, that I have a soul. . . ."

"The lack was in him, not in you," Brocard said firmly. "Would a lifetime have changed that?"

Gonard stilled. "But I shouldn't have had to prove anything.

I was his son. I shouldn't have had to earn his love. Why didn't he love me? Why?"

Brocard took a step forward. But Gonard whirled. Claws wrenched free from the ground, threw dust and gravel into Brocard's face. He ducked, then started after the dragon, mouth opening to call him back.

A hand clasped his shoulder. "Let him go," Dom Cherril said quietly.

"He needs me—"

"No." The brother's eyes were dark with a memory of his own. "He must find his own answers. He is in the hands of the Lord now."

Brocard bent his head in reluctant agreement. Together they watched the dragon gallop away, heading toward the mountains. "Lord, his heart is in Your hands," he whispered.

* * * * *

He didn't love me. He didn't love me. The jeering litany echoed through Gonard's charge, breaking as his limp broke his strides. Why didn't he love me? How dare he not love me? How dare he die before he loved me?

Almost without notice he had left the valley of the chapter behind him. The smooth plains of grass were rising up into mounds and hills. He threw himself forward, savagely forcing his way up slopes, claws tearing loose clods of earth.

At the crest of a hill he halted, panting. You don't need to pant, you don't need to breathe, he told himself harshly. You're only a machine, a toy for a man to play with. Of course he didn't love you. Why should he? You wouldn't dream of loving a plow, for all its usefulness. A tool, a thing, that's what a dragon is. That's what I am. Nothing more. I am not important.

But still he panted, drawing in deep breaths. The clean smell of water made him blink. He focused his eyes on a

wide river running below him. His ears flicked to the sound
of water sliding over rocks and forging through earth.
Water. Rust. Death. Gonard took one last breath, then
plunged down the steep slope.

He did not pause at the bank, but dropped himself into
the water. The river was shallow at first, rising only to his
first knees, so that water splashed coldly against his chest as
he stumbled across the uneven riverbed. Then the bottom
suddenly plunged away, and Gonard dropped down into it,
seeking the oblivion of its dark depths.

The current, stronger here in the middle of the river,
caught at his heavy body as his head dipped below the surface. A strong tug rolled him over, water foaming into nostrils, ears, throat. Other loose debris tumbled over him,
slammed into his sides, bounded off his close-set scales.

He began to sink, sickened, battered. The roar of the
water above was a stark contrast to the sudden silence of his
mind. He was waiting, he realized. Waiting for the voice
that had spoken to him before, when the Barrier had held
him, when the City had refused to let him go. But the voice
was gone now. There was no father to urge him to surface, to
live.

Because I destroyed him. He did not love me, so I
destroyed him. Now I will destroy myself.

A snap of current rolled under his wings, wrenched them
open. Water billowed into his left wing, forcing it up, back.
Steel bone ground against steel bone. Gonard screamed in
pain, and the last air squeezed from his lungs to rush in
bubbles to the surface.

Without any conscious decision, his legs churned, driving him through the water. His wings clung to his sides;
his tail thrashed behind him. The surface was a mottled,
shifting barrier of light above him, and he fought to reach
the light, to leave the darkness behind.

The shifting ground of the bank was suddenly under his

feet. He stumbled to shore, left wing throbbing, his body heavy with pain, black water wheezing from nose and mouth. Legs straddled, he hung his head and coughed, water gushing over his tongue until his lung sacs were free from liquid.

I survived, he thought dully, looking at the river churning past him. I survived without you, Father. Not that you know. Not that you'd care. Not that I care, either.

Gonard closed his eyes. A breeze had picked up; it chilled the water beading on his scales, and he shivered. What now? What place was there for a son unloved by his father? What place was there for a creature unforgiven by the Ultimate?

He opened his eyes. He had crossed the river; the land rose again before him. His gaze wandered up the steep slope, noting how it curved around to a sheer cliff, high above the river. Then he began to limp up the long distance, absently flipping his wings onto his back. The river had returned his life to him. He did not think the earth would be so forgiving.

He continued his pace tirelessly, through the sunset and into the night, the light from his eyes directing him around rocks and bushes. All conflicting thoughts were gone; his mind was now clear, fixed on one goal, one purpose. To the end of the cliff he would walk, and then he would keep on walking. His existence should have ended long ago, in a cold laboratory, deep within a cave. He would now apply the necessary correction.

Dawn found him finally near the cliff edge, looking down the slope to judge the cleanest drop. To one side, the earth fell away gradually, which would give his claws too many opportunities to catch, to preserve himself. But here, facing back over the river, the cliff was a sheer drop for five hundred meters, the rest of the earth having fallen away long ago. One more stride, and he would follow.

Why?

He halted as he felt the Presence that had touched him briefly in a desert, long ago. Gonard lifted his head, looked defiantly up into the lightening sky. "Why shouldn't I? Even You won't forgive me."

It is not my forgiveness that needs giving.

"I don't understand," Gonard protested. "I killed him. I need his forgiveness, and his creator's."

Who is the injured one? The one dead, or the one left living?

Gonard stared down at his left foot, the toes curling loosely through the long grass. What sort of man accepts solitary exile, far from others of his kind? he found himself wondering. His vision flipped, changed. For once, he looked at Rumfus Max not as creator and Master, but as a man, with hopes and fears of his own. He saw him stand back from Lord Citizen Merril Lange, nod nervously as the taller man boomed instructions for the next Hunt creature. A shy man, Gonard suddenly realized, a man uncomfortable around others, who sought instead to construct creatures who could provide him with the companionship he sought.

Then he saw himself, the product of Rumfus Max's greatest effort. His creator had poured everything into him, all the knowledge saved and accumulated since the Destruction—not even withholding his own mind. And on the day of Gonard's birth, a connection incorrectly inserted had overloaded in his left forefoot, his left wing, making a mockery of all the man's hopes, all his dreams. And yet, he was alive, he did exist, and the Master, staring up at his creation, panicked and sought immediately to assert his control. *Rust. That's all you can do without me.*

But he turned away, Gonard recalled rebelliously. He could have healed me. Instead, he created the next creature, and the next. He forgot what he made me for. He forgot that I was meant to be his son, his heir. How could he forget?

Because he was no more than human. Gonard swallowed. He was the Master, his father—but also human, with human weaknesses. After his disappointment, he had thrown himself into other creations, trading them to Lord Lange for the raw materials to create yet more. Never realizing that his first dragon was slowly gaining a separate consciousness, developing a life of his own. Perhaps even the beginnings of the soul Rumfus Max had hoped for . . .

Gonard bent his head, felt an old anger begin to ease. You did not love me, Father, but neither did you know me. If only you had been less frightened of failure, more willing to fight for success . . . If only you had not deserted me to create the others, maybe you would have realized that I was starting to Awaken.

If only, if only. Gonard shook his head. His father was dead now, by the fire chamber he had himself given his creation. There were only could-have-beens, but no way of determining what would have been. Rumfus Max could no more help being as he was than—than Gonard could being what he was.

"I love you, Father," Gonard said into the dawn, his voice low, but strong. "I love you, even if you can't love me. That doesn't matter; that doesn't make what I feel any less important."

He felt at peace now, ready for what he must do. Gonard lifted his head, limped to the cliff edge. A few grasses tumbled down from a clump of soil, waving in the breeze. Far below, the river shimmered in the weak sun, unwinding like a serpent between the green hills and stark mountains. I can forgive you, Father, he thought, his hindquarters bunching beneath him. Perhaps, in time, I can even learn to forgive myself. But the one to whom we are both ultimately accountable will not forgive me, and I cannot survive without that. He closed his eyes and launched himself out over the cliff.

The wind flapped his ears, threw out his tail. He gathered his legs up close beneath his belly, willing his fall to quicken, the ground to welcome him. Soon he would no longer be a menace to others around him.

Then the Presence returned, surrounding him as he fell. *I forgive you.*

Of course, Gonard thought, until I forgave, another's forgiveness would have meant nothing to me. But, he told the Presence balefully, you could have said so sooner, before I jumped from the cliff. It's too late now.

Too late, all too late. His chest filled with sudden anger. To have come so far, to have learned so much, and now it was all to be lost, scattered into pieces across the ground. He threw back his head and roared with frustration.

His fire chamber responded to his anger, expanding with his rage. He snapped his jaws shut. What use are you to me now? he thought. Can I flame the ground and make it give way to me? Your only purpose is to destroy.

But the chamber expanded farther, gases pumping in, mixing. His belly scales spread under the pressure, sliding past one another, until edges no longer overlapped but met. And still his body created the deadly mixture. Gonard felt a series of small pops along his neck and back as valves suddenly snapped open. His neck and body spines swelled, raised themselves upright, accepting the gases his fire chamber could no longer hold alone.

A gust of wind blasted his body, swept his wings back from his shoulders. Gonard looked down, blinking as the dizzy whirl of blues, greens, and browns slowed, stopped. Was he imagining it, or was his fall actually slowing?

His wings were still wet from his river crossing. He spread them farther; the left felt strange. Gonard craned his neck, glancing back at the elbow. Loose skin flapped between elbow and shoulder but . . . He caught his breath. But the bones were realigned, and other than for the skin, the wings were a matching pair. The river, he thought numbly. The water had realigned the joint.

The wind was no longer rushing past his ears. He looked down, found the earth only a hundred meters away. The river was before him, his shadow rippling the moving waters, touching one bank. The wind was beneath him, supporting him. He stretched his wings, the wind billowing into the folds, and the ground was no longer rushing toward him but past him. He was flying.

Flying! Gonard watched the ground pass for a few minutes, unable to believe it was true. He was airborne, maintaining his altitude, heavy body no longer plummeting to earth.

Heavy body? No, in fact, he felt light. My fire chamber, he thought dizzily. It wasn't designed to destroy. I wasn't made to kill. The chamber is to lighten my body, my wings only meant to direct my flight. I was made to fly.

He lifted his wings, then swept them down. Air cupped beneath the skin folds, was forced beneath his body. The ground receded slightly. He pressed down again, and again, rising steadily into the air.

Quickly, with growing confidence, he learned to interpret the air pressures above and below his wings, bending the supple leathers to compensate for any changes. A large portion of his brain that had before lain dormant was now alive, gathering information from the multitude of sensors spread through the skin. Within a few hours he was flying as if he had been airborne for a lifetime, gliding on air currents, pumping his wings to change direction or when an updraft ceased. His tail, held aloft behind him by its own gas-filled spines, served as a rudder, enabling him to make crisp turns.

This was where he had been created to be. The sky was bright blue above him, the earth a patchwork of dark forest and lighter valleys below. Here he was not large and awkward, nor crippled and limping. In flight he was graceful, perfect, free. This was where he belonged.

But it was not enough. He was not made to be alone. He needed companionship, someone to share this with him. So he swung to the west and began the journey back to the chapter.

* * * * *

Brocard had come to the hill beyond the chapter buildings after sext, remained through dinner and none, and was now in danger of missing vespers. He glanced back at the buildings, not far below, the cathedral's eastern window deep in shadow. This is the direction in which Michel departed, he thought. This is the way from which he must return—if he returns.

Leave him in the hands of the Lord, indeed, Brocard mocked himself. Here you stand, awaiting his return, ready to offer whatever healing you can. The Abbot was right. Michel is too close to me, his healing wrapped up too much with my own. But to have come so close, so close . . .

A glint in the sky made him turn his head, squint at the darkening blue of twilight. The sun flashed again off an object high above the far hills. Brocard was suddenly reminded of the way the dragon's scales flashed in the sun. He watched, dry-mouthed, as the mass came nearer. Could it be?

The object grew, came lower. Now Brocard could make out the wings, stretching to either side of a thick body. He frowned, for Michel was much thinner, almost too thin. But before he could doubt for long, the creature was suddenly coming low over the treetops, and the setting sun sparkled from a green crystal twisted through a long ear.

Brocard lifted his arm in salute, in exaltation as Michel flew ten meters over his head, the wind of the dragon's passing ruffling back his hair. Then Michel swung up into the air, came past again, blue eyes glinting down at Brocard. For the first time, Brocard heard Michel's deep laughter, the dragon's flame spurting as his wings lifted him above the hill. "Look at me, Brocard! I can fly! I can fly!"

Brocard lifted up both arms to the dragon, feeling his joy. He threw back his head and laughed, capturing some of Michel's freedom, claiming part of it as his own. The dragon circled around and around, swinging in close and then away, gusts of wind slapping Brocard's robe against his knees. Their laughter echoed down the hillside, mingled with the bells ringing loud and clear for vespers.

* * * * *

Gonard hummed softly to himself as Brother Angles stitched the last piece of wing skin together, the thread glistening as it pulled through the membrane. Protection from rust, Gonard reflected, eying the drops of clear liquid that stood above each of the small holes running either side of the new join. So long as his body continued to manufacture the sealant, he could even throw himself into rivers.

Not that he would ever need to wade through water again. Gonard glanced wistfully at his left wing. It would take about a week for the skin to knit together, forcing him to remain earthbound for that time. But then I'll have matching wings, he consoled himself. I won't have to compensate for the tear.

"You will be in the air again shortly," Angles promised him, wiping his needle and dropping it into a bottle of blue fluid. "A swim repositioned the joint, you say? The Lord does indeed work in mysterious ways." The physician gave him a smile, then strode from the stables.

Gonard stopped humming, grateful that the operation was over. He turned his gaze to Brocard, who stood against a stable door, arms folded across his chest. "The Lord does indeed," the man said quietly. "You appear to have finally found a measure of peace, Michel."

Gonard nodded, shifted his weight from his left forefoot. "I remember my birth, now, and my father's death. I've forgiven my father. I've forgiven myself." He paused, surprised still by his new acceptance of his deed, the lack of anger and pain. "I've remembered my birth name."

"Do you wish to reassume it?"

"Yes." He paused again. "My father gave it to me, so I want to use it. But my chosen name is part of me as well." He lifted his head, coming to a decision. "I will call myself Gonard Michel."

Brocard inclined his head. "Do you remember anything more?"

"Not after my father's death," Gonard admitted. "I remember only parts." A bright grin in a dark face, a City of gleaming towers, a grim man with dull, silvery eyes . . . "It'll come back to me."

"I am certain that it will." Brocard turned to leave.

"Wait," Gonard protested. "Aren't you going to ask me what happened?"

Brocard studied him for a moment; then he smiled. "Do you wish to tell me?"

Gonard blinked. "I . . . don't know."

"I will always be ready to listen," Brocard continued. "But you appear ready to assume care for your own soul. You no longer need me."

"I'm sorry—" Gonard began.

"There should be no sorrow, only celebration, when healing has taken its course." Brocard smiled again, then left the stables, leaving Gonard to realize belatedly that he hadn't expressed his thanks.

* * * * *

The week seemed to drag by. Gonard Michel resumed the duties of a novice, attending services and instruction times.

He also explored carefully the use of the chemical sack he was coming to regard as his flight chamber. He found that he could maintain a constant level of gases in his spines, which held them erect above his head and back. The buoyancy was enough to ease some of his weight, making his steps lighter, his limp less noticeable. But he couldn't maintain a level in his flight chamber and talk; the egress from lungs and from chamber was the same. Valves prevented leakage from the spines, but there was no such precaution on the chamber itself. Gonard shook his head at Rumfus Max's design fault. I'd know better, he thought.

On the day of his second flight, the first with whole wings, he limped out of the stable block. Though the chapter was busy with the preparations for Easter, the Abbot had announced at dinner that, after none, all those who wished could watch Gonard Michel launch himself from the courtyard.

Gonard halted outside the wooden doors, his eyes roaming over the brothers who stood, silent and respectful, around the edges of the stone-paved yard. Memories of other gatherings crowded at the edge of his consciousness, hostile voices and accusing snarls. . . . But all these faces were friendly. All were his brothers. He had sung with them, plowed their fields. And now he could try to give something back to those who meant so much to him. With a new sense of confidence, he marched into the center of the courtyard.

The sky was gray with unbroken cloud, and Gonard could taste moisture on the air. I don't need to stride into a river to get wet, he thought wryly, raising his head to gauge the direction of the wind. He swung his head, acknowledging calls of well-wishers with a nod, a smile. If only he could give them a taste of his new freedom, his joy, it would be worth the effort it would cost to rise into the air from a flat, standing start.

He took a deep breath, his last until his flight was over.

Then he exhaled, clearing his lung sacs, before he opened his flight chamber. The gases churned in, expanding his chest, rounding his belly. His claws flexed, opened onto the ground, although he knew that the flight chamber alone was not enough to prematurely raise him into the air.

Gonard opened his wings, arching the leathers across the courtyard. He heard murmurs from the brothers as they compared for themselves left wing with right, finding both now perfectly matched. A breeze started to fill the skins, rippling the strong material, information shivering down electrical pathways to Gonard's brain. The wind grew, as if the sky were reaching down to him, inviting him to soar above the gray clouds, the dull earth. Gonard smiled, ears flicking, as he enjoyed the tug of the wind on his wings.

Time to go. He rocked back, gathering his hindquarters beneath him, and took a final glance around to ensure that his flight path was clear and no brother was in danger of being hit by a wing. Then he leapt into the air, powerful leg muscles thrusting him high above the ground. His wings swept down, stopping short of a full beat to avoid slapping the stones. But it was enough to send him past the cathedral, and the next wing sweep sent him over the chapter's fields.

Beyond the cathedral a second group of men watched, their black robes contrasting with the young green wheat. Gonard felt a surge of affection for the lay brothers, for all in the chapter who had been willing to accept him despite his great dissimilarity to themselves. He dipped a wing to circle over the fields, then rose above their heads, trumpeting a quick, flaming fanfare into the sky. His gesture lost him height, and he pumped his wings to regain altitude as his flight chamber refilled. He set his sight for the gray clouds above, determined to rise above them and feel the sun on his back.

Flight, he decided, was pure joy. Coming back to earth

was like a defeat, returning to limp painfully from place to place, others always dodging his large, unwieldy body. But once again, he felt that flight was not all. Something was missing. A name, a face, someone he had sworn a promise to. Someone he must find.

CHAPTER 13

They struggled up the hill late one evening, the setting sun flicking their shadows long across the grass. Gonard, his head bent in concentration as he discussed a few points on flying with Brocard, did not see them at first. The man's sudden lift of head made Gonard pause, look up as well.

As if their attention had been a signal, the two figures halted, a dozen meters of grass separating them from Gonard and Brocard. One was a man, his face worn and haggard, skin sagging unnaturally from cheeks and chin. The other was a woman, her skin almost as dark as her silhouette against the red sun. They stood quietly, as if waiting.

Gonard found himself frozen where he stood, unable to move. Their faces had danced through his dreams, and voices echoed from some part of him still in shadow. Brocard glanced back at him, seeming almost resigned. "So, they have at last come for you. Or do you still not remember them?"

Gonard took a deep breath, aching to remember. Brocard touched his muzzle lightly with his fingertips, then strode forward. The man turned politely to acknowledge him; the woman still locked gazes with Gonard. "It has been imparted to us that he was found lacking access to his memory," said the man in a weary, dusty voice.

"Gonard Michel has recalled much," Brocard said. "But not yet all."

The woman began to laugh. Her sudden gaiety seemed to ease some of the stiffness in Gonard's chest. " 'Course he don't 'member me! Missin' somethin', ain't I, dragon?" She dropped her pack to the ground, ripped open the bindings to rummage inside. Gonard watched, intrigued, on the verge of knowing, remembering, being . . .

"Got it!" She pulled a tattered bit of once-green cloth from her pack. "Got too bitty to wear, dragon, but since ya always liked it, I brought it 'long." She carefully shrugged into the vest, even in its faded condition a startling contrast to her gray shirt. "There, dragon, 'member me now?"

Gonard's ears flicked at the concern in her voice. He took a deep breath of her sweaty, dusky scent, studied her dark face, black hair. Then he stepped forward, slowly, carefully, each step rolling back the shadows. She stood defiantly by a lake in his father's domain. She flung curses at the Council as they tried to sentence him. She argued with the medtech, moved a chess piece by firelight, reddened her arms as she gutted a buck. Then he stood before her, feeling her presence ease an ache within him that even flight had not filled. "Itsa," he breathed, almost unable to believe that she had been returned to him.

"Good to see ya too, dragon." The thump she gave his leg was real enough. "How've ya been doin'?"

"I am very well, thank you."

"Is it to be my understanding," asked the medtech, "that your name has been altered?"

Gonard reluctantly moved one eye from Itsa. "I'm Gonard Michel now."

"It is not your place to name yourself," the medtech began icily.

"Crack off, tech," Itsa interrupted. "Don't matter what he calls himself, do it?" She glanced away, dug a toe into the grass. "Is it true, what they say?" she asked quietly, looking up at him again. "They say—ya can fly."

In answer, Gonard turned and broke into a gallop, running down the hill. He launched himself into the air, wings flinging him from the ground as the gases swelled his chest. Within seconds he was several hundred meters above the hill, three small figures watching him from below. He swooped a quick pattern across the sky, his tail flicking wildly as he traced a series of circles and loops. Then, expelling the gas in a long flame, he dropped back down, neatly backwinging to land near Itsa.

The wind of his passage blew strands of hair across her face. She smoothed them back, but her hands did not hide the glow in her eyes, the wonder softening her face. "Ya're . . . fixed," she said softly.

"Almost." Gonard limped back to her.

The medtech's dull eyes roamed over his body, making Gonard's skin twitch at the intense scrutiny. There was a fierceness in the gaze, almost an anger, that Gonard couldn't understand. "Am I to comprehend," he demanded of Brocard, "that it was your crude technology with which you undertook to repair the wing?"

Gonard winced at the sharp tone, felt his two worlds rub painfully against each other. He realized suddenly that he would have to choose between the two, and that there was only one choice he could make. With a pang, he knew that the chapter would soon be no more than another memory, another place he had loved and left. When will I find a place to stay? he wondered once again. When will I have a home? The laboratory was the only home I've ever had.

Brocard was studying the medtech. "The Lord uses what tools He has been given. Brother Angles is a very experienced physician, and Gonard Michel possesses a great capacity for healing." He paused, then added, "I can understand your regret, if you desired to heal him yourself. But now that the deed has been done, can you not take pleasure in his wholeness?"

The medtech glared at Brocard a moment longer. Then he shuffled to Gonard's side. Gonard obligingly extended the left wing. Unlike the brothers, the medtech didn't run gentle fingertips down the leathers; Gonard winced as the medtech jabbed stiff fingers into the yielding skin, probed the struts for any weakness. "How did you know to roughen the edges?"

"I undertook his initial healing when Gonard Michel was first found. I noted then that a clear fluid arose to seal the edges of wounds together." Brocard shrugged, and Gonard admired his calmness, such a contrast to the medtech's anger. "I judged that the same would be necessary to bind the portions of wing skin together."

The medtech walked back to Brocard, allowing Gonard to fold the wing. "It has been done remarkably well, under the circumstances," the medtech admitted grudgingly.

"I was equally pleased at the lack of scar tissue."

"It is understandable that none would appear." The medtech's voice was beginning to thaw slightly. "Once the connections were reestablished, the program would ensure the correct readjustments."

"A master plan for the body structure?" Brocard mused. "Do you speak of DNA?"

The medtech blinked. "What knowledge can this community possess regarding deoxyribonucleic acid?"

"There he goes again," Itsa muttered to Gonard. "Think he'd get tired of hearin' his own voice, like the rest of us do."

They wandered down the hill together, Brocard and the medtech deep in conversation at the fore, Gonard and Itsa following. Gonard was happy simply to walk beside Itsa. He could see new lines worn into her face, noted the new heaviness in her strides. We will talk later, he decided. For now, it's enough just to be with her.

But the arrival of his companions was already causing difficulties, he discovered upon their return to the chapter. "The medtech may take lodgings with the lay brothers," Brocard told Gonard as they halted in the courtyard. "But Itsa may take only the most temporary of accommodations there, preferably for no more than this one night."

"Why?" Itsa demanded.

"The order is pledged to celibacy—" Brocard began.

Itsa laughed. " 'Splains why ya all look so old. Nothin' to keep young for." She lifted her chin defiantly. "C'mon, dragon, let's blow this place."

Gonard took a deep breath. "I can't."

"Why not?"

"I have taken temporary vows." He saw her eyes slide to his neck and for the first time register the brown cloth draped against his scales. "I have promised to remain here for twelve months."

She stiffened. "Like ya promised to come back to me?"

"I'm sorry I didn't . . ."

"What're we s'posed to do, then? Stay here with ya?"

"This is a community of healers," Brocard said equably. "The medtech would be welcome among the lay brothers, at the least. If he felt so called, whatever skills he possesses would be welcomed to the order proper."

Gonard was startled by the look on the medtech's face. "Welcomed?" he repeated incredulously.

Brocard nodded. "You would be valued for the knowledge you could bring to us."

"Hey, how 'bout me?" Itsa stepped forward aggressively. "What'm I s'posed to do?"

"We have a sister order," Brocard said gravely. "You could test a vocation there."

Gonard winced in anticipation. But Itsa merely stared at him, as if too shocked by the suggestion to think of an appropriate response. "We'll talk about that later," Gonard said hurriedly.

Itsa flicked him an icy glance. "Ya mean, ya need time to think it over first."

"Yes." Gonard cocked his head. "Is there anything wrong with that?"

"Yeah, if it gets in the way of doin' anythin'." She glanced back at Brocard. "Show me where I'm s'posed to go, then."

* * * * *

A knock on the stable doors after compline made Gonard sit up, surprised at the late visit. The light from his eyes flashed across Brocard's face, and he quickly dimmed them as the man squinted. "You don't usually knock," Gonard commented.

"I usually do not come here at night." Brocard closed the door softly behind him. "I have apprised the Abbot regarding our two guests."

"I remember them now," Gonard said. "I remember everything."

"Yes. So I understood. You are now well on the road to healing." He smiled at Gonard's blink, which plunged the stables briefly into darkness. "The wounds are closed over, but you must remember that the scars still remain. Do not despair if the pain returns occasionally."

Gonard tightened the fold of his left wing, though he knew that the man was not talking about physical injuries. "I hope my—guests—aren't causing any problems."

Brocard waved away his concern. "I had expected that Itsa would be one of your own kind."

"She is my own kind," Gonard said. "Only our shapes are different."

Brocard rubbed his beard. "Do you wish you were human

in shape as well as in being?"

Gonard shook his head. "I used to. But if I were human, I wouldn't be able to fly. Humans aren't built for flying." He cocked his head. "My vows bind me for another ten months?"

"Not strictly. You may petition the Abbot for an early release, stating why you wish to be permitted to leave the order."

"What sort of reason should I give?"

"The truth, of course."

Gonard stared, uncomprehendingly, at Brocard.

"You wish to leave because of your love for Itsa, do you not?"

Gonard jerked back his head. "No, that's not why."

"You need not lie to me," Brocard said sharply. "Or is it to yourself that you lie?"

"You must understand." Gonard ran one eye down his body, light glancing off his scales. "She's a human, and I'm a dragon."

"Why limit yourself?" Brocard countered. "Why limit her?"

Gonard shook his head, light sliding across the rough stable walls. "We are limited."

"Only if we choose to be." Brocard shrugged. "I suggest that you spend a day in contemplation of your choices. I will explain to the novice master that you will be secluding yourself from all services and duties tomorrow. Use this as an opportunity to become reacquainted with Itsa."

"But we know each other already," Gonard protested.

Brocard raised an eyebrow. "Are you the same person as you were when you came here? Is she the same, for her own journey?" He strode to the door to leave. Then he turned back, one hand still resting on the dark wood, frowning at some thought. "What relation is the medtech to you?"

"He's my brother."

"Does he accept the death of your father?"

"He never knew him." Gonard wondered how he could explain. "Our father left him before—before he was born. I was born later."

"He did not live with you, then, in your father's home?"

"He's never had a home." Gonard mulled over the thought. At least I once had one.

"Then he also never knew a father's love."

"That doesn't affect him like it did me," Gonard said. "He's not like me."

"Is he not?"

Of course not, Gonard wanted to say. He wasn't made to have a soul. But Brocard wouldn't understand. "He isn't."

"It may not be wise to limit him, either." Then Brocard excused himself with a nod, the door closing quietly behind him.

* * * * *

Gonard found Itsa sitting on a corral fence, watching the coursairs grazing. She looked up as Gonard approached. Her hair was tied back from her forehead with a simple string, as tattered as the clothes she wore. "They letcha out, then," she said as he halted.

"I've been given leave of my duties for the day."

Her eyes slid to the left forefoot, still curled awkwardly into itself. "Your wing might be all right, but they couldn't do the full job, could they?" She looked up again. "Why'dcha join them?"

"The chapter has been a family to me."

"Golly gee for ya."

He felt a brief flash of anger at her dismissiveness, and it startled him. If Brocard could stay calm with the medtech yesterday, he told himself, I can stay calm with Itsa. He said quietly, "Yes, we're both orphans, you and I."

Her eyes flashed. "I didn't kill my mum."

"But she showed you as little love as my father did me."

Itsa stiffened. Then her face flushed. "Ya got no right to talk 'bout my mum, or me. Got it?"

Gonard sighed inwardly. "I don't want to argue with you."

"Ya ain't doin' bad so far." She turned away. "Look, dragon, I came for ya. Right? I came for ya. I left behind—I left things behind. I was decidin' things too, but I came for ya. What 'boutcha? Ya've been doin' nothin' but sittin' here, makin' plans without me."

What had happened to her during her time at the settlement? "I want to go somewhere with you. I want to talk."

"Yeah, great. All right." She dropped off the fence. "Where'dcha wanna limp to? There's the fields, the barns, loads of places."

"There's no need to walk," Gonard said, watching her closely for her reaction. "We don't have to stay around here. The sky is a much more even surface."

Some of the tense lines eased from her eyes and lips. "Ya mean—fly?" she asked incredulously. "Ya mean—fly with me?"

Gonard recalled her light weight, riding on his back out of a parched desert. "I'm willing to try."

"Try, huh?" Itsa muttered. They trudged away from the lay brothers' dwellings and through the chapter courtyard. "And if ya fall flat and break my neck?"

Gonard felt laughter dance along his throat. He swallowed it back with difficulty, respecting her attempt to cover up her excitement. "I'll apologize."

"Ya'd better."

In silence they climbed the hill beyond the chapter. Gonard bent down obligingly, and she climbed awkwardly onto his back, wriggling into place between the two spines by his shoulders. He ignored the boot heels scuffing his neck, her sweaty hands gripping the spine before her.

"Okay," she said, her voice giving away none of the fear he could smell sweating her body.

Gonard gazed down the slope, gauging weights, speeds, inclines. He took a deep breath, released it. Then he started down, gaining speed with each stride. His flight chamber expanded, and he unfurled his wings into the wind. The hill dipped suddenly; he leapt forward, using the gap to bring his wings down for the all-important first sweep. Wing tips brushed the tall grass. Then he was climbing, pulling free from the ground.

The wind carried away anything Itsa might have said, but he felt her moist palms grip more tightly around his spine. This is her first flight, he reminded himself. He quickly settled his flying into a steady rhythm, searching for a wind current on which to glide. Itsa was not heavy, but already he could feel an extra strain on his wing muscles from the additional weight.

He found a strong current and glided on the wind, noting that it was carrying them eastward. An hour of gliding restored his muscles, and when they came to the river curving through the eastern mountains, he decided to follow its flow as it curved back toward the west.

Itsa began to shift, disturbing Gonard's balance. She must be getting uncomfortable, he thought as he readjusted. But he didn't want to land. As long as they were in the air, they couldn't speak, couldn't argue. Why is she angry at me? he wondered.

The river widened. Here and there near the banks, Gonard could see the scattered remnants of an older civilization. Rubble outlined the square forms of buildings, longer lines of dark stone between them showing where roads used to run. He recalled some of his father's old books, showing pictures of tall cities, millions of people crowded into small concrete-and-steel boxes. What happened to all those places? he wondered. Have they all been destroyed by five hundred years of neglect, or do some still stand?

The land rose, then suddenly fell and disappeared. Gonard found himself flying over an expanse of blue-green water, stretching away as far as he could see. An ocean. I have reached an ocean. The word seemed so inadequate to describe this new domain.

He turned, flew along the shoreline for a while. Itsa grew more insistent, drumming her heels against his neck. Reluctantly, he finally chose a cove, circling down to settle in the still-damp sand exposed by the receding tide.

Itsa swung a leg over and dropped to the ground before he could help her. She staggered away, complaining, "Your spines are too close together!"

"I didn't make them."

"No, s'pose not." She flopped to the sand, rubbing first one leg, then the other. "My feet don't feel as if they're there anymore. I don't jive ya're made for carryin' people."

"Perhaps not," Gonard agreed solemnly, a light thought teasing through his mind. "Would you rather walk back?"

She glared up at him. "Don'tcha dare leave me here." Then she squinted at his wrinkled nose. "Are ya funnyin' me?"

"Yes." He felt laughter tickle in his chest. "Shouldn't I?"

"No." She struggled to her feet, slapped wet sand from her clothes. "Ya don't funny. It ain't part of ya."

He wondered at the strange tension, almost fear, in her voice. "I've learned about laughter recently."

"What else've ya learned?"

Nothing that changes how I feel about you, he wanted to say. But he couldn't tell her. She was human. He was a dragon. A companion, sometimes a guardian, but nothing more. "I'd like to tell you. That's why I brought us here."

She looked away from him, gazed out across the sea. A breeze swept back loose strands of hair from her neck, exposing a newly healed scar just below one ear. Gonard wondered where it had come from, decided that this was not the time to ask. The silence stretched out between them, broken only by the rasp of waves against the sand. "I 'member," she said finally, "when I first met ya. Ya didn't even wanna talk 'fore bein' given a say-so. 'Member?"

"I remember."

"And ya were all big on findin' a new Master, or dyin', or both." She turned to him. "Why'dcha run 'way from us?"

"I—"

"I mean, we used to talk, didn't we, sometimes? Not run 'way."

"Because I—"

"Then that fardlin' tech," Itsa went on. " 'It is apparent that Gonard did not feel inclined to examine his thoughts in your presence.' So, why didn'tcha talk then?"

"I'm trying to now," Gonard said patiently, "but you're not letting me."

" 'Cause ya jig what happened, 'cause ya'd gone 'way?" She was speaking quickly now, not looking at him. "I found a hunter, a man, nice bod. And I was goin' to stay with him, maybe, who can jive. But 'cause of ya, he left me. 'Cause I was with ya and so what happened to the tribe was my fault, too." She glared up at him, eyes bright with mingled pain and anger. "I don't like nobody leavin' me. Got it?"

"I am sorry," Gonard said softly. "I would have been happy for you."

She brushed stray hair out of her eyes. "Yeah, maybe." Her eyes searched his for a moment, as if seeking some reassurance. "Ya've changed."

He dipped his head in a nod. "So have you."

Itsa grinned, suddenly more like the Itsa of old. "Blame the tech. Worn me out, he has. Hardly talks at all anymore." The grin dropped away. "He's dyin', ya jive?"

"Ceasing to function," Gonard corrected automatically. But an awareness of the loss to come made him take a deep breath, seeking to ease a sudden tightness in his chest. "He must be conserving energy."

"Yeah." Itsa shrugged. "Not that I care lots 'bout what happens to him, ya jig. Just makes me jive that I'll die too one day, but ya'll just go on, won'tcha?"

Gonard found himself turning away the image of Itsa's dying and leaving him alone. "I tried to destroy myself."

"Should of asked my say-so first," she declared.

"But I didn't," he challenged in return.

"And so ya didn't do it," she retorted smugly. "Why'dcha wanna, anyroads?"

Suddenly it was easier to speak, the mock battle easing some of the tension. "Because I found out why I'd killed my father. That's what made me run away, as well. I was trying to hide it from myself."

"Thoughtcha killed him 'cause he was pointin' a laser at your head." Itsa shrugged. "Good 'nuff reason for me."

"No, it was not that." Gonard lifted his head, watched the waves coil, then unleash, in an unceasing pattern. "He— betrayed me. I loved him, but he didn't love me, or he wouldn't have tried to kill me."

Itsa scowled down at her feet. Gonard held his breath, wondering if she was going to snap a retort, once again put a distance between them. But she bent suddenly and unlaced her boots. She hopped on one foot, then the other, removing shoes and socks. Dark toes stretched out into the white sand, and she grinned up at Gonard. "That's better."

She started to walk along the sand, Gonard following. He found progress difficult; the dry sand shifted under every step. He ducked behind Itsa and marched over to the sand only recently revealed by the tide. The wet sand compressed under his weight but was easier to walk on.

Itsa came to his side. "Ya used to follow me," she said wryly.

"Used to," Gonard acknowledged.

"S'pose ya were lookin' for a Master, then." She glanced at him. "Ya found him now?"

"I'm no longer looking for one."

They strode over the sand in silence. The sun climbed into the sky, warming the air around them. The shoreline began to narrow, the cliffs drawing in closer. An occasional clump of seaweed appeared in their path, washed up and deserted by the sea. Gonard wrinkled his nose at the pungent smell, laying back his ears as flies buzzed away from the green-brown tendrils.

Gonard finally stopped. He closed his eyes, drinking in the sound of the waves, sweeping across the sands again and again. The rhythm was somehow soothing, marking an interaction between land and sea that had begun when the world was young. He had the sudden urge to sample the ocean for himself. A quick internal check confirmed that all scales were whole, watertight; he opened his eyes and limped purposefully to the foam outlining the extent to which the last wave had washed.

The water had receded at his approach. Now another wave crashed apart, spilling its contents. The water rolled up the beach, foamed over Gonard's toes. He took a deep breath of its salty tang, felt the coldness ease the strain in his feet. Bits of sand, loosened by his weight, were pulled away by the waves, and he began to sink into the shore.

Reluctantly, he pulled his feet free. A sudden shout jerked his head up. Itsa ran past him, bare legs flashing in the sun. As the next wave hit the beach, she jumped over the swell, water splashing away from her body to break against Gonard's legs. "Golly gee, dragon," she said, grinning wickedly, "looks like I gotcha wet."

Gonard cocked his head, smiling as he remembered another sunny day, a splash of water that had hit him. But Itsa waded out of reach. "Shat, it's cold!"

Gonard merely dipped his head in agreement. He watched

the foam swirl around his legs, cling to his toes when the water had returned to its source. Despite her complaint, Itsa was giving herself a quick bath, her clothes piled on the dry sand.

As she turned her back to him, Gonard suddenly plunged forward, seawater splashing up his feet and chest. Itsa glanced up, startled, and turned to run. But he caught her in a few strides, closing his eyes and scooping his muzzle through the cold water to send a spray across her back. As he lifted his head again, she skidded her hands through the surf, sending an answering splash across his chest. Then she retreated to a safe distance, laughing at him. Gonard laughed in return, suddenly glad to be alive and to be with her, the first person to have accepted him as a being in his own right.

Afterward they returned to the beach, the strange tenseness between them gone. Itsa pulled her clothes back on, shivering slightly in the only just warm spring sunshine. They started back the way they had come, crossing over their earlier footprints.

Clouds skipped across the blue sky, flocks of fluffy white occasionally covering the sun. The tide was beginning to turn. Gonard headed farther up the beach, onto the treacherous dry sand. Itsa stopped to reclaim her boots, and he wandered a little farther as she pulled them back on. He was reluctant to leave this place, end this day.

He halted, turned his head to look back at Itsa. A cloud crossed over part of the sun, leaving him in the light, but casting a shadow over her. She seemed suddenly remote, cut off from him, plunged into a world of darkness that he could not enter. Alarmed, he turned and stepped forward. "Itsa?"

"What?" She raised her head. The cloud blew past, and the sunlight was bright upon her again. She straightened. "What's up?"

"Nothing," he mumbled, ashamed of his strange alarm.

"We should be going back now."

She winced. "Jig I won't be able to walk tomorrow."

With his assistance, she mounted. A wind was beginning to blow inland from the ocean; Gonard launched himself into it, using the current to help him rise above the cliffs and begin the long journey back to the chapter.

On the beach behind them, the waves began to methodically remove all traces of their passing.

* * * * *

Gonard limped slowly up the nave, his eyes fixed on the three men awaiting him just before the choir. The cathedral was otherwise empty, for this was essentially a private ceremony. He knelt before the Abbot, Lybrand's quick smile and Brocard's nod lending him strength.

"Gonard Michel, my son in the Order of St. Thomas," the Abbot said quietly, "for what reason do you come before me this day?"

"I regret that I must petition you for release from my vows, most Reverend Father," Gonard said steadily.

"For what reason do you seek release, Gonard Michel?"

Gonard had carefully thought out his response. "Most Reverend Father, I have come to realize that I cannot give myself wholly to the Lord and to this order, either now or when the time comes for me to consider the taking of permanent vows. I have left my former life unfinished, and I must return to the world to complete duties left to me."

"When you have done so, my son, is it your intention to return to us?"

"Most Reverend Father, I regret that it is not." He raised his head, met the man's gray eyes. "I cannot give my heart wholly to the order, for it has already been gifted to another. I can obey only the letter, not the spirit, of the vow of celibacy."

The Abbot bent his head for a moment. Then he raised it. "Gonard Michel, temporarily of the Order of St. Thomas, I release you from your vows. May the blessing of the Lord go with you, and the love your brothers have shown you give you the strength to serve the Lord outside this chapter."

Brocard and Lybrand stepped forward. They untied the brown cord, slid it free from Gonard's neck. He stood, dizzied by the speed at which yet another part of his life had ended. The mark of the order had been only a small thing, yet he felt bare without it, as if a part of himself had been cut away.

He numbly accepted Brocard's and Lybrand's blessings, mumbled polite words of gratitude to the Abbot. Then he stumbled from the cathedral, blinked in the bright sun outside. Without any conscious decision, he leapt into the air for one last flight over the chapter. He had learned so much here. . . .

A small figure staring out over the fields caught his attention. He released flame, then spiraled down, landing gently at Itsa's side. She smiled up at him. He took a deep breath, startled by the smile, that it was given simply because he had come to stand beside her. We stand together, he thought, remembering a chamber of Citizens where she had first lent him strength. He felt the sense of loss ease, then disappear. We stand together again.

CHAPTER 14

"Right, so the dragon's free," Itsa said. "Where're we goin' to go now?"

The light of the eye Gonard kept fixed on the medtech revealed the robot's frown as he looked at Itsa. "It is patently obvious that we must return to the Domains. Even an Outler with your low capacity for rational thought must be able to recognize that."

Itsa leaned back against a stable door, crossing her arms over her chest in mimicry of the medtech. "Yeah, sure. We were in such a flash to get outta there we forgot our socks."

The medtech glared at Itsa, prompting Gonard to add, "You did say then that it was important for me to leave. Why should we go back now?"

The medtech transferred his glare to Gonard. Then the lines softened, and the look became appraising. "You have just illustrated why it was necessary to leave the Domains. That creature which stepped through the Barrier held his queries to himself, nor ever sought to challenge another's statement. Only since our departure have you matured. Only now are you ready to challenge the assumptions of the Lord Citizens and prove to them that you do indeed possess a soul."

"I might have a soul," Gonard acknowledged. "I think I

have one. That doesn't mean I need to go back to the Domains."

The medtech cocked his head, silver eyes gleaming dully. "It is imperative that you return to the Domains. It is imperative that you prove to the Lord Citizens that you possess a soul. Is it not a matter of importance to you to establish that the Master's work upon you was not in vain? Is it not essential that the exile he chose for your sake is finally justified?"

"What's *really* chewin' ya, tech?" Itsa demanded. "Didcha really love Daddy so much that ya care what a bunch of Lord Cits jive 'bout him?"

There was a moment of silence. "Love," the medtech finally mused. "I do not know the emotion. I cannot love. Nor can I hate. I feel only varying degrees of indifference. Beyond those, I know only anger, envy, despair." He lifted his head to Gonard. "It is necessary that I speak to you alone, Gonard Michel."

The medtech spoke as a subject seeking a favor of his superior. Gonard took a deep breath, turned to Itsa. "Would you mind leaving us for a while?"

" 'Course," she snapped. But she pushed herself onto her feet and strode to the doors. "But he'll only play mummer if I don't, won't he? I'm out countin' stars." She slammed the door behind her.

"She would not understand," the medtech explained softly. "She has never been as you were, or as I am. She has always possessed a soul, despite her wishes otherwise."

Gonard shifted restlessly. "What do you want to say to me?" he asked, suddenly wishing Itsa were with him, lightening the darkness that seemed to cling to the medtech.

"How different we are." The medtech's voice was strained with weariness. "Are we truly both products of one man's hands? But of course we are. It is for me to diminish, and for you to increase. I was the beginning; you are the fruition. I was the experiment; you are the reality."

"What do you want from me?" Gonard demanded.

"What I have always wanted. Lord Citizen Rumfus Max abandoned his first creation and accepted exile so he could continue with his second." Teeth flashed in a brief, mock smile. "I have ever known that. I have always accepted that the creation of a being with a soul would be a far greater accomplishment than the construction of a robot that can express some limited emotional states. A far more important task."

A moment of silence followed. Gonard's tail rustled over the loose straw. Was the medtech looking for some reassurance, some acceptance? But he hesitated and felt the moment slip away.

"Indeed, a far more important task." A harshness now crept into the medtech's voice. "I am ceasing to function, Gonard Michel."

Again, the feeling that he should say something, that the medtech was awaiting some sign. "So Itsa told me," he said lamely.

The dull eyes glowed, full of self-mockery. "I urged you to depart from the Domains so that you might have time to develop into maturity the personality bequeathed to you by the Master. It was always my intention, however, that we should one day return to the Domains so you might prove that our Master was not in error. You must return for judgment and prove that you have a soul."

"But *why* must I?" Gonard asked. "I don't want anything from the Lord Citizens."

"It is not for gain that I advise return. You have misunderstood my words."

Gonard narrowed his eyes. "Maybe," he said slowly, "you aren't saying what you really mean."

"The Master must be vindicated," the medtech stated. "You must prove that his actions were justified."

Gonard shook his head, confused. "Why's that so important to you? You never even knew him. He left you to go into exile long before——" Gonard stopped; he blinked as a sudden thought came to him. Anger, envy, despair—betrayal? He looked at the medtech. "To whom do you want him to be justified—to the Lord Citizens or to yourself?"

The medtech looked up at him, his face clear of emotion. "He abandoned me half-complete," he said calmly. "Deserted me to the clumsy attentions of his minion. I was only a dalliance; you were his vision, a creature capable of developing a soul." His voice suddenly cracked over Gonard like a whip. "And I will know if he was successful!"

Gonard winced. "But why go back to the Domains?" he persisted. "Can't you decide for yourself whether the Master was successful?"

"I? A robot without psychic substance?" The medtech's voice was hoarse, vocal apparatus obviously damaged by his shout. "On what knowledge or experience can I base my judgment? No, I must seek the wisdom of my betters. Only the Lord Citizens possess the necessary qualifications."

"And after the Lord Citizens have proclaimed their judgment?"

A brief smile, without warmth, crossed the medtech's face. "My task will have been accomplished, and my existence will no longer have purpose."

"You'll die?"

"I will permit myself to cease functioning." The dull eyes mocked him. "Existence without a soul is a burden, Gonard Michel."

Gonard bent his head, feeling some rebuke hidden in his name. He limped forward, blindly pushing his way through the stable doors, out into the dark night.

The rusty sound of a bolt being slid into place brought his head up again. Itsa dusted her hands against her trousers as she turned away from the doors. "There. He's stuck inside. So, what's he gotta say?"

Gonard took a deep breath, discovered that he was trembling. Anger, envy, despair, betrayal. Such a darkness within which to exist, with no hope, forgiveness, acceptance. He possessed choices; the medtech did not. "He presented his reasons for returning to the Domains."

"Yeah, I jigged that. What'd he say?"

Gonard studied her for a moment, weighing obligations. "I can't tell you," he said finally. "I think the medtech would want only me to know."

Itsa shoved her hands into her pockets, squared her jaw. "So what? Why should what he wants count? He's only a 'bot."

"So am I," Gonard reminded her.

"Yeah, butcha're diff, and ya jig it."

"His confidences are as safe with me as yours are." He lifted his head, picked out constellations above them. "I owe it to him to return."

"You don't owe him nothin'."

"Anything," he corrected. "He helped us escape from the Citadel—have you forgotten? He preserved your life throughout our travels and a long, bitter winter. If he now asks that we retrace our steps, is that too great a repayment?"

Itsa made a face. "Ha, ha. So, the great G. M. has decided, has he? Golly gee."

Suddenly alarmed, Gonard asked, "You'll come with me, won't you?"

" 'Course." She turned away from him. "Where else'd I go?"

Calling to mind another decision made long ago, Gonard said to her softly, "I want you to come with me. If you wish to."

Itsa slowly turned back. "Yeah, all right, I'll go with ya. I always do, don't I?" Then she frowned. "Just don't trust the tech, right? He—"

Gonard waited a moment, wondering what she had been about to tell him. "He has always worked to protect us."

"Maybe." Itsa shook her head. "Just, whatever he says, don't trust him."

* * * * *

Brocard met them in the courtyard. He looked weary, face lined with the days of fasting and nights of prayer he was required to spend as the day drew near for his consecration as Abbot. But he quirked his smile as Gonard stepped forward, leaving Itsa and the medtech standing behind him. "So, Gonard Michel," he said, "it has come time for you to take your leave of us."

Gonard bent his head. "I can't stay. I have—obligations."

Brocard nodded. "Yes. An uncompleted task."

"Thank you . . . for all you've done for me," Gonard said awkwardly.

"The chapter owes you thanks also," Brocard replied, the sound of hooves striking stone suddenly undercutting his voice. "And we have a gift for your departure."

Gonard's nostrils dilated at the thick scent of coursair musk. He glanced back over his shoulder, finding two of the beasts being led forward by several lay brothers. "Coursairs?"

"I understand that your journey will be a long one," Brocard said. "You cannot fly both of your companions at once, so the beasts are meant to ease your passage."

"But the chapter needs them," Gonard protested.

"The lay brothers have already reminded us that we would have only half a harvest this season were it not for your assistance. The gift was their suggestion. We can replace the beasts."

Gonard eyed the coursairs dubiously. But Itsa had already claimed the reins of the shorter beast, grinning up at the small red eyes. "Then—thank you."

One of the lay brothers was explaining to Itsa how to mount the high saddle, the medtech listening closely. Gonard brought his head back to Brocard. The man beckoned him to follow, and Gonard limped after him.

"Gonard Michel," Brocard demanded, stopping behind the dormitory, "do you renounce all that is evil and rebels against the Lord?"

Gonard blinked, startled. "Of course I do."

"Do you renounce all sinful desires that draw you from the light of the Lord?"

"Yes, I do."

"Do you vow to battle against the evil powers of this world, which seek to corrupt and destroy the creatures of the Lord?"

"Yes," Gonard answered, growing more and more confused.

"Do you turn to the Lord as your savior, trusting in His love and grace?"

"I've already done so."

Brocard nodded curtly. He drew a small vial from a robe pocket, undid the glass stopper. "Bend your head to me."

Gonard obeyed. He felt Brocard trace a cross on his head, just behind the first spine. "Gonard Michel, thou art sealed to the Lord by baptism, and marked as His own forever. 'When thou passest through the waters, I will be with thee; and through the rivers, they shall not overflow thee: when thou walkest through the fire, thou shalt not be burned; neither shall the flame kindle upon thee. For I am the Lord thy God, the Holy One of Israel, thy Savior.' "

Gonard raised his head, the cross of oil sticky moist on his scales. Brocard restoppered the vial, slipped it back into his pocket. "You have been received by the sacrament of baptism into the care of the Order of St. Thomas. You are welcome to any of our chapters, brother to us in rebirth by blessed water and anointment by sacred oil. Go in peace, my son." Brocard sketched a cross in the air. Then, with one final smile, he disappeared into the dormitory.

The realization that he had seen Brocard for the last time made Gonard lower his head in sorrow. Then, taking a deep breath, he turned and limped back to the courtyard where Itsa and the medtech were waiting for him.

* * * * *

"We must travel southwest," the medtech explained to the lay brothers. He took a stick and drew in the dust next to the corral. "This is where we came from. Here is where we are now." He sketched jagged lines for mountains and hills, long lines for rivers and streams. "It would be my intention to travel directly." He drew a straight line from the chapter to the Domains, through uncharted territory.

One of the brothers shook his head. "High mountains, treacherous land," he explained. "And, sometimes, raiders." He took the stick and drew a line south, then west. "Much better to go like this."

"It is perhaps a wiser route," the medtech acknowledged. "It has the advantage of familiarity, as we have already followed much of it to come here."

Gonard stepped back. "It'll take us past the City." The tall green towers, the personality that existed at the heart of that beauty and to which he had nearly lost himself . . . "Is there no other way?"

"Travelers have nothing to fear from the place of Singers," the lay brother said. "Brothers have been given shelter there."

"Ya can take it, dragon." Itsa punched his leg. "Just keep mummer 'round her."

The lay brothers placed packs full of dry travel bread and smoked meat behind the coursairs' saddles, hung several waterskins from the saddlehorns. Itsa pulled herself into the saddle, the medtech copying her action with far less grace. With final farewells, Gonard led them from the chapter.

The first few days seemed to pass by very slowly. Gonard missed the talking, even the arguing, that had often marked their journeys together. But as he had expected, the coursairs reacted unfavorably whenever he came too near, rolling their eyes and rearing in alarm. Nor could they be tethered too far from the campsite at night, for the lay brothers had warned him that spring was the time when the traders traveled the wastes—and raiders seeking easy prey were often not far behind.

But after a week, the beasts seemed to grow somewhat accustomed to Gonard. He was able to venture near his companions at night, though he still kept his distance by day. Itsa cocked her head at him one night as the coursairs snorted in the darkness. "Ugly don't like ya, does he?" she commented.

"Ugly?" Gonard repeated.

Itsa grinned. "Yeah. Good name, ain't it? Whatcha name yours, tech?"

The medtech stared at her. "It is inappropriate to ascribe names to simple animals."

"Just jealous 'cause ya ain't got one." Itsa tore off a piece of travel bread, chewed it loudly. "Dragon's named himself. Why don'tcha do the same?"

"It is inappropriate to ascribe names to manmade devices." The medtech shifted his gaze to Gonard. "It is equally inappropriate for a manmade creature to name itself."

Gonard's ears flicked the criticism aside. "My father gave me the first name. I chose the second."

"It may not be to your benefit to give two names when you face the Council," the medtech said.

"Yeah, that's right," Itsa broke in. "Only Lord Cits get two names. Everyone else's got a name and a number."

"I am now Gonard Michel," Gonard said calmly, but he felt a twinge of nervousness. Would he be as confident when ringed by a Council full of hostile faces? "What I am, I am. I have to be true to myself."

"Yeah?" Itsa challenged. She rocked back on her heels, gazed up at him. "Then sing somethin' to us."

Gonard obligingly sank to his hindquarters, lifted his head, and broke into song. He chose one of Lybrand's compositions, twelve voices soaring from his throat. There was a release in song; he felt tension lifting from his shoulders, aches easing from his chest. The song finally came to an end, one last, long, high note echoing through the trees.

Gonard turned his head to look at Itsa. She snapped her mouth shut. "Thought ya weren't ever goin' to sing again."

"I've changed my mind."

"Right." She gave him a sidelong glance. "Just 'member ya've got other promises to keep. And ya owe me one, 'cause I came for ya, this time. Right?"

"Right," Gonard said solemnly. "I shall remember." But her grin made his chest feel light.

The medtech grunted and shuffled off into the darkness. Gonard looked a question to Itsa, but she only shrugged. Anger, Gonard thought, envy, despair. Does the medtech envy us? Anger I have felt, and envy, but never despair.

"Chill it, dragon," Itsa advised. "He ain't worth it."

"Perhaps not to you."

"Not to hisself, neither." She scowled at the remnant of travel bread, then shoved it into her saddlebags. "So don't waste the thinkin' space."

But Gonard could not help looking into the night, wondering at the darker depths within his brother creation. Does he ever envy me, he wondered, that I have so much, and he so little?

* * * * *

Itsa leaned back against the tree. Down the hill and across the valley, all but a smudge in the distance, was the camp of Naylor's tribe. Was Rygor with them? she wondered. Had he joined the hunt, leaving Rydeth behind in the settlement? Or had he stayed with her?

Why do ya care? she asked herself. He wasn't the great love of yar life, after all. Sure, he was friendly, and great in bed, and ya really liked his kid, and—

She deliberately ended that line of thought. No point goin' on 'bout what ain't, she told herself. Ya're goin' with the dragon to help him get what he wants, and the medtech what he wants. Then maybe it'll be Itsa's turn.

Footsteps swept through the grass behind her. "I ain't told him, ya jig," Itsa said without turning around. "He don't jig 'bout that man ya killed."

"Why have you not spoken to him regarding the incident? I expected you would tell him at once."

" 'Cause he's goin' to have 'nuff to think 'bout, what with him facin' the Lord Cits and everythin'." Now Itsa moved to face him. "But ya watch yar step, 'bot. 'Cause I am. I'm watchin' ya."

"That is a comforting reassurance," the medtech said dryly.

He shuffled back up the slope, grass snapping under his heavy tread. He's in the winter of his life, Itsa found herself thinking. He's not got much longer to go, now. And what about me?

She sighed, looked down. Among the bright green of the young grass, small flowers pushed through, tumbling sparks of blues and yellows down the hill. I'm far from gone. She smiled. Winter's over, and I'm still here. There's lots I can still do. See the dragon through to his Lord Cit, and then we'll see what happens.

With a new lightness to her step, she headed back to their camp.

* * * * *

Hills and forests, valleys and glens, the land passed steadily under their feet as the days passed by overhead. Gonard marveled at the speed with which old, familiar landmarks came and went. He was beginning to appreciate the coursairs; the beasts could keep up with his pace better than a human. Or even a medtech.

Halfway through their journey, they passed through the hunting lands of what must now be Naylor's tribe. Gonard tried not to think of the lazy evenings by the cooking fires, Ranalf pontificating with easy familiarity. If only he had been able to sing, then. But he had never really wanted a home with either the tribe or the settlement.

But now the passing kilometers were bringing them steadily closer to the place he gladly would have called home. The coursairs, which had begun to accept his presence, sensed his tension and once again bared their teeth if he came too near.

"Can we not go over the hills?" he asked the medtech one night.

The medtech looked up from the fire he was attempting to prod into life. "The most direct route to the Domains requires passage across the hills. The steep inclines would, however, prove difficult for our mounts to climb, and thus slow our journey. The pass into the valley will lead us to level terrain through which we can easily complete our journey."

"He jives all that, tech." Itsa expertly drew her knife through the rabbit's fur. Gonard turned his gaze away from the dull, dead eyes that stared mutely at the now flickering fire. "He just don't like the City gettin' to him. Do ya, dragon?"

"She cannot touch me," Gonard said stoutly, "unless I sing near her." He flicked his left ear nervously, the crystal earring dancing in response.

"Then whatcha antsed 'bout?"

"I may wish to sing to her."

"Ya won't go to her," Itsa said confidently.

"Why not?"

She grinned up at him. " 'Cause ya'd have to leave me."

Gonard swallowed words that he knew she wouldn't welcome. "And I've given you a promise."

" 'Xactly."

But Gonard found it hard to share Itsa's confidence as they toiled up the hill above the City. His pace slackened, forcing his companions to halt their mounts several times to allow him to catch up with them.

Finally they crested the hill, the trees parting to reveal the City glistening below. The medtech did not halt his beast, but urged it onward, down the slope to the plains. But Itsa halted, her shoulders stiff as she stared down at the City. "All right, dragon," she said without turning around. "Do whatcha gotta do."

Gonard halted several paces away, mindful of the coursair's agitation. Then he allowed himself to look down at the City, drinking in the sight of her pure towers, her beautiful walls. "I think—I think I loved her," he said quietly.

Itsa laughed, a harsh, brittle sound. "Took ya a long time to jig *that*."

"The City does not possess the capacity to return such an emotion," said the medtech, riding back to Itsa's side.

"Why not?" Itsa challenged. " 'Cause she's made from crystal, not flesh 'n' blood?"

"The medtech is right," Gonard said, cutting through the medtech's reply. "She . . . cannot . . . love. Not yet." He took a deep breath. "But that does not affect how I feel."

He began to sing, reaching across the distance to the City. The crystal in his ear began to tingle as she turned her attention to him, attracted by his song. There was a moment's incomprehension; then she located her memories of him.

Gonard felt his control begin to slip at her touch. But he had deliberately chosen one of Lybrand's compositions to sing, rather than one of the songs she favored. As he had expected, the strangeness of his song was a block between them.

He felt her puzzlement at his song, her query as to why he had returned. Was he now ready to become a part of her?

Gonard brought a note of regret into his voice. His experiences since leaving her had only strengthened his need to be a separate entity. He could not sacrifice himself to her as her other Singers had done.

Sacrifice? she repeated. His song wavered as she drew him effortlessly into herself, through her glittering mind. There was a crystal for every Singer who had ever served her, and all the humans' memories were preserved forever. Their essences continued to exist, long after the deaths of the bodies that had once housed them. There was even a crystal for Gonard, in which the City housed her memories of him. There was still a place prepared for him. Waiting.

I cannot, he repeated firmly.

Not for now, she acknowledged. *But part of you will always be with me.*

Part of me will always be with you, he agreed, his voice trembling with some of his old longing.

She brushed his mind one last time, with something close to affection. Then she was gone.

Gonard let his song trail away, took a deep breath as he returned to the hilltop. A breeze blew past, tickling Itsa's musty scent past his nostrils. He opened his eyes, finding her standing beside him, concern etching lines across her face. "Dragon?"

"She hasn't . . . taken me," he said slowly.

She nodded. "Right." She strode back to her coursair,

tethered roughly to a tree. The beast, red eyes calm, eyed Gonard as she mounted.

Gonard moved slowly toward the coursair. Neither it nor the medtech's mount reacted, allowing him to step between them. My singing? he wondered. Whatever the reason, he was grateful.

* * * * *

They set the coursairs free at the desert's edge, leaving discarded bridles and saddles in a pile. The beasts stood stupidly beside them for a long moment, seemingly unable to comprehend their new freedom. Gonard finally sighed. He took a deep breath and growled at the animals. With wild snorts, they turned and galloped away, disappearing into the forest.

"Smelly things," Itsa said, hoisting her saddlebag over her shoulder.

"Considering your own unsavory state," commented the medtech, "I would not have thought your nasal faculties sufficiently acute to distinguish between your scent and theirs."

Itsa shrugged. "Least I'm not fallin' apart, 'bot."

"I shall continue my existence until such time as my duties have been fulfilled."

"And what're those?"

"We should start," Gonard interjected before the medtech could answer. Hearing him lie made Gonard uneasy. "It'll be night soon."

"We're ready for the desert this time." Itsa patted her saddlebags, liquid sloshing inside the waterskins.

The sunset reddened the sky before them as they started out across the shifting sands. They walked for a while in silence. The moon rose, its bright disk casting monotone light onto their path. "When we reach the Barrier," Gonard asked the medtech, "how will we get through it?"

Itsa snorted. "Great job, dragon. Wondered when ya'd finally ask that."

"It seemed appropriate at the time of our departure to prepare for our eventual return." Gonard noted once again how weary the medtech's voice sounded. "I programmed an area of gradually increasing weakness in the Barrier. We will be able to return through that portion."

"Gradually increasing weakness?" Gonard repeated, alarmed. "How large will it grow?"

"The Barrier will eventually be broken down, should I not alter the programming shortly."

"Let the fardlin' thing come down," Itsa said bitterly. "There's loads of room for them outside. Room for them and everyone stuck at the bottom of asteroid mines, coughin' their lungs out for nothin'. All this great talk of one day gettin' us all back to Earth—they could of done it ages ago."

"A very emphatic speech for an Outler, pledged to consider the needs of no one but herself."

The moonlight caught in Itsa's eyes as she flashed a glance at Gonard, striding between her and the medtech. "Yeah. Right."

"The Domains are at any rate doomed," the medtech continued. "The growth of this desert is the result of the drain on the water table to allow the Citizens' gardens to flourish. Soon the sources of water will run dry."

* * * * *

They halted near dawn. Gonard remained standing, spreading his wings to provide shade. Even the medtech sat down, sheltered from the intense heat. "Would have to be shattin' spring again," Itsa said once, mopping up sweat with one grimy sleeve.

"It is incumbent on us to return at this time," the

medtech responded from under the other wing. "Outstanding petitions to the Council may be challenged after the period of two years. We have not much time left."

"Petition?" Gonard twisted his neck to look under his wing. "What petition?"

"It is evident that you do not utilize your memory to its full capabilities. I informed you at the outset that Citizen Reefe had filed a petition to the Council, declaring that the charge of murder against you must be dropped. The petition stated that you were merely defending your existence. A necessary adjunct to such a petition was the declaration that you possess the necessary soul to defend. Citizen Reefe furthermore placed a restraint upon the domain of Lord Citizen Rumfus Max. You are potentially the Master's heir, and if you become a Citizen, you will be able to lay claim to his domain."

"I would inherit the domain?" Gonard was suddenly filled with a longing to return to the place that had been his only real home. But—would Itsa be willing to come with him? Or would she try to prove her own claim and become a Citizen, then eventually a Lady Citizen, with a domain of her own?

"It is the law of the Domains. If any Lord or Lady Citizen leaves an heir of the body—"

Itsa snorted. "Yeah, the dragon's a 'xact image of his dad."

"—that heir inherits the domain. The heir would still be required to first become a Citizen. I, however, anticipate that you will have little difficulty passing the Theological Examination."

"Then what stops the Lord Cits from havin' litters to set up after them?" Itsa asked.

The medtech said grimly, "Before any man or woman is permitted to become a Citizen, he or she is arbitrarily sterilized."

There was a long moment of silence under Gonard's left

wing. He twisted his head around, concerned by Itsa's silence. He found her staring down at her hands. "Oh."

"Surely you must have been aware of the price you must pay to come to Earth."

"No. Don't tell ya those things."

"The edict was devised by the earliest Lord Citizens. They feared unrest should unlanded Citizens begin to breed."

"And if I prove my claim and pass the T. E.?"

"It will be my dubious pleasure to sterilize you."

Itsa shrugged. "Wasn't goin' to have brats anyroads." But there was a note of bitterness in her voice that startled Gonard. Even after all this time, he thought, I still don't fully know her.

They continued their journey as the sun set. Gonard found himself taking deep breaths, filling his lungs with the scent of hot sand. So different from the artificial smells of the Citadel, the staleness of air consumed and exhaled repeatedly over centuries. Why am I going back there? he wondered. Because you owe it to the medtech, he answered himself. Because you should give Itsa her chance for a better life. Because you haven't found a home anywhere else.

Dawn was warming the sky behind them when the Barrier came into sight. By unspoken agreement they continued their march, finally halting just before the hazy, blue-black mist as the desert wavered under the sun overhead.

Itsa swung her saddlebags to the ground, removing only her knife and a waterskin. Then she hefted a handful of sand, threw it at the Barrier. The grains bounced off the mist as if it were a wall, falling back to the ground at their feet. She glanced at the medtech. "Looks pretty solid to me."

"The entryway will be not far from here," the medtech said. "I programmed the weakness to form near our original exit." He trudged along the Barrier. Itsa glanced at Gonard, then shrugged and followed him.

The medtech halted after a few minutes. "The entryway is now before you."

Itsa studied the mist dubiously. "Where? I don't see it."

"I can see it," Gonard assured her. "The difference shows up on the ultraviolet spectrum."

"Human sight is remarkably deficient," the medtech agreed.

Itsa crossed her arms. "Well, since ya can see it, ya can try first, tech. And don'tcha take a breath this time."

The medtech studied her for a moment. Then he turned and stepped into the Barrier, the mist swirling back into place behind him.

"Right, one down." Itsa looked up at Gonard. "Hope it's big 'nuff for ya."

"It is." Gonard slid his tail forward, lifting the disk to Itsa. "Hold on to me."

"It wasn't *me* who breathed the stuff last time," she reminded him haughtily. "My head stayed on straight."

"I only did so because I was looking for you." He nudged her with his tail tip. "Take it."

She obeyed reluctantly, scowling as he wrapped the disk around her right hand. He took a deep breath, glanced at her. At her nod, he limped into the Barrier.

He was prepared for the voices this time. What he was not expecting was the stench of rotting meat, wafting past his snout at every step. He forced his nostril slits to shut, hoped that Itsa had not gagged on the smell and taken a breath. Her hand still clutched his tail; he picked up his pace, tendrils of mist swirling away from his thrashing legs.

The medtech was waiting for them as they broke through the Barrier. Gonard exhaled explosively, trying to rid his nostrils of the stench. Itsa unwrapped her hand and sneezed loudly. "Shat, tech, didcha have to make it *smell?*"

"It was my intention to create a portion through which we could return. It was not my intention to permit any another creature access to the Domains, so I considered it appropriate to construct a deterrent."

"Ya could of warned us." Itsa unstopped her waterskin and took a deep drink. "Okay, now what?"

Gonard looked around with interest. They were back in a domain forest. But he had never before realized how hazy the Barrier turned the sunlight, making the human-planted forest seem dark and gloomy when compared to the natural ones through which they had traveled. "Do we march to the Citadel now?" he asked, suddenly longing to be back in a real forest, far away from here.

"It would be my suggestion that I venture on to the Citadel on my own."

"Ya want us to wait here," Itsa said. "Why?"

"I am the least likely of our trio to be detained by guards upon my reappearance." The medtech shifted his gaze to Gonard. "It is my expectation that Citizen Reefe will be sympathetic to supporting your return to appear before the Council and there lodge a claim for you to the domain of Rumfus Max."

"Not prove he's got a soul?"

The dull eyes flicked her a glance. "The claim is the manner by which Gonard Michel will challenge the Council for a ruling on that matter. To gain the domain, he must establish that he is the rightful heir. To be the heir, he must prove that he possesses a soul."

"You've still not told me how I can do that," Gonard said.

"I have not, nor will I." The medtech met his gaze calmly. "It has been my task to devise a means by which the authenticity of your claim can be established. I have completed this task, but the success of the operation is dependent upon certain aspects remaining unknown to you."

"So whatcha're sayin' is, ya're hidin' somethin'."

The medtech studied her for a moment. "Yes."

His short reply seemed to startle Itsa into silence. Gonard stepped closer to her as the medtech trudged away. I must trust him, he told himself. He only wants the same as I do—to prove that I have a soul. But Gonard was aware of Itsa's scowl as she sat down on the dark earth.

CHAPTER 15

He was coming to the end of his energy reserves. The medtech knew this with a calm awareness. He had calculated long ago that his energy stores would be more rapidly depleted outside the Domains than in the undemanding duties he had faced in his laboratory. The need to adjust his programming after the brush with the Changewinds had further diminished his reserves, and he had calmly accepted the inevitable shortening of his existence. But what he could not accept, would not permit, was a cessation in functioning before he had seen his Master exonerated, his desertion justified. Nothing must be allowed to interfere with that driving goal. Nothing.

Do you not know, Gonard Michel, of the original destiny for the glittering brain that you possess? he thought. It was once meant to be my own, before it outgrew the Master's initial designs. I was left behind as a decoy, to detract from his greater heresy, his more important plans. So, I will know if he was successful in his intentions. I *will* know, at any cost.

But determination did not ease the stiffness of overworn joints or restore energy levels. The Master might have used less precious materials for the dragon's frame, but his second creation had benefited from expenditure on a self-sustainable energy source, and a self-repairing structure. Gonard Michel had been designed for permanence.

He is the more important experiment. The medtech stepped around a fallen branch, the trees starting to thin as he reached the end of the domain. *When he proves that he indeed bears a soul, all will be justified.*

The forest ended abruptly, a short swath of grass leading up to the formal gardens marking the surface of the Citadel. A few Citizens were walking along the tiled paths. The medtech ignored them. A few clipped syllables uttered to the main entrance opened a ramp to the corridors below.

As he had anticipated, he was able to progress down three corridors before a half-dozen guards met him, their hands ready on blunt-nosed weapons. "State your name and your purpose, stranger," the leader ordered.

The medtech slowly analyzed each of the men and women, deciding that entry standards to Earth had plunged yet further. "I am known as a medical technician, which adequately expresses both my position and my purpose. A name has not been given to me."

"The robot medtech," a short woman said, turning her head to their leader. "He disappeared several years ago."

The man nodded, his hand tightening on his gun. "I hereby take you into custody in the name of the Council of Lord Citizens."

"Is it permissible to enquire as to the grounds for custody?" the medtech asked mildly.

"You disappeared at the same time as that other robot."

"Both events occurred in the same time frame," the medtech acknowledged. "However, no charges were ever brought against the medical technician."

"Must've been," the man asserted, glancing at one of his subordinates. She strode away.

"I assure you, there are none." Three corridors had been sufficient for him to consult an information point, easily breaking through the computer access codes to check through Council records.

The woman trotted back a few minutes later. "He's right," she reported, breathing heavily. "There's nothing against him."

The leader chewed his lower lip. "But there still might be a connection with that other—thing."

"It is apparent that you have no justifiable reason to detain me," said the medtech. "Nor do I find your company enlightening. Kindly therefore withdraw yourselves from my path and allow me to continue my quest in peace."

"Maybe you could use a guide," the short woman said quickly, with a glance at her leader. "The Citadel might have changed since your—departure."

The medtech gave her an appraising glance. Perhaps one of this sorry lot had potential after all. He bent his head gravely to her. "A guide may be appropriate. Perhaps you would kindly lead me to the chambers of Lord Citizen Reefe Grant." He flicked his eyes over the leader. "There is no need to further inconvenience your companions."

With ill-grace, the leader stood aside, his subordinates milling around him. The medtech's guide strode forward confidently. As he expected, the remainder of the guards followed at what they assumed was a discreet distance. How will they react, he wondered, when I bring Gonard Michel into their midst? There was a crude human phrase for the reaction, but his memory was beginning to decay. The term was somehow connected to a loss of control over urinary functions. . . .

"Here you are, sir," the woman said, cutting through the medtech's musings. She palmed the door comm.

"Lord Citizen Reefe Grant is currently resident," an artificial voice responded. "Who seeks an audience with the Lord Citizen?"

"The mechanical medical technician," the woman

responded, her eyes meeting the medtech's.

There was a pause while the door consulted with the Lord Citizen. Then the voice replied, "Lord Citizen Reefe Grant will grant an audience to the medical technician. He may enter. His escort is dismissed."

If the woman did not welcome the command, her expression betrayed no sign. She stepped to one side as the door slid open.

The medtech had never entered the chambers of a Lord Citizen before. Those he had treated had always come to his laboratory. He took in with a quick glance the colorful wall-hangings, the thick carpet, the well-padded chairs. A computer console was set into the wall above a utilitarian-looking desk, and a few books were set in glass display cases.

The Lord Citizen came into the room, a door shutting silently behind him. "I have been fortunate to never have required your services," he said, picking up a glass from a wall shelf. "Which is just as well, bearing in mind that they have not been available for some time."

"I am not listed as the property of any Lord Citizen," the medtech replied evenly. "Nor was I ever designed to replace the human medical technicians available in the Citadel." He paused for a moment, then added, "It is not usual for you to question the assumption of liberties, my Lord Grant. I restored a dragon's leg at your behest, when you were no more than an unlanded Citizen."

The man studied him for a moment. Then he relaxed into a smile. "Very well, medtech. What is the purpose of your visit?"

"I have come to act as the representative of the aforementioned dragon."

"The dragon?" Interest suddenly sharpened Reefe's face. He strode over to a collection of chairs grouped around a clear table. "Take a seat," he said, flopping into one himself.

The medtech turned, but otherwise remained where he

was. "I prefer to stand." To sit and then stand again wasted precious energy. "It may be advisable for you to remain seated. We have much to discuss."

Reefe took a sip from his glass. "About the dragon."

"Lord Citizen Rumfus Max sought to create him with the capacity to develop a soul. You filed a petition in his defense two years ago on the grounds that he might indeed possess a soul, in which case he could plead self-defense in the murder of Rumfus Max." The medtech paused, but the man seemed to be following his reasoning. "After the passage of the same two years, the dragon feels prepared to prove that he indeed possesses a soul, and to declare himself heir to the domain of Lord Max."

"The robot," Reefe mused. "A Citizen."

"Lord Citizen Gonard Michel."

Reefe gave him a sharp glance. "Lord Max gave him two names?"

"He was given only the first name by his creator. The second was a recent addition that he himself chose."

"Somewhat premature, don't you think?" The chair creaked as the Lord Citizen shifted his weight, freeing a portion of his trapped green robe. "Most Citizens are courteous enough to await the granting of a domain before taking on a second name."

The medtech allowed himself enough energy to produce a small smile. "His actions may not be so much precipitous as confident."

The man stroked a day's growth of brown beard. "Where is—Gonard—now?"

"Gonard Michel has returned to the Domains." The medtech straightened, joint grating against joint. "It is his request that you support him as he seeks to gain his rightful inheritance of the domain once held by his father, Rumfus Max, entailing an application for Citizenship and the dismissal of the charge against him."

"His father." Reefe's gaze wandered away. "I filed that petition in a moment of brash rebellion. The Lord Citizens appeared so sure of themselves, so smug, so self-righteous. And the dragon almost appeared more alive than any of them, holding his head to their scorn despite his wounds. I could not allow them to destroy him."

"And you now have your own domain to possess, your own luxuries to consider," the medtech said dryly.

Reefe winced. "I must consider the challenges my fellow Council members will raise. Where will these applications end? Who will be next to press a claim—you? Other creations by Lord Max?"

"None of the other creations of Lord Citizen Rumfus Max possesses a soul." And I will not exist for much longer, he added silently. "Shall I return him to be destroyed, my Lord Citizen?"

Reefe clasped his hands behind his head, leaned back in his chair. "How is he, after two years?"

"Not as I am, my lord. His wing has been restored to him, and he has matured considerably."

"I will propose to the Council that the robot known as Gonard Michel should be permitted to return to the Domains," Reefe said finally. "I will state that I believe he possesses a soul and must be given opportunity to prove this, so that he may lay claim to his father's estate. What proof can he offer?"

"It would be my suggestion that he be permitted to establish this by his manner and actions." Reefe took a long gulp of his drink, and the medtech waited until he was finished before continuing. "The Council should allow him to wander freely through the Citadel and the Domains, engaging all Lord Citizens in discussions so that they may satisfy themselves that he is more than a simple mechanical device."

Reefe placed his glass onto the table. "You seem certain

of success."

"I am." Through means you could not fathom, the medtech added inwardly.

"The petition will require a seconder." Reefe smiled. "A new addition to Council procedures. My brashness was not welcomed in all quarters."

The medtech gave him a nod. The change fit into his plans admirably. "I will find the necessary Lord Citizen."

"Only ensure that the dragon does not harm anyone in the Domains." Reefe stood, signaling that the audience was drawing to a close. "I know that his programming is unlike yours. You at least cannot harm humans."

The medtech bent his head, deciding not to correct the man's misapprehension. "I shall return with Gonard Michel tomorrow morning. This will provide you with sufficient time to prepare your petition, I presume."

"It will. Just find that seconder."

"And will you arrange an honor guard to meet us, my lord? The dragon must not be seen to return as a criminal."

Reefe waved his hand irritably. "Yes, yes, I will see to it."

The medtech nodded, then strode to the door. No guards were visible as he returned to the corridor; they obeyed the commands of a Lord Citizen, as they had been trained. Just as well. His next call could have caused suspicion.

A comm booth was only a few corridors away. The opaque door shut around him as the screen lit to await his instructions. The medtech rapped out a complex code. As he had expected, access was denied. It took him several attempts, but he was shortly through to the private comm.

"What do you want now?" a harsh voice demanded from a dark screen. A light came on, revealing a round face, reddened eyes blinking away sleep. "You're not Marion."

"I am the medical technician—"

"How'd you get my private link? Is that woman spreading herself around?" The Lord Citizen dragged a bare arm across his eyes. "Go 'way. Had my last physical ten days ago. Got nothing I want to talk to you about."

The medtech smiled slightly. "Does the return of the dragon not interest you?"

The man had leaned forward to cut the connection. Now he leaned back, looking at the medtech with interest. His face assumed the same eager look as when he had stood in the Council, demanding that Gonard be released to him. "R. M.'s last one?"

"The same, Lord Citizen Merril Lange. I have returned the dragon to the Domains. Would my lord have an interest in a final Hunt?"

"Very much." The man leaned forward, his tone confidential. "Gets in the blood, having a good chase. Better than sex."

Having never experienced either activity, the medtech declined to judge. "I believe the Hunts have also proved successful in providing you with leverage over other Lord Citizens."

Merril shrugged. "Everyone likes a good Hunt. What's your price, 'bot?"

The medtech flicked through potential replies, this being one question he had not anticipated. "Only to be permitted to return to my laboratory, my lord, with a full pardon for my part in the escape of the dragon."

Merril's eyes narrowed. "No charges were ever brought against you."

The man was more intelligent than he had predicted. "I am aware of that, my lord. I have, however, already been subjected to harassment by guards upon my return. They certainly suspect there to be a connection between the dragon and myself. One Lord Citizen has already dismissed their attentions; I would request your secondment of his command. Then I will be able to return to my duties in peace."

"If that's what you want." Merril shrugged. "Guess you 'bots can't think of doing anything but slaving away."

"I have been programmed to serve," the medtech agreed. Never mind that he had long ago altered that portion of his programming. "It will also be necessary for you to second the petition to the Council that will agree to the dragon's return to the Domains."

"Why would I want to do that?"

"I cannot lead a dragon across a half-dozen domains without his passage being noticed," the medtech explained patiently. "A petition will be presented to the Council tomorrow requesting that his claim to the domain of Lord Citizen Rumfus Max be recognized. This will of course entail the dropping of the charge against him, as well as the declaration that he possesses a soul. It will be proposed that the dragon be given the freedom of the Citadel and the Domains, so that he might have the opportunity to convince all Lord Citizens that he has a soul."

"Utter shat," Merril declared. "You expect me to agree with all that nonsense?"

"The petition will ensure that the dragon is not summarily destroyed—"

"I'll just claim it as mine again."

"And it will ease your attempts to gain him for your Hunt. He will venture into your domain to never reappear. His disappearance will not be too closely questioned. He has vanished once before."

"With that sort of a petition, lots of Lords wouldn't mind seeing it disappear," Merril mused. "Might even thank me for it. Better and better. All right, 'bot, I'll second this petition. How're you going to get the dragon to come to me?"

Never do any thinking you can convince another to do for you, the medtech thought derisively. "There is an Outler with the dragon. Approach her with an offer: if she will entice the dragon to your domain for the Hunt, you in turn will support her claim for Citizenship."

"Your request has met with my approval," the Lord Citizen declared. "Bring the dragon to the Council tomorrow. I'll send someone to speak for me."

"Yes, my lord." The medtech bowed stiffly, as far as the narrow cubicle would allow him. "I should warn you that the dragon now possesses the ability to fly."

Lord Merril shrugged. "Then I'll clip its wings. This audience has ended."

"Indeed," the medtech murmured as the screen blanked. He paused for a moment, ensuring that the conversation was permanently recorded in his circuitry. Then he broke through the security access codes to the comm records, erasing all trace of his discussion with the Lord Citizen.

* * * * *

Gonard limped through the domain forest, Itsa keeping pace to his right, the medtech on his left. The sun filtered softly through the Barrier and the green-leafed trees, casting faint shadows over the dark, moist earth. Moist, Gonard thought. He could almost sense the vast underground pumps, draining water from the earth to feed the Lord Citizens' gardens. Are the Domains doomed?

He forced his strides to remain steady as the Citadel drew nearer. Prove I have a soul. Become a Lord Citizen. I don't want to be a Lord Citizen. I only want a home of my own, somewhere to live with Itsa, if she will come with me. Why am I going to the Citadel?

Because the medtech has asked me to. Gonard sighed, drawing a quick glance from Itsa. We both owe him so much. How could I refuse him his own chance at peace?

The trees parted, dropped away. Gonard welcomed the brush of grass against his feet, a brief respite before he stepped onto the tiled paths of the Citadel's formal gardens.

He stopped, waited. A dozen guards surfaced, a platform raising them to the garden. They quickly formed a straight line and marched down the wide path, boots clacking in unison against stone.

"I won't wear a muzzle," Gonard warned the medtech.

"They come to serve as an honor guard," the medtech assured him.

Gonard said nothing, though he didn't like the way one of the men kept rubbing the handle of his sheathed weapon. The guards halted several meters away. Gonard's nostrils slitted, the sour smell of the guards' fear reminding him of what he was returning to face.

A tall woman stepped from their ranks. "You are Gonard Michel, descendant of Lord Citizen Rumfus Max?"

"I am," Gonard affirmed.

"Gonard Michel, you come to be presented to the Council as a petition is read regarding the domain of Lord Citizen Rumfus Max. We have been sent to be your escort. However, we are charged with the safety of the Lord Citizens, and we ask you to swear by the one you hold to be holy that you will not harm, by . . ."

"By tooth, claw, or fire," one of the guards suggested as the woman faltered.

"By tooth, claw, or fire," the woman continued, "any of the denizens of the Domains."

Gonard dipped his head. "I swear, by all that I hold holy, that I will not intentionally harm any denizen of the Domains."

The woman frowned at the amended words. Then she shrugged. The guards did not noticeably relax at his declaration, Gonard noted, and he suspected that they didn't put any trust in it. The woman returned to her place, and the guards broke into two groups. Six turned on their heels and led the way across the gardens, while the remainder followed behind Gonard's tail, a bit too close for comfort, as their boots narrowly missed the disk.

A portion of the path slowly retracted ahead of them, exposing a sloping access to the levels below. The guards marched down without hesitation, the tenor of their footsteps changing to a higher pitch as they left stone for metal. Gonard took one deep, almost desperate breath of fresh air. Then he was scrabbling down the smooth slope, claws screeching against the metal as the lit ceilings of the Citadel closed over his head like a tomb.

"Shat, forgot how much it pongs," Itsa muttered beside him.

Gonard slowly released his breath, exchanging it for the much recycled atmosphere of the Citadel. The smell was worse than he remembered, the lights dimmer. I have seen grander places than this, he thought, remembering the glowing towers of the City, the intricate windows of the cathedral. The Citadel no longer awes me.

There was no waiting outside the Council chamber this time. The guard opened the doors at their approach. It is imperative that you appear calm and confident, the medtech had told Gonard last night. You are a Lord Citizen's heir, coming to claim your own. So Gonard obediently held his head high as he followed the row of guards through the entranceway, emerging finally into the bright lights of the chamber beyond.

A Lord Citizen stood as Gonard and his companions halted, the guards forming a circle around them, facing inward. "I request the Council's leave to present a petition."

The Lady Speaker inclined her head. "The Council recognizes you, Lord Citizen Reefe Grant."

"I thank the Council." The green-robed man glanced down at the note-screen in his hand, then raised his head to give Gonard a quick smile. Gonard wrinkled his nose in return, recognizing him as the friendly Citizen he had met once before. "Two years ago, the descendant of Lord Citizen

Rumfus Max stood before this Council. At that time, a ruling was made for his destruction. I presented a petition to provide him with a defense against the charge of murder. Will the Council accept that petition as read, my Lady Speaker?"

The old woman swept a glance around the chamber. There was no visible dissent. "The petition is accepted as read, Lord Reefe."

The Lord Citizen bowed to her. He readjusted his cloak, then continued, "A temporary stay of execution was then granted, prolonged by the subsequent disappearance of the accused. He has, however, appeared before us today. My Lady Speaker, I would request that it be noted that he has submitted himself before the Council under his own free will."

Several Lord Citizens stirred. Gonard was puzzled for a moment; then the reason for their discomfort came to him. Robots were not expected to possess wills of their own—that was an attribute of humans. But I, too, have a soul, Gonard thought, straightening under their gazes. And I've come here to prove it—somehow.

The Lady Speaker waited, but no one protested aloud. "The Council has so noted."

Reefe bent his head again. "I present another petition, my Lady Speaker, in acknowledgment that my original petition has nearly expired. My Lord and Lady Citizens, I petition for the descendant of Lord Citizen Rumfus Max to be acknowledged as the heir of his body and thus also heir to his lands and title, and to be declared and honored as Lord Citizen Gonard Michel."

A loud murmur went around the room, swirling up the domed roof. One Lord Citizen leapt to his feet, arms waving wildly in protest. "Lord Reefe, you cannot be serious! That—that *creature*—is not even human!"

Reefe smiled. "Not in form, perhaps. But that does not

mean he cannot possess a soul."

More Lord Citizens rose to their feet, voices raised. "Silence!" commanded one strong voice above them all. The Lady Speaker stood, repeating her order. "Silence, all my lords and ladies. Please be seated. Lord Reefe, continue your petition."

"Thank you, my lady." Reefe glanced down at his notes again. "Consider this, my lords and ladies. Consider Lord Citizen Rumfus Max, one of the great technologists of this age. Proof of his early ability is illustrated in the maniod standing below you." Gonard felt the medtech straighten as Reefe pointed toward him. "Consider also the nature of Lord Max, that he chose to live in solitude deep within his domain. Consider this combination: a man possessing unique knowledge that he felt compelled to pass on, yet unable to long abide contact with other humans. So, what could be the solution to such a dilemma?

"Lord Max devised therefore an heir, one to whom he could confide his knowledge without the need to accommodate the difference of another human personality. Not, at least, at first. For while the brain would require sufficient complexity to contain a man's knowledge, so would capacity be required to permit the development of personality—and a soul. Full well did Lord Max realize that his heir could not be Lord Citizen after him if he did not possess a soul."

Gonard's ears twitched, bemused by Reefe's argument. The Master hadn't created him to be his heir, had he?

"It was with this understanding that Gonard Michel was raised," Reefe continued. "It was for this reason that, when Lord Max's mind finally broke under the strain of his brilliance and he threatened his heir's life, Gonard Michel found it his painful duty to defend his existence. After two years in mourning for that necessary act, Gonard Michel now feels himself ready to claim his Citizenship and his domain, and to continue the work of Lord Citizen Rumfus Max, his creator, and his father."

But it's not like that at all, Gonard thought. He stepped forward, preparing to protest. The medtech's arm shot out, clenched a handful of skin and scales on Gonard's left leg. Gonard, startled, glanced down at the tense, pale face, the dull eyes widened in wordless warning.

"I conclude, my lords and ladies, with the request that you give consideration to the appointment of Gonard Michel as Lord Citizen, with all the rights and obligations given thereto."

Reefe sat down to a rumble of whispered discussions throughout the chamber. Now they will judge me, Gonard thought. He looked around at the many intent faces, their eyes flicking away from his own. For a moment, the white walls blurred, giving way to yellow stones, the floor underneath made of cobbled rock. I have stood to be judged before, he recalled, blinking away the memory of the settlement. He straightened, lifted his head high. I proved myself once; I can do it again, if I have to.

The Lord Citizen who had stood in protest before came to his feet again. "An intriguing story, Lord Reefe. But I am certain that no Citizen would accept such a blasphemous proposition—a mechanical creature possessing a soul? You insult the Ultimate."

Reefe smiled, but remained seated. "Is a soul installed by the Ultimate at birth? Or, as is taught in my School, is a soul developed only by the maturing of a personality?"

"And you think that this robot has one?"

"I cannot say, Lord Lanard. I cannot claim the honor of Gonard Michel's acquaintance, though I hope to rectify this lack as soon as possible. Our Schools may differ in the definition of a soul, but they are in broad agreement as to the signs: compassion, love, honor, bravery. I would suggest a trial period of, say, thirty days, during which time Gonard Michel is to be given the freedom of the Citadel and the Domains. Allow us to know him, and he us, so that we may judge as to whether he does indeed exhibit the attributes of a soul."

Lanard shook his head in exasperation. "Citizen Zaire," he called to a young woman across the chamber. "Surely your sponsor would wish you to disagree with this?"

The woman stood slowly, licking her lips nervously. "My Lord Merril Lange has empowered me to speak on his behalf, and in support of Lord Citizen Reefe Grant's petition."

Lord Merril Lange. Gonard barely heard the renewed murmurs encircling the chamber. For a moment, he felt anger surge through him. Claws dug deep into the soft floor as he fought to control himself. Then confusion overcame anger. Why should Merril want to support his bid to become a Lord Citizen? Didn't he want him for his Hunt?

"Does he indeed?" Lanard asked tightly. "My Lady Speaker?"

"The correct affidavits have been filed," the Speaker confirmed. "Citizen Zaire speaks for Lord Lange."

Lanard straightened. "I oppose the presented petition. Do I have a second?"

A blue-robed man stood. "I second."

Reefe and Zaire now stood as well, and all eyes went to the Speaker. She sighed, studied her clasped hands for a moment. Then she raised her head. "Gonard Michel."

Gonard met her eyes. "Yes, my lady?"

"Two options are now available to me. I can place the petition to the vote of the Council, with the majority opinion determining whether it is to be adopted. Or I may use the power vested in me by the Council to make a ruling that will allow time to consider the petition more fully."

She paused, her eyes leaving Gonard's to roam around the chamber. "Lord Reefe has suggested a trial period for his petition. I accept that the teachings of our Schools indicate that only a human can possess a soul. However, we are also taught that it is equally blasphemous to limit the Ultimate.

"Gonard Michel, it is my ruling that you are to be granted the thirty days as proposed by Lord Citizen Reefe Grant. Will you grant me your solemn oath that you will not seek to harm any resident of the Domains during this time?"

Gonard nodded. "I swear that I will not intentionally harm any resident of the Domains."

"Then I give to you the freedom of the Citadel and the Domains. It will be your responsibility to use this time in such a fashion as to prove to the Council's satisfaction that you indeed possess a soul. At the end of this trial period you are to reappear before the Council, and the petition will be placed to the vote."

Thirty days, Gonard thought. What can I do in thirty days? "My lady, how shall I prove to the Council that I have a soul?"

"That is your responsibility, Gonard Michel," she told him sternly. "However, I in turn charge each Lord and Lady Citizen to associate with Gonard Michel at some point during this period. You are not to cast your votes in ignorance, my lords and ladies. Any who cannot testify to some acquaintance with Gonard Michel will have his or her vote disallowed."

But how am I supposed to prove anything? Gonard wanted to ask again. He swallowed his questions. At the medtech's nudge, he said, "I thank you, my lords and ladies."

The guards reformed their ranks, and Gonard realized that he was now excused. He turned and limped out of the chamber, his companions beside him.

The guards left them reluctantly once they were outside the chamber doors. They don't trust me, Gonard thought. The Lord Citizens don't trust me. "How am I going to prove to them that I have a soul?" he asked the medtech.

The medtech stood a short distance away, gazing down the corridor. "I would not have returned here without a prepared course of action."

"Yeah," Itsa said, "the one ya won't spill."

"Discussion could lead to destruction." The medtech turned his head, meeting Gonard's eyes. "It is my goal to establish that you possess a soul. Do you not trust me?"

Gonard studied him for a moment, remembering the medtech finding food for Itsa, entering the City's Heart to save him. He took a deep breath, came to a decision. "I trust you. Tell me what I need to do."

"It will not be necessary for you to plan any course of action. All will become apparent to you in due course." The medtech's eyes flicked to Itsa. Despite his decision, Gonard shifted uneasily at the strange sheen suddenly lighting the dull orbs. "For the present, follow the injunction given to you by the Lady Speaker. I am overdue for a return to my laboratory."

Gonard watched the robot shuffle down the corridor, Itsa's scowl echoing the sudden feeling of foreboding creeping over him. You're only uneasy because you don't know what's going to happen, he told himself. You know that you can trust the medtech. You have to trust him.

CHAPTER 16

The medtech stood in the middle of his laboratory, analyzing his surroundings with something near to satisfaction. As he had anticipated, the laboratory had been unused since his disappearance. He had reclaimed it and now, after several days of labor, the room was nearly ready, walls and floors gleaming under the directionless light.

The door swished open. The medtech crossed over to his desk as Itsa entered. The bright silks she had acquired from some Lady Citizen suited her far less, he decided, than the practical clothes of the settlement. "Where's the dragon?" she demanded.

"It should be apparent that he is not here," the medtech said. "Why do you seek him?"

She ran a hand through her newly shortened hair. "Gotta talk to him, that's why. 'Bout that Merril bod."

So, all is proceeding according to plan. The medtech leaned over his desk, casually depressed a button. The doors closed and locked. "Why should Lord Citizen Merril Lange be of any interest to an Outler?"

"He's not," Itsa snarled. "But he's still got the dragon in his sights. He wants him for one of those Hunt things."

"It is difficult to believe that a Lord Citizen would lightly reveal such intentions to an Outler."

"Believe whatcha like, tech. He came to me." Itsa glanced around, eyes lighting on the newly acquired medical bed. She flopped onto the end, bouncing once on the mattress. Then she sat up, tucking one foot under her. "Okay, not in person—got onto my room comm, he did. Said it'd be 'advantageous' for me if I got the dragon to him for a Hunt. He'd sponsor me for the T. E. and get me my Citizenship."

"You will require the support of two Lord Citizens before you will be permitted to attempt Citizenship for a second time. The Lord Citizen could be of great assistance to you." He paused, prepared himself for the next step. "Nor have you considered whether Lord Lange could be acting in Gonard Michel's best interests."

Itsa gave him a sour look. "Yeah, and ya told him to ask me, right?"

The medtech permitted himself a small smile. "You speak with uncharacteristic aptness. The Lord Citizen did speak to you at my suggestion."

Itsa stared at him for a moment in stunned surprise. Then her face darkened. "I jigged ya're s'posed to be gettin' the dragon his Lord Cit—not tryin' to get him killed."

"My goal is as it has always been. It is imperative that I enable Gonard Michel to illustrate that he possesses a soul within the time period stipulated by the Council. Do you anticipate success by the means ascribed by the Lady Speaker?"

"No." Itsa's fingers dug into the bed sheet. "So, what've ya got planned? Or are ya still mummer on that?"

"It was necessary for me to remain silent before Gonard Michel. I will, however, require your cooperation."

Itsa slid back onto her feet. "Never fear, Itsa's here. What've ya got jigged?"

"It is necessary for you to recall that which was said in Council. 'Our Schools may differ in the definition of a soul, but they are in broad agreement as to the signs: compassion, love, honor, bravery.' It is therefore required of us to place Gonard Michel in such a position as to reveal some of these attributes."

"Don't see how takin' him to Merril is goin' to help."

"Lord Citizen Merril Lange, unbeknownst to you, has offered his assistance in establishing the Citizenship of Gonard Michel." He paused for a moment, reflecting how easy it had become to lie. "You will lead Gonard Michel to his domain for the Hunt, which Lord Lange will endeavor to make appear as realistic as possible. It will be for you to ensure that you participate in the Hunt and provide Gonard Michel with an opportunity to confront you regarding your apparent betrayal."

Her face was suddenly tense, wary. "And what's that s'posed to prove?"

"It is unnecessary for you to carry on such a pretense," the medtech said tersely. "You know that Gonard Michel holds a high regard for you, for reasons beyond my understanding."

"Yeah, maybe."

"If he is as human as I suspect him to be, he will confront you regarding your apparent betrayal. The exhibition of the appropriate emotional response will be the means by which his claim will be vindicated."

"How's the Council goin' to see all that?"

The medtech picked up a small object from his desk. He tossed it to Itsa, who caught it reflexively. "Lord Lange has placed vid-cams similar to this throughout his domain, for he records every Hunt he undertakes. The evidence will be easily obtained."

Itsa rolled the round lens in her palm. "And if Merril kills him first?"

"As I have already stated, Lord Lange's goal is not the death of Gonard Michel, but his continued existence." A twinge from his truth circuits; the medtech ruthlessly suppressed it. "It is his wish to resume his Hunts. I have informed him that our Master shared all his knowledge with Gonard Michel, and Lord Lange expects Hunt creatures to be his reward for assisting Gonard Michel to Citizenship."

Itsa said nothing for a long moment, staring thoughtfully at the floor. The medtech waited, other arguments ready should she still disagree, other courses of action held in reserve. But this was still too soon for the ultimate portion of his designs. Itsa finally moved, tossing the lens back to him. "All right. I'll take the dragon to Merril's place."

The medtech placed the lens back onto the desk, unlocking the doors at the same moment. One more step to further allay her suspicions. "It was my perception that you did not trust me."

"I don't. But the dragon does, and he jives ya better'n I do." She lifted her chin. "The dragon knows." The doors slid open at her approach, then closed behind her.

The medtech paused a moment, ensuring that the conversation was stored in the most reliable portion of his failing memory. Then he called up the comm code for the head of the medical technicians. Vidcams were still installed in this laboratory; he would have to ensure that the final scenes took place here, so that the Council could witness their proof. "Citizen Oswald," he said into the comm unit, "I wish to offer my services in the Regenerator development." Whatever he had to do to achieve it, the last part in his designs would take place here.

*   *   *   *   *

Gonard sighed. He extended a claw and carefully turned off the vid-screen. The Talmud held little interest for him today; the stories of kingdoms fighting one another thousands of years ago seemed to have little relevance to his predicament.

The door comm buzzed, announcing a visitor. "Come in," Gonard called, glad that he had been given one device that did not demand the equivalent of human fingers.

The wide door opened obediently. Itsa swaggered in, grinning widely. "Yo, dragon, whatcha doin'? Thinkin' 'gain, I wager."

Gonard stood, immediately cheered. "I was trying to."

"Oh, give it a break." She lifted a foot to slap her hand against a shiny blue boot. "Just got these from a new shipment. Wanna come see me try 'em out?"

"Where shall we go?"

"Outside, of course. Ya're 'lowed to go anywheres, 'member?" He followed her into the corridor. "We'll just pick somewheres when we get topside."

I'm permitted to enter any domain if it's to visit a Lord Citizen. But he kept the thought to himself. Lord Citizen Reefe Grant had visited him earlier, wanting an update on Gonard's progress toward proving his claim. Gonard was able to tell him how many Lord and Lady Citizens had visited him. The man had frowned when Gonard told him that otherwise the planning was being left to the medtech. "I have been studying the notes left by Lord Max," Reefe had explained. "I am concerned as to the soundness of the medical technician's programming."

But Gonard felt his spirits lift as they approached the surface. Fresh air cut through the rank of recycled, adding energy to his stride. Itsa grunted as she attempted to keep pace with him. The slope slowed him, and they emerged into the formal gardens together.

It was early morning, the Barrier breaking up the sunlight into a hazy brightness. Gonard took a deep breath of the clean air, scented with the coolness of mint from a nearby bush. He started down the path.

Itsa tugged at his tail. He stopped, turned his head back to her. "Let's go this way," she said, pointing at a grassy domain nearby.

Gonard hesitated. "I don't know whose domain that is."

Itsa shrugged. "That don't matter. Probably won't even see a hair of the Lord Cit."

"And if we do?"

"Then ya've come to see him, and I go off and play."

"All right," Gonard agreed reluctantly. He had meant to review domain boundaries before leaving the Citadel; it was one piece of knowledge his father hadn't given him. But he had had so many visitors, Lord and Lady Citizens obedient to the Lady Speaker's command. Gonard wasn't sure which was worse, those who kept near the door and said little, or those who poked and prodded his body, as if a soul were something that left a physical mark. Maybe it *would* be different if I visited them, he thought. They might feel more comfortable on their own lands.

Itsa clomped ahead in her new boots, self-importantly leading them across to the domain. Gonard wrinkled his nose, smiling at her evident pleasure in her bright clothes, tight red shirt contrasting with flaring green trousers. It was right to return for Itsa's sake, he decided. I enjoyed our journeys, but she prefers this sort of life.

"C'mon, dragon!" She jumped onto the grass and glared at him. "Ya're thinkin' again, ain'tcha?"

Gonard ducked his head. "Sorry."

"I'll getcha to stop." She marched forward. He lowered his head to her, wondering what she was planning. Her hand suddenly flashed past, patting him on the nose. "Ya're it!" she shouted, dancing away.

Gonard drew back his head. "It?"

"Yeah." She grinned. "Now ya've gotta catch and tag me, then I've gotta getcha back. Catch me if ya can, dragon!"

She ran into the domain, her boots flattening the long grass. Catch her? He could easily outrun her. She must know that.

A game. Of course, she was playing a game. He trotted several paces, giving her some extra time to place some distance between them. Then he expanded his strides into a gallop. The grass blurred past his eyes, his gaze intent on the figure running away from him.

Itsa glanced back over her shoulder. Then she put her head down and cut off at an angle. Gonard changed direction with her, claws digging deep into the moist earth. He stretched out his neck, his head drawing parallel with her own. Carefully, lest he knock her over, he brushed his muzzle against her shoulder. "It!" he shouted and quickly passed her.

She halted, her breathing loud and heavy. Gonard stopped as well, swinging around to face her. "Should of jigged," she wheezed. "Should of jigged I couldn't outrun a dragon."

"And I gave you a head start," Gonard agreed merrily. "Do you chase me now?"

She waved her hand. "Yeah, yeah, in a bit. Let me get some air first." She stumbled toward him, rubbing her eyes. Gonard cocked his head, catching sight of a small smile lifting her lips. He quickly filled his flight chamber, retracted his claws. A few meters away, she suddenly charged toward him, arms outstretched. He sprang into the air, unfurling his wings in a quick downbeat that lifted him above her head, out of reach.

"Hey, not fair!" she shouted, squinting up at him. Her hair swept back in the wind of his wings. "No fair flyin' outta reach!"

He backwinged to land a dozen meters away, expelling the contents of his flight chamber into the air. "You were going to cheat."

She glared at him. "Okay, I was. Only 'cause fair cheatin's part of the game, but unfair cheatin' ain't."

A laugh rumbled in Gonard's chest. "Shall we play again?"

Itsa shook her head. "I can't outrun ya. Better than that game the tech gave us, wasn't it?"

Gonard wrinkled his nose at the memory, the long nights of mastering chess during their first winter. "Yes. Much better."

"I loved that game."

Gonard blinked. "I thought you hated it."

Itsa laughed. "Guess ya're still too spotty to get it. Still gotta grow up a bit, first."

"Sarcasm," Gonard said, suddenly understanding. "It's not true humor."

"Whatever ya say, dragon." She walked toward him, still breathing heavily. "Might as well go on, yeah?"

Gonard glanced back the way they'd come, the Citadel gardens shimmering in the distance. "I think we should—"

Itsa suddenly broke into a run, her hand slapping his leg as she sped past. "It!" she shouted, laughing as she ran away.

Gonard whirled and galloped after her. The hazy sun was warm on his back, the grass smelled fresh and clean, and he was suddenly filled with joy to be alive. The greatest reason for his happiness ran ahead of him, her laughter still ringing across the meadow. He circled around her, blocking the way forward. She dashed one way, then another, but he cut in front of her every time, his feet plowing into the earth, tail snapping behind him.

Itsa finally halted, then strode forward. "All right, ya win," she huffed, leaning back against his good leg. "Should've given ya a handicap."

"I already have one."

"Ya wouldn't jig it." He twisted his head to her, and she touched one cheek lightly. The scales under her fingers seemed to tingle. He once again had the longing he knew she couldn't fulfill. *Not physically*, he thought. *Does that matter? Not that she would want to remain with me. She'll be a Lady Citizen one day, and then she'll be able to pick any* unlanded Citizen she wants.

"C'mon." She pushed away from him. "Don't wanna get there too late."

"Get where?"

"To the Lord Cit's, of course." She started walking. " 'Bout time ya started visitin' them."

"I don't know if it's a good idea." Gonard carefully matched his pace to hers. "What if they don't want to see me?"

"They all gotta, 'member?" She snorted. " 'Sides, maybe they'll be happier on their own ground. Ever jive that?"

"Well . . ." Gonard hedged, not wanting to lie.

"See? Ya need me."

Yes, I do, he thought. But what can I offer you? What can a dragon offer you?

Clumps of trees began to form either side of the meadow. They must be far into the Lord Citizen's domain now. The ground sloped in a gradual curve. A barrier came into view, rising from the grass in a darker shade of green. A hedge, Gonard decided. A long line of precisely cropped bushes stretched ten meters in either direction. There was only one gap in the close-set structure.

"A maze," Itsa said as they drew near. "Gotta be close to the Lord Cit's manse now."

"A maze?" Gonard peered over the hedge—only to find another beyond, a pathway running between the two rows. " 'A network of paths and hedges designed as a puzzle for those who try to penetrate it.' "

"Got it, dragon." She stepped through the entrance, frowned as two more gaps confronted her. "Tech would've been good at this, I wager."

Gonard followed her down the left opening. "Why?"

" 'Cause it's all twisty and complex." She strode down the path. "Dragon, do ya trust him?"

"Yes," Gonard answered, bemused as Itsa, without

hesitation, chose between two more gaps.

"He's always said not to."

"He wants to see me become a Lord Citizen," Gonard said. "He'll do whatever he has to do to make the Council recognize me as having a soul. So I can trust him."

"Right. Then I'll trust him too."

Gonard frowned. Her tone sounded final, as if, after much consideration, she'd reached some decision. Then he quickly swung after her as she strode through yet another gap.

Then they were suddenly through the maze, out onto a clean expanse of green. The close-cut grasses lapped around a small gray castle, the crisp outlines of the stones announcing their newness. A castle. Gonard stirred uneasily at a dim warning.

Itsa looked up at him, her face unreadable. "He's goin' to support me for Citizenship."

Gonard blinked. "I don't understand."

"Ya will soon."

A man rode from the castle gate, his bright clothes glittering even in the muted sunlight. The horse he rode was a light, dappled gray, black mane curling down the neck and a black tail sweeping behind its stiff prance. By the horse Gonard knew the rider, for his father had made the gray to serve as the personal mount of Lord Citizen Merril Lange.

Gonard straightened as the man came nearer. Itsa slowly moved away from him, not meeting his gaze, her eyes fixed on the approaching rider. Merril reined in his steed a short distance away. Gonard laid his ears back as the man analyzed him; he disliked Merril's possessive air. "Good," Merril said to Itsa. "You have led it here unharmed."

"Wasn't hard."

"Perhaps not for you." Merril grinned. "But it would not have come at my command."

"No," Gonard said, "I wouldn't have."

"Speak when you are spoken to!" Merril snapped, slapping the reins against his horse's neck in emphasis.

"I will speak whenever I choose," Gonard returned. "What do you want with me?"

"Want with you?" Merril laughed. "Why, to hunt you, of course. What else are dragons for?"

The dread that had slowly been building within Gonard finally spilled over into sickening fear. "You can't," he said, forcing the weakness back. "The Council—"

"Is far away in the Citadel, deaf and blind to the happenings in the domain of an esteemed Lord Citizen." The saddle creaked as Merril leaned back into the cantle, placing a small horn to his lips. A single brassy note echoed against the castle walls. "You will finally be put to the use for which you were made, dragon. The Outler has performed her task well."

Gonard took a deep breath, drawing strength from the crisp smell of dry grass. Itsa had brought him here to be hunted, delivered him into the hands of his enemy. *He's goin' to support me for Citizenship.* Was that all that mattered to her? He took a step toward her.

A wild barking rose into the air. A pack of two dozen hounds streamed out from the castle, their black coats glistening with tinges of blue and green. Gonard lashed his tail. He had never liked these beasts, not since the day they had been activated on his father's laboratory table, howling at the indignity of their birth. Their bulky muzzles were bald, and black tongues lolled between red teeth. Merril's own design, conceived especially for the Hunt.

"I was not created for the Hunt," he told the man. The dogs milled around his legs, harsh bodies and smooth muzzles rubbing against his scales. "I will not be hunted." He unfurled his wings.

The Lord Citizen barked a command at his hounds. They bared their long teeth, sank them deep into the trailing edges of Gonard's wings. Gonard cried out with pain, and the grass was torn under his claws as he swung around, dislodging several of the beasts. He heard metal rasp against metal; then a sharp pain sliced through his left wing, ripping his sail up to the elbow. The dogs dropped away, leaving Gonard to stare at his wing, two halves flapping loosely.

A bright glint of metal brought his head up. Merril sheathed his sword, gathered his reins in one gloved hand. "You cannot escape so easily now," he said. "And the Hunt is ready to begin."

A half-dozen riders cantered from the castle. A seventh, riderless horse followed behind them; it came to Itsa's side, and she mounted. Gonard folded his left wing awkwardly, numbly. Crippled again, Itsa no longer beside him—it was as if none of it had really happened, as if the past two years had been nothing more than a false dream. Was he no more than a Hunt creature, after all?

"I will not be hunted," he said quietly. "You will have to kill me here."

Merril accepted a lance from one of the riders. He reined his horse into position and lowered the sharp tip to bear on Gonard. "You will run, when I call the Hunt to form. They all run at that signal."

He thinks I'm nothing more than a programmed robot, Gonard realized. He doesn't believe that I have a life to lose. He swept a glance across the other hunters. They all see me as a mere machine, no more alive than the horses that bear them or the dogs that wait at their feet. Why should they believe otherwise? They don't know me.

But Itsa does. And she led me here, knowing what is the outcome of a Hunt.

He took a deep breath, forcing the anguish aside. The air was hot, still. The men were sweating, the sour scent creeping through their thick armor. Saddles creaked, reins rattled, as they shifted restlessly. The horses were still, patient, the dogs panting in a programmed sequence.

I have been hunted before. Gonard raised his head. Gray skins and yellow eyes, a canyon closing him in. The wolves did not have me. Nor will Merril. I will not be killed.

The dogs had drawn back, giving him a clear path to the forest. That's where they want me to go. Gonard carefully tucked both wings closer to his body, wincing as the torn edges of the left scraped against each other. Then he whirled, claws ripping the grass as he charged back into the maze.

Behind him, frantic orders were shouted to men and hounds. The pattern of hoofbeats informed him that, as he had expected, the hunters were racing around the maze, hoping to reach the other side before he did. He could not be allowed to return to the Citadel, not at any cost. Merril couldn't risk his reporting to the Council how one of their lords had ignored their ruling.

But he had no intention of trying to gallop across the long plain to the Citadel. The horses were not handicapped by a twisted foot. They would outrun him, and the hunters would surround him with lances and swords, holding him in place for Merril's killing stroke. No, he must gain the forest, seek to lose the hunters in the trees. But first he must give them time to reach the opposite side of the maze. When he turned and exited on the castle side, the hedges would be a useful barrier to slow their chase.

The dogs had churned into the maze behind him. Their deep voices belled, a hunting cry that was designed to inform the hunters how close they were to their prey. Gonard kept one ear flicked back, using the sound for the same purpose.

The head start he'd gained by his surprise move began to shorten. The hounds seemed to know the maze, finding shortcuts and gaps in the bushes too small for a dragon's body. Gonard came to a stiff-legged halt as they suddenly veered away, only to reappear at the end of the pathway in which he stood.

Gonard took a deep breath, then threw himself back into a gallop, straight at the pack. The pitch of their cries intensified as he came nearer; their eyes gleamed in anticipation.

At the last moment, Gonard gathered his legs under him and sprang to his left. Metal teeth bit at empty air; his tail glanced off a smooth muzzle. Then he was over the hedge, his legs brushing the top and scattering leaves onto the hounds below. Their voices shrilled with protest as he landed and galloped down another pathway.

Then the dogs' cry suddenly changed. "Going back, going back, going back!" they howled in unison.

Going back! The hunters would now change direction. He could no longer afford to spend time racing through the maze. He leapt over the next bush wall, landed, leapt the next. But the pathway was narrower than those before. He threw his weight forward, his forelegs clearing the hedge. Bushes scraped his belly, tangled his hind legs and tail. For a moment, he was perched painfully on the wall, the meadow of the castle just out of his reach. Then the bushes growled and snapped beneath him, his weight pitching him forward. He hit the ground hard, his snout digging a deep furrow into the ground. Then his back legs were free, and he stumbled to his feet, momentarily dazed.

A horn blew, calling the hounds back to the Hunt. Gonard glanced behind him, glimpsed the hunters racing around the maze. He charged away, shaking his head free of a branch entwined around his ears.

It was only once he had reached the woods that he realized the whistle Itsa had given him had been torn off in the maze. He paused for a moment, wondering if he dared try to retrieve it. But the sound of the hounds not far behind forced him to continue.

The forest drew him in like a long-lost friend. He liked

forests, even a manicured one. The branches above him comforted him, cutting him off from the sky once again denied him. The wing could be healed, he consoled himself. It's a clean cut. Stitches, ten days' rest . . .

If I have ten days. He halted, suddenly realizing that the bare ground was soft beneath his feet. He glanced back the way he'd come, saw the clean marks of his passing disturbing the smooth soil. The hunters would have no difficulties in following him.

I must find some way to disguise my path. Resuming his gallop, he glanced from one side of the path to the other, searching for something that could bear the weight of his passing without leaving telltale signs.

The sound of running water caught his attention. He changed direction, trotted beneath the trees. The stream was just wide enough; he wandered into the water, paused to think. The water would help to erase his steps and what little scent he left; should he go upstream or downstream? Or would the hunters fathom his ploy and merely follow him?

He searched his surroundings. Several large boulders were sunk into the ground a dragon-stride beyond the streambank. Gonard studied their oblong shapes, then walked deliberately out of the water. His feet sank deep into the earth, his tail dragging a line between the claw marks. Then he leapt lightly onto the rocks, balancing precariously on the uneven heights. Water dripped from his scales, darkening the gray stones. He turned carefully, filled his flight chamber to its maximum capacity. Then he leapt back into the stream.

Water splashed up his belly, ran up the banks. But not enough, he hoped, to give away his ploy. He headed downstream, fighting the urge to run. Trees crowded closer to the water ahead, branches draping across his path; he had to hope that he would be past and shielded by them before the hunters rode up to the stream. The splashes caused by going faster than a careful walk might give away his position.

I'm getting good in the role of the hunted, he thought grimly. He progressed down the stream, the water washing around his feet, silt swirling into the current as he disturbed rocks lining the bed. Overhanging branches were the most difficult obstacles, demanding great care as he wove around them, lest a snap of wood give him away.

In the distance, he heard the hounds reach the stream, followed closely behind by the hunters, the humans whooping as their horses leapt over the water. Then the hounds suddenly barked in confusion. Lost my scent, Gonard decided. Eventually, the hunters would split up, he was sure. He must decide on his next course of action. A place to hide, he decided. I need time to think.

He traveled deeper and deeper into the forest. Rocks, fallen logs, wider streambeds—all helped hide his tracks. He found a bed of strong-smelling herbs and crushed the leaves against his feet, hoping to confuse the hounds further. At one point a hunter rode past, clutching his sword and glancing around nervously. Gonard watched from behind a clump of trees, grateful that the steed wasn't a coursair. The robotic horses had not been programmed with olfactory abilities.

The stream ended in a deep marsh, mud thickening as the water disappeared into the ground. Gonard frowned at this waste of resources, Merril's lack of foresight. His frown deepened as he stepped forward, sank up to his first knees into the muck. Then the frown became a smile. Carefully expelling the contents of his flight chamber, he wandered out into the mud flats, sinking slowly up to his chest in the dark mixture. He took a deep breath and lowered himself into the mud, working his body slowly underneath the earth. So long as the disturbance to the mud was overlooked, he was safe. Now that he was hidden, he had time to think.

I can't go back by the direct route to the Citadel, he decided. Merril will have put someone there to stop me. But he can't guard all of the borders between his domain and those of his neighbors. He probably hasn't even thought of it—Hunt creatures were programmed not to leave his domain. Merril doesn't accept that I'm not a Hunt dragon. I can wait until night and leave.

But what will happen to Itsa, when Merril finds that I'm gone? Images of Itsa flicked through his mind. Itsa, holding a rose in trembling hands. Itsa, laughing as she splashed seawater across his chest. Itsa, tenderly touching his cheek with her hand. Itsa, stepping away to give him over to the Hunt.

I love her, he thought suddenly. I love her, and I thought maybe, maybe . . . It doesn't matter. I still love her. But Merril—he can't risk her telling the Council about the Hunt. Once I've disappeared, she'll try to blackmail him for her Citizenship, and he'll have to act against her. I must speak to Itsa. I must warn her.

He waited for the day to pass by overhead, his inner clock keeping watch on the hours. The hunters would bed down for the night, he was certain. Then he could leave his hiding place and try to find Itsa, speak to her on his own.

* * * * *

Itsa scowled, leaning down to her mount's neck as it blindly pushed its way through a series of low-lying branches. A thin mist formed shapes in the predawn morning. Stupid thing, she thought, as the horse made a wide circle around yet another swirl of fog. Wish I'd got Ugly back. He wasn't so dim. And he was alive. Ridin' this is like bein' on a digger, goes where ya tell it till ya tell it to stop.

But she'd gotten away from that Lord Cit for a while, like she was supposed to. He was starting to bore her, between his leers at her breasts and his talk about how important he was on the Council. He also seemed keener on sticking the dragon than she liked. She only hoped he remembered the reason for this shatting business when the moment came.

And when the dragon's got to ya, he's said his bit, and gets his very own Lord Cit—what for the Itsa then? She straightened, then swore as a branch nearly removed her left ear. Gotta work that out, she thought, rubbing her ear. Go for my own Cit, I guess. The dragon'll sponsor me, and maybe that Reefe, since I can't see Merril bein' too happy when the dragon tells him he's not gonna make Hunt things for him. Lady Cit Itsa. Ain't that what I always wanted?

She scowled again, wishing she didn't have to try so hard to convince herself. Well, if that's not what I want, then what? To go back to the mines? Or the City? Or the settlement? Or what?

The sky was beginning to lighten. She stopped the horse in a clearing. It held still as she dropped the thin reins to its dark neck and rubbed her arms. The hunters had laughed at her when she'd said she was cold. They wore thick armor— fireproof, Merril had bragged. Covered everything 'cept the least important bit, she thought. His head. No noodle to fry, else he never would have been taken in by the tech. Like the dragon'd really make creatures for him to hunt, after bein' hunted himself.

A rustle made her glance to her right, expecting a hunter to ride in. But it was the dragon, limping heavily, his left wing sagging. Buck it up, Itsa girl, she told herself. Ya're on show now. But she found herself staring uneasily at the mud-caked body, the wounded wing. It seemed almost too real.

The dragon halted just within the clearing. "I need to warn you."

This wasn't how it was supposed to go. "Yeah, 'bout what?"

"Don't trust Merril. He's never kept his promises. He'll betray you."

"Golly gee, and I jived he was an angel. Thanks." She shifted, still hoping to finally find a comfortable position on the thin saddle. "Didn't jig ya'd wanna talk to me 'gain."

He gave her a long, appraising gaze. Then the skin around his nostrils wrinkled. " 'Beareth all things, believeth all things, hopeth all things, endureth all things,' " he quoted softly.

"Whatcha mutterin' 'bout?" Itsa demanded. To her annoyance, she felt her face flushing.

"You betrayed me," the dragon acknowledged. A note of pain strained the deep voice. "But I forgive you."

Itsa coughed. Keep the show goin', she told herself. "Thanks, buddo."

"Yes, I am." The dragon stepped forward. "I will always be your—friend."

Itsa fiddled with the reins. The horse backed obediently. Something else seemed to hang in the air, words unspoken. She swallowed, suddenly breaking out into a sweat. "Yeah, guess we get 'long all right." Shouldn't a buzzer sound now, some Lord Cit appear to tell them it was all over? They must've got enough on vid now to show that the dragon had a soul. Machines didn't forgive people, say they were friends, didn't almost say—

She relaxed with relief as Merril rode into the clearing, stopping beside her. "Well done, Outler," he said, loosening his sword in its scabbard. "You have held it long enough. My hunters now surround the clearing."

"Oh, shut it," Itsa snapped. "Put your toy 'way. The dragon's said 'nuff, ain't he? Get serious."

"I am very serious." Merril drew the sword, the faint rays of sunlight glimmering down the patterned blade. He lifted it into the air, and the other hunters materialized, circling the glen, their drawn swords resting across their saddles. "I take my Hunts very seriously."

"Yeah, and now it's over. Ya've done yar bit." Itsa glanced back at the dragon. "It's all to show ya had a soul, ya see?"

Sudden life seemed to flow into the dragon. He took a step forward, head high, eyes bright. "You didn't really betray me?"

She snorted. " 'Course not. I'd never nut ya. Whatcha jive, I did so's I could get my Lord Cit?"

"I hoped not." The dragon replied calmly, but again Itsa felt something running under the surface of his words. She suddenly realized that wherever she went—to the Citadel, City, settlement, anywhere—didn't matter, so long as the dragon was with her. Her new awareness made her tremble, as she seemed to regain something she'd thought lost forever in a deep mine shaft. The dragon smiled, seemed to sense the change. "Let's go home."

The rasp of metal against metal drew harshly across the moment. Merril lifted his sword from his horse's flank. "You may have had some plan, Outler. But mine has always been to finish the Hunt. The dragon is mine."

Itsa twisted her horse backward, dry-mouthed in sudden horror. The hunters were still, their mounts unmoving, swords ready to prevent any escape. The dragon straightened, his coat of dry mud cracking. The medtech, she realized suddenly. I fell for his plan—I trusted him. I made the mistake of trustin' him.

The dragon waited, ears twitching, nostrils flaring. The forest was unnaturally quiet, the only sound that of the hunters' harsh breathing. Itsa smelled the stench of her own sweat, knew that she was strung high with fear. If the dragon were to be killed now, when she was so close to knowing what he meant to her . . .

She'd have to create a distraction, let him escape. She kicked her horse over to Merril, grabbed wildly at his sword. He tried to swing his horse around, but she crashed her mount into his, pinning their legs together, banging her cheek against his sharp, armored elbow. Then her hands were around the sword, the sharp metal cutting into her palms, blood running into the intricate designs.

Merril's face was above her, dark with fury. He swore at her, kicked his horse into her. The change in direction twisted the sword in her hands, and she watched in disbelief as it slipped past her grasp, sinking deep into her side. The cold metal slid through skin and muscle, ground past bone. I wasn't s'posed to be the Hunt, she thought as she slumped from the saddle, then crashed to the hard ground. I don't have 'nuff legs.

CHAPTER 17

The sword was torn from Itsa's ribs as she fell. Gonard found himself frozen for one long second, unable to believe that her blood was spreading across the dirt. Then he leapt forward, his legs trembling as he straddled her small form.

The hunters were motionless, faces white with shock. All stared numbly at the bloodied sword hanging loosely in Merril's grasp. "Hunters," Gonard raged, controlling his flight chamber with a great effort. "You've never seen a drop of real blood. Your killing's always been sanitized. But now—" his voice broke, and he lowered his head to Itsa's.

She stirred feebly, a hand clutching uselessly at the wound in her side. "The medtech . . ." she whispered, then coughed. "Dragon, the medtech . . ."

Yes, of course. The medtech was her only hope. If he could only get her to the Citadel, perhaps the medtech could save her, as he had so many times before. Gonard raised his head, glared at the hunters. "You," he said, selecting one young man.

The man swallowed, looking ill. "Me, sir?"

"Itsa must be taken to the Citadel, and I can't carry her. You'll carry her before you, on your horse." With his eyes, Gonard singled out two more hunters. "You and you—you will lift her carefully onto his steed. *Now.*"

The hunters glanced nervously at Merril. But the Lord Citizen only stared numbly at the blood splattered on his hands. At Gonard's growl the two hurried to obey him, dropping to the ground to raise Itsa into the arms of the third man. He arranged her awkwardly across the saddle, leaning her back against his chest.

"Now," Gonard said. "Run. Run that horse and don't stop for anything. I'll be right behind you."

The man nodded, steered his horse around. Then he kicked the brown sides, the horse responding with an almost instant gallop, and Gonard followed.

The forest fell behind them. Freed of the trees, both the horse and Gonard were able to increase their pace. The ground blurred past, barely seen, Gonard's eyes fixed on the dark-skinned woman bleeding her life out into the rider's gray armor. How long? he wondered. How long can a human bleed and not die? The information was probably somewhere within his brain, but he ruthlessly suppressed it, choosing hope over knowledge.

The Citadel finally came into sight, the pruned trees of the formal gardens rising in the distance. The young man's face was lined with strain, his legs slackening against his horse's sides. But Itsa was Gonard's only concern, and he lashed his tail at the horse when its pace slackened.

The horse's hooves rang out on the paved pathways of the gardens. The man dropped the reins from one trembling hand, swallowed noisily. "Not yet," Gonard snapped, halting beside him. "We've got to get to the laboratory."

"It will not be necessary to bring the steed into the Citadel." A gray-haired man hurried up to them, followed by several guards bearing a stretcher. "We have been informed of the seriousness of the Outler's condition. We will take her from here."

The rider gratefully allowed his burden to be lifted from his arms. The guards strapped Itsa into place, then trotted down a ramp into the Citadel. Gonard was forced to follow at a steadier pace behind.

By the time the guards admitted him to the medtech's laboratory, Itsa had been moved from the stretcher onto a thin bed set against a wall. A thick gray bank of complex machinery squatted on her right, whirring with a purpose Gonard could not comprehend. Electrodes were attached to her temples and to each arm.

"It was fortunate that you brought her here," said the gray-haired man as Gonard stopped beside the bed. "This is the prototype Regenerator, fully operational due only to the assistance of your companion."

The words brushed past Gonard's ears, unimportant. "Will she live?"

The man waved him away from the bed. Gonard followed him reluctantly to the other end of the room, one eye noting that the medtech was adjusting the controls on several of the panels. "It appears very hopeful that she will survive. The main damage is to her left lung and to her stomach, compounded by a serious loss of blood. But the Regenerator is operating as anticipated, stimulating and supporting the regrowth of cells at a rate many times that of normal healing. So long as we can sustain the growth, she will be returned to health."

Gonard relaxed slightly, the cold pit in his belly disappearing. He turned his attention to the man, wondering what seemed so familiar about him. "Who are you?"

"I am Oswald, co-creator of your predecessor and companion." The man smiled slightly at Gonard's start. "It would appear that you have heard of me."

Gonard nodded. "I'd like to ask you some questions."

A sudden shout snapped his head around. A guard had left the door, was grappling with the medtech near the Regenerator. Gonard frowned, wondering what the guard was planning. Then the medtech calmly threw her off. He turned, raised his arm. A gleam of bright blue light arched from a rod in his hand. He slashed the beam down across the whirring panels, the laser cutting through a series of delicate components.

Gonard threw himself across the room, his tail lashing out before him to wind around the medtech's legs. The robot fell heavily to the floor, the laser scalpel clattering from his grip. The guards rushed over to pull the medtech away. Gonard could only watch, numbed by yet another unexpected betrayal.

He stepped back as Oswald hurried over to the machine, calling over several technicians to assist him. Feeling suddenly very clumsy, very old, Gonard limped around to the other side of the bed. Metal covers were ripped from the Regenerator, components stripped out, new parts wired into place. But he had seen the damage, knew that the repair work could not be completed in time.

"Dragon?" Itsa opened eyes bright with pain. "Shat, this hurts."

Technicians, giving up on their repairs, called with ragged voices for surgical gear. Too late, all too late, Gonard thought, watching as blood began to stain the gray blankets red. He took a deep breath, pushed back the beginnings of a twisting grief. Later, there would be time enough to mourn. Itsa still needed him, needed him now more than ever before. "I know," he said helplessly, wondering how he could help her. What could he do?

The memory of his own great physical pain came back to him. His wing stretched out across a stable floor, a long, sharp needle relentlessly weaving through sensitive skin, in and out, in and out. His voice, rising in song, pulling his awareness away from the agony of the necessary work. Itsa can't sing, he thought. And I don't think my singing can help her. But perhaps I can take her away from the pain in some other way. "Do you remember our day by the ocean,

Itsa?" he asked quietly.

" 'Course." She smiled slightly, though sweat was beading across her forehead. Her hand clutched tightly at the bed covers, the skin stretched almost white across her knuckles. "I wish—I wish we'd never left."

"But we haven't."

"Shattin' dragon, I'm flat out."

"But we haven't left, not yet," Gonard insisted quietly. "You're standing there now, with me beside you. The sand is gritty between your toes. Don't you feel the cold waves swirling around your feet, leaving foam behind on your skin? The air's strong with the smell of seaweed, and the breeze blows strands of hair from your forehead." He exhaled softly across her sweaty face, his breath lifting her hair.

"Yeah," she replied dreamily, her hand loosening in the blankets. "Yeah, I see it."

"The sun is setting."

"Over the water."

"Over the water. The horizon is red with sunset, a red line across the gray-blue of the ocean. As you look up, the sky fades to orange, yellow, and then to blue, a few clouds scattered above tinged purple."

"It's beautiful."

As are you, Gonard thought painfully. "The tide is receding, the waves coming into shore farther and farther away. Your feet are beginning to dry, and the sun is disappearing into the water." He paused, gathered all his courage, then said softly, "Now, let your life go down with the sun, wash out with the tide."

Itsa released her breath, her eyes shutting. Then her back arched, her hands pawing through the blankets. Gonard bowed his head over her, knowing that this was only the body refusing to die. Her soul was already growing, stepping free from its decaying shell. She was going to a place he could not follow, not now, not for a long time yet to come.

He felt her whisper his name, pause briefly to touch him once. Then a dazzling light claimed her, and she was out of his reach.

Gonard lifted his head. Grief weighed his back, ached in his chest. His eyes roamed over the technicians, some now bearing scalpels, sacks of synthoblood. They stepped back, wary, fearful. The guards were back at the door, carefully not meeting his gaze. The medtech was slumped in his chair, arms hanging uselessly at his sides, legs bent awkwardly across the floor.

The medtech. Gonard felt anger build up in his chest, a welcome respite from the chill of grief. He strode over to the robot, forcing his claws to remain sheathed, his flight chamber to remain empty. "Why?" he ground out, towering over the still figure. "*Why?*"

"It would be preferable to be outside. Betrayers always wait outside." Something like a throttled laugh came from him; then the medtech slowly, laboriously lifted his head. The dull eyes met Gonard's. "Only one who has loved can feel grief. Only a soul can love. Only a soul can grieve. You have proven that you have a soul."

"*Why?*" Gonard howled. "Why is my soul so important to you?"

"I now have from you what I have always needed." The voice was thin, mechanical. "My Master deserted me. He abandoned me for you. I needed for him to justify himself to me. Only success would be justification. I now know he was successful."

"So," Gonard asked bitterly, "now you can forgive him?"

The medtech eyed him. "I was not programmed with for-giveness."

"I brought you into existence." Oswald stopped beside Gonard, his face grim. "I am your Master."

"You are not my Master," the medtech said flatly, his eyes not leaving Gonard's. "Rumfus Max was my Master. He deserted me. He left me, even as you did. He was Gonard Michel's father. He was never mine. No one was ever mine."

"So you killed Itsa," Gonard said savagely, his claws flexing. "I loved her."

"That is of no importance to me. I have simply put that emotion to use. All that has happened here has been broadcast to the Council. You will now be declared a Lord Citizen. My work is done." His head tipped back, rested against his chair. "So, this is death. Some interactions are more amusing than anticipated." The light faded from behind his eyes.

"He has only exhausted his power supplies," Oswald mused. "I could perhaps restore him."

"No!" Gonard snapped, trembling with grief. "Let him go."

A polite cough made him turn his head. One of the guards, arms clasped behind his back, flinched under the dragon's gaze. She shifted her weight uncomfortably. "Sir, the Council requests your attendance."

Gonard drew breath to tell her what he thought of the Council. But Oswald replied, "Gonard Michel will appear before the Council momentarily." In a lower tone, he murmured to Gonard, "Do not permit her death to be wasted."

Gonard bent his head in acceptance. He limped out of the laboratory, following the guard down the long corridors to the Council chamber. His wings sagged, tips drawing lines into the white floors. *She is gone*, he thought numbly, stumbling over his wings several times. *She is gone.*

All of the Lord Citizens were present in the chamber. Even Merril was in his place, slumped in his seat, his face still pale. Gonard spared him a quick glance, finding himself unable to blame the man for what had happened. The medtech had always planned for this conclusion. If not by sword, Itsa would have met death by some other manner. *Why did I ever trust him? I should have known better than to trust him.*

"Let us dispense with the formalities," the Lady Speaker said, standing. "Gonard Michel, we have witnessed what has occurred in the medical laboratory, and a vote has been taken. The majority have accepted the petition, and you are to be welcomed to the Domains as a Citizen."

"Thank you very much," Gonard said, anger and grief embittering his tone.

The Lady Speaker winced. A man stood. "Before you claim your inheritance, however, you will of course be required to pass the Theological Examination."

"Indeed?" Gonard swept his eyes around the chamber. "Shat your Theological Examination. Ask me any question, and I can answer it. Except for how to raise the dead. That's one question I can't answer."

There was a murmur around the chamber. The Lady Speaker stood again, silencing them. "My lords and ladies, I believe that there is no question that the Citizen Gonard Michel could easily pass any examination set for him. I rule that we let the Lord Citizen reclaim his domain." She met his eyes. "Let the man go in peace."

Gonard nodded to her, unable to speak. He backed from the chamber, the guard hurrying out of his path.

He found Oswald still in the laboratory, slowly dismantling the medtech. "He said he had a high scrap value," Gonard said, chilled despite himself at Oswald's calm precision.

"He possessed all the intelligence I could devise." Oswald carefully lifted an arm loose, placed it on the floor. "But I could not give him that for which he most longed."

And he destroyed what I had. Gonard's eyes flicked unwillingly to the bed. The sheets were drawn over Itsa's head, hiding her from view. Oswald said awkwardly, "The Outler—Itsa—her body is yours, to do with as you wish."

"The soul is gone," Gonard said quietly. "What use have I for the body?"

"The body housed the one you loved." Oswald sighed. "It may help you to grieve for the soul, if you bury the body."

"I'll grieve," Gonard affirmed heavily, his chest aching with tears he could not shed. "The Domains—"

Oswald paused in his work, looked up at Gonard. "Is there some information you would wish to impart to me?"

"The Domains are in danger." Gonard glanced away from the structure that held as little of the medtech as Itsa's body now held of her. "The medtech programmed a fault into the Barrier so we could return. The fault will grow until the Barrier is broken."

Oswald straightened, his face grave. "Few technicians possess knowledge regarding the Barrier. Will you assist us in the necessary repairs?"

Gonard shook his head. "I don't know anything about the Barrier."

"But with your great mental capacity—"

"No," Gonard cut him off curtly. "I'm not staying in the Citadel." He turned to the bed.

"Lord Michel, wait!" Oswald called. "Where will you go?"

"Home," Gonard replied bitterly. "I'm going home."

* * * * *

He buried them together, his strong legs heaving the earth to one side in great clumps. A small breeze rustled the trees, lifted the twin scents of decaying flesh and decomposing rubber. When the hole was many meters deep, he lowered Vomer's remains into the earth, arranging the red skin to line the bottom of the grave. Then he carefully laid Itsa's body on top, pausing a moment to gaze at them.

The present blurred before his eyes. A red snout turned toward him, asked him about souls. A dark face scowled in the light of a fire. Too late, he thought. I acted too late for both of you. And I shouldn't have. I shouldn't have. Then he shoveled the moist earth back onto them.

The mound was a blemish in the grove, a blot on his father's careful landscaping. It's my domain now, Gonard thought sullenly. I can do whatever I want to it. He limped away, came back bearing two red roses, which he laid tenderly across the grave. Then he returned to the laboratory.

The green Hunt dragon was a glittering pile in one corner, and Vomer's remains were gone; both were alterations he had made. Otherwise, the laboratory was unchanged, even a trace of ash remaining where a man had once stood. Gonard strode past the table, ducked into the passageway to his lair. There he curled up, brooding.

His eyes lit the walls. He studied the marks in the stone, remembered the life he had spent here. There were the long scratches left by a hippogryph, testing its claws. One corner had been the favored place of the griffin, its quiet voice telling Gonard stories he had never really understood. Vomer had lain against him, her body spines pricking his wing. A shimmering unicorn had never set hoof into this cave, had instead thrown herself from a ledge within minutes of her creation, refusing to accept servitude.

The unicorn would have followed me, Gonard thought suddenly. She would have traveled with me. The thought was sudden, strange, and yet he felt some dim realization almost surface, then drop away.

But he didn't want a unicorn. He wanted Itsa. Her dark face turning to the sun, teeth shining in a sudden smile. Would she have been happy here? Would she have come with him? I don't know, and I can't know, he told himself fiercely, and now it doesn't matter. Nothing matters.

He pulled himself to his feet, wandered restlessly through the laboratory. The cave is mine; the lab is mine; the whole domain is mine. He felt harsh laughter ache in his chest. Lord Citizen Gonard Michel. Was that what my father had planned for me? Does his heir have what he wanted for him?

I don't have what I want. He limped from the room, into the corridors of his father's demesne. All this means nothing to me, nothing, because she's not here, she's not here. I wasn't made to be alone.

It's all your fault, he thought at the memory of his father. Anger began to build in his chest, his flight chamber expanding. He paced down the corridor. You made me what I am, deformed, imperfect—

He halted outside the room that had been his father's. The dusty scent of the Master still hung in the air. Clothes and blankets were tangled over and around the thin bed, just as when Gonard had passed by, two years ago. A layer of dust was all that marked the passing of time. Only dust to show for the passage of two years.

Rage swelled up his throat. He opened his jaws in a scream of anger. Gases swirled into flame as they passed his teeth, fire shooting into the room. The bed was engulfed in flames. Red-yellow tongues licked at the bedcovers, raced along the mattress, leapt across to the chair. Wood cracked, snapped, and Gonard backed away from the heat, feeling suddenly cheated. As he watched a gray mist fill the room, some automatic defense dousing the fire, he realized that his anger wasn't directed at his father.

But there has to be someone at fault, someone to blame! He turned back up the corridor, flight chamber empty, but ready. The computer room was ahead of him, delicate components that would crackle and burn in dragon flame. He would destroy everything, destroy it all, so that nothing would be left behind to show . . . to show . . .

To show what? He halted, glanced into the library. The ancient tomes rested peacefully in their glassy cabinets. I destroyed that book, he thought for the first time. The book Brocard brought to me—it must have burned in the stable fire. I never said I was sorry.

He closed his eyes. Something else ran beneath his rage, something deeper, darker. As his flight chamber quieted, he could feel it tug at him, pulling him away from his anger. The memory of a laugh, water splashing coldly against his chest.

No. He opened his eyes, turned away. I don't want to remember, he thought fiercely. I don't want to remember. What's the point? She's gone now, gone forever.

The eyes of the Hunt dragon seemed to glitter at him as he returned to the laboratory. "What're you staring at?" Gonard demanded, stopping before the green-and-black hulk. "You aren't like me. You don't have to live with a crippled wing and a twisted foot. You're not—"

He stopped, listened to his own words. It's me, he thought dully. It's me I'm angry at. It's my fault she's dead. The medtech warned me not to trust him. He never said that he could be trusted. But I needed to trust him, I needed to, so I did, and she's dead now because I did. I failed her.

The scenes of all his other failures washed over him in a great wave of despair. Vomer a pile of discarded skin. The shattered tower of the City. A stire crushed by his body. Tribe members lying on the ground with red, gashed throats. A wolf begging for release. Itsa lying too still on a thin bed. And the very first, in this very room, his father a pile of ashes at his feet.

I failed you, Father. If only I'd tried to tell you that I had Awakened. Would you have made other creatures for the Hunt? Was their suffering my fault too? I could've made you understand. I'm sure I could have, if I'd tried. And you would have been proud of me, proud of yourself. You wouldn't have killed Vomer. You wouldn't have tried to kill me.

And I made promises I couldn't keep—to Vomer, to the City, to the tribe, to Itsa. I should have known better. I should be better than that.

The Hunt dragon hulked silently in her corner. Gonard gazed upon her again. The glittering eyes seemed to ask a question. "Because I'm like you, a robot," Gonard answered bitterly. "I'm made to be perfect. I shouldn't make mistakes."

Self-loathing crawled over him. How could I have been so wrong? The laboratory walls seemed to close in on him, constrict his breathing. He glanced around, seeking an escape. Was this how the unicorn had felt, refusing the heavy hand of the Master?

An opening beckoned to him. He stared numbly at the slope, the slick white path leading from the laboratory. The path the unicorn had taken. A ledge lay that way, the forbidden ledge leading to the sunrise. And to a cliff high above the forests of the domain.

Gonard turned, limped to the slope. He passed the Hunt dragon without sparing her a glance. His claws extended, screeched against the slick material as they grappled for purchase on the smooth surface.

A cliff. He grimly fought his way up the slope. And no wings to bear me up this time. He came out into the night, the full moon gleaming starkly on the rough stone of the wide ledge. The cool air cupped his wings as he opened them, the ragged halves of the left fluttering in a slight breeze. For the second time in his existence he paced purposefully to a cliff edge.

Even this I got wrong the first time, he found himself thinking. But I'll get it right this time. I'll finally get something right.

His left forefoot caught on a stone, twisted beneath him. Gonard grunted as his shoulder dipped, pain driving up his leg. And you're the worst, he thought, gazing down at his foot. You're a constant reminder that I'm not perfect. I've never been perfect.

The words seemed to return to him, calm, stripped of bitterness. *I've never been perfect.* He stared down at the twisted toes, every bent joint and roughened scale harshly exposed by the bright moonlight. Some answer seemed to be held in that awkward curl. I've been faulty from birth. From the start I've made mistakes.

But a robot shouldn't make a mistake. A computer shouldn't err. I should be perfect, flawless. I should get things right. I shouldn't have failed Vomer, my father, the City, Ranalf, Itsa . . . and the medtech. If only I had listened to what he didn't say, heard the need in him, maybe he wouldn't have had to kill Itsa. I failed him, too.

He saw a dark face lit with laughter, felt fingers gently touch his cheek. His breath seemed to be strangling in his throat. I'm flawed. I'm not perfect. What does that make me? The words were just on the edge of realization. Then I'm only—I'm only—

Human.

The face faded, was gone, buried under darker earth. The laughter was stilled forever. Pain welled up from its deep recess, and a sob tore from his chest as he rasped for air. The moonlight was liquid in his eyes. Gonard bent his head and wept.

CHAPTER 18

The days were growing shorter. Autumn was approaching. Gonard sensed it in the laboratory, saw leaves darkening when he climbed onto the ledge and looked at the forest below. But he had no wish to go outside and look for himself. He felt oddly—quiet. As if waiting for some sound, some thought, that was just out of reach. It was a silence he had become accustomed to in the chapter, when he had been waiting to rediscover his name.

The Hunt dragon seemed to draw a glance from him each night as he went to his cave to sleep. She tugged at his thoughts when he stood on the ledge and watched the sunset. Finally, one morning, he paused before her, cocking his head as he studied the body thoughtfully. The damage was not that great. One leg needed setting, a wing mended, a neck restrung. She could be restored.

The thought exploded over him. He sank down onto his haunches, found that he was trembling. The dragon could be rebuilt, perhaps even brought to life. . . . The last creation of his father, the only other dragon in existence. His father had shared all his knowledge with him. It merely needed to be reclaimed.

Gonard took a deep breath, calmed himself. He had destroyed parts of the laboratory equipment before killing his father, and other components could have suffered damage during the past two years of neglect. And while his father had shared his mind with him once, much of that knowledge was out of reach until nudged into action. There was much work to be done.

He got up and limped to the library. The glass cabinets opened at his command, and he brought out book after book, laying them across the laboratory table. In an annex, he found the plans detailing the construction of his father's creations—including himself. He carried the folios out, placing them also on the long table.

The folios were opened first, the long pages spread out across the gleaming surface. His father had written everything out in longhand, seemingly not trusting his plans to computer storage. Gonard found himself smiling fondly at the idiosyncrasy. Then he concentrated on the drawings. Neck structures, wing lengths, skeletal constructions, electrochemical connections—nothing was missing. Notes in the margins referred to sources of inspiration, and Gonard opened the relevant books, analyzing the passages mentioned. He blinked as a scribble credited him with the color chosen for a hippogryph's hide, and swallowed a sudden pain. *You did listen to me sometimes, Father.*

He spent long days drinking in the information, adding it to that which his studies called from his mind. The necessary portions of his father's machinery were still in order, and a storeroom revealed material sufficient for the plans he was forming. But one thing was lacking. *Hands,* Gonard realized. *I'll need hands.*

One day a familiar scent wafted down into the laboratory. It broke his concentration, and he straightened with a start, nostrils flaring wide. Without thinking he broke into song, raising his voice in the hymns Lybrand had taught him. *Changewinds,* he thought. *The Barrier must be down, and the Changewinds have come to the Domains.*

* * * * *

The alarm rang several days later, announcing visitors at the entrance to the complex. Gonard looked up from his books, twisted his head before he remembered that his father had never installed a vid at the entrance. "Let them in," he commanded, suddenly curious as to who could have come to his domain.

A delegation of Lord Citizens finally straggled into the laboratory. Gonard turned to meet them, bowing politely to the Lady Speaker. She looked aged, her eyes hollowed by lack of sleep. Four men had come with her, one of whom was Merril, who remained at the rear of the group, scowling.

"Lord Michel, I will not waste words," said the Lady Speaker. "The Barrier has become inoperative."

Gonard nodded. "I know. I sensed the Changewinds."

"We have come to request your assistance—"

"My lady," Gonard interrupted, politely but firmly, "I know nothing about the construction or the maintenance of the Barrier."

"Then we are doomed." The woman sagged. "Do you know the destruction these—Changewinds—caused in the Citadel? Thirty Lords and Ladies and fifty Citizens were driven insane. We are still searching the rest of the Domains for those as yet unaccounted for."

Gonard turned his head, guilt twisting through him. Of course, he thought, they don't know anything about the Winds, or how to defend themselves from the effects. But would they have listened to me, if I had tried to warn them? He took a deep breath and looked back at the Lady Speaker. "I can't repair the Barrier. But I can teach you how to protect yourselves from the Changewinds."

"Of course you can." Merril stepped forward, his face flushed. He brushed off the Lady's attempt to restrain him, coming to stand before Gonard. "You can do anything now, can't you, Lord Michel?"

The man doesn't know what he's saying, Gonard thought. As Brocard had taught him, he listened to the words below those spoken, the thoughts held back in the dark eyes. "I don't blame you for her death," he said softly, lowering his head to meet the man's gaze. "I forgave you long ago."

Merril's face froze. Gonard lifted his head, looked beyond him. "This is how you gain protection from the Winds." And he sang, the notes of one of the City's wordless tunes echoing through the chamber. With a glance at their haggard faces, he softened the song, added an almost crooning undertone. Some of the tension eased from their stiff bodies.

They were silent after he finished. Then one of the men shook himself free. "How would that assist us?"

"The singing counteracts the influence of the Changewinds," Gonard told him. "All the societies we encountered outside the Domains used song to defend themselves against the Winds."

"We have found only desert outside," the Lady said.

"Because you haven't gone far enough." Gonard was conscious of Merril's struggle for control. "Let me show you something." He led the Lady and the other men from the laboratory, leaving Merril behind.

The storeroom lit up at his approach. "I will make recordings of my singing," he told them as they stared curiously at the racks of metal bars, the rubber molds. "If anyone has the necessary talent, I'll teach him or her how to sing. But the Domains are doomed. You'll have to decide whether you want to try to stay here until the last water supplies have been used up. If not, you could go outside. But I have two conditions."

"Our people are dying," one of the men asked bitterly, "and you give us conditions?"

"Yes." Gonard met his angry eyes. "You haven't thought

beyond the Citizens in the Domains. What about the asteroid colonies? Anyone who wants to come to Earth must be
allowed to, before you also forget how to operate the transmat. But let them know what they're coming to."

"And what is your second condition, Lord Michel?"

Hands. I need hands. "The services of four technicians."
Gonard's eyes roamed around the storeroom. "One of whom
is to be the Citizen Oswald."

The Lady Speaker inclined her head. "It will be so."

* * * * *

The technicians came into the laboratory slowly, nervously, clutching bags of tools. Oswald strode confidently
in their midst, swiftly sorting out accommodations and a
cooking rota. Gonard watched him work, bemused. "You
seem to be planning to stay here for a while," he said when
the man paused for breath.

Oswald met his eyes. "I have viewed the vid of the death
of Lord Max. I think I know what it is you have called me
here to do, and it will take a while."

Gonard noted that one of the women was setting up a
recorder. "What do you think I want?"

"It is obvious that you would wish to have the other
dragon repaired and activated." Gonard looked a question
at him, and the man shrugged. "It should not be impossible
to accomplish. The Changewinds took many of the promising technicians, but I have brought the best with me." He
lowered his voice. "I will offer you what reparation I can for
the death of the Outler."

"I don't blame you," Gonard said, recalling Merril's
white face as the man had been led from the laboratory.

"The programming of the dragon is Lord Max's own, so
it should not suffer from the same instabilities." Oswald
straightened. "Have you made any preparations?"

Gonard led him to the table. "I want one addition. I want her to have a flight chamber."

Oswald studied the diagram thoughtfully. "Yes, it is as I said. We will be here for a while." But he sounded almost cheerful.

* * * * *

The Hunt dragon was lifted onto the cleared table, Gonard lending his strength to the heavy task. The skin was slit along the belly, peeled back, and then the technicians immersed themselves in the intricate components that filled the chest cavity. "There is much to do," Oswald said, leaving the others to their work. "It is fortunate that we possess Lord Max's original designs for your construction from which to work."

Gonard nodded, winced as fibers were removed. "I'm not sure I want to watch."

"There is no need for you to do so. I have faith in the handiwork of my technicians." He gave Gonard a small smile. "All technicians in the Citadel offered their services. It is considered a great opportunity to be permitted to study that which Lord Citizen Rumfus Max created." Then he became serious. "You, also, are in need of repair."

Gonard unfolded his left wing. "I'd like to be able to fly again."

Oswald nodded. "Crouch to the floor." As Gonard obeyed, the man walked the length of the wing, stretching it flat along the ground. He carefully aligned the two ends. Gonard turned his head away, awaiting the first painful rasp against the skin, wondering if Oswald had brought needles or some more advanced device along.

A low hum made him turn his head back. Oswald was holding a flat, metallic box, which he directed at the edges of skin. He followed the rip with the thick muzzle of the box, the leathers warming under its impact. In its path, the device left a join of skin, which Gonard knew from experience would quickly heal.

Oswald followed the slit up to the elbow, then lowered his arm. "You will be able to fly again in a matter of days."

Gonard sat up, leaving the wing outspread. "I never understood," he said, the pain an old and almost forgotten one now, "why my father never repaired my wing."

"It may be that he was fearful of losing you. Yet love is shown only by the willingness to allow another's release." Oswald looked away, as if embarrassed by his words. He glanced at his team; then, obviously satisfied that they were progressing satisfactorily, he left the laboratory. Gonard was mystified when he reappeared, rolling a rounded rubber mold across the floor. The man upended it in front of Gonard. He pulled his tools over, then tapped the flat top. "Now, your left foot."

Gonard found himself backing away, sudden fear spurting through him. "No."

Oswald frowned. "You have been a cripple for long enough. Why should you wish to remain so?"

"I don't know." Then Gonard bent his head, decided to tell the truth. "It reminds me that I'm—human."

"Gonard Michel." Oswald waited until Gonard looked up again. The man held out his hands. "I too am human, and I need no such reminder."

Gonard swallowed, wondering if he could explain even to himself his strange reluctance. "It's part of my past."

"And you should now look to the future." Oswald tapped the mold again. And with a suppressed sob, Gonard laid his forefoot on the surface. The technician began the delicate operation, sliding back skin and scales to repair the twisted connections beneath.

* * * * *

The technicians worked steadily, the dragon disassembled and then reforming under their hands. The flight chamber was inserted with improvements suggested by Gonard. The incorrectly set nerve coil was straightened, the leg repaired, the neck reset. The black wing-leathers were knit back together again. Gonard sang as they worked, transmitting the recordings back to the Citadel.

Finally the dragon was ready, lying motionless across the table, every component in place, the green skin stretching whole and unblemished over the long body. The technicians smiled at Gonard's thanks, accepted with pleasure the folios he gave them.

Oswald left last. He turned to the computer panels, barked a few commands. A high note whistled through the laboratory, and Gonard stiffened uncomprehendingly. The sound died away, and Oswald gave him a small smile. "You were both programmed with inhibitors, so that you could not escape from the Domains. The robot medtech temporarily nullified yours when you first came to the Citadel. I have now removed that programming. You are now free to come and go as you please."

Only temporarily nullified, Gonard reflected. I would have had to return sometime, then. "Thank you, Oswald."

The man nodded. He paused by the door, looking back at the two dragons. "You realize that it may be a long time before she develops a self-awareness, if ever."

"I know," Gonard acknowledged. "But we've got centuries."

Oswald nodded again. "Yes, you have. Your god go with you, Gonard Michel."

"And yours with you."

Gonard waited until the technicians were outside the complex, the doors shut firmly behind them. Then he left the table, striding without a limp to the equipment created by his father. With his tail disk he made the necessary adjustments, summoning the required energy levels, directing them onto the table.

The dragon shuddered. Muscles tightened; skin shone. Green scales sprouted, lapping over the skin, darkening as they hardened in the air. An ear twitched, rustling across the table. Gonard crossed over as the head lifted slowly, eyes blinking in confusion. "Dragons are born to love," Gonard said softly to the new creature staring up at him. "That is why you have been created."

The dragon carefully rose to her feet. Gonard looked up at her, his nose wrinkling in a smile. "Who are you?" she asked slowly, cautiously, as if she were sampling every word.

"I am called Gonard Michel."

"Who am I?"

"That is for you to decide."

She stepped down gingerly from the table, shyly met his gaze. "I was in a dark place, and then you called me. Why did you call me?"

Words bunched up in Gonard's throat, words he could not allow himself to say. It was far too soon. She must first Awaken, he reminded himself. "Because you were in the dark, and alone, and I was in the dark, also alone. Now we can go out into the light together."

She cocked her head, gazed around the laboratory. "Where will we go?"

"Everywhere," Gonard replied, thinking of the City, the settlement, the chapter, the many other places he had yet to visit. All the beauty of the Earth, and he longed to share it with her. "Will you come with me?"

She studied him for a long moment, her black wings rustling as she flexed newfound muscles. Then she came to his side. "I will go with you."

Gonard released his breath. He raised his head, smiled at her. She wrinkled her nose in return, imitating him. He glanced back at the stone walls, the long table, taking one last look at his past.

Then they left the laboratory together.